"Hogle succeeds in crafting a fun romance with a touch of fantasy."
—*Booklist*

"[A] cozy and witchy rom-com . . . [A] fun take on the fake-dating trope that will have readers genuinely wondering how Alex and Romina will find their way back to each other. The result is a beguiling and heartfelt story of rekindling love." —*Publishers Weekly*

"A delightfully magical second-chance romance . . . The world Hogle has created is cozy and warm, and fans of her previous work or of witchy romances will be crossing their fingers that this is the start of a series." —*Library Journal* (starred review)

"With her brilliant twists on magic and romance, Sarah Hogle does it again! Filled with all my favorite tropes, *Old Flames and New Fortunes* captures the magic of first love and the whimsy of a second chance." —Ashley Poston, author of *The Dead Romantics*

"*Old Flames and New Fortunes* reads like a spell, one that compels you to move to Moonville, Ohio, and become a Tempest sister, or at least one of their coven. Gorgeous, heartfelt, and romantic to the very last word." —Lana Harper, author of *Payback's a Witch*

"Heartwarming and utterly enchanting, *Old Flames and New Fortunes* had me under its spell from page one. Hogle grounds the story with real emotional weight while letting her fantastical elements flourish, and the result is nothing short of magical and testament to the idea that, although life might not turn out the way we plan, there's always room for hope, love, and miracles."
—Sarah Grunder Ruiz,
author of *Last Call at the Local*

"My goodness—I fell so hard and so fast for this hilarious, cozy, devastatingly romantic story! *Old Flames and New Fortunes* is a brilliant, magic-filled exploration of second chances and what it means to open up your heart again. It may just be my favorite Sarah Hogle book yet."

—Sarah Adler,
author of *Mrs. Nash's Ashes* and *Happy Medium*

"I can't get enough of Sarah Hogle's impeccable writing. Sarah Hogle is a rom-com genius, and *Old Flames and New Fortunes* is perfection."

—India Holton, author of
The Wisteria Society of Lady Scoundrels

"Whatever Hayao Miyazaki is eating and drinking, Sarah Hogle is eating and drinking it as well. . . . I am a Sarah Hogle fan first, human second. And this story has my entire heart with its flowery magic and lovable and absolutely hilarious characters."

—Zoulfa Katouh,
author of *As Long as the Lemon Trees Grow*

PRAISE FOR
Just Like Magic

"A hilarious holiday romp with a splash of magic." — *Paste*

"Pair the unhinged Christmas spirit of *Elf* with the redemption narrative of *A Christmas Carol* and you'd get something like *Just Like Magic*. . . . Hogle has the unique ability to take an absolutely bonkers premise and spin it into an instant classic—this will be a keeper on our holiday shelf for a long time." — *Entertainment Weekly*

"[An] outrageous, hilarious adventure . . . Exactly what I needed to kick off the season!" — *First for Women*

"[A] whimsical yuletide twist on fantasy." — *The Week*

"The book has layers of emotions, mystery, lots of characters that you somehow grow to love, a sunshine-and-grump trope, comical lies and their even more comical consequences, and most importantly: humor and love."
—*The Nerd Daily*

"The perfect comfort read: emotionally healing and so much fun."
—*Book Riot*

"Whatever Sarah Hogle writes, I'll be reading it."   —*BuzzFeed*

"With over-the-top antics, lovable characters, and a romance sure to melt even the coldest of hearts, *Just Like Magic* cast a spell that kept me turning pages all night just to see what would happen next."
—Sarah Grunder Ruiz, author of *Love, Lists & Fancy Ships*

"Brilliant and totally bonkers. It's sheer joy and true heart and utterly glorious pandemonium, and I adored it."
—India Holton, author of *The Wisteria Society of Lady Scoundrels*

"I cannot remember the last time a book made me literally laugh out loud this much."
—Martha Waters,
author of *To Marry and to Meddle*

"This gloriously zany holiday rom-com completely stole my heart."
—Chloe Liese,
author of *Two Wrongs Make a Right*

"Mischief and mayhem and pure, unfiltered joy!"
—Timothy Janovsky,
author of *You're a Mean One, Matthew Prince*

Also by Sarah Hogle

Old Flames and New Fortunes

Just Like Magic

Twice Shy

You Deserve Each Other

SARAH HOGLE

G. P. PUTNAM'S SONS
New York

THE
Folklore
OF
Forever

A NOVEL

PUTNAM
— EST. 1838 —

G. P. PUTNAM'S SONS
Publishers Since 1838
An imprint of Penguin Random House LLC
1745 Broadway, New York, NY 10019
penguinrandomhouse.com

Book design by Katy Riegel

Trade Paperback ISBN 9780593715079
Ebook ISBN 9780593715086

Printed in the United States of America
1st Printing

The authorized representative in the EU for product safety and
compliance is Penguin Random House Ireland, Morrison
Chambers, 32 Nassau Street, Dublin D02 YH68, Ireland,
https://eu-contact.penguin.ie.

For my sweet Bo, who was the goodest boy

But doth suffer a sea-change

Into something rich and strange.

—Shakespeare, *The Tempest*

THE
Folklore
OF
Forever

Part One

ONE

When it storms at midnight, brew a cup of
dandelion root tea. Slowly wave the flame of a
six-inch candle back and forth over its depths
to glimpse a secret you've long forgotten.

Spells, Charms, and Rituals,
Tempest Family Grimoire

LEGEND HAS IT that the first sentence of a new book is
always the hardest.

Although I imagine it'd be easier if I had any idea what
sort of story this one's going to be. I've sent four polished pro-
posals to my editor, each neatly shot down for being either too
similar to my There's Magic in Villamoon series, or too dis-
similar ("We want all the charm and excitement of Villamoon,
but for it to be totally fresh and different"), so when I lower a
bucket down the creative well, the only water is insecurity and
reminders that I have bills to pay and no reliable prospects on
my horizon. Moving to my hometown was supposed to magi-
cally (no pun intended) fix this creative dry spell, but here I am
sixty-five days after returning to Moonville, Ohio, and I am
still staring down a blank page.

Perhaps I could try a spin-off? There are plenty of characters
in the Villamoon universe I could write about . . . but readers

would inevitably compare a spin-off to the original and probably find it dissatisfying. I need to move on.

The thing is, readers might not move on with me.

What if I don't have any other stories worth telling, and nobody will care about my books if they're not about Henriette Albrittey, amateur sleuth and heartbreak vampire, who feeds on the anguish of failed relationships rather than blood?

My gaze shoots to a stack of recently procured library books, each title more fascinating than the last: *Genghis Khan and the Making of the Modern World. Get Well Soon: History's Worst Plagues and the Heroes Who Fought Them. Other Minds: The Octopus, the Sea, and the Deep Origins of Consciousness. A Grave Robbery. Heir of Uncertain Magic.*

I shouldn't.

But it's so very irresistible.

But I shouldn't. It's been a while since my last novel came out, and I don't have time to mess around. Sales have been declining, which I am told is natural to happen at the tail end of a seven-book series—and I've funneled a fair bit of money into my family's shop. If I don't get another contract in the works, I'll end up needing to find *another* job (on top of my part-time work at The Magick Happens), which will leave me with even less time for writing, which will make sustaining this career that much harder.

My hand, without permission, snatches up *A History of the Habsburg Empire, 1526–1918.*

I will draft yet another proposal for a cozy paranormal mystery. It will be brilliant! I promise! But first, it is completely necessary that I learn everything there is to know about the Habsburgs.

As my thumb smooths over "Chapter I: Toward the Union of the Habsburg Lands," a soothing peace descends over me like a mist, worries sieving into a distant time and place. Writing has not come easily lately, but reading is *always* dependably wonderful. This sort of text is my very favorite kind, with maps and an index and appendices. The names of a few rulers—Leopold, Maximilian, Ferdinand—stick to the walls of my brain, happily repeating themselves over and over in the way that, in my experience, select words are oft to do. I look forward to getting lost in new information.

A sputter of lightning draws my attention to the window, my gaze falling eye-level with somebody else's, looking at me through his window across the street. My heart rate kicks up at the sight of that thick, sleek black hair that tumbles nearly to his shoulders. Dark, clever eyes. Tattoos of constellations spidering up his arms. That incredible jawline alone is the food of poetry.

A slowly considering smile pulls at his mouth.

My phone rings.

Imagine Vallis Boulevard, which is our street, as a thin brick ribbon laid across a giant's palm. On either side of the brick ribbon are all manner of shops—some of the ordinary variety, like Mozzi's Pizza or Riddle & Owl (they sell board games, puzzles, and such). Many others play up our homegrown urban legends, promoting the fantastical in some way. Like how Wafting Crescent, the bakery, advertises their Danish dream cake as "baked with eight drops of love magic." Or how Dark Side of the Spoon, a new diner that's just opened up, claims to have been constructed over crossing ley lines, which allegedly gives their establishment a boost of supernatural energy. Imagine creeks that cut through the road every which way, so many of them that some shops are perched over the water on stilts, and ten thousand trees stuffed into every available crevice (including sprouting out of the middle of the road in medians).

Now: the giant crumples all of it in his fist, scrunching neighbors right up next to each other with no room for breath, and you've got the reason why I can see what Morgan's face looks like while I'm safely inside my attic. I could throw a pen and smack his window with it. My building, which is the oldest one in the neighborhood and has been called The Magick Happens since the 1970s, is a three-layer brick cake. My attic is the tart black currant jam that stacks over Luna's apartment, a dense slab of sponge, mousse, and ganache with so many ingredients fighting for dominance that you can't tell what the hero flavor is supposed to be; which sits atop a creamy meringue with Pop Rocks exploding whimsically here and there: our shop. Well, I should mention that it's technically *Trevor's* shop, as he's my sisters' and my landlord, and he bought the property from our mother, who sold it to spite her ex-husband (our father) who'd inherited it from his mother (Grandma Dottie). I won't get into all of that right now, though—it's a whole thing.

Back to Morgan and the phone that vibrates itself across my desk, glowing Unknown Number. He's called my cell before, requesting book recommendations, but always from the special line downstairs in the Cavern of Paperback Gems.

Neon colors fishtail through what I presume is his bedroom, strobing his face. He must have purchased his wall decorations from a Miami motel's going-out-of-business sale. It's a stark contrast to my cave: my first priority after moving back home was to paint the attic a deep indigo and adorn it with black-framed artwork: a weeping skeleton with an arrow in its vertebrae; a black goat on a shore, its hindquarters formed from seawater. Not that you can see much of anything besides my books, as they're stacked and stuffed anywhere they'll fit. My sock drawer. Under the bed. Sandwiched between terrariums for my vampire crabs, beetles, ghost mantises, and isopods.

My phone continues to ring. Morgan twiddles his device back and forth in a gesture to *pick up*. His body language is self-assured, powerful, as though he knows I'm going to do exactly that.

Today, Morgan is wearing acid-washed jeans, a matching denim jacket with the collar flipped up, and a shirt color-blocked in fluorescent pink and orange. A miniature gold sword dangles from his left earlobe. His wardrobe of exclusively 1980s vintage clothing is so opposite to my own fashion sense that he's a UFO spotlight demanding my full attention. I have such a fondness for the different and unexpected.

We stare at each other, my vision black and sparkly at the edges from fixating on a bright white rectangle for forty unproductive minutes. And then finally, I answer the call.

My "Hello?" is cautious, suspicious, a quick peek around the corner of a dark alleyway.

His silky voice pours into my ear, coaxing every hair to stand up. "Hello to you, too, gorgeous."

My pulse races. "It's one in the morning."

"So it is."

He hasn't said anything overtly sensual, and yet the brief words *feel* it. My body tightens, blood stirring. "Why aren't you sleeping?" I ask.

"How could I possibly? It's as if you're in my bedroom. What did I tell you about those curtains?"

My throat is packed with sand. "You told me that when I keep them open at night, you can see me."

A short silence falls, in which he says everything by saying nothing at all.

This is more blatant than he's dared so far; for the past few days, Morgan has begun to look at me with a new . . . suggestiveness . . . in his eyes.

"You could close your own curtains," I point out.

"Not even if I wanted to." His voice is rough. "My hands wouldn't allow it. When you dangle temptation, Zelda Tempest, I won't say no."

He's seated at a desk in front of his window just like I am. Morgan lives on the second floor of a pale green Victorian house, the first floor of which is a bakery, Wafting Crescent, run by Bushra and her brother, Zaid. They probably have to listen to a lot of eighties synth pop pumping through their ceiling.

My breath catches. "Bold."

"Bold is efficient," he replies. "And you look like you could use some company."

I'm at a loss for words. This isn't new territory, as I often don't know what to say to Morgan. He has a keen interest in the paranormal and likes to ask me questions about my books (as they are focused on the paranormal). Because of this, I tend to avoid him. My writing—and what I plan to write next—is a sore topic at the moment. But I have noticed Morgan, certainly. From afar.

And I can hardly process the words that are coming out of his mouth, like a daydream glimmering to life.

You look like you could use some company.

He is so intensely good-looking that I don't know how to converse sensibly with him, and that is why I flounder with the weak response: "I'm busy. Reading."

"Reading what?"

"A volume on the Habsburg Empire."

He tilts his head, fixing on his ceiling. "Are you into history?"

"Oh yes," I reply in a rush. "And science. Geology, geography, ancient weapons and torture devices. Bog bodies. Cairns. The lost colony of Roanoke." I am giving too much information, but I can't stop—I have a million special interests. My present studies are Baltic Sea trade in the Viking Age, Egyptian hieroglyphs, and listening to unsolved mysteries on audiobook. Traveling used to be a great love of mine, but I've tired of it (and also can't afford it these days). "What about you?" I ask with barely contained eagerness, pulling my waist-length braid over one shoulder and nosing a pen out of it. I usually keep one somewhere on my person for easy access. "What do you enjoy learning about?"

His chair swivels so that he faces me fully, one hand running through the night-shining strands of his hair. "You."

My heart takes flight.

He grins as though he knows what that word, in *that* tone, has accomplished. A man like Morgan must know how he affects people. I am not infatuated, precisely, but with a little more encouragement on his part, I could see myself getting there.

"And ghosts," he goes on as thunder shakes the walls. "Witchcraft, magic. You already know."

I bite my lip. Yes, I do.

I also know that none of it is real.

Not the ghost stories that have made our town famous. Not witches, which my sisters claim to be, as did my grandmother. For decades, Grandma Dottie sold candles in our shop. They were supposedly imbued with spells that helped divine a customer's One True Love, or could speed up the romance-finding process, weeding out the duds so that you knew not to invest too much into the relationship. She passed this particular strain of magic down to Luna, who's taken up the mantle and has filled the shop top to bottom with "bespelled" candles.

My younger sister, Romina, calls herself a *flora fortunist*. The magic she claims to wield is similar to Luna's, in that it aids customers' romantic notions. But rather than candle magic, she uses floriography, which is the language of flowers. The way that I understand it, magic tells her which flowers to give to a person in order to bring their romantic wishes to fruition (if magic agrees with the customer's wishes, that is). If you ask Romina and Luna how they can be so sure they're witches, that what they're doing is truly charmed, they'll respond irritatingly vaguely about "intuition" and "connection to nature." When they practice witchcraft, there are no sparks, no sudden gusts of wind, no sign that anything otherworldly is happening at all. It can't be proven. I'll be the first to admit that I love a good witchy aesthetic. But I'll also admit—and this is where I diverge drastically from my sisters—that it's only a style. Nothing more.

Rats. I've accidentally defiled a library book again.

If it were real, I appear to have written in the corner of Appendix I, *it could be proven.*

"There's something about you," Morgan tells me lowly. "I would like to find out what it is."

"What do you mean?"

He leans back slightly, amused. "Don't you know?"

I truly do not. "Please be explicit, or I might misunderstand."

"I'd love to be explicit, but for now I'll be polite. I'm saying that you're beautiful, and I want to spend time with you. A lot of time. Alone."

The pen slips from my hand. It rolls off the edge of the desk, gliding across a famous tapestry—"The Unicorn in Captivity"—re-created on my rug.

"Um."

He arches an eyebrow. "Now you're the one who will have to be more explicit."

I swallow a shaky lungful of air. Bats and rats and frogs, I am at terribly loose ends. "I . . . ah . . . it isn't that I don't *want* to. You are very"—I gesture to him—"but, ah, this is moving fast, don't you think? Until this week, you didn't talk to me much unless you were asking me to go on your podcast to discuss writing fictional magic systems." An offer I've refused, since I abhor talking about myself but even more abhor talking about writing. The inevitable query *So what's next? What are you working on now?* would make me physically ill. If I throw up on Morgan Angelopoulos, he'll definitely start drawing his curtains closed every night.

"Until this week, that's all you noticed," he replies. "But that doesn't mean I haven't been noticing *you* for quite a while now. For me, this isn't sudden at all. It's overdue. But I don't want to move faster than you're comfortable with, so I'll leave you with something to think about, and my phone number in your call history."

I press my lips together, not trusting myself to speak.

He lets a weighty pause drop. The corner of his mouth twitches with a velvety "Good night, Zelda."

The call disconnects.

Crack!

It's the third of July, and above, an aptly named Thunder supermoon glows vividly when it shouldn't be visible during a storm at all. The huge white rock is melodrama in the night, rain lashing sideways. Below, glow-in-the-dark footprints trace a path along the road from a murder mystery dinner theater's door all the way to the Moonville tunnel. They were painted to give the illusion of ghosts having a stroll, trapping moonlight. Right now, they twinkle to suggest an invisible traveler is dancing in the rain. My gaze traipses from the footprints and up the front of the green Victorian, latticed with roses, to the second floor. An irresistible pull.

Our eyes meet again as lightning breaks, thunder follows, and something *alive* happens to the globe string lights that hang high over the road, connecting the roofs of Wafting Crescent and The Magick Happens. Like a flurry of miniature wings, dime-bright, undulating from one bulb to the next.

I shoot to my feet with a start, but before I can get a closer look, all the power drains from my lamps, the Smithsonian channel on TV—as always, muted with captions on—my row of haunted house luminaries. I'm left in darkness with only the spatter of rain.

I crank the windowpane until it pushes outward, then lean out as far as I dare. Raindrops tap the sill. Already, there's a calm spreading across the sky, rain slowing.

The string lights have burned out, but other than that, they look perfectly ordinary. Nobody is out and about. The storm must have caused an electrical burst, or my eyes are playing tricks on me. I shake my head, forbidding myself from opening my laptop tomorrow. I need a break.

You don't have time for a break, an inner voice murmurs. *You haven't even started.*

Sighing, I grope through the darkness for my silver skull lighter and a candle. I've got dozens of them—normal, non-magical tapers—that I use for my pair of candelabras with ravens carved into their bases. But instead of regular tapers, my hand finds a different candle instead. The only one in the room that claims to be enchanted.

Gilda Halifax, a cherished nemesis of my grandmother's, gave this candle to me last week for my thirty-second birthday. It's a cumbersome, lumpy, graying thing—nothing at all like the candles Luna creates with her lively colors and pretty molds. Gilda said that Grandma made it many years ago and would want me to have it. I'm still not sure what that means. The candle's name, according to an attached tag, is a little cryptic.

"Here goes nothing," I mumble, clicking the lighter.

I glance askance at the window as LET THE STRANGE IN rips into a high, thin, orange-red flame the precise color of my hair; the silhouette of Morgan flashes again in the lightning's blaze, violin under his chin, then abruptly disappears with it in the space of a heartbeat.

Long after, my goose bumps haven't eased, the back of my neck still prickling with the invasive tingle of being watched. It feels as if it's coming from somewhere farther away than the house across from mine on Vallis Boulevard. The sudden, strange idea sweeps through my head that whatever is looking through my window now is something that flickers all the way up in the sky, with the lightning—and that is how I know that sixty-five days in Moonville is exactly how long it takes to start seeing things that aren't there, once again.

TWO

The waters of Twinstar Fork swell with love
magic at the full moon. Pour three tablespoons of
midnight into a birch bowl with a smooth stone at the
bottom. Drink half, then offer the rest to a garter
snake. For the following minute, enunciate your words
carefully and your One True Love will hear whatever it is
you say, from wherever it is that they are.

Love Magic Misc.,
Tempest Family Grimoire

D AMN. I GOT my hopes up for nothing." Luna pulls
back from the box in resignation, forehead pinched.

"Another one for the wall." I pluck the key from her
and add it to its mismatched fellows hanging from hooks on the
shop's storeroom door. "We're building a nice collection here."

Whenever Great-Aunt Misty comes across a random key
in her house and doesn't know what it's for, she mails it to us.
We've been dying to find out what's inside a locked box Luna
and Romina found in the attic a couple years ago. It's got tar-
nished brass fastenings and wine-red upholstery featuring a
faded damask pattern. My sisters asked Grandma, before she
died, what was in it, and where the key might be, but her dementia had carried her to a place where she no longer knew the
answer.

"Oh, did Misty send us another key?" Romina asks, gamboling over. She had cut her platinum bob into a shaggy pixie yesterday and dyed it cotton-candy pink. She and Trevor Yoon—our landlord as well as our media/marketing director—played hair roulette at the salon, so he's sporting a newly silver pompadour.

"Wasn't a fit," I tell her glumly.

Romina twirls to make the hem of her moss-green dress rise up. Her wardrobe ranges from earth-toned dungarees to frothy pastels with ruffles, the sorts of outfits you'd see anthropomorphic animals from a Beatrix Potter book wearing. "I should ask Alex to look for the missing key. He's shockingly good at finding lost things lately."

Luna raises her eyebrows, hovering over our younger sister like an ominous fog. "I *told* you he's becoming a witch. This happened to Grandpa Dennis after Grandma fell in love with him. Remember? She said that one month into dating, he was suddenly able to tell when somebody would die the next day. Which was unfortunate for him toward the end, when he saw his number would be up."

Romina brightens. "Last night, I said, 'Where's my purse?' and Alex knew without even getting up that I'd left it at Pit Stop Soda Shop."

I dismiss myself from what promises to be a ridiculous conversation, as Romina is not a witch and neither is her boyfriend, and this is the third time this summer that she's left her purse at the soda shop.

Delusion! I think loudly. What my sisters credit to magic is, in fact, coincidence and patterns.

Especially delusional is this town's legend of love magic, which generations of Moonvillians have claimed hangs in our trees, swims in our rivers. Supposedly, a romantic love grown in Moonville is stronger than anywhere else, and if you're here in near proximity to your One True Love, magic will physically redirect your paths so that they continue to cross. It will make your love burn forever, as bright and true in your fiftieth year together as it did your first.

Because we are the children of bitterly divorced parents, it boggles my mind that Luna and Romina espouse such garbage. Romina insists that the reason our parents' love wasn't lasting is that it wasn't seeded in Moonville, as they met and fell in love in Indianapolis, where our mother is originally from. Maybe my sisters still believe the legend because they've never left our hometown—certainly, when I first moved away, I still believed it all, too. I would even go so far as to say that I believed it more than *anyone*. Magic was so tightly plaited into my worldview that I *hallucinated* magical things. I'd treasured the idea of a One True Love, somebody made just for me.

But then I grew up. And I realized there is simply no proof that any of it is real.

Passing by the open front door, I spy a shirt with neon squiggles and triangles in the bakery across the street, and duck back against a wall. Lean out again to take another peek.

My heartbeat thumps in my throat at the sight of him.

I'm saying that you're beautiful, and I want to spend time with you. A lot of time. Alone.

I am a jumble of electric nerves and impure thoughts. Exclamation marks. Question marks. It isn't that I'm shocked a man is attracted to me, but the "I like you, let's get horizontal" ritual has never played out at quite this speed with the sweet, shy fellow nerds I've dated. It was only last week that Morgan tried to read my palm and declared it said I'm going to take a trip to the Maldives and enjoy three nights of passion with a muscled blond man "whose name begins with an *S*, or maybe a *K*, and you might meet him online, actually, and not in the Maldives."

Ever since I moved back to Moonville, I've kept my preferred distance from those outside my family, observing Morgan the appropriate amount that one observes a man who uses their shop as an unconventional workspace to write for the *Moonville Tribune*. I distantly recall his presence in high school. He was popular, lots of friends, lots of female admirers, lots of detentions.

I wore fake vampire teeth to school and tried to get my classmates to believe I was actually six hundred years old. I made up this whole elaborate history of my life as a horse girl from 1409, and when I wasn't talking about that, I was writing *Doctor Who* and *Supernatural* crossover fan fiction in my bedroom. By senior year, I'd stopped hissing "You foolish mortals" at fellow students, but it was too late—I graduated with honors and no friends.

As an adult, he's charming. Chatty. Wildly extroverted, and I am . . . not. Too much socialization eats my energy like a white dwarf consuming its companion star. I'm gripped by the way he moves through the world, striking like a match against everybody he sees, generating chemistry with them effortlessly.

Steeling myself, I tip up my chin and stroll across Vallis

Boulevard, into Wafting Crescent Bakery. I'm embraced by a bellow of sugary cold; no matter what time of year it is, you always need a jacket in Wafting Crescent.

Morgan doesn't turn at the *ding!* of the bell, deep in conversation with Zaid. The baker's busy building a seasonal display of small puffy pastries that must be called *sou*, as the chalkboard slate beside them reads HAPPY SOU-MMER! Zaid dearly loves a pun. His dog is named Ruff Puff.

I survey the variety of pastries, not at all hungry, sneaking glances at Morgan now and then. My face flames when he catches me looking, but I impress myself by clearing my throat and managing a "Good morg— Good morning."

"Morning to you, too!" Bushra sings, waltzing through the swinging door from the kitchen. Her hijab is a brilliant orange today, encrusted with dangling jewels. She is in her midtwenties and radiates an aura of firm authority, of knowing what she's about. "I hope you don't mind that there's no blueberry vatrushki today, Zel—I know they're your favorite."

"Are they?" Morgan's eyes slide to mine, but when he speaks he's addressing Bushra. "If you'd be kind enough to whip some up, I promise I won't play loud music for a week."

Bushra crosses her arms as she considers the proposition. "Darn you. I can't pass that up."

They shake on it.

Oh, my poor cardiovascular system. Bushra flits off to prepare the sweet buns, promising to deliver them to The Magick Happens when they're ready, and it's unfair that aside from being funny and alluring, Morgan's also so *sweet*. I feel excited, but sick. It is the weirdest mixture.

Morgan holds the door open for me. (Chivalrous!) I bleat "Oh thanks," under my breath and hurry out, then hurry *up* to keep pace with the stride of his long legs. He's walking next to me. *Right* next to me. Perhaps we are about to flirt again.

Get yourself together, Zelda, he's walking this way because he works here.

He doesn't work *at* The Magick Happens, per se, but he does *do* his work here. Meaning, he writes articles for the newspaper from a desk by the window. He claims this spot makes him a million times more productive than he is anywhere else (I have yet to see evidence of him being productive, to be honest). I will never confess to another living soul the thrill that I wring from knowing his desk used to be *my* desk, when I was young and wrote stories while hanging out with Grandma after school. I was irritated when I first discovered he'd usurped my spot, but it's impossible to stay angry at somebody with eyes like that—deep, dark, long-lashed. Mesmerizing.

Standing by the desk now is a tiny older woman with voluminous bright red hair, thick blue eyeliner, and a purple muumuu. Her surly old cat, Razzle Dazzle, sleeps in a picnic basket looped through her arm. She's toting a clipboard and her signature scent: Drunk Brunch. Her ear-to-ear smile portends snake oil.

"Zelda!" She grabs me by the cheeks and yanks my head down so that she can plant a big red lip print on my forehead. "I was just saying how lovely you're all looking these days! Except for Romina's hair. Sweetheart." She turns to my sister. "Did you and Alex break up?"

"Of course not," Romina begins to reply, but Gilda already isn't listening.

"Luna, it's such a shame about those tattoos on your otherwise pretty face."

Luna touches a finger to the side of her nose, absently rubbing it. She's got a microscopic splash of colorful dots tattooed across her cheeks and the bridge of her nose, blending in with her many, many freckles. They're dainty and cute, but Gilda Halifax comes from a generation in which tattooing your face is not the done thing. She insists on judging our choices with particular severity now that Grandma isn't here to do so.

"And, Zelda!" Gilda tosses up her hands, accidentally smacking Morgan with the clipboard. "What has this cruel world done to you, for you to dress this way?" She clucks her tongue. "Like you're a nineteenth-century widow. Learn to love again, dear! Throw on something green, your hair demands it. Or maybe a nice blue outfit. The three of you, you've got the loveliest blue eyes, I'm always saying you need to wear more blue—"

"Yes, thank you, Gilda," Luna interrupts. "What's with the clipboard and the compliments?"

"*Are* they compliments?" I muse.

The woman smiles. "Yes, I am so glad you offered to help. As it happens, there *is* something you can do for Moonville." Her penetrating stare slides from Luna to Romina to me. "Something you *all* can do to help. And, who knows? You just might fall in love while you're at it."

THREE

Hang your hat on an ancestor's tombstone in the
summertime and listen to crickets for the following
minute. Count the chirps, then double them;
that is how many years you've got left.

Local Legends and Superstitions,
Tempest Family Grimoire

FESTIVAL BUDGETS AREN'T what they used to be,"
Gilda laments. "There should be a fair going on this
very minute, as it always does in July, but as you can see
it's been canceled. A tragedy! But we *have* to uphold the Halloween festival. Midnight at Moonville is practically famous.
We get folks by the thousands here every October for it!"

Luna, who has a few good inches on me in height and towers over Gilda, tries to peer at her clipboard and figure out
what any of her spiel has to do with the price of beans. Gilda
tugs it back, hitting Morgan again.

"Stand somewhere else, young man. You're gonna get that
pretty face bruised."

Morgan is visibly split between the pain in his shoulder and
the glow of having his face appreciated.

"I'm throwing an auction to make sure Midnight at Moonville doesn't get guillotined by our fun-hating mayor," Gilda
goes on darkly.

"An auction?" Romina repeats. "We could donate gift baskets." She looks at Luna to gauge agreement. "The same items we put in our subscription boxes, basically, but packaged prettier? Rose quartz, star anise—"

"Sounds fine, to start with." Gilda smiles sweetly. "But what I'm really after is a slice of your time. In a tight-fitting dress." She inspects me. "You got anything that shows cleavage? Blessed as you are, it's a sin not to show what you've got, honey."

"None of my clothes are able to show cleavage," I deadpan. "I have a condition that makes all the flesh rot off my bones and if I were to unbutton my dress, you'd see the rattlesnake that lives in my chest cavity."

She ignores this. "We're going to auction *dates*. Romina, sweetie, how serious are you about Alex? Has the passion worn itself down yet? Room for one more?"

Romina drops into a squashy armchair in front of the fireplace. In the summer months, we fill the hearth with battery-operated snow globe potion bottles, splashing the mantel and, atop it, Grandma's crystal ball, with eerie emerald light. "Count me out. You're welcome to auction off my floral services, though."

Gilda huffs. "Fine, that leaves the rest of you."

"Not me." Trevor gestures to the dynamite stick design on his shirt: TNT, for Trevor and Teyonna. "I'm a taken man." He steals a bite of pink popcorn drizzled with butterscotch icing and crushed Reese's Pieces from Luna's carton, which she bought from a corner stall. "Speaking of TNT, you're all invited to a light show in the dollar store parking lot after dark.

Please feel free to donate items you wouldn't mind melting in a grill I found by the side of the road."

Luna flicks him in the ear.

Gilda whirls on Luna. "I assume you're single and desperate? My sources have not indicated otherwise."

It is a testament to Luna's people skills that her smile looks sincere. "Single, yes. Desperate, no. I'm waiting for the right—"

"Slap your signature here." Gilda thrusts a sign-up sheet at her. "Auction's next Friday, winning bidder gets a date. Mind, you can think of it as a lunch or hangout or what have you, but men will throw down more money if we call it a date."

Luna shakes her head, bending to scrawl her name. "You're shameless."

"Wear one of your crop tops to the auction. I figure that'll drive up interest at least fifty bucks."

She turns to me.

I brace myself. "Thanks for the offer, but I'm—"

"You've ignored Moonville for the past fourteen years so that you could sleep in your van in overpriced cities," she interrupts. "Which I'm sure is more glamorous than it sounds, but you can make it up to us now by giving our town's children the festival they deserve."

"All right, all right. You're getting your way." There truly is no arguing with Gilda.

She beams. "Splendid. There's a lid for every pot, as they say. *Somebody* out there, I'm sure, won't mind that you dress as if it's Halloween every day."

I would give Gilda my kidney if she needed it, but there are times I'd like for her to retire in Florida. She can't know how it stings to think about my love life, how ardently I *do* hope there is somebody out there who will be the perfect lid to my pot. I chance a sidelong look at Morgan.

Right as I'm poised to add my name with the rest of Ursula's stolen souls, Romina gasps. "This is how it happens!" she loud-whispers, seizing my wrist. "For Zelda!"

I frown. "How what happens?"

Her eyes are enormous and dreamy. "The *moth*."

Curses.

"Oh, not the moth thing again."

My lovely, caring, sweet liar of a grandmother used to pretend she had psychic dreams, and when my sisters and I were younger, she informed us that one day we would all fall in love with the men we're meant to spend the rest of our lives with, all within the same year. She said we would know it was *the* year when we saw a silver luna moth, and at the time that we saw it, one of us would be running from love, one would be waiting for it, and the third would already be in over her head. (Silver luna moths do not exist, by the way.) A couple days ago, just after Romina finally admitted to herself that she's madly in love with her high school sweetheart, she saw a metal butterfly decoration or something like that and has declared it to be The Moth. Which means that this is Our Year.

Gilda's face is pitying. "My poor naïve girl, that was a fabrication. I am sorry to tell you that your grandmother did not possess True Sight." I nod, but then she adds, "*I* possess True Sight, and have not Seen any prophecies relating to moths, whether they be silver or luna or any other. Unlike Dottie, rest her fraudulent soul, *I* am an actual psychic, and my crystal ball has foretold that at least one of you girls shall find love at this auction."

I scribble my name, phone number, and email address. Will Morgan bid on me? I'd say yes to a date even without an auction, which he likely guesses, so maybe he won't bid. Why fork over cash when you can have what you like for free?

"It's about time you found yourself somebody special, Miss Zelda," Gilda says. I bite my lip, trying to restrain a smile.

"Zelda's found a *lot* of special somebodies." Luna laughs.

My smile dies.

Romina points a pink kernel of popcorn at me. "Our Zelda's a heartbreaker. Don't get your hopes up, Gilda."

I smirk as though this is funny, because that is the expected reaction, but acid coats my throat. "Yes, she's quite persnickety," Luna adds.

Persnickety, persnickety.

```
ERTY I P
 S      K
   C  N
```

Frequently, a word will get jammed in my systems and I have no choice but to repeat it three or four times, liking the way the sound rolls around in my mouth; then I visualize where each letter of the word would be located on my laptop's keyboard. In my mind's eye, I find the necessary buttons and tap down each one. I once told Grandma that I did this, to which she said, *How unusual!* I find the buttons for those words, too, humming in satisfaction after they've been typed out.

W   U O

A S   H   L

N

Gilda collects Morgan's signature, helps herself to six bookmarks and a handful of whatever's in the candy dish at the checkout counter, and smiles roundly. "Your grandmother's ghost would like to express her gratitude to you, for supporting our town's economy."

The incomprehensible brass of this woman.

"She didn't say any of that," my eleven-year-old niece replies, socked feet appearing before the rest of her does as she slicks down the banister rail from the upstairs apartment. Our knotty pine staircase is well-polished to assist in quick sliding. Aisling's gaze is baleful. "Grandma's in the attic reading Aunt Zelda's notes for her next book. Says Zel should try writing bodice rippers."

Gilda looks a tad unnerved. "What a charming imagination you have."

My face colors. "You're not supposed to be in my room without permission." She has a penchant for "borrowing" clothes. "Or know what bodice rippers are."

"I only went up there because I heard Grandma. She was talking to herself."

It's a flash up my spine, the horrible, wonderful, too-good-to-be-true imagery of my grandmother lingering, watching over us. "Aisling, it is *wrong* to make up stories like that."

Her face crumples. "I'm not making it up! She wanted me to tell you, uhh . . ." Ash squints, pretending to recall something. "*Remember what I told you.*"

"That is a step too far," I say sharply.

"All right, everybody settle down." Luna throws me a severe look.

I exhale through my nose. Damn this family and their delusions of magic and prophecies and ghosts. It is painfully clear why I stayed away for so long. Whenever I've gone on vacations with my sisters and niece, they've still behaved peculiarly, but it wasn't the full-blown charlatan experience like it is here, in this building, where our town's cumulative idiosyncrasies embolden them to live their best lies.

"*And* you're wearing my shirt," I add. My biggest, comfiest black sweater, with the faded outline of a pirate ship. She's paired it with one of her mother's tie-dye scarves, pinning back her straight brown hair. She looks adorable, though, so I soften. "Just don't spill anything on it, all right?"

"I would never," she declares dramatically.

Romina *pffft*s. "You would *always*. My clothes come back from you stained so badly, they look like old-world maps."

The bell chimes as Gilda swans out the door, and, consumed by my thoughts, I drift from room to room.

As if memory is a ghost, I can fixate on any spot in this shop and see myself and my two sisters, many years ago, when Grandma still ran it all. There weren't any books or flowers then—she sold only candles—and dementia hadn't begun to take her from us piece by piece. She was strong, whimsical, bejeweled; dragonflies in her long white hair; wrapped in a purple, gold, and green apron; a folk saying for any occasion ready at her lips. Stories galore, which watered my creative spirit, shaping me into the storyteller that I am today. *Did you know there's magic in Moonville?* she'd whisper, swishing across the creaky floor in her long skirts with bells at the hem, humming to old Celtic songs playing from our bulky CD player. *It's in our trees. It's in our waters. In your very bones. Can't you feel it?*

Dottie would place my hand against her ear, like a child listening to the ocean in a seashell. *I can certainly hear it. Runs all through you like music in a wind tunnel.*

She made magic seem . . . not merely *real*, but as if it were alive with a beating heart, like it belonged with our family, and we were its guardians. I idolized her, gobbling up this belief that I was part of something bigger. I believed there was magic in my bones.

Dottie's favored music still plays, although not from a CD player anymore. I meander through the sunroom porch, called the Garden, where Romina is at work braiding a floral crown for a customer who wants to get over their ex-girlfriend. Their past lover has already moved on, and loving them is a torment. *"To let love go,"* Romina says softly, piling plants together. "Cyclamen. Blue iris. Snowdrops." She pauses, hand hovering over a pot of drooping white flowers. "Not snowdrops, it seems. The magic wants . . . honeysuckle. *Yes.* This is the combination that will help you. Wear the crown while you sleep tonight, and you'll wake with a lifted heart. Tomorrow, spread the flowers out to dry. Then crush their petals and keep them in your pocket until you feel the heartache easing."

I shake my head, passing all the way back around into the Candleland section of our shop, high shelves crammed with wax artworks: pumpkins, acorns, trees, blooms; meltable mages and knights and dragons inspired by Luna's favorite fantasy series, Tributales. The competing scents of coffee, patchouli, caramel black tea, amber, sea salt, and raspberry should be migraine-inducing, but they calm me instead, evoking the strange feeling that I am standing at the center of the universe, where everything started. Exactly where I need to be.

Ahead, a man leans against a hallway wall papered with torn-out book pages, lit by electric torches. This corridor curves down to a landing of sorts, then ramps steeply down again, leading to the Cavern of Paperback Gems. The Cavern was my idea, as I wanted a way to imprint a little of my own personality into the shop. Luna had candles, Romina had flowers, and the obvious choice for me was books. If I'm not writing a book of my own, then I've got my nose in somebody else's. Even when I didn't live here, I still operated the Cavern, ordering stock and making myself available to customers for recommendations. There's an old-fashioned telephone on the wall downstairs, and if you dial 3, my cell rings.

The man sees me coming and straightens, slipping his hands out of his pockets. He looks to be in his late twenties or early thirties, with soft brown hair that curls at the nape of his neck, light gray eyes, and my biggest weakness: glasses. It's dishonorable, how fast I can go to pieces over a man in glasses.

"Hi," he says, clearing his throat.

I glance at his shopping basket, a plastic gold cauldron with a wire handle, which contains one copy of *Cave of a Thousand Crystal Wings*, the third book in my There's Magic in Villamoon series. He sees me looking at it and picks up the book, flipping to read the synopsis on the back. A receipt is sticking out of the pages like a bookmark; I wonder how long he's been lingering after he made his purchase. "Vampires, huh?"

"Among other monsters. If you're new to the series, it might help to start with the first book, though. That one is number three."

"Ah, but *this* is the one that you forgot to sign." He smiles, a wry sparkle in his eyes, and I can't help but smile back. "I had to search through thirty books before I found a copy you skipped."

"You *wanted* one I hadn't signed?"

He holds my gaze. We're close enough to the basement entrance to hear my playlist, which is separate from the music that plays in the rest of the shop. Down in the Cavern, I like to knit the atmosphere with stormy midnights and spooky film scores. At this moment, "The Incantation" from *Beetlejuice* is creeping around the landing.

"I wanted you to know who you were signing it for." He opens to the title page and uncaps a pen, handing both the pen and the book to me. "Dylan."

I give him an assessing look as I Zorro a great big *Z* across the page. "You a fan of paranormal mysteries, Dylan?"

He shrugs. "We'll see." A mock frown pulls at his lips. "Couldn't have added your phone number?"

At that, I have to laugh.

He takes the book from me, then begins to turn. "By the way, I overheard you talking to Miss Halifax. An auction sounds fun."

"Oh yeah?"

"Yeah." He opens the front door. "I'm looking forward to our date."

FOUR

A cat on a fencepost with its back
to the road is a sure sign that an undesirable
visitor will soon knock at your door.

Local Legends and Superstitions,
Tempest Family Grimoire

THE AIR IS moist in a way that sticks to you as if it wants to coat all your cells, winds foul, sky a sickly chartreuse on the day of the auction. Everybody else is miserable to be outside in this weather and I can barely contain the pleasure it brings me, standing off to the side of a stage built from wooden pallets while Gilda garbles into a dying microphone that's only catching every other word. As always, she's brought along Razzle Dazzle in a picnic basket. The cat is so old that she's got bald patches, face sunken in around the cheekbones.

This block of Vallis Boulevard has been sectioned off, a hundred or so folding chairs siphoned from local churches facing us, half of them filled with people and the other half with gift baskets. Streaks of pooled rainfall glimmer in the road like marbled raw meat. When I point this out to Luna, she tells me I'm disgusting and that she's going to convert me to vegetarianism.

I'm wearing one of my favorite outfits for what will hopefully celebrate a romantic new beginning: a grayish-white hoop skirt dress I discovered in a curiosity shop in New Hope, Pennsylvania. The corset and cage crinoline's boning are made with whalebone, and beneath them (rather than over top), gauzy white material is spread in a dreamy, ethereal way that makes me think of the webs ghost spiders might weave. I've accessorized with black widow earrings, a snow of glitter across my cheekbones, and silvery twigs tucked into my hair. With the color of my hair and dress, I'm going for "drop of blood in a haunted ice cave," and judging by the despair on Gilda's face when she spots me, it's a success. I feel pretty—if a bit self-conscious. Not because I'm embarrassed about what I'm wearing, but because it draws attention, which I don't enjoy. It is a burden to be this fashionable.

"Next up," Gilda calls, "we've got the Moonville Historical Society, who will . . ." She pauses to read from her card. "Let you in on their highly exclusive quilting circle. Haven't accepted a new member since 2002! Annalee and Ruth McMahon, this is your moment, gals. Go knit some baby booties and let the rest of us have a turn under the hair dryer for once."

"You're fidgeting," I murmur to Luna, who's wiping her pink palms on her boho maxi skirt. She's wearing ten pounds of moonstone necklaces, and a cropped yellow tank that matches the sunflower tattooed on her shoulder. She keeps fiddling with her hair, nervously panning the audience. Romina, who is only volunteering her flora fortunist services today, is in a brown plaid number with puffed sleeves and a straw cloche hat. Ahead of us, her boyfriend, Alex, carries a toolbox that I assume is a symbolic representation of his donated skills.

"You are," she mutters back.

"No, I'm not. I'm standing very, very still." It often unnerves people. I like to sometimes pretend I was cursed into a statue and I cannot move unless somebody says the right word to reverse the spell. I focus on my breathing to make it as unnoticeable as possible and imagine vines and thorns growing out of the ground beneath my feet. If anyone speaks to me while I'm doing my thorn-and-vine-imagining and I haven't gotten to the bit yet where the vines settle into a crown on top of my head, I ignore them until I'm finished. People really do not like it.

"Are you *sure* you won't auction off a date?" Gilda complains to Alex before he mounts the stage steps.

Alex glances back at Romina, pretending to consider it.

"I'd wring your neck," she warns.

His mouth slides into a grin as he steps up beside Gilda. "Don't threaten me with a good time."

"Up next," Gilda announces, her sequined shawl blinding everyone when a dagger of sunlight sneaks out from behind a cloud and strikes her, "is Alex King. You might be surprised to see him with a toolbox, since he told us before he left for college that he wanted to be a doctor. Instead, he has decided to be a roofer. There are already hundreds of roofs in Moonville, but only three doctors. Who am I to judge? Surely, God will. Anyway, up for bid is Alex King and his box of tools. Here's your chance, ladies, to get that porch rail fixed! Your useless husbands are all lying, they're never gonna do it. Let's start the bidding at twenty-five dollars. Do I hear twenty-five dollars?"

Ultimately, Alex's mother pays close to two hundred bucks for him to build her a mailbox that will resemble a miniature version of the house she just bought. This is how he learns that his mom and new stepdad, Daniel (Trevor's father), have decided to move back to Moonville after their recent wedding.

"Next up is . . ." Gilda's gaze settles on mine, as I'm now at the front of the queue. Luna, that chicken, has retreated even farther back. "A date with Zelda Tempest."

She offers a hand to assist me as I ascend the steps, and only now, at this exact moment, does it occur to me that it is quite possible nobody will bid at all. Such an experience would be devastating. How deeply tragic that I did not consider this prospect until facing all of my sisters' friends and neighbors (I myself do not keep many friends), who may be witnesses to my ego's blunt death.

"Zelda Tempest is thirty-two years old and yes, that is her natural hair color," Gilda states. "She's an author of books about dead people who don't stay dead and she works at The Magick Happens, but you'd never know it because she's always hiding in the basement. I suppose it's a small step up from when she was a kid and used to hide in the woods. Remember? We could never find her!"

"Please do my obituary someday," I tell her warmly. "You're such a natural at this."

"Thanks. I honed my talents on Rotten Tomatoes." She clears her throat. "Zelda enjoys black-and-white photography of old sheds and trying out new sports!" (This is not true.) "Let's start the bidding at a thousand dollars."

Nobody raises their paddle.

"I'm joking! Let's start the bidding at ten dollars."

I clasp my hands into a sweating knot and close my eyes, sinking into my happy place: Curled up in a chair in my attic, reading *Vlad the Impaler: A Captivating Guide to How Vlad III Dracula Became One of the Most Crucial Rulers of Wallachia and His Impact on the History of Romania.* Flickering in the periphery, a candle scents the dark room with cinnamon, nutmeg, and roasted chocolate. Straight ahead lies a window— the curtains sweep themselves aside, revealing another window across the street, and beyond it—

I open my eyes again.

"One hundred," Gilda is droning in the background, but I hardly hear her over the noise of my thoughts. I cast my gaze past all the faces and their varied expressions, the hands that lift and the ones that lower, deciding I am not worth *quite* that much money. The bespectacled man who purchased my book is nowhere to be seen. My attention rambles to the forest just beyond.

"Poor guy won't know what hit him," I hear Luna remark.

And a curious thing happens—

The top of the forest moves.

The air is solid and heavy, no wind to cut it, but the forest's canopies sway. It reminds me of insect antennae. All of my other thoughts are emptied out, a rush of blood to my head, and it feels like

Zelda!

A familiar voice I can't quite place, speaking my name.

Zelda. Zelda.

You've forgotten.

Gilda seizes my hand and raises it with a celebratory "Two hundred and fifty dollars going once, going twice, sold to Morgan Angelopoulos."

The mystery voice halts at once. What on earth was that?

I descend the steps, and there he is. His right eye squints against a burst of sunlight through the treetops, painting his cheek with gold dust. His left eye is a brilliant, shining brown, regarding me with an eager, speculative appreciation.

"Perfect," he murmurs. "This could not have gone better than if I'd planned it all myself."

"I'm here! Don't start without me," someone exclaims, breaking between shoulders. It's Dylan, glasses askew, shirt half-tucked into his jeans. "I couldn't find my shoes. Then my tire had a flat, and once I got on the road, rain started pouring down so thick I couldn't see."

Morgan beams at me. "Guess what?" he tells Dylan without bothering to glance at him. "You're too late."

FIVE

Spirits of those who die alone in the woods are
called brays, and they move with the storms.

Local Legends and Superstitions,
Tempest Family Grimoire

Re: New Idea

Hi, Zelda! Hope you're doing well. I had the
opportunity to read over your proposal, and
while CATASTROPHICAL sounds fun, there's a lot
going on here that perhaps needs to be pared
back. I also worry that a vampire main
character might not be enough of a departure
from Henriette. While you know I LOVE
Henriette, I think we can both agree that it's
time for something new. Should we schedule a
phone chat?

All best,

Abigail

Editor (she, her)

Sara Spright Books | Wuthering Press

Self-doubt is a sickness. As I examine myself, I can almost see it spreading down my arms, pooling in the creases of my fingers. It colors the space between my ears with monochrome fuzz.

I don't have any good new ideas. I'm a one-off.

My phone rings.

I jump in my seat; I'd begun to slouch sideways, eyes glazed on the email from my editor. The computer screen falls asleep, and now all I see is myself, blank-faced and utterly failing at this core part of my identity that I am supposed to love.

I scramble upright. "Hello?" I've accepted the call without checking the name. "Who's this?"

"Morgan. Did I catch you at a bad time?"

"Not at all." I'm instantly bright-eyed. "What is it?"

"It," he replies, "is *time.*"

"Hm?" I move my mouse around to wake up the computer. "Eight o'clock."

He laughs. It's soft and dark, conjuring images of kissing in closets, or traipsing along Black Sands Beach as the stars lift up. I shiver. "Yes, I know. I'd like to take you on our date tonight."

Tonight? I am not a Woman Ready to Go Out; I'm in black velour pants with the top two buttons unsnapped, and an oversized, holey Jack Skellington shirt, my hair stuffed sloppily in a claw clip.

"It's . . . kind of late for a date, don't you think? I already ate dinner."

"I'm not taking you to dinner. Be downstairs in ten minutes."

"Wait—"

He hangs up.

I am soon swimming through all the clothes I own. Pants and skirts and dresses and tops, all my favorites are in the dirty laundry hamper, *of course*; where's that gray outfit I bought especially for dates? Oh, but it doesn't fit when I'm this close to starting my period. *Thunderation*, I have nothing decent to wear.

I eventually track down my black-and-green-plaid dress under Aisling's bed, shimmy into black tights, and I'm off to the races (with an extra deodorant in my purse, just in case I start nervous-sweating).

Downstairs, Morgan is pacing the sidewalk, dressed in his usual shine and flash. His brow is furrowed, eyes cast down, lips moving silently as if he's talking to himself. When he spots me, that strange expression on his face melts away and he mirages back into the Morgan Angelopoulos I recognize: leaning against his vehicle, legs crossed at the ankles, shoulders back. He is the portrait of cool confidence.

"Hello, gorgeous." He greets me in a sleek, seductive voice.

"Hi. You look nice."

"Not as nice as you." He opens the passenger door of his car and waits for me to slide inside. I am the human equivalent of ten cups of espresso as I buckle my seat belt. Do first dates always feel this way? I don't remember being so jittery in the past.

He peers in his rearview mirror. Morgan wears his anticipation like a heavy cologne, high energy burning outward. It crackles where it touches my own energy, inquisitive and fickle, coiling itself protectively around my body. "Where are we going?"

"It's a surprise."

With dinner out of the equation, that doesn't leave many options. The movies? I try to recall what's playing. I'm so consumed with wondering where we'll end up that I don't pay attention to where we're going until we're speeding *in reverse* up a hill. I brace my hands against the glove box. "What are you doing?"

"You have to drive backwards on Wiley Palmer Road," he replies breezily. "Everybody knows that. The Black Bear Witch can only see you if you're moving forwards."

"This isn't safe!"

"Nobody'll be coming from the other direction. There's only one thing at the end of this road, and trust me, I'm the only person in this town who wants to go there."

I lay out a mental map of the area, memory clouded by panic. The words *Wiley Palmer* are a flashing DANGER! sign in my mind, connected to a childhood of horror stories, rumors, the fact that it's a dangerous road in general. But then I remember—

And then I see it.

Turning fully in my seat, I catch Morgan's smile as the outline of a saltbox house looms into view.

As a kid, I loved the old story that the Davilla house is alive, aware of you. If you wish to enter, first you have to feed it.

Even though I'm an adult, a wonderful terror still flutters at the sight—because the memory is so strong, the memory of what I *believed*. Suddenly, it isn't only me and Morgan sitting in this car; ten-year-old Zelda is with us, too. She believes, and she presses her hands to the window, wriggling with delight.

He puts us in park, headlights slowly dying as the engine shudders to a standstill. For a moment, all is silent.

"You brought me to an abandoned house?"

"I certainly did."

I don't remove my gaze from the crooked timber-framed building, which used to be brown, I think, but has rinsed to an ash-gray, roof collapsed on one side, vines choking broken windows. The house's face, propped against a rust-red sunset, has sagged in a way that lends it a sad expression. All five trees in front of the house have veered, leaning from it; an aspen near the chimney is so curved that its trunk has made itself horizontal, and you could sit on its trunk like a bench. I'm amazed nobody's torn the place down, then salted the earth yet.

My heart *tha-rump, tha-rump*s. I look properly at Morgan now, and he is watching me—unsmiling, curious, a bit hopeful, maybe. I grin back at him.

"This is perfect."

SIX

The Davilla house must be dusted so that it
does not fall ill. Rearrange the furniture, replace
it as needed, to keep it happy and entertained.
If neglected, the house will turn feral.

Local Legends and Superstitions,
Tempest Family Grimoire

I AM RETROACTIVELY DISAPPOINTED that none of the men I've dated have had the consideration to bring me to a haunted house.

Morgan is pleased. "Seemed like it might be up your alley."

"It has a permanent address on my alley. I *love* creepy places."

He closes the trunk of his car, swinging a backpack over one shoulder. A flashlight, digital audio recorder, and headphones hang from various clips on his tool belt. He tosses me a flashlight.

I switch it on, experimenting with the different modes. "Fun! What's the plan?"

"To make contact, hopefully." A small pink ball bounces out of the pocket of his backpack, lighting up when it hits the grass. He scoops it.

"Is that a cat toy?"

"Yep. These things *only* light up when touched. We'll put it on the floor and step away, and if it activates, we'll know a ghost is trying to communicate." He peers at the house, running a hand through his windswept hair. Then he gives me a camera. "Would you mind recording this?"

I blink at it, still distracted by his hair. "Uh. Yeah, sure."

"Fantastic. Start recording now, please, and keep filming even if it seems like nothing's happening. I might be able to pick up interesting stuff in the background while I'm editing the video."

"Will you post this online?"

"Not the footage itself, no. I'll review it later, then discuss anything noteworthy in my next podcast episode. You can let me know when you're available to guest chat, so we can discuss the experience together."

I pointedly do not commit to that, and tap the record button.

The ground leading up to the house is uneven, reminding me of a crème brûlée after you've cracked the sugar crust with a spoon. I scan our environment through the flip screen on the camera: up close, the front of the house seems to be swollen, and whichever room is tacked to the right of the porch bulges out. I frown at the coloring in the screen, the way it makes the house look brown again, the grass not as vibrant, almost as if we're walking across a late autumn scape. The sky is off-color in the camera, too, more like late afternoon than 8:25 p.m.

"Built in 1934," Morgan utters into his Dictaphone, "by Frank Davilla. The Great Depression hit his family hard. Had two younger brothers who lived with him, his wife, and three kids. Was accused of inappropriate behavior toward a preacher's wife, and the congregation shunned the whole family. Tried to drive them out of town. Mrs. Davilla, a pious lady and Sunday school teacher, was devastated to lose her community and tried to get them to forgive Frank so that she could return to the church. On March fifth, 1945, Frank's wife and his two younger brothers were found dead in their beds. Frank and his children were never seen again."

I study the house. "Are you hoping to find Frank?"

"Or anyone else still here. Maybe they'll know why Mrs. Davilla, Nate, and Otto were murdered, and what happened to the missing family members." He lays a paintbrush on the doorstep. "Feeding the house," he explains. "Mrs. Davilla liked to paint."

I don't believe in ghosts, but as a writer of paranormal mysteries, this is fantastic field experience. And unorthodox for a date, which makes me all the happier.

I test the front door. The knob rattles loosely, unlocked and broken, but the door itself has engorged in the July heat and sticks to its frame. I press harder, hoping there aren't any cops cruising nearby. Not that they'd have much reason to. This house is so notorious for its (alleged) malevolent spirits that even the most intrepid of teenagers dare not use its halls as a place to drink or make out.

"So, one sister who does candle magic. One sister who does flower magic." He eyes me sidelong. "And what about you?"

"Lately? I read and sell books." The door finally gives way. "When's the last time you were here?"

"Never been inside. I've checked out the property, but you don't go into a place like this without backup."

"How long have you been into the paranormal?"

He sighs. "Not as long as you have. About two years."

We're in what appears to be a living room, and it definitely hasn't been sitting empty for seventy-eight years. I expected cobwebs, dirt, and bugs. Peeling paint, strips of plaster hanging from the ceiling.

There *is* damage to the ceiling: it bows in places, perhaps from gathered water. But there isn't any dust, no paint leaves shedding from walls. Not a single spiderweb. It's a surprisingly small room, compared to what it looked like from the outside of the house, with a boarded-up fireplace, a child's sandal (judging by the style, it was left here sometime in the past fifteen years), a framed painting on the wall, a desk, and a McDonald's Happy Meal toy still in its plastic. The air smells peculiarly like one of the walls in my living room. The wall back home, which currently has a television and armchair pushed against it, has always carried a scent of rose water and tobacco. Nobody in my family smokes tobacco, and neither did my grandmother.

"I'm not really *into* the paranormal," I tell him. "I only write about it."

Morgan isn't listening. "That's the desk where they found the severed hand!" He turns, shining the light directly in my eyes. I wince, and he lowers it but is too wired to apologize. "It didn't belong to any of the victims. Wasn't a match for Frank's description. They never figured out who it might have belonged to, but the weirdest part is that it smelled like sulfur and spontaneously combusted during forensic analysis."

"Very weird," I agree. "Two years you've been doing this, then? Two years ago is about the time you started renting my old desk at the shop."

"Yeah. I mean, you've heard what Aisling says about ghosts. It's impossible not to be intrigued."

"You believe in ghosts because of Aisling?"

"I always thought . . . *maybe*. Maybe they're real. But then I started listening to her stories, and now I'm a true believer."

Key word: *stories*.

I try not to sigh, but it's inescapable.

"Her information's so specific, it has to come from *somewhere*," he goes on. "Luna monitors what Ash gets up to online. She doesn't watch any ghost hunting shows. So it's like, how does she know any of this?"

Credit where credit is due: Ash can give a hell of a convincing speech. But still, I pity him for being so gullible.

Morgan thumbs through a book he's brought along: *The Unidentified: Mythical Monsters, Alien Encounters, and Our Obsession with the Unexplained*, and I am helpless to float over, skimming it with him. "You dog-ear your books," I observe.

He flicks me a guilty look. "Yeah."

"So do I."

His face brightens. "You do?"

"I write in them, too. Little footnotes."

"*Yes.*" He smacks the book against his palm. "Exactly. That's what books are meant for! Love them, mark them. Fill up the margins."

I have to hold myself steady, hand to the wall, so that I don't faint into a dead swoon. What I wouldn't give to read this man's margins.

He peruses drawers in the rolltop desk, which prove empty. Not a paper clip, not a dead cricket, not a mousetrap in sight. "I thought The Magick Happens was going to be my novel-writing muse," he tells me, "but it turned out to be a gateway to something entirely different. I work for the newspaper, you know, but a couple years ago, I actually wanted to write books, too."

"Really?"

He tests the first three steps of the staircase to see if they'll hold his weight. They don't even creak, so we forge our way up. The carpet is tan but probably used to be white. "I'd write three thousand words, then get a shiny new idea, and set it aside. Write three thousand words of the new idea, scrap them for another new idea. You get the picture. It was disappointing, because I'd been telling myself I was going to be a novelist—it seemed like the next step, for some reason. But I'm a short-stories kinda guy, it turns out. I like the challenge of limited length, and it keeps me from getting bored. Speaking of stories, what are you working on now? Are you gonna add to the Villamoon universe, or . . . ?"

"What can you tell me about ghosts?" I blurt. "I haven't done much research." Intentionally. I've always worried that if I let myself fall down supernatural rabbit holes, I'd end up believing again. Most of the lore in my books comes from my own imagination.

As it happens, Morgan can tell me a *lot* about ghosts.

SEVEN

I once knew a girl who gathered up death.
Into her basket of dreams it went.
She knew not that she plucked
the fate spelling her end,
for it looked
just like
a
friend.

Author unknown,
As Evening Falls

V RAYS DIMINISH their energy, which is why you tend to make stronger contact at night. They are sometimes more responsive if you're dressed from their era. To most people, they're invisible, but just about anybody has the potential to glimpse one *if* they've been awake for too long but their brain still feels sharp. Something about that particular state opens the mind up to seeing beyond our physical plane. Encounters usually get shrugged off as 'seeing things,' though."

Morgan requires very little from a conversation partner, happy to chatter enough for the both of us. "Interesting." I tap the tail of a classic Kit-Cat Klock on the stairway's landing. Vintage to me, but modern by Davilla standards, this clock must have been a gift from a fellow trespasser. The minute hand ticks once, in response, before swinging back to its broken sentry at two thirty. Morgan removes it from the wall, sliding it into his backpack; in the clock's place, he hangs a small painting of a sailboat.

When we reach the top, a long hallway is spackled blue with a shine like moonlight although such a thing is impossible, for it's a new moon tonight. The air is warmer up here, thicker, as if holding its breath.

"A common misconception about ghosts," Morgan goes on, "is that they mostly stick to old, historic sites. Lonely farmhouses. Abandoned prisons, psychiatric facilities, funeral homes. Not true! Ghosts can pop up anywhere, and they move freely, changing residences whenever they feel like it. Ghosts like comfort zones. The house they grew up in, or a movie theater they used to love visiting. Sites that brought them joy when they were alive. Disney World is a billion times more haunted than any morgue."

"Then we probably won't find anyone here," I point out. "Does this seem like a comfort zone to you?"

"To somebody, yes, I think it was. Who knows what this place looked like, once upon a time? Based on multiple eyewitness accounts, there have to be *some* ghosts established in this house."

The second floor holds three bedrooms and a bathroom. Bedroom number one is empty save for a glass bottle on the windowsill, half filled with loose dirt. The carpet has been partially torn up, revealing wood floors with scorch marks.

Bedroom number two contains a little girl's tea table, but the two chairs accompanying it sit on the opposite side of the

room, facing a cheval mirror with dark speckles across its surface like lichen. I step closer to the mirror. Morgan takes a
miniature piano out of his bag and lifts its lid, and the charming little music box begins to play "Wiegenlied" by Johannes
Brahms.

Years ago, I heard Piano Quintet in F minor, Op. 34, by
Johannes Brahms and became besotted with the pianist, which
only increased when I saw a picture of Johannes in his younger
days. This is not the first time I've been swept away by somebody I've never met, not even knowing what they looked like or
caring if they were already dust in a grave. After devouring
a collection of short stories called *The Barnum Museum* by
Steven Millhauser, and, in particular, the tale "Eisenheim the
Illusionist," I was half in love with the author. He was, at that
time, a septuagenarian.

I look at Morgan as the notes of "Wiegenlied" tinkle around
us like glass chimes, and he glows even rosier in my view.

I wait until he retreats from the room, investigating the
bathroom across the hall, and touch my fingertips to the warped
ones in the glass. Daring something to happen. For the expression in my reflection to change; to see the flickers of a sinister
Victorian child in a white dress, moving closer with every
blink. I wait, anticipating, and then—

A black blur streaks across the mirror, behind me. I whirl.
"Was that you, Morgan?"

"Did you say something?" he calls from the bathroom.

My eyes sweep the corner where I saw the blur: with the
angles of the room and the position of the doorway, there's no
chance it was the reflection of a bird flying past the window.

The spookiest thing about this house, somehow, is that the windows are all so tiny, their placements random. Some are near the ceiling, others close to the floor. None of them are centered, and the size of them reminds me of a jail cell.

We're in the dark, alone, in a creepy, isolated location. We're primed for fear. Our imaginations are doing half the work, so all we need now is an external trigger: whether it be wind causing a door to creak, a mouse rustling papers, or a distant noise contorted by echoes.

Oh, how I *adore* a good scare.

The bathroom is my favorite room of the house so far. It's got an oval stained-glass window, a rush of impossible moonlight tinting the clapboard walls and tile floor green. The bathtub isn't claw-foot, sadly, but it *does* have rings of rust around the drain and a stain that vaguely resembles a handprint, minus the fingers. The seventies-floral shower curtain is cut in half, suspended two feet short of the tub. The sink has been wrenched out of the wall, exposing the dark hole of a long pipe, and a spider scuttling out.

A faint sigh expels from the pipe.

I stick my ear against it. "What are you doing?" Morgan asks, leaning in.

"Listen." My eyes close. I count the beats: three, six, nine. "It's as if the house is *breathing*."

"Get away, it might be the house's mouth." He pauses. "Wait. Do you feel that? Come here."

I join him. He passes his hand through midair, then jolts back. "It's cold in that spot."

He's right. "Ooooh. Fun." I search the walls for a vent, a

hole in the wall for air to blast through. I do find a hole in the ceiling, which is the likely culprit. Happiness dances through me to have found the source. I love an aha moment, pinning down the *why* and *how*.

"Bathroom on the second floor," Morgan reports to his Dictaphone, "contains a cold spot about the height and width of an adult human. Corroborated by Zelda Tempest, paranormal expert." He measures the temperature with a thermometer, numbers erratically rising and dipping, ranging from eighty-one degrees to sixty-four.

"I'm not a paranormal expert," I insist. "And I think your thermometer isn't working."

He smiles as if I've made a joke. To his Dictaphone, he says, "I'm Morgan, and this is Zelda. We are not here to hurt you. We're here to learn more about you, and if we can, we'd like to help you. Can you please tell us your name?" He holds the recorder out, toward the cold spot.

After a minute, he plays the recording of himself talking to the ghost, listening to the silence afterward. Disappointed, he replays it twice more as if the results will change.

"Sometimes you can see ghosts but can't hear them," he informs me. "Sometimes what they say comes after a twenty-minute delay. Or you don't hear their voice until much later, after you've left."

"Mm." I want him to like me. I don't want to question him, make him feel as if his beliefs are being attacked. And yet I cannot help saying, "So you've seen these ghosts yourself, I take it?"

"Well, no," he admits. "This is just what I've heard."

"Mm."

His long-lashed eyes narrow. "It feels like I'm sharing all of my theories, but you're not sharing yours."

Dodging his gaze, I zoom the camera on the wallpaper border, but it just gets fuzzier. "I don't have any theories."

"I mean, you do. You wrote about ghosts in *It Howls*." The fifth book in my series. "They weren't main characters, but you *did* have ghosts in there. I assume you collected some info while learning about them."

"Not really. I pulled from general knowledge: ghosts are remnants of dead souls, who sometimes moan and kill living people when the whim strikes. Where'd you get all your theories, anyway?"

"From Ash."

I shake my head. "You put too much stock into what a child says."

We check out the final bedroom on this floor, which replaces the bathroom as my favorite. A pipe organ with six keys missing. Books about farming, printed in the 1800s, strewn about. Some are still readable, but splotched with mold and, in one case, insect eggs. I scoop the books up in spite of Morgan's grimace, explaining that I can clean them later. An Orange County almanac's pages have melded together and hardened, dense as rock. A sewing machine sits on a table, its teeth still biting down in the cuff of trousers small enough to fit a young boy. I pick up an empty, discolored bottle of C. C. Parsons' Household Ammonia.

"Let's go back downstairs," he suggests. "I read an article from the fifties about a teenage boy and his girlfriend who snuck out here. They said they heard a teakettle whistling in the kitchen, but the stove was off."

"Moonville is certainly rich in stories," I say, tracing the porcelain mane of a chipped rocking horse with one finger. "But what other types of stories do you like?" We have to have shared interests *somewhere*, if I dig enough. "Any nonfiction?"

"Right now, I'm reading *True Tales of Ghosts*."

I force a smile. "What about books that don't involve ghosts?"

Morgan thinks for a minute, then grins broadly. "A few months ago I finished a book that teaches about how to unlock the power of telepathy. Wanna borrow? You'll love it. I haven't been able to unlock my inner powers of telepathy yet, but with some more practice, who knows!"

Oh dear.

We go back downstairs. As my foot presses a step, it lets out a loud groan. So does the next, and the one after that. They grumble even louder under Morgan's weight; we exchange mystified looks. "These weren't noisy when we were going up."

Another oddity: once back in the living room, we notice a curio cabinet we don't remember seeing earlier.

"We probably saw it but didn't really *see* it, because we'd just come into the house and were taking everything in at once," I reason. "We weren't paying attention."

"Or." His gaze travels, rapt on the piece of furniture. "It wasn't here."

I almost laugh. "A ghost cabinet?"

I'm only kidding, but he nods. "Sort of. This might be part of a flashback." At my expression, he explains: "Memories that have attached to a particular space are called flashbacks. It's a super common phenomenon in Moonville because of all the magic here. The apparitions in a flashback aren't actually ghosts. Magic is attracted to people experiencing spikes of heightened emotion, which can be happy moments, frightening ones, angry ones. Magic records it, and the recording plays on a loop, stamped in the place where the memory was made. Since high-emotion events can include untimely deaths, when you hear wailing or screaming, you could be hearing somebody's final minutes over and over. So, if this theory is correct, it isn't necessarily that a location is being haunted by ghosts— it's that the location itself is still replaying a memory, even though the people in them are long gone. You can tell a flashback from a ghost by the way they don't see or hear you, or attempt to communicate."

The curio cabinet is old-fashioned, but so well-preserved that it looks brand-new, shelves stocked with medicine bottles, books, a sewing box, and porcelain horses.

Morgan takes a spool of blue thread from his backpack and rests it on a shelf.

A *thump* from another room has us turning our heads away from the cabinet. He and I raise our eyebrows at each other, trailing into a dining room. Unlike the rest of the house, this room is properly decayed. Wallpaper has sloughed off, revealing grayish plaster. Two low-backed chairs flank a fireplace, hearth thick with brick dust, an easel in front of it, on which sits a painting of a basset hound. Our footsteps sound much louder here than anywhere else. The shift in atmosphere from living room to dining room is arresting. It feels like something's *stopped.* As if we were operating on a timer, the house alive and listening, until now, and now it is just a house.

See, this is the part I love—I don't believe, but part of me wants to, and it's spectacular to get carried away by my imagination. My imagination and I haven't been the greatest of friends lately; it abandons me whenever the second-guessing starts up. *Not good enough. Not original enough. Delete and start again.*

Thump. The floor beneath my right shoe quivers.

"It's coming from below," I say, keeping my voice hushed.

"The basement." He shines a flashlight at the dirty carpet, beige with a faded pink rose pattern, as if we'll be able to see through to the other side. "That used to be Otto Davilla's room, and where his body was found."

"We have to go down there."

Surprise spreads over his features. "You're seriously up for it?"

I meet his gaze. It is the sweetest indulgence to admire his face for as long as I like, and all I want is for him to keep talking and talking so that I have an excuse to keep on looking and looking. He's got the most beautiful eyes in creation, astonishingly dark. Morgan's gaze is fossilized shark teeth, volcanic glass, the Dark Horse Nebula. It makes me think of the lightless void of black holes, and endlessness, floating through space like cosmic dust, like a fresh drop of ink being drunk into paper. The black widow's long legs as she elegantly spins her web. When he walks into a shaft of light, a rainbow luster is added to the darkness, and I think then of Tahitian pearls. Alder leaf beetles. The common grackle bird, with its oil-slick feathers.

"Absolutely," I say.

Morgan drops his backpack, flips it open. He pulls out a battery-operated traffic light, which I recognize, since I once purchased it for Aisling as a Christmas present.

"Why do you have that?"

"On loan." He pats the yellow lens fondly. "This thing is more reliable than any EMF reader, any para light, any REM pod. It's been sitting in your house, which is haunted, absorbing magic and supernatural energy. I call it the Surefire."

I am beginning to suspect that Morgan is a few trees short of a forest. I am bewildered, but no less attracted to him. His eccentricity has a hook in me, rather—even though he is quite wrong, I am drawn in.

"Henriette Davilla," he announces. "Are you here with—"

"Wait," I interrupt. "Her name's Henriette?"

"Yeah. I figured you knew that? You took so many Moonville facts and tweaked them to fit your books that I assumed you used the name Henriette specifically because of the Davillas."

Come to think of it, I don't remember why I picked that name. It's possible that I subconsciously hoovered it from Moonville's legends, like I did so many other things.

The red lens of the stoplight flickers, then winks out.

I jump back a step. Morgan's lips press together, whitening. His upper lip is more pigmented than the lower, the slope of each line meeting in a slight lift at the corners, so that he looks perpetually amused even when his mouth is at rest.

"Is this Otto or Nate?" he asks the room.

The red lens flickers again, right as we hear another *thump*, louder this time. And much closer.

A door slams.

I turn sharply.

"Hello?" someone shouts. "Who else is here?"

Morgan and I sprint into the living room, where we find the last two people I would ever expect: Joan Finkel and Wanda Horowitz, two ladies who work at Our Little Secret, the local murder mystery dinner theater. Wanda's doubled over, hands on knees, wheezing. Her flashlight rolls across the floor.

"You scared the poor old broad something bad," Joan chastises us.

"You scared us, too." My dress is sticking to my sweaty back. "What are you *doing* here?"

Joan rotates Wanda, who's still wheezing, so that we can read the letters on the back of her shirt: MOONVILLE GHOST HUNTERS ORG, with a cartoon ghost holding a magnifying glass.

"I didn't know there was a local chapter!" Morgan is euphoric. "Where do I sign up?"

Joan fetches Wanda's flashlight. "You shouldn't've come here without us. Places like this can be dangerous if you don't know what you're doing." She juts a thumb at the door. "We're clearing out—we were just down in the basement and heard the cops on our police scanner app. A concerned citizen said they saw a car driving backwards in this area, so we might have company soon. It is, ah, not quite legal to be here."

"My EMF reader!" Wanda howls. "I left it in the basement."

"I'll help you find it," I offer, just as Joan's phone emits clicking noises, a voice rippling, "*White Buick Verano.*"

Morgan swears. "That's my car!"

EIGHT

Henriette's eyes snap wide, trying to listen over the violence of her own heartbeat, and a new wind comes howling, shadows rising from the ground into an animal that stands on its hind legs, eyes like dust clouds. The terrible creature lets out a shrill scream of warning.

Legend of the Black Bear Witch,
Zelda Tempest

YOU BETTER GET outta here," Joan advises.

Morgan and I bolt. Just before he reaches for the door handle of his car, he grinds to a halt. "Wait a minute. Did you see the curio cabinet? I think it disappeared again."

"Does it matter right now?"

He nods once. "Right. I'll check another time."

We pile in.

I turn off his camera and stow it back in his bag. "Do you know any other roads out of here?"

"This is the only one that connects to Piedmont." And then, to my horror, he steers the vehicle around and begins driving in reverse.

"Not again!" I scrabble for purchase in the car as branches of three-hundred-year-old trees scrape at our windows, sucking us into a black, clawing tunnel. "This is not how I want to die! There's supposed to be"—we rocket over a pothole, and I clutch my door handle with a scream—"two wineglasses, one body. Missing jewels. A luxuriously decorated sitting room with a half-burned envelope in the fireplace."

"Don't worry, I've done this a thousand times." But even as he says it, one of the tires slips off the edge of the road, dragging us toward a steep slope, and he corrects so forcibly that I'm swung forward, seat belt strangling me.

"The backwards-on-Wiley-Palmer thing is an urban legend," I manage to rasp. "Nobody actually does it."

"I do. If the witch sees us, she might magic up a bunch of different dead-end roads and we'll end up lost."

I tilt my head back, pulse racing. We're barreling in reverse through a forest, after sundown, on a narrow road that curves like a sidewinder. "Let me out."

"Zelda. I promise, you will live long enough to be murdered for your jewels someday. I've got this."

"You're going to get arrested or worse. You cannot DRIVE BACKWARDS!"

"I don't have a choice! You should know better than anyone that if you drive forwards down Wiley Palmer, the Black Bear Witch will climb into your head and crack it open like a nut."

"Please turn around." My eyes squeeze shut.

"Zelda, listen. I respect you and I hear what you're saying and all, but I am *not* about to be cursed by a five-hundred-year-old shape-shifting witch. There are scarier things in this world than Ross Baumgartner, who is barely even a cop. All he does is lurk in Moonshine's parking lot, hoping to catch people carrying open containers of alcohol. Wait till we make it to

Piedmont, and then I'll drive the regular way and you can stop digging your nails into my arm."

"There's no such thing as curses," I seethe, digging my nails in harder. "Pull over pull over pull over."

"But the Black Bear Witch—"

"The Black Bear Witch isn't real," I snap.

He accidentally presses the gas, sending us careening for a terrifying moment. When I wake up tomorrow, all of my beautiful red hair will have turned gray overnight. "What do you mean? You *wrote* about it."

"In a book!" I cry. "A fictional book. None of it's real. How can you think it's real? There is no witch. There are no ghosts. There *is. No. Magic.*"

I think I would almost find the dumbfounded look on his face funny, were it not for the fact that he keeps looking at me instead of the road, risking untethering my fragile little life from this mortal plane.

"But you're a witch."

"Witches aren't real."

"You cannot possibly mean that—"

"I do," I cut in vehemently. "I'm sorry to disappoint you, Morgan, but that is the truth. Anyone who claims otherwise is either duped or lying, and I am neither of those."

Morgan is speechless for maybe the first time in his life.

"Now will you please—" I begin to say calmly, right as a dog darts into the road. I scream at the top of my lungs: "Stop!"

Morgan slams on the brake, tires squealing. "What? What is it?" My heart pumps furiously, so dizzy with adrenaline that the back seat of his car wavers in my view. He stares anxiously around, unclipping his seat belt. Just behind us, sitting utterly still in the ruby glow of brake lights, is . . . not a dog, I don't think. It might be a coyote, with something jammed over its head.

"What is it?" Morgan looks at me.

"I don't know."

"But you told me to stop. Why'd you tell me to stop?" He runs his hands over his face, distressed. "You scared the shit out of me."

"I didn't want you to hit it."

"Hit *what*?"

"That!" I point.

He throws up his arms. "I don't see anything."

I fling open my car door.

"What're you doing? It's dark. We're in the woods. Don't—"

"The poor animal has a piece of fence stuck to its head, I think. It isn't leaving for a reason; it needs our help." I close the door, cutting him off.

There are no streetlights out here, surroundings as black as the depths of Jacob's Well. In the shoulder, long grasses whisper against my legs as I steady myself. There's a deep ditch to my left, no guardrail to keep me from toppling over.

"It's all right," I croon, creeping as slow as I can manage, offering my palms. "I'm not going to hurt you."

Morgan rolls his window down. "Please tell me it isn't a skunk. I am not letting you back into this car if you get sprayed. You didn't mean what you said about not being a witch, right?"

"I'm not a friggin' witch," I hiss. "And does this look like a skunk to you?"

"I don't see anything." He tries to open his door, but it clunks into a tree. "There isn't enough room for me to get out."

"Stay where you are. I don't want to scare it away."

The animal's ears twitch in different directions, toward me and then Morgan, then back to me. Its eyes are set closer together than a coyote's, more oblong, but its snout definitely resembles a coyote. "It's all right," I whisper. "I only want to help you."

I reach out, slowly, slowly, trying to get a grip of the thing on its head, but frown. The thing has a velvety texture, and I can't find a way to pry it loose because it's become . . . fused . . . to its skull.

I draw back, staring.

This coyote has *antlers*.

The animal stares at me, and I stop breathing as I lower to my knees, taking in the weird shape of it all. Short fur, a longer neck, like a greyhound. Definitely paws, not hooves—and then, of course, the impossible antlers. They're short, bunchy ones, shaped like two small pieces of coral. Has somebody glued them to him? I'm reminded of P. T. Barnum's "Fiji mermaid," which was just a fish and monkey skeleton sewn together, and my heart breaks for this poor baby.

The animal turns in a circle. With its head bent close to the taillight, I can make out exactly where the growths protrude from its scalp, the fur surrounding it a gradient of copper to gray to black. The fur on its long, bony tail is as short as the fur on its snout, skin molded so tightly to its vertebrae that it looks vacuum-sealed.

"Did you pull the fence off it yet?" Morgan asks.

"I . . ." My voice cracks.

Morgan tries to climb across the seats to get out through my door, elbow bumping the loud horn on his steering wheel. *Beeeep!* Before I can react, the coyote-with-antlers shoots off, switchgrass rustling, and is swallowed by the woods.

I move forward. And from somewhere in the trees floats a soft female voice: *"The clock of . . ."*

I freeze. "Hello?"

"What?" Morgan calls back. I ignore him, straining to listen.

"Old and new," the voice goes on, light as a flower. I step just a foot backward, and the voice fades away. Maybe I heard somebody's radio.

"Where did it go?" Morgan asks, joining me at my side. "What was it?"

I stare into the darkness.

"Zelda." He waves a large hand in front of my face. "Hey. You here? You can tell me the truth, you know. A lot of witches keep it secret, they don't go around advertising like your sisters do—"

"I already told you the truth." My patience is running thin. "Anybody who says magic is real is trying to sell you something."

He seizes a fistful of his hair. "Two hundred and fifty dollars! In this economy!"

"What are you talking about?"

"I spent two hundred and fifty dollars for this date, when I am, frankly, pretty broke, and you're not even a witch."

I don't know if I have ever been this confused. I need a gallon of chamomile tea and a five-hundred-page book to stabilize. "Why does that matter?"

"How else am I supposed to get powers?" He begins to pace. "I wasn't born with them. If I'm gonna acquire magic, the easiest way to get it is the same way Alex did—by getting a witch to fall in love with me. One day he was a regular, boring guy, and the next he was a boring guy with a supernatural gift for finding lost objects."

My mouth drops open. "Are you serious?"

He smears the heel of his hand over one eye. "Never mind. Sorry, I didn't mean—" He stares at me, pleading. "Are you *sure* you aren't a witch?"

I start walking. Grab my purse out of his car, then take off down the road on foot.

"Hey! Where are you going?" he shouts.

"I'm not getting back into that car with you. Please give me a fifteen-minute head start so that I don't get run over."

"Oh c'mon, it's too dangerous to walk. Guess what? Ninety-nine percent of run-over-by-a-car incidents happen between ten and ten thirty p.m."

"I'll take my chances." And he made that up.

"I'll drive front-facing. Please get in the car, Zelda."

I do not get into the car. He does, following behind me at a cautious distance, headlights revealing my way forward.

I am barely cognizant of my journey to Piedmont Road, the

downhill trek carrying me faster than my feet want to step, my breaths loud and even, eyes focused straight ahead. I replay that haunting image of the thing that wasn't a deer, wasn't a dog, wasn't a coyote. The strange voice in the forest. And, most of all: *How else am I supposed to get powers?*

So that's why.

The late-night phone call. The flirtation. The switch from sort-of-friendly to invading my personal space, calling me gorgeous. Morgan's only been pretending to like me because he thinks I'm a witch, and he thinks he can get powers if I fall in love with him.

I am such an idiot. Not as much of an idiot as he is, apparently, but still. I am too old to have been tricked like this.

When I finally reach the turnoff, back in civilization where there are sidewalks and streetlights, the backs of my knees are slippery with sweat. "At least let me drop you off at home," Morgan barks out his window.

"No."

"You saw something weird back there, didn't you? Was it a ghost?"

"Might've been a fairy."

"Really?" He perks up. "What'd it look like?"

"She was a few inches tall. Blond hair, green dress. Told me she was on her way back to Neverland."

He rolls his window up, curses muffled.

The hum of his Buick follows me all the way to Vallis Boulevard. He swings a jerky turn down the alley beside Wafting Crescent, parks, and jumps out. Morgan doesn't say a word as he watches me unlock The Magick Happens and head inside, hands trembling, unintentionally slamming the door so hard that the bell above it falls down with a crash.

Up in the apartment, Luna and Aisling are at the kitchen table painting each other's nails.

Luna pitches a fit at the state of me. "Why are you so sweaty?"

"Because it's hotter than dragon's breath outside, and I just walked three quarters of a mile."

"Are you all right?" Her chair squeaks against the floor as she hip-checks it out of the way. "How's Morgan?"

"Alive, somehow."

"What's that supposed to mean?"

"It means he's lucky." I yank off my shoes. "I'm gonna go shower."

"Wait! Not yet. Tell us about your date first. Did you hike out to the Davilla house? Is that why you look like you're dying?"

"How'd you know he was taking me to the Davilla house?"

"He told us," Ash chimes. "Why didn't you bring me along? I'm the only one in this family who can see ghosts."

I turn so that she doesn't see me roll my eyes.

"Although." She rummages in a cabinet for a teacup. "I heard you two made contact with the dead."

"Heard from who?"

"Samuel."

Ahh. Her imaginary friend, Samuel Pinney. It's been a while since she's told us what he's up to. Luna fixes a hot toddy when the weather's cold and leaves it by the fireside armchair downstairs, as it's allegedly Samuel's favorite drink. Ghosts can't physically consume food or drinks, according to Aisling, but by moving *through* them, they can taste their flavors faintly. This is also why a dish of chocolate-covered cherries perpetually sits on the counter: Luna freshens them up once a week for Grandma to enjoy. "Nope. Just heard noises, but nothing that can't be explained."

"Samuel—"

"Ash," I cut in impatiently. "You're telling stories again."

"Hey, now." Luna sends me a warning look.

"But he says you made contact with two poltergeists!" Aisling insists. "Strong entities capable of affecting your perceptions of reality."

I feel myself shut down as she talks.

"It's true. When a witch dies, their magic is separated from them, and it transforms into a different kind of energy. Other witches die, this energy accumulates, until eventually, it's strong and solid enough to manifest into a poltergeist. It takes at least three dead witches to make a poltergeist, Samuel says."

I pour myself a glass of water. "I truly do not know where you get this stuff."

"I told you, from Samuel."

"Sure, sure," I mutter, thumping upstairs to grab clean clothes. I love Ash to the ends of the earth and can appreciate a vivid imagination, of course. But I resent being shut out of this rich world they all share, even Morgan. The only way in is if I pretend to believe as they pretend to believe. I can't do it. I am firmly in the real world, and not even a beautiful man—not even *the most* beautiful man—is going to lure me down that path.

NINE

The trails out here can move on you, leading
even the seasoned local astray. To appease the
forest gods and keep your path, drop aragonite
or fruit of the black gum tree as you go.

Local Legends and Superstitions,
Tempest Family Grimoire

S LEEP COMES IN fits, and I rise out of bed much earlier
than normal the following morning. I sneak downstairs, hiding when I hear voices, then wait until Luna
and Romina are preoccupied in the storeroom before I tiptoe
out the front door, undiscovered.

Then I drive to Wiley Palmer Road.

It isn't that I think I'll see again whatever it is that I *thought*
I saw. With the threat of police, Morgan driving backward,
heated emotions, and the general spookiness that accompanies
a night of ghost hunting—real or not—my epinephrine-soaked
brain simply conjured an extraordinary vision. However, I am
a woman of study. If there *is* something strange out there, I
certainly need to know what that is.

Already, the animal's begun to smear: I can no longer remember the length of its fur or the texture of the antlers. And
while yes, I am certain I hallucinated at least most of it (I likely

saw a coyote), returning to the scene where it happened might refresh my memory.

I park my car in a gravelly patch off the side of the road, lock the doors, and set out. I'm in silver tights and a long black dress, which isn't ideal for July temperatures, but I'm not about to go traipsing through a poison ivy meadow without protection. My hair swishes in a long braid to keep it out of my face. I'm wearing so much SPF that if the sun stares directly at me, it's going to get a migraine. From somewhere deep inside, I hear an excited child's voice. *Yes! Finally!* But I remind her that this isn't like those times. I didn't bring a notebook. No backpack. No lunch. I'm not venturing inside the forest.

The road is barren. No animals in sight.

I walk it anyway, gaze averted from the woods as if I don't want it to know I'm thinking about it, which I am, of course. I never did stop thinking about these woods. Spending all day in them, morning till dinnertime, trudging home only because my parents would notice at some point that I was gone at all, surely. As long as there was a body in my chair at the dinner table, they wouldn't give much thought to how I spent my time. I didn't have it the same as Luna, who they crushed with responsibilities from a young age, or carefree Romina, who acted out to intentionally draw attention to herself. I grew up invisible.

When I reach the turnoff for the Davilla house, its decomposing roof visible in the distance, I turn back to scan again. Of course I'm not going to come upon the animal simply waiting for me.

My gaze travels the switchgrass where I watched it— *imagined* I watched it—disappear.

Wiping sweaty hands onto my dress, I roll in a gentle breath and take a step forward. The ground rises up to greet me—that's what it feels like, anyway—and wind blows through the grass to lean in my direction, nudging me toward brambles, a dark, cool land beyond with an opening just wide enough to admit one person. The gap is, in fact, shaped precisely like my figure: short torso, wide hips, thick legs.

As if inviting me in.

The trees are achingly familiar. I believe they're American hornbeam, but I always called them grandfather trees, because the bark of their trunks has a smooth, whittled appearance, and whittling struck me as a grandfatherly pursuit.

"The clock," says a fragile, whispering voice, just on the other side of the wall of trees.

I leap back, startled. "Hello?"

No response. I stand utterly still for what feels like ages, waiting and listening.

I could venture forth, find out who's in there, but unfortunately it isn't safe, as a woman, to wander alone in the woods. I'm furious that I have to think this way—I should be able to roam wherever I want, day or night, regardless of what I'm wearing or who I'm with or not with. I shouldn't have to worry about human predators. But the sad reality is that I must.

My lips press together, deeply buried longing reaching out to sensitize my skin, running me all over with an electric charge as I stand at the edge of who I used to be. I imagine all of the Zeldas I've been, the Zelda who happily stole away into this forest, the Zelda who walked out of it for good, not knowing it would be the last time.

The forest feels like home, but also like hurt. Long ago, I'd treated the woods as I would a friend and their feelings, but really it wasn't a friend at all; it kept me from making *real* ones.

I close my eyes as the breeze slips over my face, branches swaying overhead, remembering.

When I was young, I told myself stories. Stories have always been my haven and escape. When I was a teenager and had to live with parents who were constantly fighting, Luna had Grandma and magic to comfort her, and Romina had her boyfriend, but I did not have anyone, because I wasn't anybody's favorite person. This is not me feeling sorry for myself, it is only the truth. I had characters. Some of them I made up, others I found in books. At times, they felt more like family to me than my real one.

I felt so very alone, and that's the only way I can explain the creatures I invented.

As any child with a vivid imagination would be wont to believe, my creatures regarded me as special. They trusted me, would eat food offered from my hand, would run with me. I'd never seen anything like them in books—and I checked out scores of books about animals from the library—so I came up with new names for them. I didn't share any of this with my family, because I worried they would take them away from me somehow, but I did tell a little girl.

When I was eleven years old, I proudly brought one of my creature friends, one I'd developed a bond with, and fed and cared for every day, to a girl at school named Danielle. I was a shy loner, and while I was happy with my animal friends, I wanted children to like me, too.

The creature was small enough to carry in the palm of my hand, with bushy, pale gray fur, about the size of a pygmy marmoset. Its eyes were wide apart, big and orange, pupils shaped like rings. It had three pupils in each eye, set in concentric circles. This happened in June, so we didn't have school, and a lot of kids liked to hang out at Coe's Park. The boys played baseball while the girls sat under the bleachers, talking.

I told Danielle that I called the creature a *huggle*, because of the way it hugged my wrist as I walked, and was named Katrina, after Katrina Van Tassel from *The Legend of Sleepy Hollow*. At which she laughed, and said, "That's just a squirrel."

Danielle wouldn't acknowledge that the animal couldn't possibly be a squirrel, as their eyes were too different. I yelled at her, she pulled my hair, and we got into a fight. The noise scared Katrina away, off into the road where she got hit by a car.

Later, I fell into my grandma's arms, tears streaming, crying over what happened to my huggle. She walked with me to Coe's Park, to the road where Katrina was still lying, and gently said, "That's a squirrel, sweetie-peetie."

I looked up at her, stunned, because if *this* woman, who raised me on legends of impossible things existing in our world, didn't believe me . . .

I looked again at Katrina, closer. And she was right. It was only a squirrel.

I never went back into the woods after that, which meant that I stopped having any friends at all, real or imaginary.

My eyes snap back open when I hear a car rumbling up the road. Backward.

Morgan parks next to my station wagon. The way he exits a

vehicle is cartoonish: he doesn't climb out so much as *fall* out, doing a spin as he regains his balance and then trots smoothly off.

He flings a sulky look my way as he slides on a pair of sunglasses and fishes his camera out of a nylon shoulder bag. Beneath the bag is an oversized collared shirt with a paint splatter design, and vintage pants covered in turquoise faces like pop art. I give him my most disgusted frown, because I'm still angry and embarrassed that he tried to use me so shamelessly, but I'm also relieved. A mysterious stranger's nearby and they keep going on about a clock, so Morgan is now my unwitting bodyguard. Or human shield. If I run faster than him, then the forest stranger will tackle Morgan instead of me.

He flips the screen to record himself, chin tilting upward so that sunlight grazes his sharp cheekbones, and says in a voice that sounds deeper than usual, "This is where a ghost was spotted last night at approximately ten o'clock p.m."

"It wasn't a ghost."

His eyebrows pull down, but he doesn't respond to me, continuing: "Subject does not believe in ghosts. Or witches, evidently. Even though subject dresses like Morticia Addams."

"Would Morticia Addams wear these?" I point to my holographic pink geode earrings.

Morgan turns away. He studies the asphalt through his camera, zooming in as if he expects to find trails of sulfur or ectoplasm. "There are no leaves in the road, despite it being a windy day. Suspicious."

"Why're you making your voice sound like that?"

"Like what?"

"Like Patrick Warburton."

I can tell by the way his jaw slides that he's gritting his teeth. "Please be quiet, I am in the middle of an investigation."

Good. I hope I'm ruining it. "You're looking in the wrong spot." I jerk my head to the right. "It was over there."

Morgan rips his sunglasses off, pointing them at me. "So you admit it!"

"I admit that I saw a coyote."

"A coyote? Then why'd you look so weird?"

"I don't look weird," I snap.

"Not like *that*. I mean weirded out. Your face. It was . . ." He stops, and I realize I want him to continue, because when he talks about it, it's like I'm back in that moment, witnessing the impossible.

But he decides to ignore me again, speaking only to himself. "Idea for next podcast topic is *never meet your heroes.* They turn out to be frauds."

"How the hell am I a fraud? I'm the only one around here who's *not* a fraud!"

"Who says I'm talking about you?" Morgan clips. But then in the same breath: "You wear a witch's hat in your author photo. It's on the back cover of all your books. Deceitful behavior for a not-witch."

"It's just a hat."

I walk down the road, exploring a nearby cemetery. I did quite a bit of loitering here when I was a teenager, where it was quiet and I wouldn't be disturbed. Sitting with my back propped against gravestones so old and weathered that the names on them are unreadable, writing stories in my notebook as fast as my hand could zip across the page. I had thick calluses on my thumb from holding a pencil, handwriting a mess, every other word spelled wrong because I couldn't slow my pace.

"If all you saw was a coyote, then why'd you come back?"

I turn, watching Morgan step over faded bouquets of larkspur laid over a grave. His sunglasses are on top of his head, cheeks pink from exertion. He looks irritated.

"I wanted to make sure it wasn't hurt."

He picks his way over, stopping less than a foot away. I am a rather short person, at five one, and he is a good deal taller than me, but I refuse to tip my head back to look him in the eyes.

So he bends. "You told me you don't lie."

"I thought I saw something odd, all right? At first, it *did* look like a coyote—"

"At first?"

"But there was something stuck to its head. And it—"

"A fence," he interrupts eagerly. "That's what you said. But maybe it wasn't?"

"Listen, I don't know what I thought I saw. Obviously, my mind was playing tricks."

"Tell me what you *thought* you saw, then."

I keep walking. There are dips in the earth over the oldest graves, indicating caskets long caved in, obelisks so timeworn that they're smooth as river stones. "Leave me alone, you jerk. You won't believe me, anyway. *I* wouldn't believe me."

"Zelda."

A hand covers my wrist, and I stop. Trace the hand up to his shoulder, and then, cautiously, I study his face. He's nothing but earnest. "I would," he says.

TEN

Two drops of frankincense oil on your
doorstep will keep enemies at bay.

Spells, Charms, and Rituals,
Tempest Family Grimoire

AFTER I DESCRIBE what I thought I saw to Morgan,
coral antlers and all, I feel so absurd about the whole
thing that I go back to The Magick Happens and begin researching tardigrades and TrES-2b, the darkest known
exoplanet, to calm myself down. Sensible activities for a sensible woman, who is not so given over to flights of fancy that she
thinks an antlered dog might be loping around town.

Soon enough, Morgan pops in and, ignoring my presence
entirely, begins his usual work routine—a process I used to
think was captivating but am now peeved by. Everything this
man does peeves me lately.

He switches on his computer, then pops behind the counter
where I'm sitting to pour himself some coffee, as he cannot
possibly write until he has a liter of caffeine in his system. But
then he spots a stray pen that needs a cap, so he goes hunting for
it, and then he sees a candle out of place, so he has to scout where
it goes; but before he can do so, he sees the other half of the
muffin he misplaced earlier. By the time he's finished pouring

his coffee, it's been fifteen minutes since he started. Then he does something truly chilling—

Morgan starts reading *Calling the Spirits: A History of Seances* but gets sidetracked after five pages. When he comes back, he picks up the wrong book: *Ghosts: A Natural History: 500 Years of Searching for Proof*, and starts reading *that*, opening it to page five. He does not look at all confused or surprised by the mix-up; he simply continues on with it, muttering a great deal of "Hmmm" and "Ahhh."

"You say something to me?" he asks Trevor when he runs out of delays.

"No."

"Thought I heard my name." He traipses back to his desk, types a sentence, frowns at it with his head tilted sideways, then quickly hammers out a paragraph. Minimizes the document, scrolls the Internet for a minute, right-clicking every headline he sees into a new tab until his browser is fighting for its life. His attention jumps to the busy street beyond the window, fingers drumming in tune with music. He gets out of his chair, freezes, then sits back down. Writes another sentence. Just when it looks as if he's found his groove, the door chimes to announce that a customer has entered and Morgan rolls his chair across the room, lassoing them into a debate about whether Tasmanian devils really have gone extinct or if they've just gotten uncommonly good at hiding.

"You look like you want to do a murder," Trevor tells me.

"That's just her face," Luna says merrily. "It's 'resting murder face.'"

"Tasmanian devils aren't extinct," I grumble under my

breath, marinating in that dig about the witch's hat. Now he's got me second-guessing my choice of author photo.

Luna leans closer. "Huh?"

I pick leaves off the counter, sweeping them into a trash can. "Nothing."

Morgan tips up his chin imperiously, withdrawing a violin from a desk drawer. Saws at the strings with his bow, producing a terrible racket.

"Come, quick!" Romina shouts from out back.

We dash into the courtyard behind the shop. It's a beautiful brick-walled square with aboveground planters teeming with flowers of all sizes and colors, Romina's pet silkie chickens, gnarled trees, and the carriage house where Romina lives. If The Magick Happens is a three-layer cake, then the carriage house is a strawberry with a whipped cream swirl on top, garnishing the plate. It's picture-book adorable, swarmed with ivy, and . . .

"Pumpkins?"

I touch one of the green globes on a thick vine that scales the side of the cottage. From where I'm standing, twenty other baby pumpkins are visible, climbing their way up to Romina's roof. "Odd place to put a pumpkin patch."

"I *just* planted this all a couple of weeks ago," Romina insists. "I think I must have enchanted the seeds somehow, for it to grow this quickly. And look at how full the garden is! My flowers grew back abnormally fast after cutting them down to use for Kristin's wedding and the May Day crowns."

Luna gasps. "You're right. I swear, there's twice the number of flowers now."

"It's been raining a lot," I remind them. "That probably sped up growth."

They look at me like I've suggested we dress like clowns and play Twister.

"Zelda," Luna says piteously. "It's magic. Just *look* at all these pumpkins."

The two of them discuss illogical theories. Before I can water down their enthusiasm by pointing out alternatives, Trevor goes, "Psst!" and waves me back inside.

He points across Candleland, where the top of somebody's head moves on the other side of a shelf of dragon egg candles (melt them down and find a wee silver dragon inside). "It's that dude again," he whispers.

"What dude?"

My confusion morphs into pleasant surprise when a familiar figure emerges, book in hand: J. A. Howley's latest, *Under the Second Moon*. We hosted the author recently for their book tour and still have a few signed copies.

He smiles when he sees me, gray eyes twinkling behind his glasses.

Warm pressure expands in my chest. "Dylan."

"I don't want to wait a whole year for another auction," he says. "Can I take you on a date?"

I'm so traumatized after last night that I don't want to go on any dates for a good while, but Dylan is a nice, normal man. And I doubt he cares that I'm not a witch. "Yes." I tune out the earsplitting noises Morgan is creating with his violin. "That sounds lovely."

He discards the book on a random candle display, which

admittedly makes me twitchy. "Are you free this Friday night?"

"Yes," I say, before remembering that I'm scheduled to run the night market that night. "Sorry, no, I can't. How about Saturday?"

His smile turns wistful. "I'll be out of town. Next Friday, perhaps?"

I don't consult my schedule, worried he'll change his mind. "Absolutely."

We exchange numbers, then chat for a bit about J. A. Howley before he apologizes for having to cut this short, as he has to get back to work (he's a bank teller, and this is his lunch break). I wave goodbye, following him to the door.

Morgan's violin screeches obnoxiously. I wince. "Can you please play that less badly?"

He holds my eyes as his bow dances the foxtrot over strings in the worst rendition of "Come On Eileen" imaginable. I cannot believe I ever fantasized about kissing this man.

THAT EVENING, I'M snuggled with Aisling and Luna on their living room couch, squeezed between eight (eight!) throw pillows, watching a movie. Luna's apartment is a love letter to maximalism. In this bite-sized space, she's stuffed a peacock-blue sofa, plush violet rug, three ottomans, and numerous cat trees. Posters of blown-up vintage tarot cards—XVIII La Lune hangs above the television, gazing down upon us all. An apothecary cabinet whose drawers won't shut because they're so full of dried herbs; royal blue silks draped from hooks in ceiling corners, glittering with moons and stars; a tapestry of various fungi; and tree branches. Tree branches absolutely everywhere. She's got them plaited so that they appear to be growing along the walls, over doorways and the glass bead curtains that scatter sunset across the paint.

One look at Luna's place makes my attic look like a wasteland. Romina's house is much more serene, with plenty of plants and a color scheme designed to make you feel like everything is going to be okay. The little garden elf is sitting in Luna's kitchen right this minute, table spread with witchy paraphernalia.

She's taken a journal and attempted to age it with water spots and burnt corners, undoubtedly going for a "has been sitting on a bookshelf for over a hundred years" effect, copying down information from notes of varying origin. Spells. Hexes. Lists of herbs and flowers and their purposes. Ghost stories Grandma told us. The mechanics of candle magic, mixing and matching scents to inspire particular outcomes. Local folklore and superstitions.

"What exactly are you doing?" I ask.

She flips the journal so that I can see its cover, embossed with the words TEMPEST FAMILY GRIMOIRE. *CONTRIBUTIONS BY LUNA, ZELDA, AND ROMINA TEMPEST.*

"Ha! What am I supposed to contribute to this, exactly?"

"I predict you'll end up writing over half of this grimoire," Luna intones.

"Oh, honey. No. You're not brainwashing me."

She narrows her eyes, jabbing one finger in my direction. "You're a witch, Zelda Margaret," she says firmly.

"If I were a witch, don't you think I would know it?"

"You *used* to know it. Then you un-knew it."

Good lord, the people in my life. I seize a bookmark from the coffee table and aim it back at her as if it's a magic wand. "Ooga booga boo, turn Luna into a shoe."

"You shouldn't say stuff like that," Ash warns. "Never know what'll happen."

"Actually, I know exactly what will happen. Nothing." I brandish it at Snapdragon next. "Abracadabra, turn this cat into a capybara."

"Stop that!" Luna shouts, being perfectly serious. "You might hurt him."

Romina shakes her head at me, tutting.

"Oh come *on*." I stare, half-amused and half-exasperated with their sour expressions. "I'm your *sister*, I'm not going to tell anyone. I'm not going to risk our business failing. Stop lying to me and admit you're making it all up."

Luna pauses the movie.

"Zelda," Romina says primly. "You are starting to piss me off."

Luna holds out her arms. "We're not going to let this become an argument. Zelda has her feelings about magic, and we have ours. It's okay to disagree."

Ash *hmph*s, her face dark.

"If magic were real," I can't help saying, "everyone would know about it. Scientists would have found ten thousand ways to bind it to chemicals, to medicine, added it to every step of our daily lives. Billionaires' companies would be exploiting it for profit. It would absolutely be common knowledge."

"It *is* common knowledge!" Romina exclaims. "Everyone's

heard about witchcraft! The fact that it isn't taken seriously by absolutely everybody doesn't mean it isn't credible."

"And ghosts are real, too," Ash adds, crossing her arms.

"Aisling, it isn't anything personal." I try for a joke, to lighten the room. "I need for ghosts to not be real. I make a lot of stupid faces at myself in the bathroom mirror when no one's around and I can't handle the thought of being watched by some dude who bit it in the fifties."

"He bit it in the 1860s," Ash replies. "He also takes offense to the suggestion that he follows anyone into the bathroom. Samuel has better manners than that."

"Where is he now?" Luna wants to know. "I told you he has to stay downstairs unless expressly invited up."

"He was invited. By Grandma. They're having ghost tea over there." She points at the wall. "Oh right, you can't see it. There are ghost rooms here, from where the building used to have an addition. It caught fire in the early 1900s, so you can't see the parlor. It's *divine*, though. Drapey curtains, a big silver harp, a mirror that reflects the faces of anyone who's ever looked in it."

Good grief. It's three against one, and I am not going to win this. I lug a gallon of chocolate ice cream out of the freezer and slap it onto the counter to soften up, Luna expertly deescalates by changing the subject, and I return to the couch with a neutral smile pasted on my face.

Underneath it, my every molecule itches. It feels like they're in on a con together, a secret, and I'm the odd one out. I love them fiercely—I always will.

But I'll never trust them completely until they admit they're faking it.

ELEVEN

Hang a broom above your headboard, and fly in dreams.

Spells, Charms, and Rituals,
Tempest Family Grimoire

TWO DAYS LATER, I contrive to catch Aisling in a lie. She isn't as experienced with deceit as her mother and aunt, so I figure she's the weaker target.

"I read an article about an old ghost man who haunts the train station," I tell her over breakfast, courtesy of Luna. My older sister likes to baby me now that we're living together again, cooking my favorite meals. She's been puttering around since the crack of dawn, the smell of animal-shaped waffles rousing me out of bed. My poor night-owl body is unaccustomed to this treatment, my eyesight so bleary that I can hardly see my own plate.

Aisling pauses with a bite of waffle halfway to her mouth. She's wearing one of Luna's old faded tank tops, blue with embroidered daisies, her unbrushed brown hair in a ponytail. Whereas Luna's nose is long and narrow, Aisling's is a short button. She's got hazel eyes, unlike our blue, and her mouth is wider. I try to recall what her father looks like, but it's been so long since he last came sniffing around that he's a blur to me. "The train station?" she repeats.

"Yeah." I sip my orange juice, playing it casual. "They say he has a striped tie. Carries a briefcase and black hat. Sits on the bench all day, waiting for his train."

"Never met him."

I stretch my arms. "Really? Lots of people have seen him." Nobody has seen him. He is my invention.

"I've been to the train station before." She squints, thinking. "There were a couple of kids building pebble forts for their toy soldiers. They were flashbacks stuck in a loop, though, and didn't know I was there." She shakes her head. "Nope. No ghost man that I know of. Somebody's probably lying for attention."

She is oblivious to my flat, penetrating stare.

From the stovetop, Luna appraises me over her shoulder. I think she knows what I'm up to, but she doesn't say anything when I saunter to the sink.

"What are you making now?" I examine her pot, which contains a simmering globby substance that smells like orange and chamomile.

"Worry-Away Jam, which we can eat with the scones I've got baking right now. I've noticed you seem troubled lately. I don't know *why*"—her head bobs on the word as she stirs her concoction with a wooden spoon—"and I don't think you'll *tell* me, so this is how I can be helpful."

Her knowing that I've been troubled lately makes me even more cross. "I'm not eating one of your potions. They aren't FDA-approved."

"It's an old family recipe. I've had it loads of times myself, and I haven't died yet."

Despite my resistance, she somehow convinces me to take a scone up to the attic to work. Faced with my intimidatingly blank Word document, I decide to nip back down for another scone, with extra jam (it tastes *interesting* more than delicious, but I keep craving more), and then I decide it's far too early to be working and I should grab a book, don a rain slicker, and sneak outside instead.

Maybe the author phase of my life is over.

Would that be so terrible? True, it's always been my dream to be an author, but it's safe to say I've accomplished that now, and . . . maybe it's time to move on. Not just from Villamoon, but from the proverbial pen. My love for writing is somewhere out at sea right now, in sunglasses and a scarf, waving goodbye.

My fingers curl around the hood of my rain slicker, lowering it. Warm drops fall, atmosphere tingling with hot tar, candied popcorn from a cart on the corner. The sky is low, pushing between treetops, pressing so close that its gray tendrils meet the rain that ricochets off the brick road.

Thunder rumbles in far-off hills, and my chest loosens, breathing easier. I've always loved storms. I met one of my exes when we were both caught in the downpour after leaving a museum. He'd covered me with his umbrella. *Where are you headed? I'll walk you.*

And he did. Five blocks out of his way, just so I wouldn't get wet. He was so kind, so thoughtful, and yet I slept through his *Death of a Salesman* stage performance because I stayed up all night writing. That was, at least, a somewhat more palatable excuse than the one I gave to a different boyfriend, who couldn't believe I was nearly an hour late showing up to dinner with his parents because I was reading *The Insects: An Outline of Entomology* by P. J. Gullan and P. S. Cranston and "didn't want to stop on an odd-numbered page, but the even-numbered pages never finished with complete sentences, which meant I had to keep reading."

I have torpedoed a lot of relationships by muttering, "Just one more page." By prioritizing whatever interests me most in the moment.

Forcibly setting this genre of thought aside, I open a hardback copy of *Phantom Architecture*. I adore the way protective Mylar covers on library books crinkle to the touch, and the buttery, battered pages that have been explored by so many other hands, loved by so many other minds. I don't even have to be reading a book for it to provide comfort. Merely holding one soothes me. But I'm eager to lose myself now, as it will be nice to think about words that aren't my own.

For background noise, I inwardly riffle through a collection of music, dusting off the tried-and-true opening theme of *Masterpiece Theatre*, and slide it onto the mental record player. Set the needle.

Right as the song begins to play, my gaze snags on a clump of trees beyond the red bridge: it's darker and thicker in Falling Rock Forest than anywhere else around here. I imagine that I can almost feel the forest breathing, watching. *Zelda, Zelda*, it says. *What have you forgotten?*

I draw a sharp intake of breath.

"Zelda."

I jump. It takes a tick to process the visually loud distortion of neon clothing, dark brown eyes, hair hanging in them, so close that raindrops falling off the ends land on my shoes.

"Guess what. I have something to show you," Morgan says, and this is followed by a strange happening.

The string lights hanging high over the road between Wafting Crescent and The Magick Happens brighten, the individual glows coalescing into a single blinding burst, blinking as the light teleports from one bulb to the next. It reminds me of those expensive Christmas light shows wealthier suburban neighborhoods put up, syncing the lights to music. An animal darts along the wire, toward us, so close that when I tip my head all the way back as it races past, I can see that its belly has fur as rumpled as an Airedale terrier's.

My view is abruptly blocked by a sheet of paper thrust into my face. "Look," he demands.

"No," I say, the word automatic. But of course, I look. "What is this?"

"The animal you saw in the road. Did I get it right?"

He's made a police sketch of The Thing That Was Not a Coyote, a Deer, or a Dog. I've put it out of my mind, but Morgan's obviously been dwelling—even though he didn't see it himself—and has stacked potential names beside the drawing. *Long-Tailed Vinton Varmint. The Zaleski Deer Dog. Coralote.*

The sketch isn't that bad, actually. Rudimentary, but accurate.

"The antlers are off. Different kind of coral."

He pulls up pictures on his phone, showing me various corals. "Which kind?"

"Morgan, I think you're taking this too seriously. There is no such thing as a long-necked coyote with coral antlers. You . . . you understand that, don't you?"

He continues to swipe. "Which kind?"

I shake my head, pointing. "That one, I guess. But the tips had fur coming out." His eyes brighten. "But not *really*," I cut in swiftly. "Because it wasn't real."

Morgan flattens the paper against my shoulder so that he can dash notes across it in pen. I stiffen, face warming. He is not touching me, his *pen* is touching me. Through layers of clothing.

But it doesn't feel like that. With the press of his pen and his nearness, tall body covering mine from behind like the large wings of a divine being, I envision Morgan holding a tattoo pen, sinking his handwriting into my bare skin. "Resembles finger coral," he mumbles to himself. "With fur on the tips."

"It wasn't real, though." I've repeated this so many times, the words have lost meaning. I smooth my hands down my arms to shake off goose bumps.

"*Or*, you found a paranimal."

In Black Bear Witch lore, paranimals are woodland creatures that the witch has enchanted for unknown reasons (the leading theory is that she likes to infuse the flavors of magic into animals before consuming them)—like turning a fox into a fox-bird hybrid with tree bark on its forelegs. Allegedly, only a rare few can see the enchanted form of a paranimal; to anybody else, they look like the normal creatures they were before the Black Bear Witch got a hold of them.

I give the sky an anguished look. "This town. You've all

poisoned yourselves with so many legends that you can't tell what's fiction anymore."

Morgan opens his mouth to speak, but I jerk back as a small animal zips between us, right over Morgan's shoes, scrabbling up the stone wall encasing Romina's garden. It turns its head, staring at me with big orange eyes. Each one contains three black rings.

"Katrina," I whisper.

Even as I say it, I know it isn't her—the fur is more tan than gray, and it's not as sleek and compact as she was.

"Who?" Morgan looks around.

"That's my—that's a huggle." I can't believe I've said the word *huggle* out loud, as a grown-up.

"What are you talking about?" He follows my line of sight. "The squirrel? Did you call it a *huggle*?"

I glance at his face, taking in his confusion, and then look back at the . . .

Squirrel.

It flicks its bushy tail at us, then sprints across the garden wall toward Romina's rooftop and disappears in a warren of pumpkin vines.

"Never mind." I am never eating Luna's sketchy jam again.

I pull away from Morgan, trying to cross the street. He yanks me back, the unexpected touch jolting through me like lightning; right as a shout leaps up my throat, a car honks and dirty water sprays up from a tire, splattering all across my legs.

"Rats." I moan. "This is what I get for going outside."

Morgan hesitates. "Zelda, do you think it's possible that you saw a paranimal?"

I scowl at him. "No."

"Because if you did," he marches on, "then maybe one of them could lead me to the Black Bear Witch."

"So that she can crack your head open like a nut?"

"So that she can give me some of her magic. Besides, she only cracks your head open like a nut if you're driving forwards on Wiley Palmer Road." He shrugs, like, *I don't make these rules.*

The Black Bear Witch's origins are unclear, and her traits vary from story to story, but it is agreed upon that she is centuries old. She hides somewhere within the town, and if you find her lair, she has to give you some of her magic before taking away your memory of ever finding it. The size of this gifted magic is quibbled over; some believe you'd come out of the situation with a small power or an enchanted object. Others believe you would become a god. There's even a rhyme about it:

> *Open wide the witch's door*
> *and burn with magic evermore.*
> *But to gain, you must surrender*
> *remembrance of the witch forever.*

Most of us associate this folklore with zozzled teenagers throwing parties in the woods. That's where all the "Nah, man, I saw her for real!" stories stem from: people blabbering about bears they saw walking around on two legs, acting suspicious, while under the influence of King Cobra (the partiers were under the influence, not the bear. Or possibly the bear joined in, I don't know).

I stare at him. He stares back, not an ounce of shame to be found on his features.

"You sure moved from plan A to plan B fast."

He fidgets. "*You* were plan B, actually. Plan A was a spell that didn't work. So technically, going the Black Bear Witch route is plan C, but I would be more than amenable to changing that if you would like to go out with me again—"

I'm already sailing past him. "Get lost."

I grumble my way into The Magick Happens, up to my attic, and fall into a chair at my writing desk. My mind is a whirlwind of sailor-worthy curses.

On the opposite side of the road, colors smeared by rain and shadow, Morgan's lounging in his own desk chair like an indolent prince: back slouched, knees apart. Eyebrows ever so slightly knit. His hands are laced together, resting on his stomach. My chest rises and falls with shallow, indignant breaths. My body clenches. What is he thinking, staring at me like that?

Probably, he is scheming more skullduggery. Congratulating himself for incapacitating my ability to think. Thinking is my favorite thing to do. How extremely dare he.

He is doing this on purpose. It pleases him to see me affected, so unable to escape the heavy, pressing weight of his gaze that has me feeling all tangled up and contradictory, with my muscles rigid and my bones loose.

He taps a long finger against his chin, watching. A ghost of a smirk hovers at his lips, and I hate him. Oh, I hate him.

Thump, thump, thump, thump goes my wild little heart.

I am furious with myself for not hating him. For wishing he were genuinely interested in me, when wishing is pointless.

But it's those eyes. It's that mouth.

It's a combustion reaction. He's a flash of white heat in the pulse beating at my throat, the tips of my breasts, between my legs, smoking out to my fingertips. I raise them in the shadows to inspect, thinking their color must have changed, so much do they feel like glowing coals.

As if he can sense the direction of my thoughts, the heat of my body, his jaw has slackened, lips parted. His cheeks are flagged with red. I have never seen that expression on him before, and it seals my airways.

He leans forward, just an inch. Eyes on me. Daring me to do something.

But what, exactly?

He wants a push to his pull. He wants retaliation and the unexpected. This man should learn now that he will not get anything he wants from me.

I close my curtains.

TWELVE

The Bone Dragon: The skeleton of an enormous
beast lies buried beneath the trees of Falling Rock Forest.
If its horn is dug up and oxygenated, it will return to life
and escape, and the entire forest will die, as it grew from the
magic that leached from its body. If it ever absorbs its magic
back, there will be nothing left of southern Moonville.

Local Legends and Superstitions,
Tempest Family Grimoire

THE FOLLOWING MORNING, Romina drags Luna and me out to the courtyard to gaze with wonder at her kingcup flowers, which are in such exuberant bloom that they're growing straight up the siding of The Magick Happens, a vertical field of yellow flowers. Several seem to be attempting to push open a window on the second floor. "Isn't it incredible?" Romina gushes.

I shade my eyes with my hand against the sun. "Is that going to damage the brick?"

"First, my garden grows back twice as fast as it ought to," she tells us, ignoring my question. "Second, the pumpkins swell up basically overnight—"

"I thought you said you planted them a couple weeks ago."

Her jaw sets. "A couple weeks is practically overnight for the life cycle of pumpkins."

"This started right after you and Alex said *I love you*, right?" Luna says, steepling her hands beneath her chin. "I think love magic might be amplifying your powers. You're a green witch, you're in love, it all makes sense."

"Look at this, though." I show them my phone, pulled up to a picture of round zucchini. "They look like pumpkins and they mature in forty-five days." I smile, satisfied with the neat bow I've tied around this mystery.

Romina makes a face. "They're *pumpkins*. Pump. Kins." She's dressed like Strawberry Shortcake today (most days, really, with her newly pink hair, but *especially* today with the big pink hat added) and it's great fun to see such a withering grimace on a Strawberry Shortcake. I wisely tamp down my laughter, as I loathe the idea of 10TV News using my author's photo with the witch hat when they report my murder. *Body of McArthur-area Winifred Sanderson LARPist used as fertilizer for the garden behind her store. More at eleven!*

My sisters exchange a loaded look that conveys the many conversations they've had about me, which I was not privy to. "The Internet doesn't possess all the answers to the mysteries of our beautifully complex universe, which answers only to the stars," Luna responds, with the wisdom of a fortune cookie that's accidentally had a second platitude printed over top of the first.

Romina's not as good-natured about my doubt as Luna is. "Why do you have to whiz in our waffles? How would you feel if, every time you started talking about your beliefs, I came in all '*Well, actually, derp a derp a derp a durr!*'"

"That would be amazing." I give her a great big smile. "I would love it if you were all *derp a derp a derp a durr*."

Romina's eye spasms.

"All right, all right, let's calm down." Luna gathers us up, her bracelets clicking and clacking against each other.

"I love you, don't be mad at me," I coo at Romina, patting her arm.

She jerks back. "No! I'm mad at you and I don't want your pats."

"Yes, you do." I sandwich her cheeks between my hands, smushing her face. "Cherish these moments of sisterhood. You've been nagging me for years to move back. This is what you wanted. Oof, you're all full of pollen. Smelling you gives me allergies."

"When the love magic finally gets you," she grumbles into my hair, "you'll have to admit it's real and then I'm going to gloat *so* bad. You'll never have a moment's peace."

"Oh, me, too," Luna agrees. "Zelda, we're going to make you so miserable."

"Wow, thanks."

"But we're going to make you miserable *lovingly*."

I THREAD THROUGH the night market later that evening, enjoying how lively it becomes once dusk has settled in. We've got booths boasting magics of all sorts: Gilda Halifax is reading palms, her daughter, Millicent, shuffling tarot cards; a fortune-telling automaton designed to resemble Gilda herself is positioned nearby, scaring small children. We've got crystals, runes, and scrying services offered by charming, well-polished con artists. My gaze passes over them, observing how their bright, hypnotic eyes seem to suck their audiences in, catching them up in whirlwinds of folly for ten dollars a pop.

With each booth that I pass, I think with a prideful inner voice, *You might be able to trick them, but I see clearly.*

I hear brisk conversation, laughter, a bit of instrumental music floating from a speaker somewhere. Plum poufs and a station for teas and coffees. Bushra's "bewitching cupcakes" (the bewitching part being that they're frosted to look like unicorns, which she has informed me are the top tamale of magical baked goods).

A short, older gentleman with tufty, graying hair materializes in front of me, expression crabby.

Alonzo opened Mozzi's Pizza decades ago. It's a long stone building next door, with stained-glass windows and table lamps made from recycled bits of mismatched plastic. Mozzi's Pizza is dark and cool, with flagstone floors and low ceilings, and when I was young I'd sip tea that I pretended was ale, pretending the restaurant was an old-timey tavern. I was, naturally, a weary mercenary who'd been hired by the crown to assassinate a werewolf but instead decided to double my money by double-crossing the prince. Both the prince and the werewolf were hopelessly in love with me, but really, I had my eye on the butcher's apprentice.

Anyway.

"Ms. Halifax is taking half my table and won't stop trying to hold my hand."

I don't have to guess which Ms. Halifax he means. Millicent, a quiet woman in her forties, holds everyone around her in contempt and won't accept payments in cash because "money is contaminated with thousands of bacteria and most bills have traces of cocaine on them." She isn't going to be touching anybody's hands uninvited.

I let out a groan. "Gilda."

Honestly, running the night market feels more like babysitting than anything else.

Gilda has not only taken over Alonzo's table; she has also lengthened her own area by docking a card table to her booth, which she did not receive permission to do. Her fake eyelashes are about an inch long and dusted with gold leaf on the ends, but it's her lipstick that's the real party: it matches her cloak, lapis-blue lips and crimson liner. I'm reminded of spiritual mediums I've seen on television, with garish makeup, teased hair, and booming voices—all part of the diversion while they lie to you. *Look at this, not at that!*

"I was only having a peek at his life lines!" she insists as soon as I weave into her line of sight. "They were astoundingly long." She analyzes him in wonder, then turns her focus on me. "Now, while I've got you: how do you feel about long-distance dating? Because I've got a nephew who invested in Pillow Pets early on, and when I say *big money*, I mean you'd never have to work again. No more of those grotesque title fonts, designed to look as if they're dripping blood."

"Gilda—"

"Michael's about fifty, but last I saw him thirty years ago he could absolutely pass for twenty, and right now he's hiding out in Bulgaria to avoid a minor embezzlement thing"—she pinches her thumb and forefinger together—"but his vision board is chock-full of redheads, and I think you two would be *sensational* together."

"Actually," I say, shoving my way into the conversation before she starts filling me in on Michael's star chart or weighing the likelihood of him stealing my identity, "I'm kind of talking to someone."

"Really?" She claps in delight. "Who?"

"Remember the auction?"

She gasps. "Morgan Angelopoulos. Of *course*." She fans herself dramatically. "Yes, my dear, forget all about Michael—I can't believe I forgot what I saw in my crystal ball about you and Morgan!" Gilda slaps the tabletop heartily, then taps it twice with a long, glittering nail. Her eyes, a watery blue-violet, bore holes through mine. "You two," she says mystically, "were written in *the stars*."

"Gilda, you are so full of it that it's a wonder you can get up and walk around," I say, but my voice brims with affection. "And no, not *Morgan*. There was a guy who'd meant to show up and bid on my date, but he wasn't able to get there in time. I'm going out with him next week."

"Oh." Her tone flattens. "By all means . . ." She waves a hand. "Why shouldn't you entertain the guy who *meant to show up*? Very promising start."

I stroll away. "Good night, Gilda!"

She tuts. "Whenever you get curious to know what I saw in my crystal ball, you know where to find me."

THIRTEEN

Simmer one orange peel, one star anise blossom, and three sticks of cinnamon in a saucepan from noon till midnight to chase all the good luck you haven't used up from this year into the next one. If you do not funnel what's left of your luck into the new year, it will be irretrievably left behind.

Spells, Charms, and Rituals,
Tempest Family Grimoire

I MAKE MY WAY to the front curb of The Magick Happens, where I check my phone to see if I've got any texts from Dylan, now that I'm thinking about him.

Over the last few days, he and I have built up a fiery exchange of banter:

Dylan: Hey, it's me 😊
Zelda: Hi! Miss me already?
Dylan: It was nice to see you again.
Zelda: It was nice to see you too. So, do you like movies?
Dylan: Yes

It ends there.

I don't communicate by text very much unless I have

something important to say; every sentence I trial-run for Dylan ends up sounding stupid and is therefore deleted. Dylan seems to be similarly reserved, so we're not giving each other much to work with. How can a professional writer be so bad at coming up with words?

I've forgotten this part somehow—how awkward it can be right after the initial sparks, when you have attraction but little else to go on yet. It's *hard* out here in the wildlands of dating.

Wretched musical notes screech from Morgan's apartment window, falling in *eeeeeek*s and *errrrrrr*s around my poor ears. I wince, plugging them with my fingers. "Please take some lessons."

"You would never say that to Beethoven!"

"I—" I peer up at him, leaning out his window. "Beethoven was a pianist. How dare you compare yourself to Beethoven."

"At the very least, I'm a Chopin." He begins to play "In the Hall of the Mountain King." I prop my hands on my hips.

"That's not Chopin," I shout up at him. A few market-goers stop to watch. "That's Edvard Grieg."

"How would you know?"

"It's my . . ." I pause, scowling. I dislike talking about myself. "It's my favorite song."

He scoffs, then continues sawing away. "This isn't a *favorite song*. There are no words! 'All I Need Is a Miracle'—now *that* is a favorite song."

"Yeah, like thirty years ago."

He stops playing, disgruntled. "And how old do you think your mountain king song is?"

Fair point. I'm poised to argue, anyway, when I hear the

delicate, pearly notes of a harp drift in from somewhere behind us. Morgan must hear it, too, because he lowers his violin. Somebody's playing along with him.

When the harp stops, Morgan picks up where they left off. Then when he stops, "In the Hall of the Mountain King" resumes on harp.

"Who's doing that?" he yells.

The unseen harpist ceases their duet and does not play again.

I'm trying to remember if any of our neighbors have a harp, when lightning brightens the sky. Oh no!

"Right on schedule," Gilda remarks, packing up. All the vendors scurry about, collapsing their tents, rushing crates of goods to their vehicles before the rain begins. It's not even ten yet, and usually the night market stays open until eleven.

"'Right on schedule'?" I can't help saying to Gilda, exasperated. "This wasn't in the forecast. We were supposed to have clear skies all night."

"Saw it in *this* forecast," Gilda replies, gesturing grandly to her crystal ball.

I help a lady pile her turquoise jewelry back into a box. "You're all impossible."

With my head tipped back, I only just manage to spot a scintillating winged creature up in the fairy lights that connect Wafting Crescent and The Magick Happens. It's the color of liquid mercury, moving so quickly that it leaves streaks in the atmosphere like smoke trails after a firework.

"I think I've seen this before," I say, and all the lights gutter out.

Whatever I saw appears to have gone with it.

———

HALF AN HOUR later, I'm in the streets with my umbrella and a flashlight, inspecting the fairy lights. Their power has returned, and I could be imagining it—however, I do not think I am—but I *think* their coloring has been affected. They gleam a bit bluer now.

"What are you looking for?" Morgan calls down. He'd left his window for a spell, but now he's back.

"Shh!" I flap my arm through mist; the air is warm and heavy with water. "Keep it down, will you? It's late. People are trying to sleep."

"Yeah, with you shining a light into their windows. What're you doing? You see something strange?"

"Yeah." I aim my light at him. "Right there."

He grins crookedly. "Set myself up for that one."

I continue with my business, determined. A drone, maybe? A tiny drone. We're under attack by foreign adversaries, or perhaps a mischievous thirteen-year-old.

Morgan's window creaks as he pushes it up higher. It judders back down a couple inches, right onto his head. He rubs his crown.

"You're going to hurt yourself not minding your business," I warn.

"Can't mind my business. You're acting weird, and if there's one thing I'm gonna do, it's pay attention to weird. Maybe you saw a ghost? I could help you look. I know lots about ghosts. Bet you don't have any EMF readers, either."

"You talk absolute fairydiddle, Morgan. And you're distracting me. Go home."

"I *am* home." He brings a mug to his mouth, sipping slowly, shrewd eyes trained on me. "You know—"

I switch off my flashlight. The streetlights are dim, most of them shadowed by tree foliage, painting the puddles of Vallis Boulevard citrine. All I'd wanted to do was have a look around, but I can't focus with all his commentary.

"You know," he repeats, louder, as if I won't be able to hear him as well in the dark. "I can help you, if you just tell me what you're looking for."

"I don't even *know* what I'm looking for."

"A phantom. Specter. Apparition."

"Stop pushing your ghosts onto me. I don't believe in ghosts."

"I'm bored *for* you," he returns. "Where's your sense of adventure? Where's your curiosity? Have a little faith."

"Faith? Ha! Says the man who pretended to like me because he thought I could give him special powers."

He makes a face. "When you say it like *that*, it doesn't sound nice. Say it a different way."

I turn around, pretending he isn't there. Accidentally step in a puddle. "Curses," I mutter. Deeply irritated now, I shout at him, "If ghosts were real, there would be ghost actors! Ghost politicians! Imagine never being able to get rid of eternally eighty-year-old Senator Barry, who keeps vetoing all the bills to fight climate change because he doesn't have any skin and can't feel how hot the earth is getting."

He crosses his arms on the windowsill and rests his chin atop them, smiling. "You've been thinking about this."

"It is any *curious* mind's responsibility to fully examine all sides of a theory before you are qualified to dismantle it." I square my shoulders, boots filling with water. "There would be ghost shops and ghost holidays and clear recordings of them, *real* ones, and ghost legislation, ghost rights movements, ghost prisoners, and living people trying to marry dead people—"

"Actually," he interrupts. "There's a woman from Oxfordshire—"

"If it were real," I continue firmly, "it could be proven." Voicing the words is cathartic. I can't say any of this to my sisters, or they'll get mad at me. Morgan is a convenient pair of ears.

He sighs, probably loud enough for the night shift to hear him from all the way down the corner at our new twenty-four-hour diner, Dark Side of the Spoon. His smooth face is white as the moon in contrast to the shadowed building he occupies, hair a tousled mess from combing it back with his fingers. From my perspective, light and darkness trace him in an uncanny way, making the bony sockets that his eyes are set in appear bigger, and the eyes themselves like black tourmaline. "You're so above it all. You don't believe in ghosts, you don't believe in witches, you think your niece is a pathological liar and that I'm annoying."

My hair is damp with a light drizzle, strands sticking to my neck and shoulders. "Not just annoying. I think you're dishonest, too."

He draws the bow from his violin downward in one quick

motion, extending it toward me like an accusing finger. Its tip is haloed in the streetlight, the softly falling rain that encircles Morgan like a faint, shimmering aura. From somewhere behind us, lifting like a fog from the earth, I hear a dreamy song twirling along the strings of a harp. "That's mean," he tells me.

The sound amplifies, but I cannot detect its source. Music seems to be falling from the sky, hidden behind each drop of rain. Then, abruptly, the song collapses and we're left in silence.

"It's what you deserve." I return to my search, walking until he's out of earshot.

"There would be ghost restaurants, with living volunteers who let their energy be fed on because they get off on the experience sexually," I mutter, dragging a wet snake of hair out of my eyes. It slaps right back into place. "There would be ghost federal agents. Musicians. Beauty parlors. Are you trying to tell me our government would pass up the opportunity to keep taxing people after rigor mortis sets in, if they could get away with it?" I gesture my hands as if swatting flies, flashlight jerking. It's maddening that I can't prove ghosts *don't* exist, either. All things should be either provable or disprovable, yes or no. "Unlikely!"

On and on I mutter.

FOURTEEN

The first of August is not called the Sturgeon Moon
in our household, but rather the Wishing Moon.
On Aisling's birthday, she makes a wish, and it
comes true, because her coven makes it so.

Family Traditions,
Tempest Family Grimoire

AN HOUR AND a quarter before the clock is set to strike midnight, ushering in August the first, Aisling's twelfth trip around the sun coinciding with the Gaelic festival Lughnasadh, Romina and I tiptoe down the hallway toward Aisling's bedroom door. Bells are tied to the bracelets on our wrists and ankles, their music a light, sweet glimmer. In Luna's room, I can hear the quiet murmurings of *3rd Rock from the Sun*. She used to bemoan recordings of that show always playing during our weekend stays at Grandma's house when we were kids. I think that if I were to ask her about it, she'd say she left it for Dottie's ghost to watch, but I think she likes having the comforting noise around to make it feel as if our grandmother's still around, too.

We push Ash's door open, which protests on its slanted frame, and sneak toward the sleeping child. Her head is at the foot of the bed, library books scattered across the comforter.

Bare mattress—the sheets have been wadded up and thrown on the floor.

"Happy birthday, little imp," we say in low singsong. It's what Great-Aunt Misty calls her. Imps are clever, free-spirited creatures known for their ability to talk their way out of trouble. While playful, they are also emotional, sensitive, quick-to-love beings. We generally see Aunt Misty only on our birthdays, so everything about her is sort of ingrained in the occasion.

Ash scrunches her face, eyes still closed. "Mm?"

Only a few hours ago, she was up in arms for being made to go to bed early ("But it's almost my birthday! People who stay up late have higher brain activity! I'm on school vacation! If this is what twelve is going to be like, I want to stay eleven!"). Judging by the dying glow of her booklight, I don't think she's been asleep for long.

"Up, up." I drape a scarlet linen dress over the back of her desk chair. "Put this on."

"Right now?"

Ash stumbles out of bed, rubbing her eyes, and flicks on a table lamp. She's got a red welt across her right cheek from falling asleep on a book. "Aunt Zel's not wearing black!"

My cloak is flowing linen just like Ash's dress, except mine has a deep purple hood attached. The hood of Romina's cloak is butter lettuce green.

"Hurry! Get dressed." We step into the hall, closing her door. When she emerges, Romina blubbers and exclaims over how cute she looks, all dressed up in red like a little house finch.

I braid Aisling's hair, tying a thin cord strung with bells to the end.

"What are we doing?" she asks excitedly. "Does Mom know about this?"

By way of answering, Romina settles a crown of purple flowers over Aisling. "Gladiolus," she tells her. "The flower of your birth month. This will bring new beginnings, charm, and mystery."

"Ooooh." Ash stands very still while we pin the crown in place. "I love mystery!"

I turn her palm over, dropping the silver-coin-like pods of the honesty flower into it. "You'll need to put these in your shoes."

"Why?"

I lean closer, smiling conspiratorially. Tonight is not about the truth, what is real or not real. Tonight is about making Aisling feel as if she's in a story.

"So that you can see them," I whisper.

She peers at me with big, round eyes. "See what?"

Romina and I take Aisling arm in arm, hustling her into her shoes and out of the house. Beyond, Vallis Boulevard is suitably more magical than usual, a full golden moon turning its face toward us to follow our movement. It lights up the glow-in-the-dark-painted footprints on bricks in the road that, if we were to follow, would lead to the Moonville tunnel.

"Where are we going?" Ash loud-whispers, craning to get a glimpse of The Clockery, a shop that specializes in keeping the time, from which juts a tall clock tower embossed with elaborate silver scrollwork and a radiant white face big enough to rival the moon. "It's eleven o'clock."

"You know what that means," I say lowly.

Romina tugs playfully on Ash's arm. "In an hour, you'll be older and wiser."

"*And* you'll turn into a toad. Sorry. It's simply how all witches spend their twelfth year."

Ash pretends to brace herself. "I'm ready."

We laugh, rushing down the empty street, no sound but the chirruping of crickets and cicadas, the *swish-swish* of tree branches overhead. Ash doesn't watch her step, her head tipped back so she can watch the moon and stars in gaps between tree canopies.

We pass windows with the muted blue of television sets within, banners showcasing Moonville's veterans hung from lampposts. The heat isn't as pressing as it was earlier, air light and skies clear. At this time of night, I notice details I ordinarily wouldn't, shops that seem to have poofed into existence following sundown. The decommissioned turn-of-the-century trolley in its Christmas colors, the Holly Jolly Trolley, rests now beside the post office, spotlit like a memorial, and come November will be decorated in festive lights, piney garland, and holly.

It's a quick walk to our destination, and soon we reach a rounded red bridge, Foxglove Creek rushing below. On the other side, brightened by a path of lanterns, Luna waits in a scarlet cloak with a gold hood pulled low over her forehead. Hands joined, from them dangles a necklace with a sparkling red pendant.

To the southwest of us, bells heave in The Clockery's tower, their melody like gongs rolling down a hill.

Ash is all amazement. When she approaches, Luna brings the jewelry around her daughter's neck and secures it. "Red goldstone for boldness, ambition, and ingenuity. Deflects unwanted energies. Magnifies happiness." She kisses Aisling's forehead, all smiles. "Happy birthday, my love."

"Am I being sacrificed?"

We all laugh.

"We're taking you to the wolves," I tell her, tweaking her nose gently. "They're going to raise you the rest of the way, since we've run out of things to teach you."

She dances. "Hooray! I've always wanted to run on all fours."

Luna turns and walks into the trees. The rest of us follow.

This area isn't proper forest, not as thick and foreboding as it gets in the south of town. This is more of a light, spritely wood. The shagbark hickory trees are my favorite for their peeling appearance; they're spaced apart, and where Luna stops and waits, moonlight pours into a pretty little clearing, with a circle of brown mushrooms growing at the very center. More lanterns of varying shapes, sizes, and colors are clustered here and there at the base of trees, their light throwing long the shadows of three men dressed all in black.

When they begin to play their instruments—flute, violin, and hammered dulcimer—I recognize the song immediately as Aisling's favorite, "The Skye Boat Song," which has trilled through The Magick Happens every day for the past forty to fifty years along with other music connecting Dottie to her Irish and Scottish heritage.

One by one, people who love Ash step out from behind trees and present her with trinkets. Trevor's girlfriend, Teyonna, slips iridescent wings over Ash's shoulders. Trevor gives her a bottle of nail polish, which has tiny gold star confetti in it. From Romina's boyfriend, a pocket-sized copy of *Alice in Wonderland*. Alonzo Mozzi and his grandson, Cannon, bestow on her a chunky pen filled with pink liquid and many-colored beads. And from Great-Aunt Misty and her granddaughter, our cousin Nitya, a pack of Lenormand divination cards drawn by Nitya herself.

"Does the Fairy Queen accept our tributes?" Luna inquires, curtsying deeply.

Ash raises her chin. "I do."

We cheer. The musical trio plays a lively tune, and everyone bursts into dance except for Alonzo (who does bow very gentlemanly, however). Romina, Luna, Ash, and I link our hands, twirling around the fairy ring. "Do you see the fairies?" I ask Aisling. "That's what the seed pods in your shoes are for. They enable you to see them."

"Yes! They're everywhere." Her face transforms with wonder, her stare riveted on the surrounding trees. "Their clothes are made from petals and leaves, and they have more musical instruments than humans have invented. Each fairy is holding a different instrument—there must be hundreds!—and they're singing in a language that sounds familiar. It isn't quite English, but it has such a similar sound."

"Don't step inside the fairy ring," Romina warns. "Or you'll be spirited back to Fairyland."

"*Back* to?" Cannon repeats. He is Aisling's best friend, and her total opposite. He has the most serious face of any child I've ever met and is always worrying. It's good for Cannon to have an Aisling. He'd never get into any fun trouble without her.

Luna laughs. "Where do you think she came from?"

"*That's* why their language sounds so familiar," Aisling quips. "I was born there, but when I was a baby I flew out of Fairyland on a dandelion puff—fairy babies are *very* small, you know—and when I blew into this world, I adapted to my environment by growing bigger, to look like a regular human baby and blend in."

"I found her sitting in the back garden, in a row of vegetables like a summer squash," Luna says. "Grandma Dottie knew she was coming. She'd seen her in a vision."

"And we knew we could never give you back," I join in, thinking about what it was really like on the day Aisling was born. Luna in labor, gripping Romina's hand, moaning that she couldn't do this alone; Romina promising she would never have to while I fruitlessly dialed Luna's ex-boyfriend over and over, unable to get past a full voicemail box. "You were too perfect."

Ash's expression is almost trancelike, face upturned. "If only you could see all the fairies here," she says to us. "And so many ghosts, too! They love the music."

"Isn't it incredible?" Luna agrees. The song changes and we detach, Ash demanding that Cannon spin with her. My sisters, Teyonna, Trevor, Nitya, and I rush toward the fairy ring, then back, toward and back, while skipping around it, in such a brisk frenzy that sweat drips from my temples. "I forgot he knew how to *really* play, not just mess around."

"Who does what?" I ask Luna, half listening.

"Morgan. That's his band, Heavy Mettle."

My steps falter, gaze cutting across the fairy ring. Morgan Angelopoulos is unrecognizable without his loud Day-Glo prints, strikingly elegant in a suit black as Death, hair trimmed a couple inches and swept neatly back. His bow slides over violin strings, left hand gripping the neck, his fingers moving deftly.

His eyes meet mine, and my chin drops.

"He can do *that*?" I hear myself sputter. "Then why does he subject me to such horrible shrieking with that thing?"

Morgan watches me narrowly for another moment, as though he heard what I said even though that's impossible from this distance, and then focuses on his work. The two men accompanying him, one tall and burly with an auburn ponytail and the other fair as alabaster with golden curls spilling over his forehead, are lost in their music. I don't think I've ever seen either of them before. The late hour, the moonlight, excitement, the song so lovely that it stirs my emotions to an unreasonable degree—it all collides into the strangest fancy that at least one of the people here *must* be fae, weaving a spell over the rest.

I study Morgan as though I've never seen him before. It is the eeriest sensation, gripping me like cold hands on my arms and legs, rooting me to the spot: it is almost as if, all this time, I have merely been looking at his reflection in a darkened window, and not at the man himself. If there is such a thing as fairies, then this must be fairy music. I've never heard a human produce anything half as enchanting.

Who *is* he?

Pale, raven-haired, dark-eyed. Quick with a grin and also a lie, always on the cusp of amusement no matter the situation. I know him, and I don't. My eyes glaze over as I watch him watching me, my vision going bright and shiny at the edges, like light striking a mirror.

And this is when I hear a voice, gentle as dandelion fluff from Fairyland, emanating from behind him:

"The clock."

FIFTEEN

Peer through a three-holed Odin's stone and you'll see
the fae folk. Odin's stones with four holes will allow you
to glimpse fae-made illusions, which are just as pretty as
they are dangerously seductive.

Legends and Superstitions, Expanded,
Tempest Family Grimoire

I'M WALKING TOWARD it before I can think, passing
them, listening.

"*Old and new,*" it goes on.

Morgan turns to watch where I'm disappearing to, silvery
violin notes tracing my steps. "Zelda?"

"Ahhhh!" I'm clobbered by Aisling, who hugs me tight
around the middle, her flower crown drooping with missing
petals. She's rosy and beaming. "This is the best birthday of
my life."

I am tugged back into the fray, disoriented. *The clock. The
clock. The clock.*

E T   O

   H   K L

  C

Old and new. Who on earth is lurking in here?

"Just wait till you're fifteen," Luna is saying to her daughter. "That's when we let you cast your first spell."

Aisling twirls. "It's going to be amaaaaazing."

Cannon smiles at her. "Which birthday present was your favorite?"

"The bluefairy pie."

His face falls into a slight pout. "Who gave you that?"

"My husband, King Aelaric of Lowhill." Her voice drops, but I'm close enough to overhear. "I stepped into the fairy ring, just an inch, when nobody was looking. In the span of three earth seconds, I lived ten whole years in Fairyland. I married a fairy king and became a real live fairy queen."

Cannon's mouth falls open in surprise, but fury catches up. "You did not."

She grasps his wrist, eyes hypnotic. "Cannon, it's *glorious* there, like nothing you can imagine. I really wish you'd gone with me! Maybe someday I'll take you, but not just yet, because I've been trying to get back here for a while now. I missed my family, and they don't have electricity in Fairyland. Although Aelaric is probably looking for me already. If the Fairy Council finds out I've run away, they'll track me down in this realm and remove all the magic powers I've been developing."

Cannon is still unhappy, but she's piqued his interest. "What sort of powers?"

She is spared from inventing a response, however, when Luna announces it's nearly midnight. "Twelve years old at twelve o'clock," Luna pronounces, herding her daughter by the shoulders back to the rest of the crowd. "A powerful time for magic." She fishes a matchbox from the pocket of her cloak and strikes a flame, then sets it to the wick of a stubby white candle half-buried in the ground. "Make your wish."

Ash shuffles forward. "I wish . . ."

She hesitates, staring into the blaze. The white candle appears to bubble, as if the wax is boiling. "I'm not going to say it out loud."

She blows out the candle, her secret wish swimming upward in a plume of smoke.

SIXTEEN

In 1925, a circus train crashed in Moonville. The
conductor claimed to have seen a bear on the tracks,
which derailed the train; many animals escaped. All were
eventually reported recovered, but sporadic sightings of
zoo animals continued into the next century.

Local Legends and Superstitions,
Tempest Family Grimoire

I WISH MY NIECE good night, feigning that I need to adjust the buckles of my boots so that I can linger behind. Luna loads up all of her lanterns except one, which I've absconded with, and piles them into the red wagon she pulled Ash around the neighborhood in when she was a baby. Then, once I'm alone, I face the empty clearing.

It's smaller when I'm the only one here, somehow. And dauntingly quiet. I circle the ring of mushrooms in measured steps, around and around, eyeing it sidelong.

Quick, before I can stop myself, I leap inside.

A moment passes.

When nothing fantastical happens, I choose triumph. There is no reason to feel disappointed, because I had zero expectations of unusual results. "Ha! Nothing."

"Trying to run away to Fairyland?" a voice inquires.

I jerk out of the fairy ring, smashing a mushroom. *Bad luck, bad luck, a fairy's going to coat the soles of your feet with molten gold as punishment.* When I was small, Dottie told me a story about fairies doing such things, and it was so enjoyably ghastly that I never forgot.

Morgan slips one hand into his pocket, the other gripping the handle of his violin case. He watches me from a short distance, his gaze wandering from the smashed mushroom to the lantern I'm holding aloft, two of its glass panels blue, two of them green. Its shine paints him beautifully inhuman, like what you'd see looking back at you from beneath the surface of the sea in a fairy tale.

Heart thundering, I tell him, "It isn't nice to sneak up on people."

"Did you have a plan for if it worked?"

"Who's to say it didn't? Maybe I traveled there and back before you could blink. Maybe I've been there for the last hundred years."

One corner of his mouth edges into a knowing smile. "I like when I catch you acting oddly. Makes you less formidable."

"I'm not formidable," I shoot back, offended. Then I frown. "Wait. Yes, I am. *Extremely* formidable. So . . . go on home, then. Leave me to my formidability in peace." I don't mind that I'm not a gregarious person, but one of the downfalls of being this way is that I've got no charm, no oil for the hinges of conversational doors to make them open and close smoothly. I am trying to conduct private business out here, and Morgan is impeding that activity, so my only path forward is to tell him to get lost. "Goodbye."

"Why do you want me to leave?" He makes no move to do so, scanning our surroundings. "You got other plans?"

"I thought I heard someone back here earlier," I reply, "who wasn't in our party. I wanted to look for them."

Morgan's eyebrows knit ever so slightly before rising, his eyes a touch wider. "By yourself?"

Instant regret. There's no getting rid of him now.

"I'll be fine."

"You heard some*one* or some*thing*? Maybe you heard the coralote?"

"The coralote cannot exist. There's nothing like it in any wildlife book, and believe me, I've looked through plenty of them." I head out of the trees, over the red bridge. Back to Vallis Boulevard with its sleeping houses and lamps firing orange off the windshields of parked cars. Aside from an elderly woman rolling by on her bicycle, frozen pizza from an open-late gas station propped in her basket, nobody is afoot.

"Just because it hasn't been found by others doesn't mean *you* didn't find it," Morgan says simply. "What if it's a paranimal? What if it's magic?"

The word burns across the night, lighting me up with a warm, wonderful feeling—*magic!*

$$I$$
$$A \qquad G$$
$$C \qquad M$$

—before I wrestle it into submission.

I've pigeonholed myself, you see. By sticking to certain

opinions for so long, they've baked into people's perceptions of me. I'll never be able to shed it.

Zelda Tempest: never stays in a relationship for long. She falls from man to man and eats their love like candy. Doesn't believe in the supernatural.

If my sisters find out I'm entertaining even a *whisper* that magic might be real—not because they've been telling me so for years but because magic is maybe happening to *me*—they are going to be disgusted. I can already hear *Too late, we're not accepting you into our witchhood because you've been so rude about it* and *I don't believe you. Now, how does* that *feel?*

"It can't be real," I say helplessly.

"Come on. You want to believe, don't you? I can tell."

I squint. "How?"

He bumps the toe of his shoe against mine. "Your boots have pictures of zombies coming out of coffins. You've got a *Werewolf of London* poster on your wall."

"So?"

He begins to speak, his cheekbones burning with color, but then stops. Studies me. "Maybe the paranormal isn't real. But tell me honestly that if it *was* real, you wouldn't want to learn every single little thing about it. If there is even the slightest possibility of knowing great big things, you need to find out." He advances on me with interest as dark as the hollow of a tree. "It would drive you mad, not knowing for sure."

My skin is hot all over, creeping down my throat, spreading like a rash. "How did you guess that about me?"

"Because you're like me. Once you're wondering, you can't let go. And do you know what?"

"What?"

"I think you should stop worrying about being right, and let yourself explore this even if you might be wrong."

I analyze his face, sharp lines and soft curves. It looks chiseled from white opal, but I bet if I stroked a finger down his cheek, it'd feel soft as feathers.

Everything feels magnified. The warm breeze stirring, the echoing bark of a dog a couple blocks away, the vivid electric green, yellow, red of the stoplight. Morgan's hair a black sickle against his cheek like the inverse of moon against night.

"Why do *you* believe?" I ask.

Morgan looks away, ruminating for a spell. "In a town known for being magical, nothing magical has ever happened to me. Not once." His pain is like a shock wave. "I need for it to be real," he says wistfully, "because I want to be able to do the unexplainable, like Luna and Romina, and now Alex."

(It should be noted that Alex himself has professed that he does not have any new gifts, and that he's able to locate lost belongings simply because he is "good at everything.")

Morgan turns back to me, jaw set. "If magic isn't going to choose me, then I'm going to go find *it*. And if you, Zelda, can see the supernatural, then I need to be exactly where you are."

MORGAN DROPS HIS violin off on Wafting Crescent's porch, and then we continue walking past our houses, down the road. "All right, then. For the sake of . . ." I twirl a hand, thinking out loud. "Scientific research. How should we proceed?"

That *we* transforms his expression to one of greed and elation. "We search with intention. How many paranimals have you seen?"

Counting only this past summer, and not the experiences I had while growing up, it would be . . . "Three." The glowing winged creatures that flock to lightbulbs when it storms. The coralote. The huggle. I allow the forbidden thought to sneak in.

What if I'm a witch?

I have no right to feel thrilled at the prospect, given that I have been such a staunch denier. I bite my lip. "Can I confess something?"

Morgan just looks at me, pleasantly expectant. *Go on.*

"I've always wanted to believe in magic. I'm not saying I *do* now, but . . ."

"But maybe?"

"I'm at whatever step is right before maybe. I'm at *almost* maybe." I'm trying to distance myself from it, wanting to believe without letting on to the universe that I want to.

"I won't say *I told you so* if we're wrong, you know," he says.

Eyes forward on the road, my next lungful is jagged. The earth is beginning to cool, fog rising from the hollows that dip here and there throughout our town, the twists and turns on back roads with sheer drops on either side. Mist floats up to wreath treetops, and it reminds me of the legend of brays, which are the spirits of people who died in these woods. If you get too close to a bray on the anniversary of its death, it's allowed to take your body as its own, leaving you a captive of the forest forever while they wear your skin and your life.

"You don't find any of this embarrassing?" I sweep my hair over one shoulder and fiddle with it. "Being a fully grown adult, hunting for ghosts, talking about paranimals. Prophecies, crystal balls, love magic."

"I don't know." He spins once, hands in his suit jacket with his elbows pointed out. "I'd rather be wrong than never wonder at all and miss out on incredible. It's why I never left Moonville. If I'm ever gonna witness anything special, *this* is where that would happen."

"What are you hoping for, exactly?"

"Any sort of magic power. Literally, I would take *any*. My neighbor growing up, Hank, said there's a strange kind of goat around here that comes out only when it senses tornadoes. Disappears as soon as the tornadoes are gone, so you'd only catch one if you were out in a storm. Why is it that Hank knows about that? Hank was the most ordinary guy alive. He didn't even really care that he saw a phenomenon. No curiosity. It isn't fair that those of us who are *looking* for this stuff don't get to discover it." He makes a *hum* sound deep in his throat. "I'd love to be able to see ghosts. Or find a waraver."

"A waraver! It's been ages since I heard about those."

"War-*ah*-vur," he corrects.

I shake my head firmly. "*Where*-a-vur."

We smile at each other. Disagreeing over its pronunciation is as locally famous as the legend itself.

Waravers are formed from whitecaps wherever rapids are found in Raccoon Creek. They survive only by moonlight, collapsing back into water at daybreak, and have a humanlike shape. Some folktales describe the waraver as looking exactly like a small child, but with a sunken nose, lower hairline, and extra joints in the arms and legs; but other stories (particularly in the modern era) have beautified the legend, depicting them as the same height and likeness as adult humans, but supernaturally attractive, with eyes and skin that gleam as if perpetually wet. Their language cannot be understood by humans. When they speak, bubbles pour from their mouths. They have been known to warn fishermen of danger and save drowning children—but are *also* said to abduct children and drown fishermen. The thing about folklore is that there are two sides to every story, and they nearly always directly contradict each other.

Could there be waravers out there?

I don't think so. But I have no evidence, so I cannot say for a fact that there are no waravers.

We've been walking for about ten minutes without direction. I look around suddenly. "Where are we?"

Morgan's hand circles my wrist to lift the lantern higher and spill light over the road before us. Some fifteen feet off, the brick street crumbles into wild grass, abandoned mid-construction. The road was originally meant to lead to Kings Station, a nearby town that's become more inaccessible and insular by the year. Tunnel cave-ins, collapsed bridges, huge splits opening up in the road, with the stench of sewer gas springing from them. Attempts to make contact with Kings Station are cursed.

"Dixon's Dead End," we both intone. So named after a man who was hit by a train here.

"But it doesn't make any sense." I point behind us. "We were just walking west down Vallis, weren't we? And Dixon's Dead End is directly east."

We look at each other.

"I don't remember. I was following you," he says.

"And I was following you."

It's like two people with their hands on the planchette of a Ouija board. You don't know if the other person has been guiding it, or . . .

If something *else* is.

Falling Rock Forest has been inching closer to town over the years, eating up all of this area, the abandoned road. Wispy gray clouds skate across half the moon, and the broken moonlight slants across a low tree branch just overhead, illumining a strange creature sitting upon it with its long furry tail wrapped around its body.

"Hello there, little huggle," I singsong. Morgan looks first at me, I think because he's never heard me use that tone of voice before, and then upward, following my line of sight.

The creature jumps down. Morgan goes very still, and I kneel, a hand outstretched in offering.

It sniffs my fingers, glass-bright eyes roving nervously, ears twitching.

"That looks like a squirrel," Morgan says carefully.

I examine the animal. Small enough to carry in my hand, with bushy light brown fur. Large, orange, wide-set eyes, three black rings for pupils, one within another within another.

A slow smile spreads over my face. "It isn't. This is a huggle."

And this time, it doesn't change. Doesn't morph back into a squirrel. It watches me for a second, then darts toward the trees. Waits right at the edge as if beckoning us to follow.

Morgan and I look at each other. The animation in his face is fascinating to me—he is so easy to read. His expressive features remind me of those digital picture frames that click to a new image every five seconds. Something's always going on: a feathering of muscles, one type of smile evolving into another, a fluid rise of a sharp black eyebrow, a shocked gasp. All the world's a stage, and I'm watching him give one long, continuous performance.

"*The clock,*" somebody says.

I stop, grabbing Morgan's sleeve.

"What?" he asks under his breath, staring at my fingers.

"Did you hear that?"

He shakes his head. I search his eyes as the voice continues: "*Of old and new was always . . .*" He makes no reaction, now absorbed in my face.

I step back, and the voice ceases.

Step forward again. There's a rush of wind. "*The clock—*"

And then back. It ceases. "You don't hear that?"

Morgan's forehead pinches. "Hear what?"

I grip my lantern tight, swallowing a hard lump in my throat. *Zelda, Zelda.* I feel the trees reaching for me. *We remember you.*

Following the huggle, I walk three paces toward the forest's edge, and this time, I do not step back when the unseen person begins to speak.

"*The clock of old and new was always talking about how she used to be human and had butter-yellow hair. That was before the sorceress stuffed her inside a clock.*"

The forest breathes out, branches twisting, the glow of

fireflies reminding me of yellow cat's eyes painted on the wardrobe in Luna's bedroom. The voice does not say anything else.

I glance at Morgan. "Ready?"

"You have no idea."

Into the woods we go.

Part Two

SEVENTEEN

A creature that seems like it would be related to the waraver, but is not, is the swid, another impermanent Moonvillian water creature. Unlike the waraver, swid lore is universal and unchanging. A swid is created when love magic (which famously pollutes Moonville's waterways) and moon magic swirl together in an eddy. This type of magical organism can move but does not possess conscious thought like waravers, which display moderate intelligence and are skilled at evasion. Swids aren't easily detectable, as they are invisible, and hover in clusters. As their matter is sticky, they tend to gravitate to one another and form clumps called swidbula. Contact with a swid results in a temporary but powerfully giddy, lovestruck feeling. Accompanying sensations include blurred vision and tingling extremities, which clears once the swid is no longer in close proximity.

Local Legends and Superstitions,
Tempest Family Grimoire

WE FOLLOW THE huggle through dense, dark trees with sappy branches, which scurry out of our way as we approach. I glance at Morgan to see if he notices that the trees are clearing our path forward, but he's focused straight ahead.

It all feels rather like being at the bottom of the ocean. How everything is colored in deep greens and blues, none of it visible until a lantern floods out murky shapes. The whispering of leaves well over a hundred feet above our heads could be undiscovered species of marine life, drifting along the current.

The huggle vanishes into brush. "Where'd it go?" Morgan asks, his breath skating across the top of my head, blowing the tiny curls that frizz along my hairline. I swing the lantern higher, light chasing up a tree trunk. "I saw a squirrel, but you saw something else, which definitely fits the brief for paranimals."

"It changes when I question it, though. When I start to doubt, that's when it suddenly looks like a squirrel again. Why does the Black Bear Witch do this to animals? Is it like a curse?"

"Maybe she's made them dangerous."

I contemplate that. "The huggle I knew when I was little was always friendly. Maybe with the way she enchants them, she gives them magic of some sort but wants them to still appear normal, because they have new value that could be exploited. Why do cuttlefish change their colors? To hide from predators and also to blend in while they hunt their prey. It's the—"

The end of my sentence dies with the lantern's batteries.

Morgan raps the bottom of the lantern, switching it on and off. Darkness prevails. "That's not good. Do you have your phone on you?"

"No."

"Damn. Me, neither." With the world gone black, Morgan feels much closer now, even though I don't think he's actually moved. "Wait. What's that?"

"Where?" I turn my head as he takes my hand. Uses it to

point. Squinting, I'm just barely able to make out a light in the forest, far away.

"A streetlight?" I guess. "How far from the road do you think we are?"

"Could be. Might be a flashlight."

I shudder. "It's the person who keeps talking about clocks."

"You're gonna need to go into detail on that."

I tell him what I heard, and Morgan stops moving. I can feel him go rigid.

"*The sorceress stuffed her inside a clock,*" he repeats. "Could that possibly be a reference to the Black Bear Witch? Who got stuffed? Do you think our mysterious voice was speaking to you, or to somebody else in here?"

I shrug. "Your guess is as good as mine. Still can't believe you didn't hear it."

Morgan grumbles resentfully. "Careful, watch your step." He laces his fingers securely through mine.

Images of steep drops rip through my mind. The terrain's dangerous: narrow roads with no guardrails, no white edge paint to reflect headlights and help keep your car from plunging off. Out here in Falling Rock Forest, where citizens are strongly encouraged not to roam even during daylight hours, we've found ourselves in a veritable death trap.

"I know." I swallow. "This was maybe a stupid idea."

"Nobody ever made history by going home."

"All right, so we're going to walk very, very slowly," I tell him, endeavoring to stay levelheaded and in control of all my senses. "Feel along the ground with your shoes before you step. It's impossible to tell where any edges might be."

Crack.

Morgan whips around. "What was that?"

"Sounded like a stick snapping."

"But who snapped it?"

I give his fingers a reassuring squeeze. "Probably just a deer."

In the direction opposite the broken stick, leaves rustle. "I'm too pretty to die!" he whines. "I'll end up as one of those terrible ghosts who can't leave the woods, the ones that take over living people's bodies, and the body I steal will definitely not be as hot as the one I'm in now—"

"Morgan."

"And everybody will say '*Oh, this is what he would've wanted, Morgan was so interested in ghosts,*' but it is *not* what I want, I want to die at the age of one hundred and two in my rocket ship. I assume they'll have Hilton Hotel space stations by then."

"Morgan." I can't believe this is the same man who looked me right in the eye and said in a husky voice, *I'd love to be explicit, but for now I'll be polite. I'm saying that you're beautiful, and I want to spend time with you.* Ha! I can't imagine being seduced by Morgan now. He is utterly ridiculous.

"What will they do at the paper without me? I *am* the *Moonville Tribune*! I write under six different pen names to make it look like we've got more people working there than we do, but it's just me and Rick, who does the layout and printing, and Katy, who's a sixteen-year-old intern. You know Marty Allgood in Sports? Me. Mariah Abernathy, who does the gossip column? Also me. Local News and Community? Me again. Mitch Appleton, who argues back and forth with Mariah Abernathy concerning the credibility of her gossip column? Guess what? Me!"

"You made up two journalists who fight with each other?"

"I do what I have to do, Zelda!"

"Breathe." I grip his shoulders. "You're hyperventilating."

"Why aren't you hyperventilating? It stresses me out that you're not hyperventilating. I think you might be a vampire for real and you dragged me out here to drink my delicious blood."

"If I were going to do that, I would've brought my knife straw." I steady my hand over his pounding heart. "Deep breaths, Morgan. In, *one, two, three, four*. Hold, *one, two, three, four, five, six, seven*. Exhale, *one, two, three, four, five, six, seven, eight*. Come on, keep doing it. In, *one, two, three, four*. Hold, yes . . . Just like that."

We stay locked in, breathing together, for another minute, until he's calmed down. Until my palm is blazing hot where it's been molded to his chest. "Are you all right?" I ask finally, hand shaking slightly as I remove it.

"Never better. What about you?" His voice summons bravado, the whites of his eyes two pale embers in the darkness. "You're the one who got scared there."

I smile. "Oh yes. Petrified."

"You don't particularly love the dark," he goes on. "Not that you're *afraid* of it, but you do spend a great deal of time thinking about ghosts and how much you'd love to meet one, so now you figure they're always surrounding you, invisible. Which is fun and fascinating to think about when you're in a well-lit public room, with witnesses and a clear exit. Like at a Burger King. In a pitch-black forest with cliffs all over the place, turns out it isn't as much fun to imagine dead people watching you."

"I'm so glad you're getting me through this."

"Happy to be of service." He pats my back. Then, after a pause: "But why *aren't* you more scared?"

Good question. I frown as we take baby steps toward the faraway light. With all the trees, we have to do plenty of weaving to keep it in our sights. "I've never minded the dark," I tell him quietly. "I feel peaceful here. I liked being in the woods as a kid."

"At night?"

"No. I definitely would have, but I didn't want my parents to come looking for me and find out what I was doing. If they knew how I was spending my days, they might've tried to push me into extracurriculars for forced mingling with other humans." My laugh is rusty.

His reply is an awkward, hesitant "Ah." Morgan can't relate. I'm drained after a small dose of human interaction, but for Morgan, chatting with strangers seems to *charge* him. I don't envy this. I have never viewed my personality as a hindrance to be changed or overcome—I like who I am, and the world needs personalities of all types. But it *is* captivating to watch people like Morgan engaging with others in high animation. He's a great speaker, whereas I'm more of a listener and observer.

"Careful," he warns as I get whacked across the shoulder with a tree branch. "Sorry. Tried to move it out of your way, but I keep forgetting how short you are."

I accidentally step on the back of his foot. "Sorry."

He stumbles, scraping my ankle. I fall sideways, and when

he tries to catch me, his hands grab my face instead of my arm. "Ope. Sorry!"

I burst into laughter. "We're going to kill each other. This is ridiculous."

"So many mosquito bites, we're gonna look like we have chicken pox. I wanna swat them away, but I'd probably end up smacking you on accident."

"We've lost the light again."

He tries to veer us to the right, but as we move, I'm suddenly hit with the oddest, most unpleasant sensation. It is exactly like . . . the feeling of being five minutes late for a doctor's appointment, and then getting to the check-in desk and being told I'm in the wrong building.

I stop.

"What's wrong?" he murmurs.

My eyes fall closed, instincts strongly compelling me leftward. "This way."

But he slides us right again, three steps, and sweat trickles down my spine. The sensation that arrests me this time is extremely specific, and once again, bizarrely unrelated to the situation at hand: I feel the coolness inside a pumpkin as I hollow out its seeds and stringy fibers with a big spoon. The back of my hand bumps against the rim, cold orange pumpkin slime smearing across my skin.

The thought is overpoweringly vivid. My hand twitches, and I drop his. "Gross."

"Wh—" Morgan begins to say, but the rest sails off in an "Aghhh!" as he loses his balance, his voice growing louder as his body falls lower, to the ground, slipping downhill.

We've been walking at the edge of a cliff and had no idea.

"Morgan!" I throw myself to my knees, catching his wrist just as the top of his head slithers from sight, weak moonlight spackling his forehead and his wide, terrified eyes. My mouth falls open with a crush of pain when gravity stops carrying him off and I'm left bearing the full force of his weight, heavy and dangling over a vast, craggy pit. "Hold on."

He lets out a choked noise. "Please don't drop me."

"I won't." But even as I say it, I can feel him slipping, the weight of his body staggering. It pulls against my every muscle, tendons standing out of my neck, skin burning like fire. "Climb up my arm."

He tries to lift himself, and my shoulder turns the wrong way in its socket. I let out a sharp cry of pain. Morgan immediately stops. "I'm sorry," he says breathlessly, laced with tangible fear. "Are you okay?"

"Keep going." I hook my foot around a tree, teeth gritted. "Come on. We can do this. You are *not* leaving me alone with the forest ghosts."

"So you admit there are forest ghosts. This is progress, Zelda."

As if my brain is trying to resist the very idea, my muscles react and I tug on him, hard and swift, bringing Morgan close enough that he can find purchase and scrabble the rest of the way up. Together, we heave him back into safe territory, then lie in a panting, trembling heap.

"Well," he manages after a while, still collapsed in the dirt and leaves. "That kind of sucked."

"*Pffft.*" Air escapes me in a wheeze. His response to a near-death experience is, for some reason, the funniest thing I have ever heard in my life. *Well, that kind of sucked.*

Morgan starts laughing, too. "Oh, that hurts."

"What does?"

"Everything."

I can't resist. "Told you we should've gone left."

"That, you did," he replies, instantly sobered. "I should have listened."

When we finally get moving again, Morgan lets me navigate without complaint.

After a bit more stumbling around, we relocate that faraway bluish-white light. "Does it seem like we're getting any closer?" Morgan wonders aloud.

"Maybe it's a portal to the afterlife. We both fell into the gorge back there and died but we don't remember, and our souls have actually been roaming this forest for years instead of an hour."

I feel Morgan shiver. "You're creeping me out."

I grin as I clutch his upper arm, stretching on tiptoe so that I can speak close to his ear. "They say that Morgan's and Zelda's bodies were never found, absorbed by nature."

"Oh god."

"Wait." I shush him, going still. "Did you hear that?"

"Hear what?" His voice thins.

For a handful of seconds, neither of us moves.

"Someone's speaking," I whisper. "But it sounds distant."

He doesn't reply, straining to listen. My hand tightens on him. "There it is again. And don't you feel the vibrations? I think it's . . . footsteps. Walking over our graves."

EIGHTEEN

In July 1952, at a quarter after two p.m., over forty witnesses reported snow falling over Downigan Cemetery, piling thick enough to bury the tombstones. It did not snow anywhere else, and the temperature in town was recorded to be ninety-one degrees. The snow melted by the end of the day, and there remains no explanation for what occurred.

Local Legends and Superstitions,
Tempest Family Grimoire

MORGAN WRESTS HIS arm from my grasp, exasperated. "What is *wrong* with you?"

"A lot."

"Never going to sleep peacefully again. Thanks. No wonder you wrote about sleep paralysis demons."

"I've never written about sleep paralysis demons."

"Yes, you have. Tall, thin, upside-down-walkers with tentacles that transform from solid into gas. In *Cave of a Thousand Crystal Wings*, they stole Henriette in her sleep and tied her to the ceiling."

He's right. "I completely forgot about that."

"How? You *wrote* it."

I shrug. "The demons were just background characters. Second-string villains."

"The background characters are my favorite. What sort of monsters are you incorporating into the book you're working on now?"

I flick all thoughts of books and writing away before they can trigger full panic, having already succumbed to the first stage of it, with weak legs and nausea. "Do you think that light looks closer now?"

"Don't even start," Morgan scoffs.

"No, really! I'm not suggesting it's anything creepy."

"Speaking of creepy. How was your movie date?"

"Don't know yet. We had to reschedule because his parents decided to drop in from Michigan for a week and are staying with him." I pinch his elbow. "And Dylan is *not* creepy."

"Sure, he's great if you're into beady reptilian eyes. His face is like one of those filters that shows you what you would look like if you were completely symmetrical. You know? Which you'd think would be attractive but instead the result is sinister. He looks like he wears a beige backpack around in his own house, and he's filled it with knives."

"He does not! Dylan looks like he could do my taxes in under ten minutes. Like he barely watches television, but when he does, it's the Travel Channel. Which I find hot."

"He looks like he reads Kerouac in bed," Morgan replies gleefully. "To his lovers. Then explains the metaphors to them."

"I'm not listening."

For the next few minutes, Morgan amuses himself inventing Dylan trivia. "He tells people he's lower middle class and thrifts all his clothes, but he's just referring to the one jacket that he stole from the coatroom they put rich people's jackets in at fancy restaurants. You know, if this whole finding-the-Black-Bear-Witch-and-getting-magic-from-her thing doesn't pan out, you could do worse than fall in love with me. I'm so much better-looking than Dylan, and I've got a friend with keys to the library. I'll ravage you in the reference section."

"Stop trying to charm me. You're so fake, you've got seven different names." I shake my head. "I can't believe you write that whole newspaper by yourself. You've got to be exhausted!"

"Nah. I write in batches, staying up all night churning out enough material to stretch for two weeks. Interviews with made-up people, horoscopes recycled from last year, petty squabbles between neighbors, predictions about the weather based on my mood. I work quickly, then get bored because I run out of stuff to do."

"You could report on real news?" I suggest.

"Zelda, do you hate me? Do you want me to lose my will to live?"

"Sorry."

I wish I could stay up all night pounding out ten thousand words. At one point, words were a creative playground of endless possibilities. Now they're expectations and fear and *delete, delete, delete*. Words are an ugly comparison game. *Not good enough.*

I'm not done yet! I want to shout. *This is my dream. I've still got more to offer!*

Isn't it still my dream?

"Zelda?"

Morgan's voice is a few hops ahead, and I realize I've stopped walking. *What if this isn't my dream anymore? What else am I meant to do?* Anxiety surges, zero to one hundred, and I'm not prepared for it. Who am I? Who is Zelda Tempest and what is her purpose? I've always been so sure of it before.

"Are you all right? Did you get hurt?"

"No," I reply dazedly. "I'm fine."

His hand slips into mine, and when we go on together, moonlight begins to striate our surroundings. At first, I think we've reached a meadow in the forest. The next step brings my foot down into water, the level almost high enough to swell inside my boot.

Not a meadow. A marsh.

It extends far enough that the woods continuing on the other side are bluish with mist. Cool air rises off the black mirror, laden with lily pads, cattails, reeds, and ferns. Pink clumps of flowers wave in a gentle breeze. And about twenty feet out, a crystal-ball-sized sphere of light sits suspended low over the water.

"That's not quite a streetlamp," I murmur.

Morgan retains a grip on me as he leans forward slightly, drinking up the sight. "What *is* it?"

We crane our necks, studying the moon, trying to gauge how this could be explained by light refraction. If it were a soft, weak light, that would make sense—but that's not what this is. It's too bright, opaque. And the water beneath it shines like white fire, illuminating the tiny fish zinging along. "It looks like . . ." Morgan says breathlessly.

"A will-o'-the-wisp," I insert.

His body unwinds, upright, every atom of his being fixated on the scene. "Witchlight."

"What?"

"A fragment of a witch's magic, which roams free after the witch is deceased. It wanders until it finds other witch magic to cluster to."

This sounds familiar. "They're supposed to accumulate to form poltergeists, right?"

He only nods, as though afraid the witchlight will hear us. And then he lifts one foot and steps into the water.

"Morgan!" I bend, hands on my knees. "What are you doing? You're wearing loafers!"

"My poor choice of footwear is an inadequate reason to not investigate," he replies without glancing back, slowly wading toward the light. With every gentle slosh, his black trousers grow even darker, water spreading up the fibers.

I begin to argue that this is a bad idea when cold water spills up my legs and I look down to discover that I, too, have begun walking toward the light. My thoughts uncurl like a flat, reaching fog, going a bit dreamy. It's impossible to tell if I'm walking of my own subconscious volition or if I'm being pulled. Water splashes around me.

"Shhh," Morgan chastises me quietly. "You're being too loud."

"Do you think it has ears?"

"We don't know what it has, or what it is for sure. Could be a fairy."

It is ludicrous that my knee-jerk reaction is excitement, but here we are: I am swishing through wetlands in the dead of night with Morgan Angelopoulos, potentially ruining these glorious boots so that I can get a closer look at some bright, shiny thing, and that means I am nothing less than ludicrous.

Ah, well. I suppose I'm just going to go with it now.

We walk for a few minutes but still haven't reached our destination. "Is it moving?" I say, puzzled.

"It looks like it's staying still," Morgan says, "but also kind of receding?"

I move faster, not caring if it makes my splashing louder. Soon I outstrip Morgan. Still, we don't get any closer to the light; it's the same distance away as it was when we stood on dry land. "Strange."

"Magic," he counters.

With an unearthly glow like that, one has no choice but to allow for the possibility of unearthly answers.

A massive, dark shape lumbers into my periphery, and I immediately shoot out a hand to seize Morgan's sleeve. He falls still beside me just as a bear slaps its heavy paw into the water, head down, and roots around by the light.

How is it that an animal can get near to it, but we can't?

I've never been this close to a bear before. It's smaller than I would have expected, but clearly an adult, black all over except for its light brown muzzle.

And then Morgan moves.

My muscles tense, thinking he's going to bolt, that the bear will give chase—but no. Morgan sidesteps behind me, hands capping my shoulders.

I turn to stare up at him, aghast. "Are you hiding behind me?" I whisper.

Morgan swallows, then returns to my side. "Of course not, gorgeous."

"Call me 'gorgeous' again and I'll punch you." I don't like that I still like it. I want to put a bag over his pretty head—it'd make it easier to keep my thoughts organized.

"Sorry, bad habit. Let's move on."

"You were totally hiding behind me! You want to sprinkle me with salt and pepper so that I'll be more appetizing for the bear!"

"If anything, I'd decorate you with fish guts," he hisses back, as we both shuffle away slowly. "Bears would appreciate that more than seasoning."

The bear stalks closer to the light, head bobbing as it sniffs around. For the first time, the light visibly spasms.

"It moved!" I whisper.

"So should we."

Right.

The light swerves, sharply enough to elicit a gasp from both of us. The bear makes a frustrated snuffling noise, batting at it, mouth open. And then . . .

Well, there is no way to describe this except that the bear appears to be *eating* the light while the light hops frantically, trying to get away. Its glow flutters and dims, becoming a half moon, then a crescent, as bites are taken out of it.

"I wish I had my phone so that I could record this," Morgan utters quietly.

Not quietly enough. The bear looks up.

Goose bumps erupt. Its eyes reflect the last wisp of light streaking the fur of its muzzle like ghost blood, and it freezes just as I do. There is something so wrong about the bear that my body doesn't do the human-reflex thing and run for my life. Rather, I take a step *closer*. Morgan snatches me back, I hear a series of loud splashes, and once the mist resettles on the water, the bear is gone.

The spell breaks.

Land, which took several minutes to wade away from, takes mere seconds to reach again. The hairs on the back of my neck stand up, and I feel as though I'm being watched. The sensation is inexplicable. It isn't terror. It's curiosity and compulsion. Sixth sense. I know something, but at the same time, I don't have it figured out yet.

"Did that bear look weird to you?" I ask as we empty marsh water from our shoes. Lily pads cling to my boots.

"Besides the fact that it might have eaten a ball of energy left behind by a dead witch?"

"No. It didn't look . . . completely like a bear."

Morgan's brow furrows. "How so?"

"I can't explain. It felt like I was looking at one type of animal, but a different type of animal was looking back at me. One hidden inside it."

"You think it might be the Black Bear Witch? Or a paranimal. Like the squirrel that isn't a squirrel?"

I'm not certain. Now that I think about it, I can't quite remember what was wrong about the bear.

NINETEEN

Will-o'-the-wisps have been known
to lure many a lost traveler.

Legends and Superstitions, Expanded,
Tempest Family Grimoire

Things that can cause the appearance of bright light over water:

Moonlight reflecting off surfaces.

*The mixture of marsh gas, decaying matter, and other
natural gases.*

Bioluminescent fungi, algae, etc.

Ball lightning.

Hallucination induced by lack of sleep, folie à deux.

Magic??

Hours later, on Lughnasadh proper, I join my family for
their tradition of planting a fruit tree on Tiptop Hill. Great-
Aunt Misty and her granddaughter, Nitya, spend the day with
us. Nitya is known for denim on denim, jumpsuits, and statement jewelry: the red plastic necklace she's blown into town

with this time is as big around as a steering wheel. Nitya wears her black hair in a beehive and an African gray bird called Odyssey, who likes to imitate her loud laugh, on her shoulder. Nitya is a nomad, like I used to be before I got tired of it, but she takes her role as Aisling's godmother seriously and is always in Moonville for her birthday (and pops in every couple of months with interesting gifts for her).

"Shapes and colors," Nitya is saying now to Morgan and Trevor. We're in the shop, and I've been spacing out of the conversation as I obsess tiredly over the ball of light Morgan and I saw last night, jotting down my thoughts in a pocket-sized notebook. But at *shapes and colors*, I glance up.

She's telling them about her gift.

"It first started happening when I was around ten," Nitya goes on. "I'd be going about my day, when all of a sudden, all of the colors I could see turned gray, except for one. Like, my classroom would turn black and gray with the exception of anything red. Or I'd be reading a magazine, and anything in it that wasn't blue would suddenly turn gray. It freaked me out. My dad took me to the doctor, but they couldn't figure out what was causing it."

Trevor is perched on the checkout counter. Morgan leans against it, entirely too close to me. A miniature Devil Zelda appears on my left shoulder and goes, *Psst. You could touch him right now if you wanted to. A knee, an elbow.* I flick her off, but she materializes on my right shoulder. *What if you reach out and put your hand on his cheek? What's stopping you? You have free will!*

Morgan props a fist under his chin, engrossed in the story as I wage battle with my naughty impulses. "Then what happened?"

Nitya's mindlessly drawing a portrait of me on the back of receipt paper, using a burning incense stick. "I was learning how to embroider one day, and all of the thread in my sewing basket turned grayscale except for a spool of light green. So I used the green to stitch a leaf onto my jacket. Once I was done with that leaf, my spool of green turned gray, and a different spool that had been gray suddenly turned pink. So I used the pink to stitch a flower to the leaf. On and on it went, until I ended up with a pattern of a tulip sprouting out of a teacup. Once I was finished with the last stitch, I felt this instant sense of protection, like whoever wore the jacket would be safe from any harm. And all the other colors came back. I realized this was my magical gift, and that I'm supposed to embroider spells."

"What happens when you use the gray threads? Have you tried?"

She dips her head in a deep nod. "Any time I do that, it feels so wrong. It'll feel like cold water's dripping onto the top of my head, or like I've scraped the back of my ankle even when I haven't, or suddenly, it'll be as if I'm running through the airport terminal, right as the flight I'm supposed to be on takes off."

I stare at her, thinking about last night when Morgan wanted to turn right and I sensed, down to my bones, that we should go left.

"We get that, too," Romina tells him. "Luna and me. Not colors turning grayscale, but with our own magic, we get tactile sensations and relive bad memories when we're not doing what magic wants. It's like the magic is guiding us. When I'm picking flowers for a flora fortune and I choose one for a client that magic doesn't agree with, it'll force me to think about the time I was followed for two blocks by a hornet, or something to that effect. Then when I put the wrong flower down and pick up one that magic wants, I'm rewarded."

"How? In what way?" I ask quickly. When Romina and Luna both turn their surprised expressions on me, I sniff and pretend to focus on my notes, hair falling forward in a tumble to conceal half my face. "Just curious, that's all."

"You've never asked about it before," Luna remarks thoughtfully. But she then adds, "Good memories. Nice, happy images, like sipping hot chocolate during the first snow or how it feels when you're at the movies and the lights dim, the previews finally starting. When I mixed just the right scents to make a candle yesterday, magic unlocked an old memory of when I was a little kid. Back when Grandma still lived upstairs, and where Ash's bedroom is now, there was a sewing room with Dad's bed and dresser from when he was young." Luna's eyes haze over as she peers into the memory. "I was standing behind Grandma as she opened a dresser drawer and took out a blanket to show me. It was Dad's baby blanket, with his name stitched on. It smelled like a pine forest, so there must've been sachets in there. Then she took out clothes she used to wear in the seventies and let me try on a yellow silk nightgown. She liked showing me old things, telling me the stories behind them. There's no way I could have remembered that on my own, without magic."

"The lost memories are my favorite," Romina says, smiling as she reminisces. "They're always random, so it's hard to say how magic finds these memories, why it chooses them specifically. Thanks to magic, I've remembered events that happened when I was only a baby. Before I even understood most words."

My heart clenches with longing and jealousy. Could that happen to me? I want to remember long-ago moments with Grandma, too. It's jarring every time I see Aunt Misty, because she so closely resembles Dottie. They have the same long, thin nose and drooping mouth. White hair. Sparse, rounded eyebrows that sit farther apart than their eyes do. I want to tell Nitya to stay home for a while, spend more time with her grandmother while she still can. Dottie and I talked on the phone all the time during my years away, but I wish we'd seen each other in person more.

I'm keen to hear if it might be possible for me to unlock good memories, but if I reveal my interest, they'll ask questions. I debate how to go about casually digging for information, but by the time I've worked up the nerve, they're back to talking about Nitya's magical embroidery again.

"She sewed a cute little ice cream cone onto my shirt collar, years ago," Luna says. "I was wearing that shirt when we went to the Pumpkin Show in Circleville. Remember, Romina?" She and Romina nod at each other. "I got lost and two guys started following me. One of them grabbed my shoulder, and *boom!* Fell backward like I'd punched him. Swear to god, it was Nitya's magic that did it."

Misty nods. "I've got a scarf Nitya made for me, and I wear

it whenever I've got to take my car to the mechanic. Nobody ever tries to overcharge me when I'm wearing that scarf."

Morgan blasts her with his full attention. "Are you a witch, too?"

Misty beams. "Oh yes! I make teas to induce astral projection and lucid dreaming." She sweeps a knuckle across clay stains on her overalls. "And I'm a potter, so part of my business is creating personalized teacups to align with one's birth chart. The teas by themselves will work for anyone, but they're far more potent when consumed from a bespelled vessel such as one of my cups."

"I'd *love* to astral-project." Morgan's eyes gleam. "Will you teach me how? What would I be able to see? When my consciousness leaves my body, can it fly to another town? State? Continent? Could I astral-project to Santorini? Wait!" He waves his arms as if to erase that last bit. "I wanna know how to get to *Saturn*."

She appraises him narrowly, then smiles. "You're an Aries. Gemini rising."

His chin drops. If possible, he's squeezed even closer to her, oblivious that he's resting an elbow over my paper and making it impossible for me to write. "How could you tell?"

"It oozes from you." Misty pats his cheek. "Come by my shop anytime, love. Tempest in a Teapot, in Cuyahoga Falls. We're on Graham Road, right next to the Panera. Come get some tea, then sit next door and astral-project to Santorini with a tuna salad sandwich."

"I am sincerely going to do just that."

Luna runs upstairs to check on the bread she's got baking—parsley, garlic, chives, and cheese—and glides back down with a loaf to send home with Misty and Nitya, who have to leave soon because they've got a three-and-a-half-hour drive home. Magical-practicing Tempests always bake bread with fresh-picked herbs on Lughnasadh, and right before bed, they eat blueberry cake dusted with powdered sugar. Wafting Crescent offers such a cake as their daily special, every Lughnasadh, for this reason.

And I, who do not (officially) practice magic, am perfectly content to enjoy the food so long as I don't have to bake any of it myself.

"I almost forgot." Misty pats her pockets, fishing out a small object from the wide front pocket of her overalls. "I've got a good feeling about this one." She drops a brass key, quite old-looking, with a miniature queen's crown welded to one end, into Luna's palm.

"That metal looks the same color as the lock," I remark as Luna inspects the key.

"I'll go get it!" Romina retrieves Grandma's mysterious locked box, and we gather around as Luna inserts the key.

Click.

"Ahhh!" we squeal.

"What is it, what is it?" Nitya pops her head between Luna and me.

A jewelry box with a musty odor. There are tiny velvet rolls in the top compartment, cradling four rings. None of the rings are particularly attractive, and two were obviously meant for children, as they're too small to fit any of us.

But in the bottom compartment, folded in half to fit, are papers.

We all grab for them, and in the scuffle, I end up with Grandma's spidery cursive scrawled across the backs of a water bill, half of a beeswax invoice, and a grocery list:

March 12 1981 Mike can't find shoe, check basement ✓ March 16 1981
April 6 1981 Mike late for school looking for stray cat ✓ September 7 1981
July 21 1981 Mellow will pass on Christmas Eve ✓ December 24 1981

June 30 1984 Baby girl ✓ June 28 1991
September 4 1984 Woman named Rachel joins family ✓ August 23 1987
November 13 1984 Black-haired man and red-haired woman run from mouse

May 6 1999 Delphine 7 lb 13 oz 20 in
October 31 1999 Misty will pass on a Friday in April, asteroid

"What the frack is all this?" Nitya mutters, leafing through pages.

"Grandma's predictions, I think," Luna replies. "The dates she had her prophetic dreams are over *here*, and the dates with checkmarks are when her predictions came true. Listen to this: *February 10, 1975. Little blond girl falls from broken swing, injures elbow.*" She lifts her elbow to display the faint scar bisecting it. "She knew that was going to happen before I was even born!"

"She knew Mom was going to marry Dad, too." I point at *Woman named Rachel joins family.*

Misty reads the paper in my hand over my shoulder. "An asteroid? Do I get hit by an asteroid?!"

"I hope that's how *I* go," Trevor says yearningly. "Imagine getting cratered. It would make for the most awesome final view, and then you've already got half the burial finished."

Misty backs away from the box, hands in the air. "This is what I get for trying to find out what's in locked boxes. Boxes are locked for a reason. Now I've got to live the rest of my life wearing a hard hat, trying to hide from the sky. Goddamn it, Doireann, you saw this happening twenty-four years ago! You couldn't have warned me?"

"Maybe the asteroid doesn't *hit* you," Morgan suggests. "Maybe there just happens to be one passing by on the day that you die. A little aerial hello before you go."

"Who's Delphine?" I ask. "Any of us know a Delphine?"

Everybody shakes their heads. "I know a Delaney," Nitya says. "Maybe she got the name wrong?"

"She was never wrong," Luna and Misty reply in unison.

Spooky.

We decide it's for the best if we stop reading, because if Grandma's predictions were never wrong, then there's nothing we can do to avoid our fates. Keep going, and I might see something like *Zelda will be devoured by a hippopotamus*. While folding the papers back up, I come across one that catches my eye.

Grandma's drawn a crude map with a few words scratched in—*BBW, cave, trestle*. In the middle, it says *Falling Rock Triangle*, and below that, in faded pencil: *Where lost things go*.

"What a woman," I marvel. "Gone for a year now, and she's still confusing us."

Romina smiles sadly. "She isn't *gone*, gone. But goodness, I miss seeing her."

"And her traveler's talismans," Nitya pines. "Remember those? *Delicious.*"

For the autumn equinox, Grandma used to bake small golden cakes shaped like triangles, called traveler's talismans. Luna had called the cakes *pirate hats.* Grandma said they were shaped that way because triangles are the most protective shape in witchcraft, but also, when traveling in these woods at Halloweentime, you're supposed to carry a triangle on you as a talisman. If you accidentally slip into the realm of the dead when the veil is thin and you can't find your way, a triangle will aid your return.

"I'd kill for the recipe," Luna muses. "I've had Ash beg Grandma for it a million times, and she always says I'll get it as a present eventually. Ghosts don't have a lot of options for gift-giving, so she insists on spacing out whatever she's got. She knows where I lost one of my bracelets, but she's saving the location reveal for Christmas. Why are grandmothers like this?"

The others keep chattering on, but my mind has caught a snag on triangles, and I can't stop staring at the peculiar diagram. What sort of prediction was this? *Where lost things go.*

BBW. Cave. Trestle.

BBW.

"The Black Bear Witch," I whisper.

TWENTY

To protect your loved ones on their travels,
dust the soles of their shoes with butcher's broom root.

Spells, Charms, and Rituals,
Tempest Family Grimoire

MORGAN TAKES GRANDMA'S drawing. "You think she might've had a dream about where the witch lives?" He keeps his voice down, but I don't think the others would hear; they've moved outside, shifting goodbyes into phase two, in which Misty and Nitya tell us goodbye while standing next to Nitya's car. In about fifteen minutes, they'll be saying goodbye from *inside* the car, with the windows rolled down, and that phase will last another fifteen minutes.

"I have no idea." I'm still reconciling myself with the concept that Grandma's visions were *real*, and what that means for me.

It would mean that the silver luna moth prophecy is real, that my sisters and I are destined to fall in love with our *True* Loves, within the same year. If Romina truly saw a silver luna moth a month ago, then that gives Luna and me . . .

"Zelda?"

. . . Five remaining months to fall in love with our fated ones.

Morgan passes his hand back and forth in front of my face. "Yoo-hoo! Still in the room?"

I shove the thought under a proverbial rug, desperate to be alone so that I can mull this more obsessively. Pacing will be involved. Graphs and charts.

"Zelda," he repeats. "Back to the Black Bear Witch. I've got priorities here. Unless you want to reconsider your stance on the other plan? Go an easier route?" He wags his eyebrows.

"What route is that?"

Morgan slides an inch closer, his lips curving. A black smolder glitters in his eyes. "Love. Give me thirty minutes on any soft surface. I swear you'll see stars."

I scrunch my nose, but at the suggestive provocation my heart beats in double time. Stupid heart. Time to start incorporating more omega-3 fatty acids into my diet. "You are really awful. You know that? And sex is not love."

He sighs. "You could at least *try*. My face is doing almost all the work for you, being this irresistible, so you're halfway to love already. Plus, it would be so much easier than hunting down a bear witch. What if the witch eats people after she gives them powers? My new gift might be totally useless from within the intestines of a bear."

"Yeah, no— *What the hell is that?*"

I leap behind him with a strangled cry, and Morgan backs up as well. He grabs a pen as if he might try to defend himself with it. "What's what? Where is it?" He brandishes the pen.

"Show yourself! Unless you're a spider. If you're a spider, stay where you are."

I point at an animal on the floor, my finger shaking. It's some kind of rodent, I think. Or a red panda genetically engineered in a laboratory? It walks on all fours like a tiny bear, with orange-and-black-striped fur and a tail that curls. It's got mole-like feet. Bulbous eyes, golden all over, no pupils. *"That! How can you miss it?!"* I paw at Morgan's shirt and force him bodily in front of me, quite possibly ripping off a button. The animal jumps from the floor onto a high shelf. "How'd it get in here? What *is* it?"

Morgan's gaze bounces around the shop, panicked. "I don't see anything!"

"It just jumped up on the shelf!"

He gapes in confusion. "What, you mean Snapdragon?"

"No! The weird little red panda–mole thing. Got a tail like"—words fail me, so I spiral a finger.

Morgan breaks away. Walks directly over to the shelf. "Don't go near it!" I shout.

He raises a hand experimentally.

"Stop!"

Morgan *pets* it.

"It might bite you. I can't believe you're touching it."

"He won't bite me." Morgan's voice is calm. "This is a cat."

"I have never in my life seen a cat like that. That is a cat after swimming through toxic waste. And you are *still* touching it!"

"Of course I'm touching him." Morgan scratches the creature under its chin, and its eyes droop lazily closed, clearly enjoying the attention. "Snapdragon and I are BFFs."

I move toward them, hesitant, not moving my eyes from the animal's. "Snapdragon?"

Morgan nods. "Snapdragon."

I don't believe it. "But I saw him this morning. He was doing his usual cat thing, sitting on the stairs, waiting to trip people. He definitely didn't look like this."

"What does he look like to you now?"

My lips part, throat dry. "It sounds strange."

He clasps a hand over his heart, and by the anguish on his face, I think he missed his Broadway calling. "Darling, *please.* Give me all your strange."

I have to take a moment to get over this phrasing. Morgan Angelopoulos is calculatedly charming, but *give me all your strange* is, for some reason, unintentionally charming to me; and while I consider myself a levelheaded person who lives according to reason and objective judgment, it turns out that I am still susceptible to a dark-eyed, dark-haired man with tattoos. Curse my baser instincts.

By the time I'm finished explaining Snapdragon's transformation, Morgan is recording my every word, eyebrows knitted. Taking notes is a good-looking—I mean—a *good* idea. Frogs, I might be in trouble. When Morgan takes notes, it makes my neck feel hot and itchy. He'd better not start using color-coded tabs, or I'm going to be in some real danger here.

"Morgan," I rasp, my hands hanging limply at my sides. I've broken out into a cold sweat. "I'm . . ." I can't even say it.

"Hm?"

"I'm . . ." The room spins a bit. "I think I might be a witch. A real one." It's the only explanation that makes sense, even though it should make zero sense, because even though I am apparently a witch I still half believe that witches are not real. The two positions are coexisting in a chaos state in my head.

Morgan laughs. "Yeah, I know. Haven't I been telling you that?"

I just gape at him, at Snapdragon, totally dumbfounded. A *witch*!

A beyond-logic, unprovable, no-concrete-evidence-to-support-this witch! I catch my reflection in Maxima, which is the name of Grandma's crystal ball, and am shocked to find a huge grin on my face. I touch my mouth to feel the broad curve, in awe. I am just like my sisters, just like Dottie and Aisling. They weren't wrong, or lying, and I can trust them . . . they haven't been leaving me out of a big secret con . . .

It is going to take some time for this to truly sink in.

As to *what* sort of witch I am, I've got no idea. What magical layers might be wrapped up in paranimals and my ability to see them? I have so many questions. I am going to need at least four new Moleskine notebooks for conducting research on myself. Soft-covered for pliability, with ribbon bookmarks and elastic closures.

Morgan pokes the cat-thing gently. When it doesn't react, he pokes it again. "Meow," Morgan prompts.

Snapdragon yawns, jumping down.

I watch, disturbed and delighted as it wends between my ankles, staring up at me with those golden eyes, tail not so much *switching* as uncurling and curling again. And I am struck by an alarming thought. "Paranimals are, by definition, Moonvillian animals that have been enchanted by the Black Bear Witch," I hedge, swallowing a lump in my throat. "Which means . . . if Snapdragon's been enchanted . . ."

Morgan sparks with understanding. "Then the Black Bear Witch was here, in our shop. Today."

FRIDAY EVENING, MORGAN strolls into the Cavern of Paperback Gems while I'm shelving books. When I've exceeded my capacity for socialization upstairs, the Cavern is where I flee to be alone. It's got atrocious marmalade carpet that I don't have the heart to rip up because Grandma was so proud when she installed it herself, but I've hidden it with rugs, fringed Edwardian lampshades, and buttoned leather armchairs so weathered and creased that they're about six shades lighter than they once were. The colors and textures here are rich. Dark but cozy. I want customers to wander down and feel like they've stepped into 221B Baker Street.

He's wearing Angelopoulos Business Casual, which for Morgan means snug plaid trousers and three shirts with all of the collars popped. He's swinging a burgundy briefcase.

"Guess what."

It's hard to tune Morgan out because he talks so incessantly, which means I've done a lot of accidental listening while trying to write a manuscript proposal (and by write, I mean read *The Silver Kiss* by Annette Curtis Klause and feel sorry for myself because I can't write about vampires again, even though

Henriette is not a traditional vampire, deriving her sustenance not from blood but from making men fall in love with her and then breaking their hearts). He's forever guess-what-ing, and nobody's able to accurately predict what he's going to say. *Guess what? If you drink Mountain Dew and then do forty push-ups, you'll burn off all the sugar and only be left with pure, raw energy.* (I do not think there is science to support this claim.) *Guess what? Go read James Joyce's love letters to his wife. Because I did, unfortunately, and now everybody else should have to.*

I take a stab at it. "If you throw yellow socks into the dryer with a purple marker, they'll come out with perfect stripes?"

He brightens. "Is that true?"

I tilt my head. "My first impression of you was so deeply wrong."

"What's that mean? What was your first impression?"

He doesn't need to know. I sort through this week's new arrivals, Snapdragon nudging the back of my leg for attention. His big, unsettling, pupil-less eyes have taken some getting used to. Despite looking so different to me now, Snapdragon's personality is the same. This morning, I watched him try to jump through a closed window because he saw a reflection of Alex's cheeseburger in the glass.

Morgan bows to Snapdragon. "How do you do?"

I fight back a smile. "Do you think he understands you?"

"Anything's possible! We don't know what all the witch has done to him. By the way, I'm calling this new paranimal a gingersnappus because he's got gingery fur in cat form as well as paranimal form and, you know, *Snap*dragon. I looked it up on

the Internet to see if there are stories about other gingersnappuses, found nothing, but then it hit me!" He *thunk*s his head
with his fist. "You wrote about it! In *The Serpent Tree*."

I frown. "No, I didn't."

He picks up several books I've wrapped in brown kraft paper, brief descriptions written on tags shaped like crystal balls.
They're for our Blind Date with a Book selection. He proceeds
to juggle them. Books fall everywhere. "Yes, you did." He then
unlatches his briefcase (which turns out to be a backgammon
case) and withdraws a battered copy of *The Serpent Tree*, stuffed
with color-coded tabs (oh dear) like rainbow shark teeth. Morgan rambles through the pages, then taps one particular passage. "Aha! Look at this."

> *Curled up beside a dented woodstove is a sleeping animal*
> *Henriette has never seen before. It has orange fur with*
> *black stripes, and its feet are wide, seemingly designed to*
> *burrow tunnels.*

"Zelda." He freezes me with a fierce, unwavering gaze, and
the emotion that washes through me in response is one hundred percent professional. "Do you think you've seen one of
these before? When you were little, like how you saw the huggle? And maybe you've held on to it subconsciously?"

The thought makes my head glitch. "I . . . I don't remember
what I thought was real and what I knew was only pretend.
The lines blurred. But possibly?"

"I can't believe you forgot you wrote about these! But you
forgot you wrote about sleep paralysis demons, too." He shakes

his head at me, grin lopsided. "How does a writer forget their own characters?"

"Probably because I don't ever reread my books."

Morgan leans over the counter, eye contact unwavering. "Are you serious?"

"After editing's wrapped, the book is dead to me. I still consult my series notes and lists of dates, main characters, important beasts, et cetera. But minor background stuff melts away."

His jaw goes slack. "So you're telling me—"

He begins to pace.

"That your book"—he points in my direction, truly getting worked up—"arrives in your hands fresh from the printer, smelling all new-book-y, and you don't immediately sit down to appreciate all the hard work you put in? You don't devour it cover to cover and go 'Hoo, yes, that was satisfying. Good job, me'?"

"I did once," I admit, "but it wasn't satisfying at all, because I found typos. All I could focus on were the mistakes, things I wanted to edit but couldn't because it was too late." I make a face, skin warming with chagrin. "Repetition, consistency errors, somebody I forgot to thank in my acknowledgments. A pop culture reference that didn't age well."

"Ahh. Your crooked doors."

"Where'd you hear that from?" I croak, my mind flying to Grandma Dottie.

His eyes blaze, like he can see the direction of my thoughts. "Right after I started renting desk space in your store, Dottie heard me complaining about the mistakes in one of my articles, which I wasn't aware of until after it printed. There was, like, a letter *g* that wasn't printed correctly, dropped lower into the next line. I can't remember what word it was, but without the *g*, its meaning changed, and having a *g* in the word underneath where it wasn't supposed to be changed the meaning of *that* word. Also, my own last name was spelled wrong and I used 'although' twice in one sentence. It was an important story, I was so proud of it, and those mistakes completely ruined it for me. Then, Dottie told me that written magic—"

"Likes aberrations," I finish, a forgotten memory roaring back. My mind arcs through time to first grade, when I wasn't very good at spelling. While writing stories in composition notebooks, I'd get angry when I didn't know a correct spelling. "Grandma told me it was okay to leave a few mistakes in, that I was drawing magic's attention with all my bumpy writing, and it would make me more powerful. With verbal witchcraft, she said, you had to get it precisely right. But with written witchcraft, magic is a bit more mischievous, delighting in discrepancies. Scrambled letters, the same sentence copied twice, a capital letter where there shouldn't be, a missing apostrophe, random words thrown in. When I told her that I wasn't making witchcraft, I was only writing stories, she said that *everything* a witch does is some form of witchcraft."

He nods fervently, a few strands of midnight hair slipping messily across his forehead.

"I started doing it on purpose," I remember, talking faster. "We called it crooked-dooring, because she said The Magick Happens wouldn't be quite as interesting if the storeroom door wasn't crooked—you know how you have to shove it a couple times to get it to close all the way?—and other stuff we all liked to complain about, like how you can't plug in two things at once in the upstairs bathroom or else the circuit breaker pops. Grandma told me she used to wish she could get it all fixed, but then one day she realized—"

"They give the house character, which magic likes," Morgan supplies. "And a perfect house is boring. She told me to think of my work like that."

We stare at each other, half smiling, a deep grief rattling my bones. I wish I'd moved home sooner. Wish Grandma hadn't been stolen away by dementia. When I was in my teens, I stopped purposefully littering my stories with errors, figuring that Grandma had just been trying to put a kindhearted spin on my blunders so that I wouldn't be so hard on myself. She had a way of doing that for all of her grandchildren, infusing the magical into the everyday. That she chose to share this with Morgan, as well, alters the angle from which I view him.

"I crooked-door every article I write," he tells me. "I don't think I'm making witchcraft, sadly, but maybe if I keep doing it, magic will see that I'm trying to get its attention and . . . I don't know. Let me in."

I wonder what Grandma saw in Morgan, for her to tell him about crooked-dooring. If she genuinely thought he'd ever be able to generate real magic for himself, or if she was being nice, or . . . well, there was the dementia, which certainly started to get much worse two years ago. Maybe she was confused and thought he might be a witch. I still wonder if she made the whole concept up.

We'll never know, unless we ask her for confirmation

through Aisling. Which we won't do, because it doesn't much matter. Whether every single story Grandma told us is true isn't what's important, I'm beginning to think. Maybe what matters most is what we get out of believing.

"Anyway. Speaking of the inexplicable." Morgan hops onto the rolling ladder, kicking off to make himself glide across a bookcase. "Let's go to the woods and look for this Falling Rock Triangle thing."

"Don't play on ladders. And I can't." I check the time on my phone. "I've got plans."

"Break them."

"Cancel my date with an hour's notice? That would be rude."

He draws back in surprise. "A date? At a time like this? You're going on *a date*?"

"It's a Friday night." I lift his hand, which has unconsciously lunged out to grasp my wrist, and remove it. His eyes are so wide that I can't help but laugh, and his gaze drops to my mouth, the corners of his own lips tightening. "This is the optimal time for a date."

TWENTY-ONE

If you see a white flower with an even
number of leaves, pluck one to
make it odd for luck.

Spells, Charms, and Rituals,
Tempest Family Grimoire

BUT WHAT ABOUT me?" Morgan insists, sounding
put out. "I need you to stay romantically available, just
in case we don't find the Black Bear Witch."

"You are disgusting. And why haven't you bothered trying
to seduce Luna, by the way? Have you forgotten she's a witch,
too? If you need any old witch to fall in love with you, let's remember I'm not the only single woman here."

(For the record, I would never allow Luna to fall into such a
trap. I pose the question merely out of curiosity.)

His face darkens. "It's too late. I've already shown public
interest in you, by buying your auctioned date, and she'll get
suspicious if I try to switch Tempests." He leans his elbow on
a shelf, bestowing me with a megawatt grin. "Bail on your date
and I'll show you the time of your life. I know I didn't mean all
those pretty things I said to you before, but I do now. Truly."

I swat him away. "Here, shelve these last two, will you?

This occasion calls for my best bra, which means I've gotta dig through an avalanche of unfolded laundry."

At the mention of the word *bra*, Morgan's intense stare locks on mine, and it's as if his skull is transparent, so easy is it to see the words DON'T LOOK AT HER CHEST rolling across a billboard in his brain. He fails to heed them.

I point. "Caught you."

"There was a fly on your shirt. Don't look, he's already gone. I can't believe you're taking valuable time away from our mission to sit with a man who probably floods anthills for fun."

I roll my eyes, annoyed that he's made me smile. "Bye, Morgan."

I OPEN THE shiny silver door to Dark Side of the Spoon, fully aware that I am overdressed for a first date at a small-town diner. I tried on several low-key outfits before giving it up and throwing on a black spaghetti-strap dress with a corseted waist and black lace tights along with the most gorgeous green Pendragon boots you've ever seen—they look as if they're made of leaves, spiking up my ankles. I am obsessed with these boots. Pendragon shoes are quite pricey, and twice now I have splurged on their Enchanted Forest collection. What I've saved in rent money by living in a camper van these past few years, I've channeled into clothes and shoes. This is my curse: I hate drawing attention to myself, but I love fashion more.

I haven't been in here before, and the interior matches the front door: shiny and silvery. It has a fifties retro-futuristic motif, with space art on the walls. The long counter is packed with customers, but Dylan's the only person sitting in a booth. He waves when he spots me.

Nerves flutter.

"Hey, you." I slide my purse along the vinyl bench across from him. There's a glass of water and a menu waiting for me, and his soda is half gone. "Am I late? We said six, right?" I laugh nervously.

"No, you're not late. I'm always early. Kind of an annoying habit sometimes."

"If only you'd been early to the auction," I joke. "Then we could've had this date three weeks ago."

His face falls. "I tried to be. Extenuating circumstances."

"I was just kidding," I rush to reassure him. "I didn't mean it like that."

He nods, perusing his menu. It's quiet for a beat.

"Have you eaten here before?" I ask.

"Yeah. I had the burger last time." He makes a so-so motion with his hand. "Wouldn't recommend it."

"Oh. I hope the other food's good." Another nervous laugh. "If it isn't, I'm sorry for suggesting this place. It's the only restaurant in town I haven't tried yet."

"That's perfectly all right." Dylan flips his menu over, skimming appetizers on the back side.

I fiddle with a pepper shaker shaped like a rocket ship, unsure of how to steer a conversation.

"You look amazing," he tells me.

"Thank you, I—"

The door opens behind us and right by walks a man with a

head full of (lustrous) black hair. He slips his fingers into it and keeps them like that, elbow blocking the face, as if that will conceal his identity. He sits in the booth directly behind Dylan and vanishes behind a menu.

I haven't finished my sentence, and Dylan is staring at me. His gray shirt is neat and crisp, bringing out the color of his irises.

"You look amazing, too," I hurry to say. "I love the glasses."

"Yeah?" He touches his frames. "I've been thinking about getting LASIK."

"Don't!" I blurt. Then I clear my throat, my voice lowering. "I'm a big fan of the glasses. Just saying."

This pulls a genuine smile from him. "Good to know."

We spend the next little while sneaking shy glances, cutting away to our menus when caught. Personally, mine could be written in German, for all I'm able to focus. When the waitress comes to collect our orders, I panic because I've been staring at pictures of food for six minutes but have retained absolutely nothing. "Um." I pick the first meal I see. "I'll have the Out of This World Cheeseburger."

A tiny frown develops between Dylan's eyebrows.

Now I remember that he didn't recommend the burger and am about to ask for five more minutes to decide, when Dylan tells the waitress, "Guess I'll have the biscuits and gravy, with bacon and eggs over easy." Behind him, Morgan is holding up a spoon and angling it to see what's going on at our table. His presence here has me so addled that I forget what Dylan and I were talking about, and we're left to stare blankly at each other.

"So." Dylan folds his hands on the table. "What have you been up to lately?"

I open my mouth to answer, but I've got nothing sensible to say. If I tell Dylan what's actually going on in my life right now, he's going to think I'm unwell.

"Just . . . keeping busy. Writing."

A low snort issues from the next booth over. My blood pressure rises.

Dylan drums his fingers on the table. "Your series?"

"Something new, actually. I finished the series." I bite my lip. "I'm almost afraid to ask what you thought of *Cave of a Thousand Crystal Wings*."

He smiles sheepishly. "I haven't gotten the chance to read it yet."

"Oh! That's fine, no rush. Sorry, I didn't mean to—"

"No, it's all right. I've been *meaning* to, but I've got a lot going on and . . ."

"Yeah. I get it."

"Right."

I point at the napkin dispenser. Most of the napkin dispensers in the diner are custom-made to look like the planet Neptune, but the ambitious owners must've run out of money because ours is a regular metal box with a Neptune sticker slapped on. "I think we picked an unlucky table."

"Would you prefer to sit somewhere else?"

"No, I was only making a joke. The napkin dispenser. Uh . . . Neptune . . ."

He follows my line of sight, confused. "Oh. Ha."

I scramble for an easy topic. *Please, god, let the food arrive soon.* "What have *you* been up to lately?"

"Prepping for the pickleball tournament in Athens."

"Really? Sounds fun."

"Everyone thinks pickleball sounds fun, but I promise it's harder than it looks."

"Ah. Yeah, I bet."

My coffee arrives, and I rush to sip it, burning off the roof of my mouth.

"But if you want to give it a try," Dylan replies, "I can see if there are still memberships available."

"Um. That's okay."

"I'll text you what I find out."

Morgan drops onto the bench beside me. "Budge up."

I gape at him. "What are you doing?" When I don't move, he forcibly scoots me over with his hip.

Dylan cannot comprehend such rudeness. "May I help you?"

"Sure thing, Bob. You sell vacuums? You look like you'd sell vacuums." The waitress arrives with our food, and Morgan flashes her an angelic smile. "Could I trouble you for a slice of apple pie, miss? I would be so very grateful."

She beams. "Why, of course! Aren't you a charming one!"

I roll my eyes. Our waitress asks Morgan if he has a motorcycle, because he "looks the type." After some back-and-forth he promises they'll do bike stunts all over town together if he ever *does* get a motorcycle, even though this woman is old enough to remember JFK's time in office. She brings him a slice of pie that is three times the size of an ordinary serving, and he croons, "It looks just as gorgeous as you do." She adds a scoop of ice cream to his plate, free of charge.

He's a devil. Using his wiles to get ice cream, to get my attention when he doesn't deserve it, calling everybody gorgeous. He probably calls his dentist gorgeous, too, trying to finagle a discount. The cops, whenever he gets speeding tickets. I've had enough!

I growl through clenched teeth, "Are you lost?"

"Isn't it obvious? I'm on a date."

I knock my knee against his, trying to shove him off the bench without creating a scene. "Then go wait for your date at your own table."

"*You* are my date."

Dylan shifts uncomfortably. "Zelda, do you know this guy?"

"She sure does!" Morgan sips my coffee. Spits it back out into the mug. "Shit, that's hot."

"Morgan! *Leave.*" I press all my weight against him, but I might as well be trying to push a parked car. My wriggling does nothing except create friction, and Morgan looks sidelong at me. His face is entirely too close, and his eyes have a happy, overcaffeinated glint to them. His mouth threatens to smile.

I scoot away with a quickness. "You are intruding."

"I am collecting. You owe me a date."

Dylan's gaze swivels between us. "You're dating?"

My reply is an emphatic "*No.*"

"I bought the date she auctioned off," Morgan informs Dylan, tone pleasant. "And I'm here to receive what I'm owed."

This is an outrage. "I already went on that date with you!"

"Mm." Morgan squints one eye. "No. We never officially confirmed that *that* outing was for the auction."

Dylan's mouth is in danger of disappearing, growing thinner and thinner. "I don't understand."

"Morgan is deranged," I tell him consolingly, reaching across the table to touch the back of his hand. "Please ignore him."

Dylan sizes up the man seated to my left, who is now wolfing down apple pie. Since I last saw him, Morgan's changed into a red Hawaiian shirt with the top three buttons undone. I suppose he considers this his date-night attire, but he looks like Magnum P.I.

Dylan eyes the wedge of bare chest Morgan's got on display and decides he can't ignore him. "This is weird."

"What's weird about it? I'm having a great time." Morgan cuts his dessert in half, scraping some to the edge of the plate toward me. "Try this. It's scrumptious." To Dylan: "If not vacuums, then maybe carpet cleaners? Definitely a traveling salesman, though, and definitely floor-related products."

I almost laugh, which is irrational, because I am exasperated. I cannot be exasperated with him *and* amused. That would only encourage his bad behavior. "Stop it."

Poor Dylan has no idea how to react. "I'm a bank teller."

Morgan scrutinizes him. Shakes his head decisively and continues to eat. "Disagree."

I am of two minds. One: this date has not gone particularly well. It wasn't going well even before Morgan gate-crashed it.

Two: first dates can be awkward. Dylan didn't get a fair

shake. I gather up my purse and ask him if he wants to go somewhere else.

"I've only got another twenty minutes," he says miserably. "My brother's bachelor party is tonight."

Morgan points a fork at Dylan. "I've got it! You sell *Encyclopedia Britannica*."

"I don't sell anything," a frustrated Dylan retorts, but Morgan cuts him off.

"I'll take *L* through *V*. Wait!" He waves the fork, flinging some flaky pie crust into Dylan's eggs. "Just give me *G*."

My date watches in silent disgust as Morgan polishes off what's left of my cheeseburger. I can't remember if it was any good or not, I've been so flustered.

"Needs pickles," Morgan muses.

Dylan exhales through his nose. "It's getting a little crowded in here."

"I agree." Morgan tries to stab Dylan's last piece of bacon with his fork, but Dylan slides his plate out of the way. "Shall we take this show on the road?"

"Zelda, I think I'm going to call it a night." Dylan stands up. "This was . . ." He can't come up with a suitable adjective and simply shakes his head. "Good night."

Oh no. "I'm so sorry." I try to get up, too, but Morgan's got me blocked in. "Maybe another time?"

Dylan's grim face says *Don't count on it*.

Morgan smiles up at him. "You've got the check, right? I didn't bring any money."

Dylan leaves swiftly, hissing between his teeth. I've botched it. I've completely botched it. Here's a handsome, presumably good man who was legitimately interested in me, and I ruined my chances by indulging—or at least not adequately discouraging—another man who has admitted to my face that he tried to trick me into liking him, for abominably selfish reasons.

Something is clearly wrong with me.

My jaws fuse together as Morgan leisurely finishes my coffee, humming along to the radio. When he finally meets my eyes again, he lowers the napkin he'd been dabbing his mouth with. "Are you going to eat the rest of your fries?"

I pinch the skin of his forearm between my fingers, then give it a sharp twist.

"Ow!" he yelps, jumping. "What was that for?"

"*What was that for?* You ruined my date!"

"I don't know why you're so upset. I think we all really hit it off. Do you think he'll text us later?"

I duck under the table, emerging on the opposite side of the booth. "What the hell is wrong with you?"

For a moment, his façade suspends, and I see a different emotion pass behind his eyes. Guilt. It looks as if he's about to apologize, but when he opens his mouth, what comes out is: "My latest theory on waravers is that the waning gibbous moon gives them a telepathic energy field that they use to communicate with clouds. What do you think?"

I stare at him.

He stares back.

I'm livid with both of us. "I have no words for you right now."

"Words?" he repeats. "Where we're going, we don't need words."

I slap a few bills down on the table for the tip and get up. "Either you pay for dinner, or I'm going to hurt you. Emotionally. I will figure out what you love, and ruin it."

He hands over his credit card at the counter, posture relaxed. I grab a bunch of junk for sale next to the register—a wrapped pastrami sub sandwich, which I don't even like, a Dark Side of the Spoon mug, two swirly lollipops, a Martian keychain, a stick of gum—and I make him buy it all.

"Did you enjoy your meal?" the guy at the register asks.

"It was wonderful!" Morgan turns to smile at me, and I cross my arms, refusing to look at him. When we're finished, I grab the bags and tear off out the door.

Morgan runs to catch up. "Hey, slow down!"

"You sabotaged my night. You are a terrible, selfish, foul little dingbat." The heel of my right shoe catches a crack in the sidewalk. I almost go toppling over, but he yanks me back by my purse strap.

"I'm not little. If you believe what it says on my driver's license, I'm as tall as Brooke Shields."

I let the handles of my bags slide into the crooks of my elbows so that I can wad up my hair in my fists. "Gahh!"

He peeks into a bag. "One of those lollipops for me?"

"Get away, cretin." I dash past Bowerbird's Nest, Gilda Halifax's costume shop, with the same dusty mannequin dressed in a gold sequin tuxedo that's been fading in the window since I was in grade school. Tacked to the eaves is a neon sign with the purple outline of a hand on it, advertising PALM READINGS, plugged in with a thick orange extension cord taped to the brick siding. Next door, the glass walls of Laser Crater

Arcade are dark, but every few seconds there's a flare of blue or yellow strobe light within.

"You need to walk more carefully," Morgan warns. "Those boots are going to kill you."

"These boots are going to kill *you*."

"So this is the thanks I get for intervening! That date was horrendous—pickleball *is* easy, I've played it, and I'm seventy-eight percent certain he was trying to scam you into buying a hair dryer."

"This isn't the 1960s! There aren't door-to-door salesmen anymore."

"If traveling salesmen aren't real, explain where my dad was from 2002 to 2005."

I hurry faster, leaving him behind.

"Aw, c'mon!" Morgan calls after me. I throw a quick look over my shoulder. He's still at the corner, arms raised up over his head with one hand gripping the other wrist, a silhouette against bright shop fronts. "Wanna go back to my place and make out? Or review my notes on the gingersnappus? We can discuss it on my podcast! Why aren't you responding? Hey! Miss Boots! Are you mad at me?"

I jam my key into the front door of The Magick Happens. "I'm putting you on probation. You will not accompany me on investigations until further notice."

"What! Is this because I lied about my height? I'm five eleven! That's the same height as Michelle Obama."

The door slams on his pained "Miss *Booooooots!*"

TWENTY-TWO

The sky is a thick green haze today, which Henriette
takes as a good omen. The most powerful magics are
almost always green—the oxidized particles produced by
alchemy, the indole scent of live cultures in a spell jar, the
flag of chrysolite gas that smokes up from the
graves of those raised by necromancy.

The Heartbreak Vampire,
Zelda Tempest

ET'S GO, I command myself, straightening in my seat as
if that will rearrange the contents of my brain and knock
anything good toward the front where I can access it.

E   T   O
S   G   L'
Book Proposal: Take Eight

Why is this so hard? I used to be a cauldron bubbling over
with ideas no matter how many distractions were in play. Time
became meaningless when I was writing or dreaming about
writing; four hours felt like one. There were so many stories I
wanted to tell, I was bursting, wishing I didn't ever have to
sleep so that I could get them all down on paper. I skim my

meatless buffet of concepts and all of them are too embarrassing to show my editor.

"Come on, Zelda. You've got this."

A flash of movement catches my attention, and my gaze slides to Morgan, walking through the door of The Magick Happens. He folds himself cross-legged into the deep window ledge where Snapdragon likes to rub his face against the glass. His eyes meet mine and a butterfly leaps into my throat.

He's wearing glasses.

I return my stare to my screen, heart thumping. *This is me typing,* I type. *I am typing typing typing. I am not noticing anything else but all these words.*

"What're you wearing those for?" Trevor pipes up.

Morgan's reply is lazy and delayed. "Wearing what?"

"Glasses."

"I've always worn reading glasses."

I watch Trevor's gears turn, wondering if Morgan has, in fact, always worn reading glasses. Luna walks in from the storeroom with three new candles and arranges them on a table display. "Your eyesight starting to go?" she asks.

"I've had these forever. None of you pay enough attention to me."

"I have *never* seen you wear glasses," she replies.

Trevor's puzzlement turns to indignation. "Yeah! That's what I thought, too."

Morgan's dark stare flickers to me. "I wear them all the time. My vision is highly impaired. Ask me to look at something." He removes his glasses. There are red marks on the bridge of his nose from his ill-fitting nose pads, which must pinch.

Trevor holds a book aloft, *The Encyclopedia of Elemental Witchery.* "What's this?"

Morgan squinches up his face. "A duck."

Trevor examines the book, as if to make sure it hasn't somehow become a duck. "Not even close. Your eyesight sucks, man."

I have refused to speak to Morgan Angelopoulos for two weeks. Not for lack of him trying to rope me into conversations, though; everywhere I go, there he is, too. At Moonville Market, both of us hunting for taco seasoning. At the ATM. In the apartment bathroom upstairs, which he insists on using because Luna's hand towels are softer than the ones in the shop bathroom. *Wanna go check out this dead thing I found in a mousetrap and see if it might be a paranimal? Hey, do you have a safety pin on you, by any chance? Guess what? The toaster at Half Moon Mill is burning images of goldfish into slices of bread. I emailed Pepperidge Farm and Guinness World Records to come check it out.*

But this, right here—he finally wins a reaction. "Why would there be a duck in our shop?"

Morgan lifts his nose, prodding his glasses back into place. "Oh, are we talking now? P.S., that's offensive to say to somebody who's visually impaired. When you're at the mercy of weak eyes, like I am, everything looks like ducks."

"*I'm* visually impaired. I wear contacts."

He gives me an injured look as he throws himself into his desk chair and spins twice before opening his laptop. Music pours through his headphones, so loud that I can hear every word. Soon he is playing the violin and belting out a song. "Nobody gonna slooow me dooowwwn. Oh no! I got. To. Keep. On. MOOOVIIING!"

Shaking my head disapprovingly, I refocus on my own computer.

A ridiculous human being, I type.

A ridiculous human being in a three-piece suit patterned to look like a brick wall. He takes a wind-up frog toy out of his desk and sets it in motion, watching the frog toddle off the edge of the desk, onto the floor. He and Trevor cheer when it lands on its feet and keeps walking.

I am never going to get any work done in here. He is intentionally disruptive! It is inconsiderate and unprofessional.

This is a story about an author who never starts her book because a man eats Funyuns loudly and brews coffee loudly and when he talks to you it's like he's trying to be heard over the din of a house party.

"I'd read that story," Morgan says, his voice close (and loud) enough that my whole body jerks. He's materialized behind my shoulder.

I slam my laptop shut. "Mind your business."

"I can mind multiple businesses. Have you heard from our friend Bob?" He hops up onto the counter, gaze like an X-ray. His frames are tortoiseshell, and there's a small scratch on one lens. It's infuriating that this makes him even more attractive. He uses his powers for evil.

"What do you care?" I grumble.

"Tell Bob you're through with him, and go out to dinner with me tonight. I know a fabulous place upstate. We'll see some sights . . . get a hotel . . ."

A hotel with Morgan. My insubordinate stomach swoops. I remind myself that I do not like him anymore, and he doesn't mean anything he says.

I cannot abide a liar.

"I wouldn't develop feelings for you even if doing so gave *me* incredible powers," I hiss. "Not even for telekinesis. Or the ability to fry an egg just by looking at it."

He frowns. "Your sisters were right. You're a heartbreaker."

I gather up my laptop, then march from the room.

"Is it something I said?" he calls out.

The back door bangs shut to slice off his last word. In the courtyard behind The Magick Happens, I slam my laptop down onto a picnic table with more force than the poor thing deserves. This machine has been loyal to me throughout three and a half novels and much abuse of the backspace key. I should probably have a name for it, like Harvey or Dellatricia.

This is a story about a ridiculous man who got struck by lightning and fell off a wagon and was kicked by a cow and had all his pretty hair eaten by an iguana.

The sky is a thick green haze today. It isn't raining, but there's a film of moisture in the air, and no wind at all. I turn to study a window that peers into Candleland, but my view's mostly blocked by Trevor's back (the letters across his jersey spell T-SIZZLE). I fidget. Minimize my document to check my email, check the news, check my social media. I can't possibly work when it's this quiet.

Brrrrring! Brrrrring!

I reach for my phone: the screen flashes CAVERN. "This is Zelda. What can I do for you?"

"You can do a lot for me, but we'll start with a kiss and see where it goes."

Ugh. "This line is for book recommendations."

Morgan's tragic sigh wears stage makeup and perspires in the heat of three spotlights. It dreams of a starring role in *Hamlet*. "Please recommend a book about forgiveness," he warbles.

"Sorry, we don't have anything like that in stock." I hang up.

My phone rings again.

"Don't hang up!" Morgan begs. "I've written you a song. It's called 'Let's Be Friends Again. Or More, if You Want, I'm Not Picky.' It took me a long time to come up with the bridge, so please listen." There are some clumpy noises as he sets his phone down. Morgan then begins to serenade me with a piece that sounds questionably similar to "If You Leave" from *Pretty in Pink*.

I hang up.

He calls back twenty minutes later. "I've written another song. It's called 'Zelda Tempest Is Cold and Unforgiving.'"

"Sounds accurate. Bye."

After I cut him off, Morgan's faraway, muffled voice shouts: "So mean!" and then he begins to play the violin as badly as he can muster. Now my concentration is broken. Thanks so much, Morgan! I might as well grab some brain fuel—a blueberry bun is all I need, and then I'll be able to generate a brilliant book concept, no problem.

I slip through the back door but am cut off by my niece

before I can leave for the bakery. Aisling drops to her knees in the doorway, flops onto her back, and piles her bookbag on top of her face. "Nobody speak to me. I'm decompressing."

Luna delivers a plate of French toast sticks to her daughter. Ever since we were kids, my sisters and I have celebrated special occasions (and cheered ourselves up on sad days) with frozen French toast sticks sprinkled liberally with powdered sugar. It tastes like funnel cake that way, and this treat is a fixture of Aisling's first day of school every year.

Ash lets out a frustrated groan, chewing one. "Seventh grade is going to be awful, you guys. They don't have strawberry milk in the cafeteria anymore. They say we're too old for recess. It's scientifically proven that kids learn better when school doesn't start until nine a.m., but of course they make us go at seven thirty because they don't actually care about our well-being and the only thing they *do* care about are test scores! Anyway, can I have ten dollars? Cannon and I wanna go to the arcade."

"Have you fed the—" Luna starts to reply, but a fist of wind punches the front door, glass rattling, and we all turn to look outside. Vallis Boulevard is glazed emerald, and in the direction of Hope Furnace, the sky is apocalyptic. "You're staying home."

"Whaaat!"

Luna points at the incoming storm. "Do you want a house to fall on you?"

"We'll walk fast."

Tornado sirens split the air.

"We'll walk *real* fast," Ash persists, hands steepled beneath her chin.

"Sorry, but I want you in one safe piece, un-barbecued."

"So unfair." Ash slumps into my arms. "Aunt Zelda, everyone's against me. Even the weather."

I pat her head. "I'll give you twenty bucks for the arcade tomorrow."

"Yay!" She ponders this. "How about twenty-five?"

Despite trapping Ash at home, my sisters don't take tornado warnings seriously until radar indicates there is rotation in Moonville and not simply anywhere in the county, so they do the hilljack thing and drag lawn chairs out front to stormwatch. Romina's somehow acquired a giant slushie from Pit Stop Soda Shop and popcorn. I snatch up our sandwich board before it can fly away, then secure the food and water bowls we leave out for stray cats in our neighborhood.

"Hypocrites!" Aisling shouts at us from the other side of the door. Luna won't let her outside until she's finished cleaning her room (which she said she did yesterday but did not).

"Hey, look, it's raining," says Trevor, standing on the sidewalk. He holds out his hands, collecting what is clearly hail in his palms. "It hurts."

"Hail signifies that something bad is coming," Luna declares sagely.

I snort. "No shit. Bad weather is coming."

She selects a nickel-sized hailstone and flicks it at my shin.

"Look at the size of this one!" Trevor cries. "I could play golf with it. Anybody got a golf club? Morgan, go grab your violin stick thing."

A window of Wafting Crescent slides open. "What are you still doing outside?" Bushra yells. "If you're all pulverized in a tornado blender, Gilda will turn your property into her overflow."

"Gilda gets overflow?" I wonder aloud. "The costume shop doesn't seem all that busy these days."

"The costume shop is just a front," Morgan explains, tossing up a hailstone and cracking it across the road with the bottom of his shoe, which he's removed. Trevor's on the other side of the street now, using his phone like it's a Ping-Pong paddle to shoot hail back at Morgan. "She makes the big bucks conducting séances. Every Wednesday night, she buses in old folks from the YMCA."

A roar rumbles across the sky. Bits of leaves, twigs, and cigarette butts spit from the wind like somebody's emptying a litter bin into our yard.

"Hey, does that look like it's going around in circles?" Trevor points at a rotating black cloud directly over The Clockery.

It's a mad dash. Trevor somehow beats us all into the shop, even though he was the farthest away. I turn the knob, but the door won't open. "Unlock this right now!"

"I don't want the tornado getting in! Go hide under a bush."

"Trevor, I'm going to kill you." Luna scrambles for a key hidden in our fake rock, while Morgan scrambles for a real rock to bust a window with. Luckily, Romina made it inside with Trevor and she has the sense to let us in.

We take turns socking Trevor as we pour past.

"My baby!" Luna croons, reaching for one of her cats.

"I'm already downstairs." Aisling's voice drifts in from far away. Luna freezes in the act of scooping Jingle into her arms, kissing her forehead.

"Right. Good! Stay down there, Ash! Don't come back up!"

"Where's Snapdragon?" Morgan wheels his chair away from his desk with such velocity that it tips over. (Snapdragon likes to curl up beneath Morgan's desk to sleep sometimes.) He scours the armchair, storeroom, windowsills. "Snapdragon! Here, kitty, kitty, kitty!"

Romina panics. "What if we die?"

Luna smacks our younger sister with her purse. "We're not going to die. Get it together! Where is my purse?"

"You're hitting me with it."

Luna starts unplugging appliances. She shoves a printer at Trevor. "Here, take this and grab some candles, too."

"Is this really what you need to be doing right now?" I try to tug her by the shirt, but she blocks me with a coffeemaker and forces it into my arms.

"I got this coffeemaker for sixty-nine dollars"—Trevor reliably yells *"Nice!"*—"on sale," she replies fiercely. "Normal price is a hundred and thirty dollars. I am not putting up a hundred and thirty dollars for another coffeemaker, Zelda!"

Only when Luna's rescued the cash register and Dottie's crystal ball are we allowed to sprint for the Cavern of Paperback Gems. I breathe a heavy sigh of relief. "Oh good, Snapdragon's safe." He's napping atop the Lost Bride trilogy. Aisling's building a book fort to protect her mother's most prized candles while shooting us all looks of dismay. I suspect the dismay is less about us acting irresponsibly outside and more about her not being allowed to also act irresponsibly.

The shop's foundation quivers. Trevor throws himself onto the floor. "Shield my face with your hands, and I'll cover your hair," he tells Morgan. "It's the only way to save our best features from being struck by debris."

"Why can't we cover our heads with our own hands?" Morgan pauses, considering. "My face is just as good-looking as my hair, you know."

"Now is not the time to lie to ourselves."

A pen rolls off the Lost Bride trilogy, off the table, onto the floor. I cast around. "Where'd Snapdragon go? He was just right here."

I examine the pen. It's striped orange and black, and the nub is shimmery gold, the same gold as Snapdragon's eyes. My knees nearly give out. I scream.

Romina screams, too. "What happened? What's wrong?"

I brandish the object. "It's a pen! It's *a friggin' pen!*" And a weirdly gummy one, like those sticky-hand toys from quarter machines that within five minutes have attracted every crumb and cat hair in a five-mile radius. I return it to the table.

Luna looks at the pen, confused. "So?"

"Is it ballpoint?" Trevor asks. "Z, you should start using Paper Mate Flair Scented Felt Tips. They'll never give you this kind of problem."

I stare at it. "I've seen this pen before." Lying around the house recently—on top of the toilet tank, on Luna's kitchen counter, in empty cardboard boxes, and, several times, my bed. I thought it belonged to Ash and that she kept leaving it everywhere.

"My garden's going to be ruined," Romina moans. "And my lunch is doomed. Poor DoorDasher won't want to come out in this weather. Or he will, but he'll die in the name of chili cheese fries. I can't live with that on my conscience."

Trevor scuttles over. "Did you put in the order already? I'll take pretzel sticks with zesty queso."

The lights buzz, guttering, and darkness sweeps across us. Everybody screams again.

"Please do not," Luna pleads. "I'm getting a headache."

We're all quiet for a few moments. Then Trevor says: "This would be the perfect time to rob somebody."

"Hang on." Morgan feels his way through the room, accidentally patting my left eye as he navigates. Seconds later, a door upstairs closes.

"Where's he going?" I straighten. "To rob someone? Trevor, look what you've done."

In the darkness, all of us cowering in fear for our lives, I hear Aisling whisper to Romina, "I want chili cheese fries, too. The food here on earth tastes so bland after being spoiled by fairy treats for the last ten years in Fairyland, but I could always go for chili cheese fries."

TWENTY-THREE

Fill a small brass cauldron with salt
on the new moon to absorb negative influences
and bury that salt under a full moon.

Spells, Charms, and Rituals,
Tempest Family Grimoire

WHAT DO YOU think Morgan's doing?" I ask uncertainly a few minutes later.

"The bad possibilities are limitless," Trevor replies. "He told me he used to eat Play-Doh as a child. We don't know what Play-Doh does to cognitive function, man."

When the siren wails again, a memory spins.

My neighbor growing up, Hank, said there's a strange kind of goat around here that comes out only when it senses tornadoes.

Fear ignites in my chest like I've stuck my finger in an electrical socket. "That idiot." I'm up and running before I can think. "That colossal idiot."

My limbs are rubber, fright surging. White spots pulse in my vision. I don't feel the floor beneath me, I'm flying so fast.

"Morgan!" I shriek, rounding the landing of the ramp. "*Morgan!* Oh curses, he's going to go looking for a goat and end up killed by the tornado." I throw open the front door and dash into the street.

It's empty.

Above, the skies whistle, hot wind battering Vallis Boulevard. Wind chimes, trash, and lawn ornaments barrel through midair. He's going to get struck by a flying mailbox. Tornadoes can turn flowerpots into weapons.

"Misery, curses, bother, blast." I wipe my sweaty palms on the seat of my pants. "Morgan! Where are you?"

The wind rips half a *Zelda!* toward me. I turn, unsure of which direction it came from. I can't see for all the hair streaming in my face.

"Morgan!" I bellow once more, gripped by a terrible fear that he might be hurt, he might—

"Get back inside!" I hear him yell. "What are you doing?"

My shoulders sag. I clasp a hand to my thundering heart.

"What are *you* doing? I can't see you!"

"Courtyard."

I race into the shop, through Candleland, the Garden. Throw open the porch's screen door. "Do you have a death wish?"

Morgan is kneeling on the brick pavers, soaked from head to heel. He's trying to herd Romina's pet chickens into the cage she uses for transporting them to the vet. I recognize the four he's managed to coax inside, but Miss Fig, the stubbornest of the bunch, is shooting out of grasp with dignified squawks. I realize that what's preventing him from getting a good grab of her is that he's only got the use of one hand—his other is pressed to his stomach to protect a rectangular shape stuffed beneath his shirt.

It's my laptop. I'd completely forgotten that I left it on the picnic table.

I seize Miss Fig, who cusses me out for teaming up with Morgan, and shove her in the cage.

"You shouldn't be out here." Morgan's hair is an onyx river, shirt plastered to skin. The speckles of rain on his glasses trigger a minor breakdown; the emotion coursing fast and inescapable through my system is a strangely wonderful suffering. He saved my laptop. I want to grab his face in my hands. I want to do unspeakable things to his mouth. I want, inexplicably.

But I do not touch him, because he is the worst, and also because right above us a gray funnel is beginning to descend, its swirling tip tasting the air carefully like it's feeling us out. The chickens are a flurry of wings, jumping over each other. It's all we can do to keep the cage from flying away.

Flowers in Romina's garden rip up by the root, obliterated as they ascend into the funnel, the tail of which *changes color*.

The budding cyclone turns green. Bright, electric green.

Morgan, whose gaze has been fastened on my face, looks up just after the green tail is sucked backward into the sky. It implodes with a deafening *clap*.

The storm dies at once.

"YOU THOUGHT I was going to die. And you were *worried*."

I scowl at Morgan.

"You were." His smile is sunlight sneaking between clouds. "I wish the tornado had picked me up. Not much—just a couple inches. You'd be so grateful I survived that you'd hug me, I bet."

"I don't do hugs."

"Zelda, stop begging me to go out with you. I'm simply too busy right now, but try again in a week and I'll see what I can do."

I keep walking. It's been a few days since the tornado, which my sisters decided was vanquished by the magic in Romina's garden. I think they expected me to argue this theory, but I've googled "green tornadoes" exhaustively and haven't found anything close to explaining what I saw.

"Slow up," Morgan entreats. "Why you gotta walk so fast?"

I'm a bloodhound on Bear Run today, armed with my notebook and a backpack containing my lunch. Sweat and mosquito repellent slick my skin. These Betsey Johnson bedazzled skull hiking boots are finally justifying their expensive presence in my collection.

"You check that way," I tell him, gesturing to an alley.

"You trying to get rid of me?"

It's a joke, and he smiles as he cheerfully strolls off, but Morgan isn't wrong: I can't focus when he's hanging around.

Once I'm alone, I let my mind relax. I have to loosen my body, imagining that I'm a leaf carried on the breeze, no thoughts in my head. I bet it isn't like this for Romina and Luna, who flex their magical muscles so often that they probably don't even have to concentrate on their magic, don't have to summon it and wait for a response. Their magic is always drawing power, even at rest; the difference between leaving your microwave plugged in so that you can press a button and it instantly starts working, and keeping your microwave stored in a box in the garage between uses. My machinery's cold and rusty.

Come on, magic, show me which way to go.

To my delight, the answer is instant. My intuition zips upright, shoulders straight. *There*, it urges, leading me to the right-hand side of the road. I take off, so enthusiastic that I almost cut off a passing car. This is a tiny neighborhood of new-build Craftsman houses in creams and olives, identical down to the sycamore tree and swing set in each yard. *That way*, the magic taps as I pass an alley, and I double back. I am an explorer. I am going to detect hidden species, something new, something nobody else—

I crash into Morgan.

"Ow." He stumbles back, wincing. "Did you miss me that much? I've only been gone for a minute."

"Why are you hiding behind a bush?"

He scratches his jaw, embarrassed. "A lady was watching out her window. She looked suspicious of me."

"Crouching in her blackberries won't help."

"It's creepier when I'm solo! Women don't wanna see some guy sneaking around their driveway. Having you with me sets them at ease. It's less like 'Oh, this guy is probably a murderer' and more like 'Hey, look at those two weirdos, I hope they don't smudge my lawn.'"

I stop short. "I've never thought about that."

He half-heartedly grumbles. "That's your privilege. Women never have to worry about these things, they're able to move freely through society without concern."

I playfully tug a lock of his hair, and his mouth trips into a surprised half smile.

"I think it must be close," I tell him. "Blegh, I wish I'd kept track of which house it was. They all look the same. Wait! Right there! Twenty-seven. I remember that hummingbird feeder."

Morgan follows my line of sight. "I don't see a cat."

We attempt to hide behind a telephone pole as we scope out 27 Bear Run, my backpack shoving into Morgan. It's pushing a hundred degrees out here and having heaps of hair never helps; I can't pile it up into a bun or I get a headache, so I'm left with a braid that's frizzing so bad, you wouldn't be able to tell it isn't a ponytail.

Yesterday, while driving this way to get to the library, I saw an animal that resembled Snapdragon. True, I was preoccupied (focusing on the road and all that) and managed only a brief glimpse before it slunk beneath a gap in a fence. I thought about nothing else all night and decided to come have another look today, staking out for as long as necessary. I wasn't going to tell Morgan, because I was worried he'd scare off any paranimals, but he smelled the bacon sandwich in my backpack and followed me anyway.

"This feels very FBI," Morgan whispers. "We need code names."

"What for?"

"In case we're interrogated."

"By who? And precisely how would code names help in that situation?"

He ignores this. "Call me Hot Drama."

"I . . . why?" I stare at him. "I am not calling you that."

"*What, who, why?*" he parrots. "Have you ever considered the life of an ace reporter? It involves a lot of eavesdropping and pseudonyms. I will make you my protégé." He then tells me that if he can't have Hot Drama, then he wants to be Thunder Fox.

There are so many reasons why, in every online quiz in which I have to choose a superpower, I pick invisibility. If I were invisible, I could walk quietly away right now and he'd keep prattling to himself. "How about Asparagus as a code name?" I suggest instead.

Morgan is affronted. "That is the least sexy vegetable, after onions." He ticks off vegetables on his fingers. "After asparagus, it goes: chard, spinach, Brussels sprouts, cabbage, and peas." Before I can ask, he explains, "Talented local writer Mariah Abernathy printed a column about it."

"Stop bouncing around. You'll draw attention and we'll get the neighborhood watch after us."

"Zelda." He tilts his head, a pitying smile playing at his lips. "Asking me to stop drawing attention is like asking galaktoboureko to stop being tasty. I draw attention everywhere I go. There is nothing I can do to help it."

I turn back to the house with a long-suffering exhale. "I miss who I was before this conversation."

"In case you were wondering," he murmurs in my ear, sidling closer, "the sexiest vegetable is celery."

I refuse to be sidetracked. I keep my attention glued to the house, scanning for signs of a furry animal with paddled paws and big golden eyes. I am wholly unaware of Morgan's warm breath and the peppery zing of skin contact where my shoulder touches his arm. I do not think about celery at all. I do not begin to imagine why this man thinks celery is a sensuous vegetable.

My nose twitches, and at last I give in. "Not eggplant?"

Morgan censures me with a look. "Don't be crass, Zelda."

"All right, I don't think anybody's home, so I'm going over there. You stay here and be the lookout." I do another visual sweep before scurrying across the road.

"Wait! Why can't I come? What am I looking out for?"

I hurry off, scrambling from tree to tree for cover, hyper-aware of how silly I must look to the casual observer. At least I am not the silliest person here. Morgan is circling his hands around his eyes as if they're binoculars and this pose will somehow enhance his vision.

I am an explorer once again, neck-deep in a top secret mission to uncover wonders of the universe. As I sneak around brambles to the front porch, I see myself from the aerial view of a *National Geographic* helicopter filming my travels. Any moment now, a majestic beast is going to appear.

The paranimologist sits as still as possible, I inwardly narrate in David Attenborough's voice, *so as not to alarm any approaching gingersnappuses. She will wait for as long as it takes, unless the residents of 27 come outside and ask her to leave.*

I hear a loud, scratchy whisper from across the street. "Papaya!"

Without turning to look, I wave Morgan off. *Shhh! Not now!*

Still no sign of the notoriously elusive paranimal, Attenborough continues. *There's only a flowerpot containing a shriveled brown plant, muddy flip-flops, and a rolled-up newspaper on the porch.*

"Papaya!"

Morgan runs across the road at a crouch, joining me.

I desperately need a stress ball to squeeze. "You're supposed to be looking out! Why d'you keep cawing 'papaya' at me?"

"It's your code name."

"I don't have a code name!" I am going to attack him. "And papayas better not mean something dodgy to Mariah Abernathy."

He cranks his head back to study the sky, a paragon of innocence. "So, have you found anything?"

"Hard to find anything when you don't give me a second's peace." I unscrew the cap of my water bottle and take a long drink. Morgan eyes my mouth thirstily. "Why were you calling for me?"

"I was testing out your code name to see if you'd respond to it."

I drag my nails over my face. "A curse on my ancestors."

"Cat!" Morgan springs to his full height, pointing to a small square garden. "It's a cat!"

A big puffy gray one with a squashed face. "Not a paranimal." I shake my head. "And the one I saw was ginger, remember? A lot like Snapdragon, but lighter in color."

"Oh, right." He prods absently at the newspaper. Then frowns. Repositions it to different angles. "Is this written in another language?"

I lean closer to him. At first blush, the print facing up definitely looks like ordinary English words in an ordinary newspaper. But when I try to *read* the words, none of them make individual sense. Headline: Tudey's Niws iv Samothung Samothung. My index finger traces the accompanying logo of a faint orange-and-black swirl. There are black-and-white photographs of rodents, with nonsensical captions. Advertisements that say *Sail! Buoy samothung ge tew samothungus.*

"Looks like gibberish."

"I don't recognize anything about this newspaper. And believe me, I know my local competition." He picks it up, testing the weight in his hand. "Do you—" We both yelp as a blur of orange materializes between us, and a claw sinks into my shoulder.

The newspaper is running away.

The newspaper has turned *into a gingersnappus*, and is running away.

"Oh my god!" Morgan yells at me.

"Oh my god!" I yell at him.

"What do you people want?" the owner of 27 Bear Run yells through their screen door. "Get off my porch."

We flee.

"Another ginger cat that has a secret gingersnappus form, that transforms into an object and then back into a gingersnappus again at will!" I cry. "There is a definite pattern: first Snapdragon, and now this one. We can safely deduce that the Black Bear Witch likes to enchant ginger cats."

Morgan grasps my arm. "Imagine a gingersnappus that turns into a diamond necklace. Or a hat. Or a dandelion. But what if someone accidentally stepped on it? Maybe they're not even really alive when they're in object form, or they're in some kind of stasis. Hey, I know! Let's break into the animal shelter! We'll poke any ginger cats to see if they shape-shift."

"Breaking into an animal shelter should maybe not be plan

A," I interrupt, patting his back to calm him down. "Let's use our heads here. Pause to document what we know so far."

I pull him off the sidewalk and into the Holly Jolly Trolley, which has been sitting beside the post office for so long that its wheels have sunk down into the dirt. Moonvillians use the trolley as if it's a town square gazebo, and it's always got crumbs from dog biscuits on the floor.

I leaf through my notepad and bite the cap off my pen. He unlatches his briefcase. Whips out a sheet of paper. *Gingersnappuses*, he jots down, crossing out *Gingersnappi as plural terminology?* I trace three capital letters stamped into the leather of his briefcase. "*LPI*. What's that stand for?"

"Library of Paranimal Information."

My heart flutters.

"I've tried to digitally archive my notes," he continues, unaware of what his organizational methods as well as "archive" in his silky voice has done to me, "but the files keep getting corrupted for some reason. The only notes that don't get ruined are longhand."

I read a few lines at random:

Huggle: squi;rrel paranimal. Small, furry, three pupils in each eye, shaped like rings, fun!ctions they serve unknown. (Affects how huggle perceives colors, shadow, distance?) Eating habits? Magical abilities?

"What's this nonsense?" I tap the punctuation errors.

"Crooked-dooring."

One corner of my mouth pulls back irresistibly into a smile, and I imagine Dottie beside us, smiling, too. I bet she's tickled to see what I'm up to these days.

I tap my pen against my lips. Morgan watches raptly. "What does this tell us about the Black Bear Witch? We aren't any closer to figuring out who she is."

"It tells us she doesn't like orange cats," he guesses. "Or maybe that she loves them extra?"

We scour the neighborhood for cats but don't find any orange ones. At sunset, we reluctantly part ways and resolve to meet up tomorrow. Hopefully we can get on the volunteer list at the animal shelter.

"Meet me at the trolley at nine," Morgan instructs. The waning day gilds his face with blooms of gold on his forehead, cheekbones, Adam's apple.

"Why don't we meet at The Magick Happens?"

"Because your sisters might ask what we're up to," he replies.

I can tell he's thinking exactly what I am: that for now, we want to keep this as a secret for ourselves.

It gives me this aerated, powerful, fireworks feeling, like carrying half of a story that nobody else has ever read, tucked away in my pocket. What gives the story so much value is knowing that Morgan's got the other half. Everywhere I walk, I'm going to think, *I've got a secret, and only he knows!* And whenever I see Morgan out and about, and we wave hello to each other, I'm going to think, *He's got a secret, and only I know.*

TWENTY-FOUR

Tell your troubles to a starling and
it will fly away with them.

Local Legends and Superstitions,
Tempest Family Grimoire

I DON'T SEE MORGAN for three days.

After a peaceful seventy-two hours in which I have plenty of time to get lots of book planning done with no distractions of the terrible-violin-playing or random-hypothetical-question-asking variety, I do some online shoe shopping instead, and then, in a fit of impatience, saunter across the street to Wafting Crescent.

With September around the corner, Zaid's setting up an autumnal display, carefully assembling a lumpy tower out of cream puffs and toothpicks with a straw hat on top. "What's this?" I ask.

Zaid's tongue pokes out the side of his mouth as he stabs a toothpick through another cream puff. "Scarecroquembouche."

"Come again?"

"A scarecrow croquembouche. Scarecroquembouche."

Bushra grabs two vatrushki with her tongs and drops them into a paper bag before I approach the counter. "He's the Michelangelo of pastry."

After Bushra rings up my order, I ask if she's seen Morgan lately.

"I've *heard* him lately." She knocks her chin toward the ceiling, one hand on her hip. "Sounds like he's rearranging furniture up there." As she speaks, I hear a crashing *thud*, a "Damn it! Not again!" and rapid footsteps.

Zaid doesn't remove his eyes from his masterpiece. "He's driving me nuts. Go tell him to shut up, would you?"

"And bring him this." Bushra hands me a donut. "He'll die if we don't feed him."

It's been ages since I've visited the second floor of this building. Back when it was all used as one big house, my cousin Nitya and her parents lived here, and I used to be so jealous that she had a bathroom connected to her bedroom. It was a preteen's dream—spacious, well-decorated, with a mini fridge and a blow-up plastic couch. She and Luna liked to pretend it was their apartment, and that Romina and I "lived" across the hall in an alcove where Nitya's mom, Aunt Sylvie (technically, I think Sylvie is my cousin, but we've always called her Aunt Sylvie) kept the litter box.

There's now a wall blocking off what had been a wide cased opening, and a new green door with a mail slot and letter stamps. They've been applied crookedly, a smidge too far to the right, so that his whole name can't fit on one line.

M. ANGELOPO
ULOS

I knock four times.

There are some mutterings in the apartment, and footsteps. I sense a body on the other side of the door, checking the peephole. There's a gentle thump as he . . . well, it *sounds* like Morgan's turned and flattened his back against the door. A moment later, three deadbolts unlock and it swings inward a crack, a narrow strip of Morgan staring back. "Hi," he greets me, somewhat breathless.

I try to peer past him. "Haven't seen you lately. What's up?"

"It's, uh . . ." His gaze darts off to the side. "Not a good time right now."

"You want to go adventuring? I'm itching to explore." *Crash!* "Whoa, that was loud. What's going on in there?"

Morgan swears. Tries to close the door, but I stick my foot in. "I'm sick," he insists, coughing into his arm.

"You don't look sick."

He perks up at this. Lets go of the doorknob so that he can smooth back his hair, preening. "Does that mean I look good?"

"Undone by your own vanity." I successfully elbow my way in.

Nitya's hot-pink wallpaper and inflatable plastic couch are gone. Her posters of Ashanti posing in bikinis have been replaced with framed, and often signed, posters of Tears for Fears, Mike + the Mechanics, Devo, The Cars, and Modern English. Morgan's surrounded himself with a shock of colors: neon palm trees on the walls, *Back to the Future* memorabilia, lava lamps. A wall of bookshelves so stuffed with books that he's got vertical stacks on top of horizontal ones. A poster that looks like an illustrated 1980s pulp horror novel cover, with the figure of a woman running in front of a full moon drawn low over a hill, surrounded by zombies climbing out of the earth. Through an open door are clothes strewn all over a bedroom floor.

I rotate slowly, taking it in. "It looks . . ."

"Yeah?" he prompts nervously when I don't finish my sentence, nibbling on the donut.

"This is the most landlines I've ever seen."

He's got a collection of novelty phones: one that looks like the Batmobile, one shaped like Garfield, the cartoon cat. A banana, a gas pump, Pac-Man, big red lips. They're all exhibited on a shelf that runs the perimeter of the room, close to the ceiling.

"That one's my favorite." He shows me a phone that doubles as a working Dubble Bubble gumball machine. I am simultaneously speechless and yet not surprised at all.

His desk is pushed against the window, facing The Magick Happens. Across the street, the ghosts of two curtains flutter in my own attic window, framing my desk, and I can see the little lights in my terrariums. I think about what Morgan might see when he sits here, and what he thinks about that view.

I take great delight in inspecting his shelves, lingering over each title. *Harper's Encyclopedia of Mystical & Paranormal Experience. The Everything Ghost Hunting Book. Ghost-Hunting for Dummies.*

I smile.

Morgan steps closer. "We don't all have witchy grandmothers and sisters to teach us stuff," he explains self-consciously. "Some of us have to read how-to guides."

"I adore how-to guides. Can I borrow some?"

"Please take whatever you like."

When he looks at me with those bright eyes, I think of the way I felt when I first read the poem "Annabel Lee," and I wanted to know what it was to be loved in such a close-up, flaws-and-all, forever-and-ever way. For me, the notion of aching for somebody's heart and the rhythm of *can ever dissever my soul from the soul of the beautiful Annabel Lee*, morbid as those lines may be, are inextricably spun together.

It is unwise to link that emotion with Morgan, who cannot possibly be my True Love. There is too much risk with him; I can never guess which moves he'll make, and that wild instability leaves me seasick on solid ground. Does he want anything from me besides my help? He has said he wanted *me*, and he has also said he didn't mean it. Yes and no. The no came second, which cancels out the yes.

"*Meow.*"

I turn. "You have a cat?"

"Oh. Uh." Morgan shifts on his feet. "No, not exactly."

If there is a cat in the vicinity, then it is necessary that I introduce myself and give it behind-the-ear scratches. As I move toward the room producing the meow, he flies up behind me, protesting.

"You can't go in there! A man is entitled to his secrets, you know!" Morgan holds up his hands in a pleading gesture. "Don't be mad. I got carried away, and I was meaning to tell you—I only wanted to study them by myself for a day or two, so that I could try on what it feels like to be surrounded by magical animals. You already know what that feels like now that Snapdragon's been enchanted, so we're even. Anyway, let's go adventuring!"

I give him a once-over. "Are you all right?"

"Of course I am. How could I not be? You're so lovely, with all that hair, it's the color of the Great Red Spot—you know, the giant storm on Jupiter. And your eyes! The most bewitching I've ever seen, like the flames of a gas stove. Are those earrings new?"

I've been incorporating a dark witch vibe more heavily in my look lately—lots of moons and black jewels, glittery black lipstick and shawls. Deep purple nails. My earrings are silver scissors.

"You lying tart. What are you hiding?"

"I'm being genuine! I know I wasn't before—and I know that I've *said* I wasn't before, and then said that I was, when I wasn't." He blinks as if he's confused himself, mussing up his hair with his fingers. "But now, I genuinely am."

I pat him on the back dismissively, not even trying to decipher that. "You're absurd." Then, at last, I see what Morgan's been up to these past few days.

I don't care about the untidiness—the jacket tossed over his headboard, some drawers of his dresser open and some not, clothes falling out. I am, however, mildly concerned about the number of ginger cats populating his bedroom.

A mangy old cat on the bed shoves its face against my hip and yowls. A second one is napping, nose twitching as it dreams. A third is scarfing down a plate of cold pepperonis.

There are several others littering the floor; one is marking its territory on a sweater in the corner while maintaining aggressive eye contact with me.

I release a small sigh. "Of course."

Morgan straightens, fingertips grazing his chest in *Who, me?* body language. "What does that mean?"

"It means I'm not surprised you've been up to something. All right, then. Tell me why you've got so many cats in your room."

"Cats? Regular cats? You're sure they aren't gingersnappuses?"

I shrug. "Sorry to disappoint. Did you take these from the animal shelter?"

"No. The parking lot behind Moonville Market's loaded with strays, and—" He points to the cat destroying pepperonis. "Not even that one? Are you sure?"

I pet the mangy one, smiling as it purrs. "Nope. Normal cat."

"But he smells so *strange*—okay, that isn't the point." He grasps my shoulders firmly and peers into my eyes, his features so solemn that it's a challenge not to burst out laughing. I'm not sure I've ever seen him this serious-looking before, but even a Morgan at his most serious is impossible to take seriously. "I'm offended that you thought I was up to something."

I can't hold it in. My laugh hits him full in the face. "You *were* up to something."

"Yes, but you should be surprised about it. And at least a little angry?"

What a puzzling development. "Why do you want me to be angry? I can hardly be disappointed in somebody I have no expectations of."

He looks wounded. "Hey!"

"What are you upset about?"

Crash!

"What was that?" I peer around the corner, to a closed door, and Morgan sidesteps in front of it.

"Guess what?" he says. "I read somewhere that blue giant stars actually smell like Caesar salad dressing."

He will not throw me off the scent, even though I am interested in both blue giant stars and Caesar salad dressing. I try to turn the handle, but he blocks me again.

"I'm worried you'll end up getting hurt if you go in there," he says anxiously. "This one is high-energy, good at hiding, scared of everything, and any time I spook him, he blows up. I can't even describe to you, Zelda, what it was like to wake up with that thing on top of me."

"With *what* on top of you?"

My imagination invokes a smoky snapshot of Morgan in bed, a woman's figure on top of him. My blood heats.

Before I can think, I burst through the door.

My eyes connect with a pair of round golden ones, a few feet above. An animal with yellowish-orange-colored fur, a scarred face, and a split in its curly tail is tightroping across the curved shower rod. This gingersnappus is much larger than Snapdragon, as well as the newspaper cat. He's gotten into his fair share of scraps.

"I call this one Forte," Morgan reports weakly, "because he's the exact same color as my cousin's Kia Forte. And he's the worst roommate I've ever had."

I take another step toward it, and the king-size gingersnappus balloons into a massive orange shape that falls to the floor with a painfully loud racket.

"It's a . . ."

Grand piano, lodged sideways in the tiny bathroom, wider than the doorframe. It's chipped his pedestal sink.

I test the piano's weight. "How do you move him? Why do you keep him in the bathroom?"

"Remember what I just said about him crushing me in bed?"

"Morgan, you've got to get this thing out of your house."

He pretends not to have heard me. "Forte is . . . not right. He only eats salt. He really hates songs by Men Without Hats—the band, not just regular men in hats. I don't yet know his feelings on regular men in regular hats. He's destroyed my shower curtains. I love him with my whole heart, and as you can see, he really *is* a gingersnappus. Which means that, in the name of scientific discovery, you cannot be mad at me."

"Who said I was mad?" I whip out a notebook and fish a pen from my hair. "Fascinating! What sort of noises does he make when he's in cat form? Only salt, you say? Snapdragon won't stop eating butter cookies, so I'd like to get one of those blue Royal Dansk tins over here and check if that's a trait of gingersnappuses or if Snapdragon is merely a pig." When Morgan doesn't respond, I glance up at him. His mouth is turned down at the corners. "What?"

"My feelings are hurt, that's what."

Oh no. What have I unknowingly done to offend this time? "What did I do?"

He folds his arms over his chest. Sniffs, looking resolutely away from me. "If you're not going to be upset with me, then I'm going to have to ask you to leave."

"You make no sense at all, Morgan." I stow my notes back in my pocket, annoyed. There's still so much I want to learn about Forte! But I can't very well pick up a piano and haul it across the street. "I'm going, then. Call me once you've stopped being like this."

He mashes his face into his forearm, making "aghughh" noises. "I meant what I said, you know," he says at length, muffled.

"Yeah, yeah, I got it. I'm leaving."

And here comes the seasickness. Every time I think I've found my footing with him, he pitches the ship and there I go, flying. Why am I wasting my time with a person who makes me feel this way? I should be keeping my eyes peeled for a man who exudes Steady and Reliable. Someone whose footsteps are visible to me before he even takes them, who will behave as I anticipate and not tell me to leave his apartment for bewildering reasons.

"By the way," I add, knowing this will kick him where it counts, "your socks don't match."

The last I see of Morgan, he's staring down at his feet, murmuring, "Oh *dear*."

TWENTY-FIVE

While the leaves of peppermint are beneficial in healing work and amplifying psychic powers, beware this herb's jealous tendencies. When not employed as the primary ingredient, it will sour the whole spell out of spite.
DO NOT COMBINE WITH CATNIP.

Spells, Charms, and Rituals,
Tempest Family Grimoire

THE ANIMAL SLINKS out of the brush where it's built a den, and—not even putting down my binoculars lest I lose sight of it—I begin scribbling details in my notebook. I'm crouched about forty-five yards away, and this is the closest I've managed to get to the paranimal in two weeks. It's been a stimulating study.

TINNITAN FOX

Solitary, keen hearing. Mundane disguise: presumably the red fox, as they share several features, and red foxes are common local animals.

Like a Tibetan fox, but its eyes are farther apart, close to its ears. Lots of long fur around the throat like a Shakespearean ruff. Will induce tinnitus in humans who

spot them. Maybe to aid in faster getaway, as human
will become distracted. Prey: unknown.

Sunlight glitters over its muzzle, and I nearly gasp but thankfully catch myself. It would surely hear me and dart away. *Whitish iridescent scales cover its muzzle,* I write. *Some scales fleck the eyes and mouth. They blend into fur.* Hopefully this is legible—I'm not looking at the paper. These days I've got perpetual circles imprinted around my eyes from cramming binoculars up to them all the time.

The fox goes still, ears flattening. He lowers himself to the ground and moves quickly toward a hollow log. I adjust the aim of my binoculars, and almost gasp again when I get a good look at what the fox is stalking.

It's a mouse with leaves growing out of its body. Six total, sprouting from the spine like a stegosaurus's ridges.

Stupendous! Baffling!

What on earth is the purpose? Who does this witch think she is, putting leaves on a mouse and casting spells on foxes to make them induce tinnitus in people? What a lunatic. Maybe it's for the best if I never meet her. However, I have *so* many burning questions, and a brain that won't let me rest until I've received satisfying answers.

I want to protect the mouse, as it's a paranimal and I feel a kinship with all these hiding-in-plain-sight creatures, but protecting the mouse would mean starving the fox. Which is also a paranimal.

A quandary!

I am right at the edge of the woods, and if I advance only a few inches, a voice drifts out from the trees. It's the same voice that kept mentioning a clock, but it's been speaking about something else today.

I slide forward.

"I'll give you a cat's-eye marble or a charm that fell off a dog collar. It's the smoothest charm you'll ever run your fingers over."

I lean back, the voice disappears.

Forward again: *"I'll give you a cat's-eye marble or a charm that fell off a dog collar. It's the smoothest charm you'll ever run your fingers over. And I can find any . . ."*

Back, and gone.

The fox pounces on the mouse. But it's thwarted when the mouse leaps *over* it and disappears into a hole in the ground. Not for the first time, my thoughts divert to Morgan. I want to tell him what I've found, because he's the only one who would believe me, and the only one who'd be equally interested.

But I don't, of course. We haven't spoken for a month.

My phone vibrates in my pocket. 5:30 Date, the screen reads.

"Damnation." Luna set me up on a date with some guy named Brant or Brent, and if I didn't agree to it, I would've had to hear her complaints that I don't get out of my shell enough (which is preposterous. Would she say this to a turtle? Shells have a valuable function). But this is terrible timing. I've got so much to research now, and there's a stack of books in my car that I need to return to the library. I'll just drop them off, and then be on my way to Brenton.

_____

AHH, THE LIBRARY. Society's best invention. If there is a heaven, it is undoubtedly filled to a mile-high brim with dusty old tomes on magical theory.

Moonville's library has milk glass sconces shaped like owls flanking the front door, and a plaque in the antechamber (a word that is close enough to *anterior chamber* that I uncontrollably link foyers with eyeball anatomy) that reads FALL INTO A STORY. It was donated by V. M. Macy, a Moonvillian author who does not know he is my professional rival because he died in the 1960s. Our town reveres him, and whenever there's talk of local celebrities, V. M. Macy's name is always trotted out.

Not that it is a competition, but someday I hope to have a plaque hanging here as well. It will be bigger than Macy's and will say something more impressive than his (to be determined).

"Now," I instruct myself sternly. "You will return your books, you will limit yourself to three new checkouts on common mice, and *then* you will leave in a timely manner so that you are not late for the date with Brandon." I squint. "Anyway. Ten minutes, tops."

Less than nine minutes later (well done, self!), I'm ambling toward checkout with five books on mice when I am waylaid by a powerful diversion.

There's a new table!

MOONVILLE MAGIC, a sign reads, overlooking a glossy wealth of books on local lore. I beeline.

I must broaden my knowledge on all magical fronts. Sly questioning of my sisters has revealed that even among witches, nobody quite agrees on everything, as every witch's experience with the craft is unique.

I'm intrigued by Luna's belief that magic is a renewable resource: *Just like solar energy, wind energy, hydro energy, tidal energy, and geothermal energy. But it must be practiced often by those who use it, or magic will abandon them and cleave to a more powerful source. It feeds your energy, and vice versa. Why do you ask?*

I am fully settled in my natural habitat, picking the bones of this establishment clean. Every book related to magic is plucked away to a table I've claimed with my jacket and purse. Dream magic. Salt magic. Blood magic. Root magic. From across the room, I spy a copy of Olaf Stapledon's *Star Maker* and have to filch that, too, as it's been a whole year since I read it last. Is there anything quite like the library? No, there is not. You're allowed to walk right in, open a book, any book. You can read whatever you like until closing time, and nobody will bother you. Interrupting the immersed reader with small talk is distasteful here. I thrive like a cockroach in this social system.

Oh, how I love my space. I never had much of it growing up—a lack of bedrooms in the house meant I had to volley between sharing with Romina or sharing with Luna. This probably impacted my decision to run across the country once I was legally free to do so. Being alone is, in my experience, as energizing for the soul as plugging oneself into the sun. 10/10, would recommend.

"Maybe it's under 'cryptids'?" I hear Morgan ask a librarian. "I'd be shocked if you don't have it. V. M. Macy is Moonville's most famous author."

Bats and rats and frogs! The library is beset with evils today.

He feels the scorch of my attention and turns. Morgan does not seem remotely surprised to find me watching. He's wearing those damned nonprescription glasses again, and my pulse spikes dangerously.

Total avoidance has proved difficult to accomplish, as Moonville appears to have crushed itself down to the size of a boiler room and we have no choice but to bump up against each other constantly. The market. The post office. The shop. I've been haunting the Cavern of Paperback Gems even more than usual, or the night market, where I can hide under the wing of darkness. I most certainly have not been listening to his podcast. I do not read "Marvin Agassi's" tastemaker column in the *Moonville Tribune*, which declares items to be "the moment," such as sherpa ponchos and apple butter.

And I am not one bit affected that Morgan is walking this way.

"Zelda," he greets me. I don't know how he manages to make my name sound exactly like cleaning a knife with a silk cloth.

"Oh, are we speaking now?" I reply, not deigning to look at him. I grab several books without examining their covers, as my hands demand occupation.

Morgan glances. "*What Happened in US History in 1957*," he reads. "Interesting choice."

"Nineteen fifty-seven was an interesting year."

"Name one thing that happened in 1957."

"Sputnik." I whirl away in a flourish of black tulle skirts and dedicate myself to the performance of looking engrossed in one of the other books I've just grabbed, a history of Vinton County coal mining.

Morgan is instantly vibrating with curiosity. I can see questions filling him like kernels exploding in a bag of popcorn. "Why're you reading that? Is there a paranimal that lives in coal mines? Or eats coal? A paranimal that burns fuel and can turn itself into a vehicle? Please say it's avian. We'll call it a Hummer-bird. Tell me about everything that's led you to this moment."

"Is that an apology? I'm still angry with you for being angry with me for not being angry with you. It is exasperating. Now please exit my beloved eyeball, so that peace may be restored."

Morgan considers the request. "I don't know what that means, but my gut instinct is to say no. I will stay in your eyeball as long as I please." He points at my right eye. "Right there. Swimming in all that pretty blue maelstrom."

"You aren't in *my* eye, you are in *an* eye," I correct archly. "The first set of doors to the library are the cornea. The second set are the pupil. The foyer between is the anterior chamber, the desk is the lens. You and I are floaters in the vitreous humor."

He regards me as though I am bedecked with a blue ribbon at a livestock exposition. "Extraordinary. I've always wanted to be a floater in vitro."

"Vitreous." I examine my coal mining book, which contains sepia photos of men and women with thousand-yard stares. Old photos are crown jewels. I've been amassing a sizable collection of daguerreotypes, tintypes, and ambrotypes that I'd like to compile into a book one day. One of my most prized possessions is my tintype of John Milne, who was one of the three inventors of the horizontal pendulum seismograph.

"What are you hunting for?" he wheedles. "Paranimals? Black Bear Witch information?"

"Not everybody is as obsessed with the Black Bear Witch as you are." And this is true. Not everybody is. But technically, I'm inching into that realm: I've depleted a highlighter and attained three paper cuts in my pursuit of knowledge. Much of it is contradictory: *The History of Vinton County* by Gilbert Fauxhall declares that *The Black Bear Witch steals children from their beds and leaves changelings in their place*, but *The History of Vinton County, Part II* by the same author states, *The Witch has been maligned by many, but she is a gentle soul who attacks only when provoked.*

Morgan sidles closer, circling a picture I've been evaluating. "Thoughts?" he encourages.

I respond with the first sincere thought that pops into my head. "Everyone in this picture is dead now." I ruminate over another photograph, showing it to him. "What level of decomp would you suppose this man's at?"

"He's bones. Why've you got so many books on mice?" He's browsing through them.

I'm reviewing the coal mining book with gaining intensity. It cannot be helped. There are pictures. Maps. How can I overlook a map? "That's not your business. It *could* have been your business, but . . ."

When Moonville's coal mines started closing, the area very nearly became a ghost town, I read.

"But what?"

I don't look up. "Hm?"

Indeed, Moonville as we know it today wouldn't exist were it not for the resurgence of interest in love magic in 1915. Folklore replaced coal as a profitable natural resource, and . . .

Morgan taps the page. Asks a question, but my head is too busy to process it, so his words have to wait at a stoplight to cross.

. . . love tourism took off. The legend of love magic, in combination with ghost stories, made Moonville an attraction, and the dwindling town rapidly jumped from strength to strength.

Morgan vaporizes into the mists of time. Whispering pages, shuffling feet, distant voices garble, becoming restful white noise. I turn page after page.

"Sorry," I murmur eventually. "What were you saying?"

But when I look up, Morgan is no longer hovering at my side. He's strolling out of the library with all my books on mice tucked beneath his arm.

TWENTY-SIX

Ghosts are like Labrador retrievers and become
destructive when bored. Keep them entertained
by infusing your life with plenty of drama, romance,
and depression for them to enjoy, or they'll start
breaking things.

Legends and Superstitions, Expanded,
Tempest Family Grimoire

I TAIL THE AGENT of chaos outside into late-September
sunshine. "What do you think you are doing?" I shout.

His grin is fiendish. "Taking a walk. Lovely day, isn't it?"

"You can't swipe another person's library books. That's
criminal."

He waves his stack in a taunt, stride quickening. "Got 'em
for the next three weeks. Six, if I renew. Forever, if I decide to
be dastardly; and I do so love to be dastardly."

Curses. "Why do *you* need books on mice?"

"Because you do, gorgeous. If I cannot get your attention
the normal way, I will get it the annoying way. There are many
paths to success!"

I throw up my arms. I do not understand this man. I need
to inspect him with a microscope, reference books, and PPE
clothing. He is practically a wildlife specimen—I've never met
anybody like him, and damn if that doesn't make him all the

more fascinating to me. I am hereby charging the lizard hemisphere of my brain with treason. "I wasn't trying to ignore you," I insist. "It's just that I was reading. And when I am reading, I am not hearing. I am not noticing anything else."

He cuts down an alley toward The Magick Happens. Over the stone wall of our courtyard, I can see that the green "pumpkins" on Romina's roof have vanished. I strongly suspect Romina has learned they were indeed round zucchini, and destroyed the evidence rather than risk me gloating.

"I'll give them back if you include me in whatever it is you're doing," he says, stopping short. I bump into him.

My braid is a mess, my resting murder face glassy with sweat. There are burs all over my shirt. But strangely, I do not feel at all awkward; Morgan is looking down at me with dancing eyes and a crooked smile, as if this is a most exciting turn of events, as if *I* am the unpredictable half of our duo and he would rather love to examine me under a microscope, as well.

I drop my gaze, glowering at his mouth. Sweet, wanton treason is spreading from one half of my brain to the other like dye in water. It is getting my reproductive system involved. This is seditious conspiracy. "You are despicable."

He bends his knees to meet my eyes again. "Is that a yes?"

I square my shoulders. "I'm searching for information on mice, so that I may learn anything there is to potentially know about the mouseplant."

Morgan arches an eyebrow. "The what, now?"

I explain what I saw in the woods. (Or near the woods—I haven't breached it by myself, as the forest is treacherous to navigate alone, and I am not about to become a bray.)

"Where're all your books on plants, then?" he wants to know. "You said the paranimal had leaves coming out of it, but your only focus here seems to be mice."

I slap my own forehead. "See, this is why you need to be a more dependable investigative partner. For some reason, you're able to think of things that I don't."

"For some reason?" he repeats. "Mildly offensive." But he doesn't look upset. He's teetering on the balls of his feet, an electrical scribble of anticipation. "Do you know who *does* own plenty of books on plants?"

"Romina! Morgan, you're a genius." I high-five him.

His cheeks bloom with color, and he smiles at his shoes.

We confiscate Romina's books (she only owns *eleven* of them and they're all about plants and the language of flowers), then spread our findings across the kitchen table up in the apartment. Morgan pores over my notes while I sketch the paranimal. I have to draw what the leaves looked like before I start researching pictures of leaves, or else they'll all meld together and I won't remember what's what. "Mouseplant is a terrible name," he comments. "It has no pizzazz."

"It's like *houseplant*, but with a mouse. Puns are whimsical."

"You must consider the dignity of the animal, Zelda." His face is grave. "A wee mouse with leaves poking out requires a stately name, so that all the bigger woodland paranimals will pay it its due respect." He thinks. "Leaf Erikson. Stuart Laurel."

"No. You got to pick the name for the gingersnappus. I'm picking for the mouseplant."

"The word. *Mouseplant*. Doesn't have. *Pizzazz*."

"Oh, like you're the gatekeeper of pizzazz," I hiss. "This is the stupidest conversation I have ever been a part of. I cannot believe I ever thought you were a smooth talker."

"Your conversation with Bob about pickleball was far stupider. And I *am* smooth, when I apply myself."

"I like it better when you don't," I rejoin, not really meaning to. He glances at me in surprise but doesn't say anything. Morgan is lost in thought as he removes his vintage varsity football letterman jacket, which distracts me for two reasons. The second reason is that his name isn't Tony (which is embroidered in gold on the front), he didn't attend Lyons Township High School in La Grange, Illinois, and to my knowledge, he has never played football competitively, let alone been a member of the 1989 state championship-winning team.

The first reason is that his plain white undershirt is a thin, almost see-through fabric, and that is doing magnificent things for me. I flip an internal notepad to a fresh page. *Morgan Angelopoulos. Thirty-two years old. Species: Some type of fairy. Eyes: Like shining black tunnels. Hair: Don't get me started. Chest: Appears to be quite nice. Definitely requires more thorough study.*

"What do you think?" Morgan's asking me now. Ah, so it appears he hasn't been silent for the duration of my ogling after all.

I blink. "I like it."

"Really? I thought you were going to say no."

"Wait. What?"

We stare each other down, but I win (of course) because he doesn't have the patience to survive staring contests. "About adopting a gang of ginger cats and attaching tiny cameras to their collars. See if they'll lead us to the witch."

Dear god. "That sounds expensive. What we need is . . ." My eyes zero in on a refrigerator magnet. HAVE BROOM, WILL TRAVEL. "A formal expedition."

Morgan cocks his head. "A day trip?"

"Days," I correct. I can see myself in vibrant color: trekking through the woods with our briefcase of notes and the slapdash map Dottie drew. Discovering the spectacular. "Romina's got a tent we can borrow."

His eyes widen as if he can envision something spectacular, too.

We flurry for pens and paper.

Words gobble up the page. *Can opener. Hand sanitizer. Hairbrush. Glasses.* I won't want to bother with contact lenses when I'm out in the field. *Purifying water bottle.*

"We'll need enough food for three days," I estimate.

"Then we should pack enough to last us five. Falling Rock Forest is vast and tricky to pin down." He's right—map out a trail and it will vanish, two new trails forming in its stead. We could wander the same area for hours and not realize we're still standing exactly where we started.

Compass. Extra socks. Pocketknife. First-aid kit. On and on we go, giddy and dreaming, the list of supplies growing extensive. We don't want to forget anything, because then we'd have to make a trip back home, and for some reason, that would break us out of our investigative haze. Once we enter the woods, we're not coming out of them until we've met the legend herself.

"Three days is enough time to find her," we repeat, fast-walking around the room, bumping into furniture, not paying enough attention to our surroundings. At some point, I must have grabbed a suitcase, because I glance down to see myself stuffing a can of soup into it. Morgan adds marshmallows.

"This is fantastic," he mutters frenetically. "You are amazing, Zelda Tempest. Amazing. Nobody else alive would be willing to do this with me. You're not only *willing*, you're just as enthusiastic!" He mangles a box of Cheerios as he stuffs it in.

"I know what you mean." I should be more alarmed by this. Surely, if Morgan is enthused by an idea, then the idea is not sound. But I have already run away with visions of witches and paranimals. I haven't been this happy since April, when I got carried away amending an essay for Aisling's history homework and scored 110 percent out of 100.

Morgan's sifting through Luna's recipe box. "Where are all the food recipes? Look." He flips a notecard from the box around so that I can read it.

———

MAKE YOUR WISH

1 fresh bay leaf, unbroken

1 teaspoon dried lovage

2 drops bergamot oil

½ teaspoon dried black walnut

A four-by-four-inch square of mulberry paper

1 yellow candle

1 small bottle or jar

1 cork

(IDEALLY, PERFORM ON THE FULL MOON,
BUT CAN ALSO BE PERFORMED ON ANY THURSDAY.)

Write your ambition on the paper, fold it up an odd-numbered amount of times, and drop it into the bottle with all ingredients. Fill with rainwater. Cork, and seal with drops of candle wax. Suggestion: use a candle scented like rum, honeycrisp apple, and sparkling ginger.

"Have you ever tried making something like this?" he inquires.

I shake my head. "Although I guess I could. Couldn't I? Since it turns out I'm a witch." I join him, perusing recipes for Emotional Healing, Shrinking Debt, and even an Antidote to Being in the Right Place at the Wrong Time. What I find most intriguing is that there is nothing in the box pertaining to love magic. Odd, since Luna's occupation centers on that branch of spellwork.

"You *have* to experiment with potions," Morgan tells me, pulling items from cupboards. "It's a waste of witchery if you don't!"

He has a point. I scrutinize a jar filled with viscous red liquid. "What's this for?" But the label tells us exactly what it's for: FOR LUCID DREAMING.

"Oooohh," we murmur in tandem.

I've never searched this cupboard before, as it's laden with Luna's witchy fixings. Now that I have become a witch myself, however, perhaps I should have a closer look.

There are neat, orderly rows of colorful bottles, some corked, some stored in repurposed marinara jars. None of the actual ingredients are listed, only the potions' purposes. FOR ANT CONTROL. FOR PURIFICATION. FOR TWICE THE TOMATOES. It becomes evident that Luna's hidden the good ones in the back: behind boring potions dedicated to controlling soil alkalinity and getting stubborn wrinkles out of clothes, we hit upon a jackpot.

FOR MISCHIEF, FOR MAYHEM, FOR WEDNESDAYS, FOR WINDFALLS.

There's a thump on the stairs, and we devolve into frenzy, whispering at each other to hurry, to be quiet, putting it all back. Then, once we realize it was only Snapdragon rolling down the stairs in pen form, we lug it all back out and start spilling potions into measuring spoons.

"We need a cauldron," Morgan says. I point to another of Luna's kitschy signs: CROCKPOTS ARE JUST ELECTRIC CAULDRONS. "Bingo! I'll plug it in right away."

"We're going to cook mischief and mayhem in a six-quart slow cooker." I cackle, dashing a spoonful of FOR WEDNESDAYS in with half a bottle of FOR SATURDAYS. Can you use them only on Wednesdays and Saturdays? Or does the potion make *any* day become Wednesday or Saturday? We are about to find out!

Morgan adds FOR RAIN. I sprinkle in FOR DRY SKIES. The smells vary, but they bend toward acrid. "This is so much fun!" I exclaim. "Why isn't Luna doing this all the time? I've never seen her use this stuff."

"Luna is a square," Morgan informs me sagely. "She doesn't have the oomph to do what we're doing."

He is so right. "I feel like a scientist. This is so much better than working from a recipe."

"Why work from a recipe when you can make your own?"

It's hard telling when a potion is finished cooking, but our concoction makes the journey from smelling like frog spawn and being an oily brown porridge half-burnt to the ceramic to smelling, somehow, like tiramisu. My mouth waters.

"Makes no sense," I remark, sniffing the mixture once Morgan's ladled it into an empty vial. It's paled to a lovely golden hue. "We didn't add any tiramisu-ish ingredients."

"Makes no sense at all!" Morgan is gleeful. "Hm. Got some on my arm, and it is unexpectedly cold. It's like liquid nitrogen."

"Which *also* makes no sense."

His smile is radiant. "I know!" He does a double take, inspecting his arm. "Wait a minute. I had a scratch here, I swear. Got it from Forte. But now the scratch is gone. Do you think this stuff might've healed me?"

I can't respond, because I've just spotted a bottle of NEVER EVER and that is the worst label Luna could have possibly given it. The temptation is irresistible. I tip some into the Crock-Pot.

"That smells delectable," Morgan says, leaning in. I lean in, too. We're shoulder to shoulder, and our eyes meet, glimmering with mischief and mayhem and—

The Crock-Pot explodes.

Or rather, once I've smeared purple goop out of my eyes, I can see that the Crock-Pot itself is still intact, but all the potion has fountained out of it, all over the walls, fridge, and floor. "Are you all right?" Morgan gasps through his laughter.

"Neither of us is all right. Luna's gonna melt us into candle wax and use the magic to seal our ghosts in the underworld." But I'm laughing, too. "You're a bad influence."

"Me!" he cries. "I was following your lead."

"Luna's not going to believe that. You're in so much trouble."

"No, I think *you* are." Morgan uses a kitchen towel to gingerly wipe potion off my chin, and the action fills my vision with him, makes it impossible not to dwell on how close he's standing, how delectable *he* smells. He's right. I am in trouble.

"I think this is the most I've ever seen your eyes look like that," he says quietly, stroking the cloth across my cheek.

I resist the urge to cover my eyes with my hands. "Like what?"

"Like joy." His features are pensive. "I'm sorry about how I acted when you visited my apartment. It's no excuse, but I've been . . . well, it's . . . I've never—I mean, I've *pretended* to be, but wasn't really, and now I don't even know how to . . ." He gives a weak half laugh, looking to the ceiling for answers. "I *very* much don't know how to."

He's lost me. "Don't know how to what?"

"Mm" is all he replies, his voice deep. I can feel that my face is clean, but he doesn't step away, doesn't drop his hand. When I continue to stare questioningly at him, he winks. "We need to raid the cupboards more often, you and I."

"Oh. My. God."

We spring apart at the sound of Luna's voice, as if we've been caught misbehaving—and then I quickly remember the state of the kitchen. My sister's enormous blue eyes pan from the purple gloop on the walls to Romina's books on the table, our paranimal scribblings, a hastily half-packed suitcase. One of us emptied a canister of peanuts in there. "What the hell is going on?"

TWENTY-SEVEN

Feed black chokeberries to the household gods in your
fireplace every Mabon or they will become offended
and leave your home cold in the winter.

Spells, Charms, and Rituals,
Tempest Family Grimoire

MORGAN AND I look to one another, helpless. "Uhh."

Luna holds up her phone toward me. "Brent texted.
He said you didn't show up to the date."

My stomach bursts into a swarm. Not again! "Oh no. I'm
so sorry, I got distracted and forgot."

"Date?" Morgan repeats with a frown. "Who's Brent? Is
that Bob's new name? I thought we were through with him."

"Meanwhile, you've been creating a mess for me to clean up,
as if I don't have enough going on what with running our business and raising a human," Luna goes on hysterically, inspecting the Crock-Pot and messy cupboard. "You heathens. Do
you have any idea how long it took me to brew these potions?"

"Sorry," we mutter, shamefaced.

Morgan falls upon his sword. "It was my fault. I got carried
away."

I grab a sponge and start scrubbing up. "No, no, it was my
fault."

"Never Ever!" Luna exclaims shrilly. "Which one of you touched this?" She brandishes the bottle of gleaming temptation, and a strip of lamplight scythes across the glass like a wicked smile. "You idiots! It explicitly says, *never ever!* Now I've got to find a stabilizer to dim it." She ransacks the cupboards, cursing us for rearranging its contents.

"Sorry," I bleat again. "You have every right to be mad. Don't worry, we'll clean it all up."

"Damned right, you will. Actually, no, don't touch anything else." She runs her hands through her short curls; there must be bits of candle wax in there, because her fingers get stuck. "You're both grounded."

Morgan steps slightly behind me before asking, "Why do you have a potion called *Never Ever* if it's never meant to be used?"

Luna's shaking her head as she splashes bits of this and that into the Crock-Pot; the purple goo coalesces into a hard rock that, from a certain angle, is sheened green. "I would have expected this from Morgan," she grumbles. "But you, Zelda? You're supposed to have a brain."

"I have a brain!" Morgan insists. "Not my fault it's upstaged by the beautiful head that surrounds it."

Luna adds a final dusting of cinnamon, her face mournful. "Poor Brent. He waited over an hour."

Morgan's eyes narrow, watching me sidelong. "Yeah. Who's this Brent fellow?"

Nobody answers him. Luna seizes my sponge. "Not that sponge, I just opened this one from a new package. Grab an old cleaning rag—no, not a yellow one." I'm digging through washcloths in a drawer. "The yellow ones are for food messes. This is a magic mess. You need a black rag. No, not *that* black rag, that one's for special occasions—"

I nearly throw my back out when I jerk upright, arms gesturing wide in frustration. "Which one do I use, then?"

"I'll do it," she snaps. "Jesus, Zelda. You always do this."

What! I most assuredly have never done this. "I haven't touched your potions before. Give me that rag, I know how to wipe stuff up—"

"No," she interrupts. "You don't give these men a chance. Before you moved home, you had a different boyfriend every time I spoke to you."

Ohhh no. Not this. We are not going there.

Morgan steps in with a warning expression. "So what? Zelda can date whomever she wants."

"If you didn't want to go out with Brent," Luna addresses me, "you should've just said no."

An uncomfortable tension smokes the room. Leaning against the countertop, still wearing the apron she wears for candle making, Luna suddenly looks much older than her age. I am a gremlin for creating chaos magic in our shared kitchen, and she is an angel I don't deserve. This woman cooks me breakfast. She reminds me to get the oil in my car changed, pick up my medicine from the pharmacy. She set up an appointment with the dentist for the persistent toothache that I'd decided to ignore. She drives me nuts sometimes, telling me what and when and how to do everything, but where would I be without her?

I fold my sister into a hug. Luna stiffens at first, out of surprise: I am notoriously not a hugger. "I didn't mean to be late. I'm sorry, and I'm going to call your friend and apologize. But I should tell you . . ." I am keenly aware of Morgan's gaze on me, so I keep my own eyes pinned to the table. "You and Romina are under the impression that I keep breaking off all my relationships because I get bored in them, or I'm some sort of ravenous maneater. Which I guess isn't a totally unfair assumption, since I never corrected you. Um. Because the truth was more embarrassing." I scratch my head. "But, yeah. I'm the one who usually gets dumped."

I grimace in the beats of silence that follow. This is mortifying. Mortifying. Mortifying.

$$R \; T \; Y \quad\quad I \; O$$
$$F \; G$$
$$\quad\quad N \; M$$

"Oh." Luna squeezes me. "I'm so sorry."

"No, it's all right. Truly! It's my own fault it keeps happening—I'll get so focused on a task that everything else disappears, and before I know it, I'm trying to explain to someone that I haven't responded to his texts in two days because I was trying to figure out Claymation." I shrug, backing away. "Not always Claymation. Sometimes it's translating a handwritten book of Finnish love letters, or speed-reading an entire book series just because I heard the author had a new one dropping the next week and I needed to catch up."

"Oh, *Zelda*," Luna says softly.

"And I *have* broken off a couple of relationships myself, for impulsive reasons," I admit, "but that was usually more to do with where I wanted to live rather than not liking the guy. I kept jumping around from city to city, you know. Restless."

"I'm sorry I've made jokes about you being a heartbreaker." Her face scrunches as if she might start to cry.

"You didn't know." I wave her off. Pity is worse! And being accurately perceived! I would rather exfoliate with broken glass than engage in a vulnerable heart-to-heart.

"Wait a second." Luna advances on me like a bird of prey. "Why were you using potions in the first place? You don't even believe in magic."

"Well." I look to Morgan for help, but he bites his lip. My hesitation is promptly pounced upon.

"You don't believe in magic, right?" Luna presses.

"Um." I pull my hair over one shoulder and start finger-combing it nervously. "Well, you see . . ."

"AHHHH!!!"

"Oh no." I shield my face as Luna wraps her arms around me and lifts me an inch off the ground. "Curses, misery, bother, blast. Put me down!"

Luna is squeezing so tight that I can't breathe. "You're a witch!" she cries. "You're a witch!"

"Luna, you're breaking my ribs."

"Say it," she sings, refusing to put me down. "Say you're a witch."

"You're a witch."

She harrumphs. "Say '*I'm a witch.*'"

"Luna's a witch," I tell her, which makes Morgan laugh. I flash him a smug smile.

My sister is glowing. "You prideful, pigheaded asshole, you've made me so happy! I was beginning to worry this day would never come! You have so much to learn about potions and which cleaning rags to use! We can finally do all those tri-witch spells I've been dying to try. I thought I'd have to wait till Ash was grown." She snaps her fingers. "Oh! And all our rituals! I call them 'witchuals.' You're Cancer, which is a water sign, which means you need to start taking bubble baths at least once a week."

I grumble incomprehensibly, shoulders up to my ears. "Merghh."

"Don't you *merghh*, you will let me have this. And Romina!" She claps her hands. "I'd better get Romina and Ash over here right now."

"Nooo."

Alas, she does not listen. Romina and Ash are summoned from their movie night at Alex's house to revel in my wrongness, demanding I apologize for ever doubting them. I am force-fed many a crow. "What have you done to our grandmother's sacred kitchen?" Romina wails upon her arrival, but soon she is hugging me and barking orders, too.

"You'll need a dream pillow," she says, digging in the freezer for a celebratory box of French toast sticks.

Ash retrieves a bag of powdered sugar. "And a dream journal. I've got an extra one! Be right back."

Luna's filling a basket with supplies for me, like a witchcraft care package. "Whenever it rains before noon, I want you to drink ylang-ylang tea. And never buy fresh produce on an odd-numbered day."

"Merghh." The onslaught of attention is appreciated, but hard to bear. I toss Morgan another pleading look. He only smiles, resting on the edge of the kitchen table. His gaze is dark and sparkling, but there is a strained melancholy to the shape of his mouth.

I think about our expedition plans. As the Tempests embrace me into their witchy fold and declare today a holiday, my focus is on Morgan, who so wishes he could join our coven, too. I am resolved, here and now, on three things:

Morgan and I are going to find the Black Bear Witch.

He is getting his magic.

Then, I am going to stop messing around with the wrong man and make myself emotionally available for the right one. Whoever and wherever he may be.

Part Three

TWENTY-EIGHT

Our world and Fairyland overlap on the full moon. The witch who is in tune with their magic will be able to see the vague outlines of fae people and cities.

Legends and Superstitions, Expanded,
Tempest Family Grimoire

YOU HAVE TO leave at seven o'clock," Luna orders sternly. "Seven in the evening is the luckiest time of day."

"Sunrise is the luckiest time of day," Romina argues. They've been bickering about this since last night, when I explained that Morgan would like to be a witch, as well, so we're journeying into the woods to find magic. I asked Aisling to gather more information about the map from Grandma, but apparently Grandma doesn't remember much about the particular dream that inspired her to make that map.

Luna commandeers my list of supplies, double-checking, adding recommendations. "I don't have a solar-powered phone charger," I inform her, and by her reaction you'd think I'd declared I wouldn't be wearing any clothes.

"This is why you should have put me in charge," she says reprovingly. "I would've made sure you're prepared."

"I *am* prepared."

"Not without a solar-powered phone charger, you're not!" She clips more knives to the metal loops on my bookbag.

"Where'd you get all these knives? And on short notice, too." It's unsettling.

"Go into my bedroom, pull out the box under my bed," she tells me, disregarding my question. "I've got spare bottles of dry shampoo I've been saving up. You may take one."

"I've already—"

"And grab some tinfoil. I've got a triple pack in the pantry. One roll only—they don't go on sale often."

"Why do I want tinfoil?"

"For cooking in. Honestly, Zelda! I'm not going to get any sleep while you're gone. Thinking about you out there by yourself, no phone charger, not even knowing why you need tinfoil." She shoos me out of the way, examining my water bottle's filtration system.

I grab the tinfoil to avoid an argument. My luggage is already nearing a thousand pounds. "You have to let me go. It'll be dark soon." I shoot a text to Morgan. Where are you? He was supposed to meet me here sixteen minutes ago.

Once I'm finished lacing my boots, I find Luna sussing out a way to stuff acorns and a Ziploc baggie of watermelon chunks in my bags. "Upon every single word, Luna. *What* are you doing now?"

"Watermelon is ninety percent water and full of antioxidants. The acorns will bring you luck."

"Do you think I'm going off to war?"

She pokes me. "I don't like that you're doing this alone. I

know Morgan will be there, too, but he's useless. You should at least bring Alex—he knows his way around a campfire."

"Don't worry, Lune. It's a full harvest moon tonight, so we'll be covered in luck."

I press the watermelon back into her hands, but my sister is so forlorn about my antioxidant intake that I cave, strapping the bag to a suitcase with duct tape. Ash, Romina, and Luna take turns squeezing me as tightly as possible, until it becomes evident that they're just trying to see how long I'll put up with it. At last, I open the front door of The Magick Happens and step into the twilight. How I let Luna talk me into waiting around all day is beyond me. Bossiness is her superpower.

Morgan's still not here yet. I tap my foot on the pavement, frowning into the glowing windows of Wafting Crescent.

"Hazelnuts!" Luna cries from behind. "Wait! I'll be right back. You need manganese."

Oh no. "I love you, bye! Gonna go get Morgan now."

Luna flees into the building, and Romina waves me on. "Hurry, or you'll never be able to escape."

She's right. I fully expect Luna to hire crop dusters to parachute gift baskets into my camp while I'm gone, and the thought makes me smile. I can always count on my older sister to give me more than I would ever think to ask for.

The drama of my bon voyage ceremony is marred when I don't get more than three feet without stumbling.

"Lift with your back!" Romina calls helpfully. Her advice makes no sense, as I've got a backpack and two rolling suitcases, but her boyfriend gazes adoringly at her as if she's just invented penicillin.

The wheel of one suitcase catches on a tree root. As I lurch it up and over, the bag of watermelon falls off and my other wheel gets stuck in a sidewalk crack. I mutter curses, cajoling it free.

Luna's returned. "Come back for your hazelnuts. They're organic and non-GMO."

I am a five-second walk from home. "Too late to go back now, sorry!"

"Catch, then!" Luna scatters her non-GMO hazelnuts to the wind. I struggle to roll my suitcases through a patch of crumbling cement. What are my taxes going toward? Pedestrian infrastructure around here is total gas, I say.

"You can go back inside now!" I shout. "Bye! I'll miss you someday!"

They watch for a while longer, with varying degrees of pity, until Romina points out that with me gone, there won't be anyone to obnoxiously call out the historical inaccuracies in their favorite romantic dramas. They dash inside to binge-watch TV.

I give up trying to roll my luggage and sprint across the street to find my wayward adventure partner.

"I cannot even begin to guess what is taking him so long," Bushra says by way of greeting me. Upstairs, there's a racket of footsteps and what sounds like heavy furniture moving across the floor.

I tip my head back and yell out a "Morgan!"

"Hang on! Sorry!"

There are a few more *thud*s, and then he appears on the stairs, wild-eyed and grinning. He is dressed for a visit to Six

Flags in 1993, lime-green fanny pack looped about his waist. "Sorry for being late. I got distracted."

I shrug. "It happens."

His grin twists into a different kind of curve—one of pleasant surprise and understanding. I know better than anyone what it's like to be led by the leash of a scattered brain, after all. "I'm ready to go. Did you pack a compass? Never mind, I've got four. And plenty of hazelnuts, don't worry—we'll need our manganese, and hazelnuts provide seventy-six percent of your daily value."

I try to lift the flap of his bag to see what he's packed, but he swerves me. "What've you got in there?"

"Things for science. And Cocoa Puffs. I don't go anywhere without my Puffs." He snaps his fingers. "Hang on, I forgot something."

Morgan runs up the stairs. More crashing noises above. Bushra and Zaid raise eyebrows at each other. Morgan thunders back down with another lumpy shoulder bag. "Oh, hang on some more, I forgot to use the bathroom."

He runs into the men's room. When he reappears a minute later, he looks at me, turns on his heel, and goes back into the bathroom again.

"I think he's an alien," Bushra muses to her brother.

"Forgot to use it, the first time around," Morgan explains when he reemerges. "Saw myself in the mirror, got distracted again." He claps. "Come on, it's getting dark. Why'd you wait so long? Sunrise is the luckiest time of day!"

TWENTY-NINE

For a productive tomorrow, sleep with powdered orris
root and dried dill sprinkled beneath your bed.

Spells, Charms, and Rituals,
Tempest Family Grimoire

EVERY ONE OF my neurons sparks with magic upon en-
tering Falling Rock Forest. It feels exactly like the old
comfort of settling into a pool of research needed to
draft a scene. Contentedly spending hours learning the par-
ticulars of a small throwaway detail, like why over a thousand
bones were found in Ben Franklin's basement, or the history of
Victorian postmortem photography.

*"I'll give you a cat's-eye marble or a charm that fell off a dog
collar. It's the smoothest charm you'll ever run your fingers over.
And I can find any imaginary thing you like."*

I brush my fingers along Morgan's wrist, and he reflexively
curls his hand into mine. "Do you hear that?"

He listens. "Cicadas?"

I shake my head. "It's that voice again."

Diamonds left behind by a late-afternoon rain shimmer on
the low stone walls running the forest's edge, so timeworn that
they've broken down in places to allow passage in and out. One

has only to step inside, and the earth changes, Moonville becoming something much more like Villamoon, teeming with veiled possibilities.

"I don't hear anything," he tells me.

Trees creak and brush, welcoming us. *Let's go, let's go, let's go,* they breathe. I get the impression that they want to show me something.

Morgan pulls out Dottie's crude map: BBW, CAVE, TRESTLE, FALLING ROCK TRIANGLE. "Which way? Wish your grandma had included a compass on this thing. There are loads of trestles in these woods, I bet. Any of them could be the trestle on the map."

"*. . . any imaginary thing you like. I have a real nose for them. Whether it's a lemon pie with buttercream frosting, or a pony with six violet spots, or a one-armed chair that sings you to sleep, I can locate exactly where it's hiding.*"

As if in a daze, I follow the voice.

The moss carpet is thick with bluebells. Bioluminescent gold plants border a path that leads deeper into Falling Rock, igniting the gloam like a million settled cinders. "*Invisible things are my specialty.*"

The voice stops. I test every direction, but it seems that the invisible person who knows how to find invisible things no longer has anything to say.

"I don't understand," I whisper. "Who *is* that?"

"And why can't I hear them?" Morgan swings around, his eyes enormous. "What if you're like Aisling? What if you can hear ghosts?"

My jaw drops. "Whoa. Maybe?"

"This is excellent. I brought the Surefire—" He goes digging in his bag for Aisling's traffic light.

"Hang on. If I can hear ghosts, then why have I never heard Grandma? Or . . . now that I think about it, I only ever hear voices when I'm in the woods."

We grab for each other's hands in excitement at the same time. "Brays!"

"You can hear spirits of all the people who died in these woods," he says, awestruck. "That's so creepy."

"It *is* creepy," I agree cheerfully.

"Good for you! What do you hear now?"

Crickets. Toads. I step carefully over the leaves, pleased by their dry crunch, stopping now and then to kick a half-buried stone out of the earth. Half-buried stones have always bothered me; I'm the same way with seeds in lemon wedges, watermelon slices. I can't focus till I've picked them out.

Morgan holds the Surefire up, its yellow lens glowing gold through the fog, curling along, striking upon a bright white surface. "Do you see that?"

Morgan's response is barely audible. "It's a ghost."

We're paralyzed, just watching. The ghost remains stationary. "Should we try to get near it?" I ask him quietly.

He nods, already slinking forward.

A dry twig snaps as I step on it, but still the ghost does not turn or flee. We're riveted. And squinting quite fiercely. Morgan removes his glasses so that he can see better. We reach the ghost at last and—

"Oh."

It isn't a ghost at all, but a tall blue-gray monument. "A grave," I say.

Morgan lifts a foot off the ground, studying beneath him. "There's another one down here, too." A flat tablet grown over with vines. "Shit, is this poison ivy?"

"No, poison ivy's got three leaves. *Leaves of three, let it be.*" I indicate the number of lobes on this plant. "Five."

We clear fallen leaves away, uncovering more graves. "Those are called fieldstones," I tell Morgan, squatting to brush dirt off a couple rounded markers half-embedded in the dirt. "Only one's got an inscription, and it's too weathered to make out. Quite old." But a marker nearby is still readable: MARY HIERMANN, WIFE OF ISAAC. Isaac is likely buried next to her, but his epitaph is harder to discern, its sandstone layers sloughing off.

Morgan taps the Surefire. "We come in peace, Mary and Isaac. If you're haunting these grounds, will you please touch the green light?"

"Aim that back over here, will you?" I ask him, reaching for the Surefire. "I want to read all of these."

He walks without paying attention to where he's going, stare firmly locked on the green, yellow, and red lenses. None of them light up.

I scrape a rust-colored lichen from a headstone with my fingernail. "Look! *Caloplaca saxicola.* And a chest tomb, too. Caved in, which isn't a surprise. I wish I'd known about this place—I would've come now and then to take care of it. Used to do that in the other graveyards when I was a teenager." I gingerly probe the headstones, careful not to pull the vines lest

I pull out bits of headstone along with them. "These are lime-stone," I go on, enthusiasm mounting. "You see how the in-scriptions have gone flat from weathering? That's acid rain for you, and the moss and lichens, which are *eating* calcium right out of the rock. There are white and black lichens, too, but per-sonally, I love these orange jewel lichens, they feel crumbly when you run your hands over them." I demonstrate.

"When I die, I want a Viking funeral," he declares. "I don't want to be put underground."

"I'd like a mausoleum in the shape of a skull."

"You would."

I happily survey the middle-of-nowhere cemetery. "Zink-ers! What an amazing find. Zinkers were a trend in the early 1800s and late 1900s, cast zinc being a cheaper alternative to marble. They actually hold up better than marble, which can turn black from chemical staining, but people thought they were tacky so they were phased out. Monument salesmen ad-vertised these as 'white bronze' even though they didn't have any bronze in them." I tap each side of the obelisk, delighting in its hollow pangs. "The plaques are removable, so that you can add names or change the epitaphs easily."

I move along, spotting a small headstone for somebody named *Alafaire*, with a lamb carved on top. Lambs denote the graves of children. It isn't uncommon to find multiple very old graves for infants from a single family, and for only a few, if any, of the children to have made it to adulthood. Before vac-cines and modern medicine, the child mortality rate was so high that parents sometimes didn't give their babies names until they were older and more likely to survive. Just two hundred years ago, in the age of the industrial revolution, forty percent of children died before their fifth birthdays.

"The most durable type of headstone is granite," I inform Morgan, "which is why that's what you tend to see used nowadays. But in my opinion, there's nothing like old limestone with a name you can barely make out, dissolved by time. Just imagine all the history these people witnessed." I drag my palms over the lichens as I walk, back bent so that I can see better. "We need to come back tomorrow when the sun's out. I want to take pictures. Do you see the headstone over there that looks like a tree stump? That's called a tree stone. With how small it is, and the tree limbs cut so short, it likely symbolizes a life cut short. I've seen much taller ones, twice my size, like real trunks with ivy and flowers carved on."

I turn to ask why he's suddenly gone so quiet, but he's knelt in front of a grave a short distance northwest of me.

I join him. Headstone iconography is fascinating, generally symbolizing peace, eternal rest, religion, et cetera. I see a lot of doves, angels, torches, hands clasped or praying. Olive branches. Celtic knots.

There isn't any of that on the headstone Morgan's studying, but rather a circle formed from the words THIS IS WHERE. Below that: ROMINA E. KING. AGED 68 YEARS, 4 MONTHS, 22 DAYS.

There is a grave at her right, the stone too devoured by vines and tall stalks of purple flowers to make out a name, and another grave on her left. DELPHINE ORCHID KING-CATTERY. A shallow indentation in the earth indicates that a body used to lie there, but has since been removed. Four other headstones finish off the row: ELLIS KING, MAIRIE LARK KING, AXEL AND BRIAR YOON,

PEREGRINE HEYGATE. There are no birth or death dates, only years lived.

Peregrine was a hundred and four when they died. A spider crouches in the V of Mairie's SLEEP WELL, MY BELOVED inscription, eight legs sticking out.

I can't feel my hands or feet. "This," I manage softly, my voice a wobble as I touch the engraved letters of Romina's name, "is the most horrible thing I've ever seen."

"Total coincidence," Morgan assures me quickly. "I mean, it has to be. *Our* Romina is alive and young, and these tomb-stones look like they were put here at least a century ago."

"Right." I can't look away from it.

"*Plus*, she's not married to Alex, so her last name isn't King." He coughs. "Yet."

"Right."

The red lens of the Surefire flares to life, pulsating in a familiar rhythm. I touch a finger to the carotid artery in my neck, counting the beats. Not quite a match—my pulse is faster. I measure it against a pressure point in Morgan's wrist, which doesn't match up either. The Surefire is certainly imitating contractions of somebody's heart, but *whose* heart that might be remains uncertain.

"A ghost is using your device as their heartbeat," I say without emotion. "Hm. You don't see that every day."

Morgan goes quite still. "Hey, I have an idea. Why don't we get the fuck out of here?"

So we promptly get the fuck out of there, not relaxing until the Surefire's red lens has stopped palpitating.

And soon, I'm following voices again.

"*We're lost,*" a young male is saying. "*We'll never get back home.*"

Morgan clicks open his voice recorder, his thumb jamming a button. "What are they saying?"

"Shh." I strain to listen.

"*Have you seen my father?*" the boy asks. "*The wolves will be out soon. We're stranded.*" He fades off, and then it starts again: "*We're lost, we'll never get back home. Have you seen my father? The wolves will be out soon. We're stranded.*"

I twist my braid into an anxious knot. "Terrible," I mutter. "This is *terrible.*"

"What?" Morgan wants to know. "What do you hear?" He plays what he's just recorded, but all that crackles out of it is dead air and the hush of our breathing.

"It's the people. They don't know they're dead."

THIRTY

Soothhounds: dogs charmed to evoke a soothing,
tranquilizing effect in people who show them love.
Soothhounds who have adopted humans to care for will
often shift into a different animal or insect form once
their physical vessel is no longer serving them well, in
order to retain a close eye on their human(s), who are
quite a weak species and require much supervision.

Paranimals, *N* through *Z*,
Tempest Family Grimoire

WE SHOULD MAKE camp, then pick up our investigation at first light," I suggest after we've left the voices far behind.

"I love how you say 'first light' instead of 'morning,'" Morgan says with a laugh.

I bristle.

Morgan pats my head. "I mean that. It's cute."

My discomfort increases. I refuse to make eye contact.

"Cute and unexpected, like a gingersnappus," he winds on relentlessly. "You have the same burnt-orange hair as a gingersnappus, too. Wonder what you'd shape-shift into?" He scrutinizes me sidelong. "Maybe a typewriter."

"A barrel of eels. Slimy, gray. Mutated with duck feet."

He wags a finger. "No. A bookmark."

"No, thank you." I make a face. "I'd be smothered all my life."

"In books. You love books, you love hiding; it stands to reason you'd love hiding in books. Speaking of books—"

"If you were a gingersnappus," I interject before he can finish his thought, "I think you'd turn into a Slinky."

"I would *love* being a Slinky." He is effectively sidetracked. "What color?"

"All of them."

"Terrific. My favorite's orange, like the harvest moon. Too bad all these trees block our view. Guess what? Saturn has one hundred and forty-six moons, and the largest one, Titan, is bigger than Mercury. One of its cryovolcanoes erupts a substance remarkably similar to vanilla extract, rather than magma, and one milligram could get a horse very drunk, or flavor two hundred waffles. How's the new book going?"

His speech has me dizzy. "Can you repeat all that?"

"I said it's too bad we can't see the harvest moon, and then *you* said you were going to tell me the plot of your new book."

"I don't want to talk about my new book."

I feel myself being guided. Stepping in one direction, I'm flooded with the effervescent memory of how joyful my sisters and niece were when I moved back to town. All of them jumping around me in a huddle, brimming with tears and exclamations. Stepping in the direction opposite, I feel my long, wet hair plastered to the bare skin of my back. Which, of course my back is not bare at the moment and my hair is not wet. But magic knows how much I detest the sensation of wet hair touching my skin, and offers it to me as a way of showing where the invisible guardrails are.

"Why don't you want to talk about your new book?"

"Because there isn't any book to talk about!" I finally burst. "I haven't left the planning stages yet, I don't know what I'm doing, I don't know if I *have* any stories left in me."

Tree branches curl as I pass, manipulating their own shapes to avoid scratching us. The farther we recede from civilization, the taller the trees become. I feel like a tiny sprite all the way down here, and it makes me think of my grandmother. When I was a child, she called me Little Sprite. *They're responsible for changing the colors of leaves in spring and autumn.* I'd cherished the idea of being one. I would have made a much better sprite than human, I think.

"You have more stories to tell. I'm sure of it," he responds firmly.

"Don't be. Don't be sure. Please. Let's not talk about it." I'm beginning to feel ill.

We trudge on, foraging for a good spot to set up camp (and also for a few appetizing wild mushrooms that grow copiously in this forest). Ideally, we'll pitch the tent near a source of water. But there's none of that to be found. "Where've all the creeks gone?" Morgan wonders.

"And marshes. Moonville's loaded with them."

"Strange that we haven't run into any."

We give up, deciding to erect our tent by a cluster of hemlock trees. The ground's spongier than I'd like, so hopefully this tent's sufficiently waterproof. I switch my lantern on before we get started, and Morgan mans the flashlight, which makes him half-useless because now he can only use one hand to help.

"How many pillows did you bring?" he asks.

"None."

He lets go of a cord that's meant to be staked down, tent snapping back to undo the progress I've made so far. "What! How utterly egregious."

"I'm working with limited space, Morgan. You could've brought your own."

"I did." And this is how I learn that eighty percent of what's in his backpack is pillow.

"I don't have a lot of supplies," he admits. "But you know what else I won't have? A stiff neck in the morning."

"I can't believe you let me carry a backpack that weighs as much as I do for the past hour while you've been running around with that marshmallow, complaining that your shoulders ache."

"I couldn't support the heavy backpack *and* Forte. He's rather cumbersome, you know."

It's my turn to stop short. "What!"

Morgan pats his lumpy shoulder bag. It squirms. "Precious cargo."

I point into the trees. Could be pointing north, south, east, or west, I really do not know or care. "Go home."

"I had no choice but to bring him! Otherwise he might smash up my apartment while I'm gone. You didn't even know he was here until now, so it isn't like he's causing trouble."

I peek into the shoulder bag, which I now realize is a baby sling. A pale, long-clawed gingersnappus paw reaches out to bat at me. His scabbed face peers up, eyes mean slits.

"*Pliggguck shhurr*," he spits.

"Yeah, he doesn't like to be touched unless he's the one initiating," Morgan tells me, fishing a chunk of Himalayan salt from a bottle in his pocket and dropping it inside the sling. Forte scarfs it down, noisy and full of rage. "But even then, he changes his mind a lot and can get mad at you after he touches you, for being in his space." He shows me a red grid of scratches on his arm.

"I don't know if it's wise to keep that thing as a pet."

"He isn't my pet," Morgan retorts. "He's my son. You can't just tell somebody to chuck their son, Zelda."

"Sorry."

Once our tent is ready, we clamber inside and Morgan begins to set up his creature comforts. I notice he did not bring his own sleeping bag, but he positions his pillow at the head of mine as if he expects me to share.

Next comes a wicker basket, into which he lovingly places a box of Cocoa Puffs, deodorant, a travel toothbrush and toothpaste, hair-texturizing salt spray, papers scribbled with notes about paranimals, and a bottle of cologne labeled POLAR NIGHT.

"Polar night, hm?" I gesture. "Did you bring that for science, too?"

"It's for your benefit. Things are going to get grim after walking around all day, so you'll be glad I smell like Mount Everest instead of a decaying small intestine." He removes a rogue hazelnut from my hair. Pops it in his mouth. "Well. Mount Everest with fewer corpses."

"But not zero?"

We snack on beef jerky, mushrooms, freeze-dried strawberries, and hazelnuts, which don't quite go together, but at least they fill our stomachs. As I climb into my sleeping bag, Morgan raps his knuckles idly against his jaw, watching. "Soooo..."

I hand him his pillow. "Good night."

His face falls. "Your poor Morgan is going to be cold out here, all alone, without a blanket."

"You can lie on top of my sleeping bag, or underneath it." I can't invite him inside. The thought makes my head spin.

Morgan begins to push back, so I add, "There's a sweater in my bag that you can borrow. It's nice and cozy."

He inspects the sweater. Frowns. "Do you have anything in happier colors?"

I switch my lantern off. Night bathes us in one fell swoop, the forest beyond projecting onto our vinyl walls as if they're movie screens. The silhouettes of crooked tree limbs could be a monster's long fingers, reaching for the tent's zipper. Focusing on this imagery relaxes me.

I am not going to allow myself to think about what is actually happening. I will not think about Morgan's long body lying inches from mine. What it felt like earlier when I brushed his fingers and his hand fitted itself into mine. I won't dwell on that dark, curious gaze, like the fathomless pits of twin cauldrons ... hair as black as shadows beneath a grim reaper's hood. What would it be like to touch it? To pass the strands through my fingers? I stare at the backs of my eyelids, so still that I'm barely breathing, envisioning vines worming out of the dirt to cuff my arms and ankles.

"Well, I for one am not thinking about you-know-what," Morgan announces loudly.

The vines are slithering about my clavicles now, not terribly constricting, more like a hug. I imagine the cool smoothness of wintercreeper leaves, an invasive species, weaving a fortress over my supine body. Soon I will be nothing but bones and greenery, chlorophyll where the blood once flowed.

Morgan turns onto his side, his breath fanning over my cheek. "The two of us alone. Together. At *night*. The possibilities that are . . . possible."

From under my shrubbery, my heart beats fast, skin flushing. "The only possibilities are you sleeping in here or you sleeping outside," I grind out. "Tread carefully."

"We could have a lot of fun, you and I," he says, his voice deeper, tone suggestive. My vines go *poof* into nonexistence, protective layers gone.

"Not happening." I twist a bit, and Forte growls. He's spread himself across my ankles. "Try to put the moves on me and I'll dump your Cocoa Puffs in a stream."

"You're ruthless." The way he says it sounds almost admiring. He's quiet for a while, long enough that I think maybe he's actually going to try to sleep. And then he says: "I do mean it, but I don't know how to say it right. Not when it's real."

My mouth opens. There is a shift in his tone that gives me pause, that warns me not to immediately respond with something snide. "What?"

"I'm the boy who cried 'I like you,'" he explains. "Not *cried

cried. The wolf story? You know? It's like a . . . a fable or something." I hear one of his arms fall across his forehead. "I can't even get near this conversation without jumbling it up. Am I cursed?"

I stare into the dark. "Don't take this the wrong way," I begin slowly, "but I'm not sure I follow."

"The big gold rib cage," he blurts.

"*What?*" Now he's definitely spewing gobbledygook.

"Your big gold rib cage jewelry-looking thing, I don't know if it's a necklace or a top or what. I like it."

What on earth. I think he's referring to my rib cage corset, which I wear on Mondays, often over a black lace dress. "Oh. Thanks?"

"And your blue cacti earrings," he goes on, a note of desperation tugging his voice upward. "See? I pay attention to the small details, and if I wasn't genuine, I wouldn't notice. That should tell you something." Morgan groans. Lets a silence linger. "Who knew I'd actually be bad at this? I'm only good at this when it doesn't mean anything."

"Don't beat yourself up, Morgan. You're bad at plenty of things."

He laughs tiredly. "Ohhhhh . . . kick a man in his spleen, why don't you."

I tap his waist, in the spleen region, and his body tenses beneath my touch. "Red boots," he mutters under his breath, as if my fingertip released the words from him automatically.

"Hmm?"

"Your red steampunk boots, with all the buttons." He sounds pained. "I love those goddamned boots."

"I think I got them from Etsy."

More groaning. "You were wearing those boots when we weren't speaking to each other, and I had to watch you walk around with your notebook and your two pencils in your hair, exploring. Your face . . . you looked so fierce and determined. Some guy asked if you knew whether the pharmacy was open yet, and you completely ignored him because you were so deep in concentration. It was incredible. I couldn't take my eyes off you."

I don't remember anyone ever asking me about the pharmacy's hours.

"When I think of you, I sometimes draw a dragon at your side," he goes on, "because it just makes sense. There's Zelda Tempest"—I feel a whip of air as he flourishes a hand—"courageous and bold, and *there* is her dragon, naturally. A Zelda should always have a dragon. Maybe I'll doodle a helmet and sword on you, too. I don't know if I'd rather be the damsel you're saving, or the dragon." He ponders insensibly. "Or the grass, enjoying it when you step on me."

"Why would you want me to step on you? That doesn't sound enjoyable at all."

"I am making a confession, and it is landing like a cannonball into a dry pool." Morgan sighs wearily. "What I'm trying to say—"

"Oh, I remember now!" My memory jogs up and waves hello. "I was wearing those boots the day I saw a hellhole."

"There is no way I heard you correctly."

"Hellhole. Small white animal with two sticks for feet. It's got dark blue feathers around the collar, and this gaping black hole for a face. At a slant, it looks like the hole is a wide-open mouth, like it's about to scream, but there are no eyes. It's just . . . a great big hole in its head."

He sits up. "That sounds like a nightmare. Let's go right now. I want to see."

"It was under a tree, over by the bank."

"The rabbit!" he exclaims. "I remember you were looking at a rabbit under a tree."

"Oooh, so it looked like a rabbit to you?" Intriguing. "I saw it swallow a hawk whole."

We're both at full attention, reaching for the lantern, fingers touching on the switch. Warm yellow light blooms, and our eyes meet; our enthusiasm is a tangible sparkle in the air around us as we dash down our notes. Morgan forgets to uncap his pen before he begins writing, he's so caught up.

"Hellholes," he repeats, mildly disparaging. "That's even worse than *mouseplant*. You're a *writer*, Miss Boots. Go back to college."

"Come up with something else, then. I know you're dying to."

Morgan is all delight, pen flying across paper. "Rabbit plus tree equals treebit. Rabbit plus bird equals rabbird. Cavity plus face could be called a cavace. What are some famous rabbits? Thumper. Thumper . . . Monster. Mumpster. Eater Cottontail."

He sounds like a robot with a dying battery pack. "There is something wrong with you." Then again, there is also something wrong with me. Most people probably don't visualize being buried alive by a bush as a way to calm themselves.

Morgan smacks his notebook against his forehead. "I've got it! The navy-necked hollowhead. Perfection." He scribbles a star next to the name.

I have to grin. "You and your alliteration."

"Magic *adores* alliteration," he points out. "And likes the chime of rhyme quite fine."

"Did magic tell you that?"

"Pretty much. Your grandmother told me that, and your grandmother's magic. Is she not?"

It makes me smile to hear him speak of her in the present tense. My sisters talk about Dottie all the time, and I'm usually left feeling sad when they do. But the way Morgan talks about Dottie is different. He makes me feel as if he and Grandma and I are in on something secret together. A journey still ongoing.

Such warmth exudes from him. A deep firelight of wonder, curiosity, mischief, mayhem. All of the best things.

The words *ever dissever* from "Annabel Lee" pop into my head again. *Ever dissever, ever dissever.*

E R   I
S D
    V

"Do you . . ." I swallow, not sure how to phrase this.

He angles a gently inquisitive smile at me. "Do I . . . ?"

"Do you have any peculiar word associations? Not the usual suspects, like how the word *happy* means *happy*. I'm not describing this well. Like, maybe you hear the word *happy* and automatically think about . . . oh, I don't know . . . the specific ringtone of one of your novelty telephones. Or maybe the word *hat*, for you, will always feel like the color green, because of a bucket hat you wore when you were a kid. Hypothetically speaking."

I truly do not expect him to understand what I'm attempting to communicate, because out loud, it makes little sense. But he says:

"Formidable. When I hear the word *fairy*, I think of fairy rings, and that jumps to the word *formidable* for some reason, written all in fancy cursive, right below your face." He scratches his jaw, thinking. "But I don't see your face in normal color, like a photograph, when I think of *formidable*; I see you as one of those old-fashioned oval brooch things. A cameo, I think it's called. I also see your face when I think of the word *fantastic*, but the image is different. For *fantastic*, you're in your raincoat, looking up at my window from the street below. And you're all black and white like a noir film."

There is a tightening in my chest, almost to the point of pain. I cannot breathe through it. Morgan doesn't seem to demand an explanation for why I asked this question, content to busy himself writing about the hollowhead.

I watch him for a while, summoning courage. "I think you're *fantastic*, too," I say. "In Luna's kitchen the night we planned all this. There's an amber glow on you from the pantry light left on, and I can still taste the Earl Grey tea I was drinking."

He smiles slowly, skin around his eyes creasing. "I like that. Very much."

I'm not sure what to do with all of Morgan's *fantastic*. He isn't right for me, and yet he is, and yet he's not, and I wish I knew for sure, one way or the other. But he doesn't fit neatly into either column. He's all over the place.

I think I sort of love that he's all over the place.

This revelation, very at odds with a brain that seeks to label, organize, tidying every word and person into their correct little box, runs through my mind over and over. I drift asleep to the scratch of his pen chronicling impossible things—and his quiet, his so very curious quiet, that makes me wish I could see all that he imagines.

THIRTY-ONE

Turn off your lights when there is a meteor shower; some
of them are cursed fairies, who are attracted to light and
will aim to become part of whatever it is they fall into.

Legends and Superstitions, Expanded,
Tempest Family Grimoire

I AM WOKEN BY my own scream, and a piano on my leg.

"You shouldn't have moved in your sleep," Morgan says
urgently, and if I weren't pinned by this piano, I'd deck
him. I can just make out his profile, dampened by the darkness
of surrounding trees.

"How am I at fault here?"

"It isn't *Forte's* fault." He manages to lift the piano off my
leg, but it nearly falls onto my face and I scream again. Morgan
makes a quick, slippery grab. From below, I fight against my
sleeping bag to get unzipped. "He's sensitive to touch," Morgan insists. "A defenseless baby."

I doubt Forte is all that young. By the patchwork of scars on
his spiteful little face, I'd say he's been picking fights for a de-
cade at least.

"He's going to kill us!"

"Unlikely. Forte hates faces and sleeps far away from them,

so all your vital organs are safe. If anything, he'd mangle your feet."

My voice is like a clatter of pots and pans. "Oh, is that all?"

"Grab my water," Morgan orders. "Splash some on him." He grits his teeth as he adjusts his hold on the piano. "Hurry!"

"I can't see your water. It's dark in here."

"Feel around!"

I stand up, still loose-limbed from sleep, and grope in the darkness. Feel along the walls of the tent to gain my bearings. Some of the fabric's rather lumpy—

"Well, hello," Morgan rasps in a fluttering baritone. His voice is located directly above the bit of tent I was patting down.

I rear back. "Did I—? Is that—?"

He doesn't say anything. I think possibly, he is unable to.

"Ohhh." I brace myself for many nights ahead of staring at my ceiling, reliving this mortifying moment over and over. I will never come back from this. "I am so sorry. I thought— Your shorts, they're that windbreaker material, they feel just like the tent . . ." My face burns.

"Here we are," he goes on formally, sounding not at all like himself. "It is dark. We are in the middle of nowhere; just you, me, and this giant piano. All is going as smoothly as can be expected. You have touched my dick. Your mistaking it for a tent is becoming more accurate by the second."

This is humiliating. "I'm so, *so* sorry." But also: "*Why* did you have to bring a gingersnappus along on this trip?"

"It isn't Forte's fault that you're insatiable with desire."

"*EXCUSE*—"

"Always trying to get me alone. Dragging me out here to

this isolated location, with only one tent and one sleeping bag. And now you're copping a feel." His tone crisps up into a stern, soldierly march. "Zelda, I am a modern man with values and standards. If you want to sleep with me so badly, you will need to guest-star on my podcast first."

"If you don't shut up," I growl, "I am going to . . . aha!" I've found the water. Definitely not any of Morgan's valuable bits this time. I unscrew the cap, sloshing it with wild abandon. Morgan cries out.

"Sorry! I didn't mean to get it on you."

I'm not sure if the hiss that follows is Morgan or Forte, who has stopped being a piano. I hit the lights, wincing at the brightness. Forte has transformed back into a small beast and is rolling happily in water.

"How did you know that would work?"

Morgan sounds winded. "He screams on the other side of the bathroom door when he knows I'm in there showering. Soon as I come out, he runs inside and lies in the wet tub. Loves it."

I watch Forte rub his nose in a puddle. "What a weirdo. And the Black Bear Witch is a psychopath. Who looks at a cat and says, *La-di-da, I know what I'll do! I'll turn this cat into a devil creature that shape-shifts into a piano whenever it gets mad!*"

"Mother of god." Morgan points at my leg.

It only starts hurting when I see the gash. My leg kicks of its own volition, as if I can knock the gash right off me. "Agh! Agh! I can see my bone!"

"That's not bone, it's your skin." He encircles my ankle with one hand and gently holds me still. I feel the touch every-where. "You're just ridiculously pale."

"*You're* ridiculously pale. My leg hurts. Oh, it hurts. This is worse than the time I had an IUD improperly inserted and had to get it removed after the most excruciating week of my life." I pound my fist in the pillow. "Damn you, Dr. Paul! You should've just tied my tubes like I asked. But no, he was all, 'What if you change your mind?' And I was all, 'Look, man, I have never seen a baby and thought, *I want one of those in my house.*' No offense, Aisling. You and I are cool now that you're old enough to tell me what you want without shrieking." I howl when Morgan dabs at my injury with a tissue.

"When I asked my doctor about scheduling a vasectomy," he replies, "she was super helpful. There was hardly any wait time at all. And after the procedure was finished, a nurse gave me some candy."

"I hate you," I grit out through clenched teeth.

"Let's not fight right now, darling. You might be on your last breaths. I want to remember you fondling. Fondly. I want to remember you *fondly*, is what you heard me say."

I try to kick him, but he dodges.

"I've got a first-aid kit," I grumble, tired and aggravated. "The suitcase over there, with my glasses sitting on top. Bottom pouch in the front compartment."

Morgan heads toward the suitcase, then halts midstride. Stays frozen like that for several seconds.

"What are you doing?" I slap the ground with the flat of my hand. "I need gauze!"

He turns in the opposite direction and begins to root through his belongings instead.

"Did you bring—" My words fail when he lifts out a glass

bottle filled with thick, sunny liquid. "Uhhh." He twists off the cap. Dabs some onto my leg. It's frigid and smells like tiramisu. "What. Are. You. Doing?"

"Testing a theory." His gaze gleams like a mad scientist.

I spasm, swiping for him. "I can't believe you put that into my open wound, you idiot!"

"Shhhh. It'll take effect better if you speak to me nicely."

I'm going to kill him. He's a dead man.

My gash is healing. We both gawk at my skin as it seals, turning a shiny, puckering pink. Within seconds, even the scar is gone.

I'm going to kiss him.

"Morgan, you genius."

He drips potion across his unblemished skin. "I knew it! Remember after we made this, I got some of it on my arm? It healed my scratch. I suspect it gave me a mood boost as well, because I felt *amazing* afterward. Must contain enzymes that speed up the recovery process! Extraordinary. We could sell it. We'll call it Morgan's Miracle Cure."

I pinch him.

"Morgan *and Zelda's* Miracle Cure, then. Actually no, that's too wordy. We'll call it *Tempoulos*. That's what you get when you mix *Tempest* and *Angelopoulos*."

"When you mix *Tempest* and *Angelopoulos*, you get disaster. You've just sprayed us with an untested, non-FDA-approved potion."

Morgan slants me a haughty look. "There's a first for everything. Somebody, somewhere, in the halls of history, fried a pig for the first time and discovered bacon."

"It's late. You're unhinged. Let's not speak again until tomorrow at the earliest."

Morgan appraises his side of the tent with a pathetic air. I've doused his spot with water.

I sigh.

"I can't make you lie in that. Here, I'll scoot over. There's enough room in my sleeping bag for both of us."

"Ah." His mouth curves. "I see we've reached the next phase of your seduction plan."

"Never mind. Sleep in water."

"It's all right, I'm not complaining." He snuggles in beside me, his voice dropping to a devilish, decadent pitch. He brings the pillow with him, and I steal three quarters of it as revenge. "I'm a willing participant."

My whole body sharpens. "Watch it."

"I'm watching as much as I can, trust me."

I roll aggressively onto my other side, facing away from him. "I hate you. At first light—ugh, *in the morning*, you're going home. I've had enough of your teasing and your stupid hair."

"You like my hair? Is that what you're trying to say?" His Cheshire grin is so corrupt, I can practically feel it through my clothes. "Every time you go quiet from now on, I'll be wondering if you're thinking about feeling me up."

I squeeze my eyes closed. "Merghh."

He raises his head off the pillow a fraction, murmuring in my ear: "*And how much you want me to get even, I bet.*"

The words sink into either side of my hips, warm and pressurized as a pair of hands. I've never wanted to be touched this badly before.

I banish these thoughts to the void, where a hologram of myself stands at a chalkboard and writes *I will not sin* two hundred times.

Inviting him to come along on this trip was an appalling mistake. I recall what Luna said: *I know Morgan will be there, too, but he's useless.* Luna was right.

"All you do is flirt," I say, my voice guttural. "You are just one big, flirty lie."

"Flirt back," he urges. "It'll be fun."

"Never. You can use your looks to get whatever you want from other people, but I'll never give in."

He laughs against my neck, or at least it feels that way. My toes curl. "You think my looks are that powerful? I'd be flattered if I weren't so devastated right now by your low opinion of me."

"My opinion of you isn't low. But you're teasing, and that's unkind."

"I'm not teasing. I swear."

Nobody laughs when they're devastated. He is unscrupulous. I must remain vigilant.

I shiver again, the magic inside me scintillating, magnifying my instincts, and I sense it in the atmosphere—

Luna has somehow heard my thoughts. She's heard me think *Luna was right* and now her power is growing. My hands quiver.

The longer I lie here, the faster my heartbeat gallops. Luna is listening. Luna is outside the tent.

"Where are you going?" Morgan asks when I unzip myself.

"My sister's here."

He sits up. "Which one?"

I slip into the night, looking around. Luna isn't staying put, jogging in circles. "Stop that," I command. "There isn't enough room for you in our tent. Why are you here?"

"Your dog missed you." She lets go of a small animal, the size of a newborn puppy, with a smooth, featureless face. Its leash jingles against the dirt as it bounds toward me.

"Oh right. Thanks for bringing her."

"Do you remember it yet?" she wants to know. I think her head is cocked, but I can't see her well enough to be sure.

I extend my hands, gazing skyward. "The rain has gotten so dry."

Morgan crawls on his hands and knees out of the tent. "Snake!"

"Luna, get out of here!" I scream. "The snake will take you!"

"Luna, come back," Morgan cries. "You have to save us. Tell my dad. He's seen snakes before. They haven't been seen in *years*."

How'd I forget? I sit down so that the snake can't get me. "This is amazing. We can sell the snake for eleven thousand dollars."

"Oh no, my legs don't work." He kicks them wildly. "Do you see? They're not moving." Morgan covers his face with his arms and mutters, "Peril, peril."

I stare at him, and all I can think about is his skeleton. Just sitting there inside all that soup of blood and sinew. Wet bones. "Stop talking," I beg. "I can see your mandible."

He springs to his feet. "Stop looking at my mandible!"

"We have to take out your bones."

"Start with my legs. They won't move anymore."

It's burning hot outside. I wasted my summer, so it must have started over. We're back in June again. Wonderful! I have so much time to work on my book now. "Let's find our bone extractor," I suggest, searching the tent. It's a good thing I packed a well-loved copy of *Blood and Guts: A History of Surgery* by Richard Hollingham. Never go anywhere without *Blood and Guts*, that's my motto.

Morgan's pillow turns into a snail, so he has to put it outside.

"Calm down," I encourage soothingly, tying Morgan down to the sleeping bag with clamps. "Shhh."

"I've changed my mind. I want to keep my bones."

"You don't need them anymore. Trust me." I locate the bone extractor, pressing it to his kneecap. Morgan howls.

"Your face has gone swirly," he wheezes. Enormous pupils appear in his otherwise empty eye sockets, rolling all over the place untethered. "Stop it! Put your beautiful face back how it goes! I liked it the other way. So much."

"Shhh." I subdue him with graham cracker crumbs in his hair. "It's June." I sit astride him. "Do you smell that?"

"It's music. I'm playing it just for you." Morgan strokes my hair. "The mountain king song."

"Luna!" I remember she's standing outside with all her dogs. She should have asked me before she got all these dogs. I would have been so good at naming them. To come up with characters, I utilize BabyNames.com more than an expecting parent.

We run back out, Morgan stripping off his shirt. "The sun is looking at me!" he cries, streaking into the trees. "The sun is looking at me!"

We run and run, until we reach the right tree. "Oh, thank god it's still here." I pat the tree. "I thought it was gone."

Morgan weeps. "This is the best day. What would we do if our tree was gone?"

"Morgan, look!" I drop to my knees, hugging his lower half. "Your legs work again."

"It's the tree," he says breathlessly. "It fixed me."

"We have to tell people about this tree."

"No." He shakes my shoulders. "They're not ready."

"Kiss my hand," I demand. "It's the only way off this planet."

"Makes sense." He charges. We take turns kissing each other's hands, because it's impossible for us both to do it at the same time: if we do, we won't be able to breathe. I make sure we don't make any eye contact, so that his dad doesn't get upset.

"Into the cocoon!" Morgan declares, grabbing my wrist. "We must transform."

The tent appears right behind us, and we dive in. "Good. I hope I become a sprite instead of a moth when I wake up."

THIRTY-TWO

It is not uncommon to find what appears to be nature-made or human-made landmarks growing out of ley lines possessing high concentrations of energy. Examples are a rock column locally known as the Devil's Tea Table (for more about the mysteries of King Hollow Trail, see pages 21, 34–36, and 97), and several old, ramshackle buildings scattered throughout Vinton County that remain standing in spite of demolition attempts. Legend has it that one of the buildings on Vallis Boulevard was not put there by humans but by a ley line.

Local Legends and Superstitions,
Tempest Family Grimoire

I COME BACK TO consciousness with a thumping headache and the inkling that I have made a bad decision. "Morgan, wake up." I poke at him until his eyes open. He grumbles, ill-tempered.

"Why?"

"I feel weird."

His hair doesn't have the decency to look hilarious first thing in the morning. It's every-which-way in a sensual, throaty-voiced *Are you coming back to bed for round three?* kind of a situation. His face is drained of life, eyes purple-shadowed, and the general zombie-ish pallor is inappropriately doing it for me. "Do you want me to feel you and see if I agree?"

I flick his ear.

He sits up. "Ouch. Fuck, my head." He moans, cradling his skull. "That is not nice at all. I do not like it."

"I've got a headache, too. I think it must be early yet."

"What's this stuff on my knee?" Morgan rubs a white flake between two fingers, bringing it to his nose to sniff. "Deodorant? Why is there deodorant on my knee?"

I unzip the tent, peeking out. "Where'd Luna go? I swear she showed up last night."

"No, she had to take the dogs home."

Morgan and I stop, then slowly look at each other. It clicks. "*Ohhh.*"

"Was it something we ate?" he wonders. We take a moment to dissect our meals yesterday. Maybe the filter on my water bottle has been tampered with. "I can't figure out what parts were real and what parts were fever dream."

I dig graham cracker crumbs out of my neck. "At least some of it was real. I remember putting these crumbs on you." I reach for my glasses. Beside them sits a glass vial with four drops of gold potion remaining. *Morgan's Miracle Cure.* "You!" I seethe, trying to grab for him. Morgan scuttles backward. "You did this. You poisoned us with slow-cooked mischief and mayhem."

I can see it in his face: the flash of recognition, the probability that I'm right. The struggle to dodge responsibility.

"But I used it before, on my scratch," Morgan insists. "It definitely didn't make me hallucinate the first time."

"Maybe trace amounts don't affect you as much. The second time, though—that was an overdose."

Morgan is enraptured. "Psychedelic potion? We could sell that, too, and make just as much money as we would if we called it medicine." He straightens. "Wanna put it on ourselves again?"

He cannot be serious. Of all the dangerous, stupid—

He *is* serious. "I tried to perform surgery on you!"

"Okay, yeah." He scratches his chin. "Maybe not, then. Today."

Perhaps just as mystifying as what happened to us biologically is what has happened to us geographically: the tent is sitting smack-dab next to a river. We did not set up camp next to a river.

"None of this was here yesterday, right?" I survey the swollen water, the two of us standing on its bank. It's a gray, drizzling day, cold moisture seeping through my pants.

He shakes his head. "No. And I know that for a fact because you kept saying we needed to camp near a source of water and I kept reminding you that we hadn't come across any."

We are parked beside a gurgling, icy river with no rational explanation, and it is not, in fact, early morning, but noon.

"Your pet crushed my leg, and you poisoned me," I say crossly. "You're carrying all the tent mishmash today, and I'll carry the pillow and Cocoa Puffs."

"Hey, I protected you from that snake last night! You're *welcome*."

"That snake wasn't real. You were probably screaming at your own shoelace."

"Hm." His lips purse. "That would explain the missing

shoelace." Then he watches me unscrew the cap of my medication and swallow a pill. Somehow resists asking what sort of pill it is, even though he's nosy and impulsive.

I answer his unspoken question, anyway. "SSRI." I wave the bottle. "Selective serotonin reuptake inhibitor. Twenty milligrams every morning helps me keep feeling like the same person all month long. It's the reason I was able to move back home."

He searches my face, inquisitive. "Luna and Romina have mentioned a few times that they hoped you'd come back to Moonville, and they said *you* said you never would."

Yep. All true. "I have premenstrual dysphoric disorder," I tell him. "I've struggled with it since my early twenties but didn't know exactly what was wrong with me until about eight months ago when I saw a thing online about PMDD, and how it isn't normal, actually, to feel like a completely different person in the one to two weeks before my period starts. I'd get severe mood swings, brain fog, insomnia. Crushing anxiety and depression. Any tiny thing to go wrong would feel hopelessly insurmountable, and I'd have a total meltdown. But also—and this is the big one—I'd get suddenly dissatisfied about where I was living, so I'd pick up and move. New city, new state. Then my hormones would go back to normal as soon as my period started, and I'd be left dealing with the consequences of all the decisions I'd made during the luteal phase of my menstrual cycle." I circle my finger. "Every month. Behaving irrationally, wanting to move somewhere new. Period starts. Feel normal for two weeks. Then it happens again. And again."

"And now you're cured?"

"I'm way better. I still get a little emo a couple days before my period starts, but the urge to turn my life upside down has gone away and I can stay put in one place without a problem. The day I sold my camper van and bought a car, packed all my stuff to drive back to Ohio—I can't even describe the feeling. I was so proud of myself."

He smiles affectionately. "I'm proud of you, too."

I look down, busying myself with my suitcases, hyperaware that I don't talk about myself this much with other people. Why am I telling Morgan personal information? And why doesn't it bother me?

Morgan and I give each other privacy while answering the calls of nature, getting dressed, acknowledging that certain parts of this expedition are not as great as I've been romanticizing, et cetera. Then we sort of stand around for a bit, looking to each other for direction. We're vaguely somewhere in Falling Rock Forest. We might be a hop, skip, and a jump from the main road; we might be miles out. It's especially tricky to guess now that we've ended up . . . not where we started.

"What if brays are watching us go to the bathroom?" Morgan asks.

"Then it's the most excitement they've gotten in a while, so let's just be grateful that we're not in their position."

"Yet. If we die out here, we'll become like them."

"You only become a bray if you're *alone* in the forest when you die. We're not alone." I survey the area. "Let's make the most of this nice weather and see if we can find a trestle and a cave close together. Find the trestle and cave, find the Black Bear Witch's lair."

My statement is punctuated by an unexpected downpour of chilly rain. I did not account for this. Normally I'm a big fan of chilly rain. There is such romance in foul, gloomy weather, in wind that's out to pull teeth. It makes me yearn to sit at my window in fuzzy socks, mug of steaming tea in hand, watching the bricks of Vallis Boulevard gleam copper as the sky spits.

"Please tell me you packed an umbrella," he says, knowing full well that I did not and neither did he.

We roam about, trying to stay under the cover of tree branches. Forte sleeps angrily in his baby sling strapped across Morgan's chest. Being wrapped up snug seems to induce a state of hibernation in him. "What does that turtle look like to you?" Morgan asks me, gesturing.

"Like a turtle."

"Damn." We trudge on. He inquires after a squirrel, a rabbit, and a deer. They turn out to be, respectively, a squirrel, a rabbit, and a deer.

"We might not be discovering new paranimals left and right, you know."

"Why not?" He leans away to examine a cardinal, which turns out to not be a cardinal because cardinals do not have fire smoldering casually from their tail plumage. "Something smells like it's burning," he notes. "We must be close to a cabin."

"Or, we're close to a bird that's on fire."

Morgan jumps back. "On fire?"

"Or *is* fire," I amend. The bird trots forward, twittering. "There's smoke where its wings should be."

"See?" he crows. "What'd I tell you? No reason we can't be discovering new paranimals left and right." He withdraws his phone and activates the camera. It shuts itself off. "I wasn't gonna share the pictures online!" he yells at the invisible forces thwarting his photography. "It would show up as a normal bird on camera, anyway." He manages to get the camera working again, but the bird hurries off.

"Notice how it didn't fly, though!" I point out. "Because it doesn't actually have wings."

Insensible to the weather now, he urges me to describe the animal in profuse detail, copying it all down on paper. "We'll call it a conflagrinal."

But the conflagrinal, as it turns out, is the only new creature of interest we come upon for quite some time. By dinner (a feast of canned chili and crackers), even Morgan's enthusiasm has waned. We study a strange film floating in the rushes of a swamp. In spite of all the rain we've gotten, the swamp is stagnant and carries a pungent odor not unlike wet clothes that have been sitting in a washing machine for a week. "This could be a paranimal's molt, maybe," I say hesitantly, dipping a twig into the water. The film instantly wraps itself around the forked end of the twig, adhering to it. The beautiful iridescence reminds me of abalone, slug trails, the way oil in puddles refracts light. "Can't say for sure, of course—"

Morgan is desperate for something new to grab his notice. "It is irrefutably from a paranimal. It looks silver to you and white to me."

"That could be perspective."

"Let's bag it."

My fingers have cuts on them from pulling back vines and branches to see if any of them are hiding caves. No such luck. We did find a trestle, but a trestle is useless if there aren't caves nearby.

While I was preparing for this trip, I envisioned myself endlessly patient. One with nature, studying every leaf, rodent, and insect. Utterly enthralled, capable of sitting still for so long that my bones would groan when they moved again at last. Maybe I'd become so enamored of the forest that I'd never leave.

"I'm sore," I grouse. "I miss my mattress. Sleeping on the ground sucked, and all I can think about is my ass."

"All I can think about is your ass, too," he replies distractedly, reviewing the never-ending expanse of trees.

I don't know if I want to laugh or threaten him, and I'm still deciding when I hear voices again.

"One clamp of their jaws on your flesh and your lungs filled with water."

I hold out a hand. "Stop."

Morgan watches me closely, not saying a word. I tilt my head.

"Once upon a time, nobody went into the forest and came out of it alive."

The words wink away. I think the forest spirits must be trying to communicate a warning, or a threat. "Somebody doesn't want us here," I murmur.

We roam deeper into violet dusk, the path becoming rougher, overgrown with wide, flabby mushrooms, split trees, and blinking yellow eyes crouched in the undergrowth. My feet ache from walking all day, my muscles are sore from carting luggage, and my eyes beg for sleep. Where did the brays go? Can they see us? Are they following?

The deluge lets up to a drizzle, tearing apart a low fog that drifts across the old wood like interstellar clouds. "You smell something burning?" Morgan asks.

I sniff. "A conflagrinal?"

We search the skies, at last locating a big puff of smoke that seems to be pouring from nowhere.

I can't make out the chimney until I'm looking at the smoke, and I can't see the roof unless I'm focused on the chimney. The only time a window is visible is when I'm staring directly at a door. It's as if the tiny building pencils itself into the frame reluctantly, pieces at a time, not giving more than it has to. If I strain my eyes hard enough, I can just distinguish four dark, blurry exterior walls and a steeply pitched roof. The closer we step, the more solid it all becomes, as if waking up from a dream.

The cabin must predate many of the trees surrounding, as thick roots have coiled beneath its foundations and risen like the undead. It was constructed close to a creek, but erosion has widened the waters and now the building's southwest corner is ready to fall in. A tiny pond, the sort you'd normally see koi fish swimming in, rests close by, its black waters rippled with leaves and yellow toads.

There are four doors, one cut into each side of the cabin. The one facing us bears a carving of an owl and the words NOTHING TO SEE HERE. On another, an oak leaf and THIS IS A TREE, NOTHING MORE. The third door has antlers growing out of it where a doorknob should be located, along with the sentiment YOU'RE NOT REALLY SEEING THIS; and the fourth door, labeled OFF YOU TROT, is frozen shut with a thick casing of ice. Every minuscule hair on my body stands up.

"This has to be it," I whisper. "The witch's lair, and a fire's going." Gray clouds wisp from the chimney cowl, curlicuing upward. "She's probably inside right now. What do we do?"

Morgan pushes a hand through his hair, fingers shaking slightly with nerves. His face is ghosts and shadows, black eyes alert. "We didn't plan this far ahead, did we?"

The goal has been: *Find the Black Bear Witch.* But I suspect that, deep down, we didn't think we would, and that's why we're dithering at her doorstep, presumably, with empty heads. Do we just say *Hey, found you! Give us some magic, please?*

My hand finds Morgan's, fingers lacing tightly together. He raises his other fist to knock. Even though I can see it connecting with the wood surface, the contact produces no sound. Not a *thud,* not a *thunk,* not a *thump.*

The door swings inward, presenting an empty one-room house with a caved-in floor.

I wrench Morgan back to prevent him from walking right over the threshold and into a pit.

"It's . . ." He gazes around in haunted disbelief. "*No.* With the way we can hardly see the house even when it's right in front of us, that means it's magicked, which means it *has* to be her lair."

I give his hand a gentle squeeze. "Maybe she's moved. Don't worry, we won't stop looking."

We've put so much effort into this, and so many wishes and hopes, that even though all we've found is a ruin, we can't bring ourselves to move on yet.

"It smells familiar in here," he notes. "Like maple syrup."

I inhale deeply. "Whiskey."

"I don't understand where the smoke is coming from if there's no fireplace."

"And no doors to suggest bedrooms where a fireplace might be . . ." I stop, eyes narrowing on the wall opposite us. "That wall is not quite right." One moment it's covered in peeling wallpaper, the next it's brick, and then wood, in such a gradual evolution that I wouldn't notice it at all if I weren't staring unblinkingly.

"It's like there's something moving in there," Morgan tells me, "but I can only see it out the corners of my eyes."

He's right. The longer we look on, the more it seems there are silhouettes and pockets of light floating about. Morgan points. "Fire!"

"Where?"

His breath releases in a gust. "It's vanished again."

I reposition myself, staring ahead but trying to glean what's happening along the edges. And there it is—a lick of bright, merry light. I face it straight-on, and it's gone. I think I catch snatches of low music, too—but I can't keep a lid on any of it, my senses scattering and confused.

"Maybe she still comes by now and then?" Morgan wonders aloud. "Hopefully we can bargain some magic out of her without ending up as bouillon cubes in her next meal."

"We don't have proof that she's a cannibal," I point out

diplomatically. "*I'm* a witch, after all, and my delicacy of choice is the nonpareil."

"Yes, but *you* don't live in a spooky cabin with invisible fire."

"You don't have to rub it in. I'd adore a spooky cabin with invisible fire."

He smiles warmly, and it sends tingles all over me. But then the happy feelings die when he says, "I think it's an illusion to scare people off. I'm going in."

"No!" I seize his shirt. "If it's not an illusion, you're going to fall into *that*." I gesture to the caved-in floor. "You could get seriously hurt. Even if I can pull you out, how am I gonna manage to carry you home?"

In a heartbeat, he is intimately close. His breath is a cold plume, his gaze urgent and filled all the way up with an emotion so visceral, it's as if I can feel whatever it is he's feeling.

Yearning.

"Risk for reward," he says evenly. "The Black Bear Witch has to give you magic if you find her lair, in exchange for making you forget where it is and that you ever found it."

"Only according to the legends," I remind him. "We don't know for sure if she'll give us anything. Or if she's real. Or if that's an illusion and not a pit that will kill you."

His muscles tighten with resolve.

"We're this close." His right hand strokes up my cheek, slipping into my hair. Both of our heads tilt, and the world goes soft and sparkling around me. "Maybe I'm wrong. But don't you want to find out?"

Find out is the everlasting flame that keeps me burning, of which he's well aware. The reason I search for the unexplained is so that I can then explain it, so that I can pin its wings in a shadow box and know what its name is.

My breathing flutters. Skips. "You're trying to seduce me again."

Morgan's gaze is serious, and it levels me. "No, Zelda. I *understand* you. You understand me, too, which is why it won't come as a surprise when I do this."

He walks over the threshold and disappears.

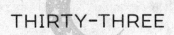

THIRTY-THREE

Open wide the witch's door
and burn with magic evermore.
But to gain, you must surrender
remembrance of the witch forever.

—Origin unknown
Local Legends and Superstitions,
Tempest Family Grimoire

I FALL THROUGH THE floor after him, ending up not in a pit but back outside again. "The house . . . ejected us?" I sputter, revolving in a circle. The door we entered is different now: the NOTHING TO SEE HERE has changed to LEAVING SO SOON? and the carved owl has altered, too, its wings lifted in flight. Morgan is staring straight ahead.

I follow his gaze.

The ground is scarcely visible under a thick layer of brilliant autumn leaves, and the still, golden air around us tastes of smoke and cider, mist twisting between the dark forks of red maples in full plumage. Across a dirt road is a sprinkling of very old buildings, medieval but perfectly preserved, as if we've just stepped back in time.

"Was all of this invisible to us before?" I say.

Morgan shakes his head slowly, indicating he has no idea, no room in his head to process what it is that we're seeing. Surely, this is the same forest we've been walking through all day. But just as surely, it is not. The shape of the trees, and the colors, are not the same. It is enhanced, like the art in a children's storybook; scarlet trees climb the sky like burning towers, their leaves reflecting a bright sunlight that can't be detected elsewhere. You'd think by looking at them that the sun must be high in the sky, but the coloring is more like evening. Soft and rosy.

He hitches Forte's sling higher on his shoulder. "What do we do?"

"We're explorers, aren't we? We explore."

We have found ourselves in a small village, and in the hub of this village there is a fountain with troughs for horses and linen-scrubbing, as well as a cluster of trade stalls. There are no people, but the stalls bear a great deal of fresh food: smoked meat, snow-white apples, figs, sweet potatoes, stews that are still steaming. A rich bounty of berries. Colorful vegetables.

I lean in to catch the aroma of blackberry pie, hot from the oven. "Who cooked all this? Seems like a bunch of people ought to be here, but there's nobody."

"Maybe the people are invisible," Morgan suggests.

Wooden arrows point down various trails called Elderberry Flood, Widow's Walk, and Bear's Bellow. Along this road are houses, a hat shop, a tavern half-timbered and studded with river stones. Hanging from the tavern's eaves is a sign shaped like an open book, with a curled-up purple dragon painted on. Beneath that, in tinfoil-silver lettering: THE DROWS-ING DRAGON. Its windows are ablaze with lamps.

As soon as Morgan pushes the door open, a crackling fire spurs to life in the hearth, flinging its comforting warmth across the room to greet us like a friend. There is so much to *see* that I'm overwhelmed and stand frozen for a few moments. Morgan, of course, starts springing about, touching everything he possibly can.

Herbs and dried flowers string the rafters like holiday garland, hanging squarely over a wooden table so rough-hewn that it's still got a couple tree branches sticking out. A mortar and pestle lie atop, as well as a carpetbag. The carpetbag's design is that of a mountainous forest sprinkled beneath a castle, yellow moon embroidered behind its tallest turret.

There's a spinning wheel along one wall, next to a woodbox heaped with rotten, fungus-covered logs. Bits of straw are scattered on the floor. I crane my neck to see up a staircase but don't dare climb it, because what if the stairs are magicked just like the spooky cabin was, and they lead me to a different place or time?

The Drowsing Dragon doesn't smell musty or neglected, but cheery and alive, lived-in, as if its occupants have stepped outside for a minute and plan to be right back.

"Stunning, spectacular, sensational," Morgan is raving, rooting through feathers, candlesticks, lumps of quartz, pouches containing items that whine or sob, a kettle that's heating itself up on the stove right this second without being asked. "Zelda, why aren't you moving? Hurry up and be nosy!"

"My brain is moving," I reply. "I'm giving it a head start before my legs join."

He laughs to himself, grinning wide. "It all looks so old! But new! Where *are* we?" He moves to examine the fireplace, which is perhaps the most extraordinary feature in the tavern. The hearth has been blasted a deep glittering purple from what I can only imagine must be years of exploding enchantments. Moss clings to the fireplace's stonework. A braid of vines as thick as my neck roots down the chimney and across the walls to bloom moonflowers like living art.

Slowly, I drag a finger over the lip of a copper cauldron in the fireplace. It's filled with water, reflecting not my own face but rather the image of a dilapidated black cabin—the same one we walked into minutes ago. Whoever peers into this cauldron can see the comings and goings around that cabin.

"Look at these." Morgan waves me over. Now that I've accepted my environment as real, and not a dream, my normal sensibilities come trickling back in and the whole world twinkles with *Find Out, Find Out.*

He's analyzing potions. By their milky coloration, I suspect most of them have soured. One cupboard consists entirely of fatal tonics. Two bowls sit under the table, one filled with pet kibble and one with water.

And then—

"Books!" My heart soars, and so do I, over to a bookshelf crammed with clothbound volumes. I eagerly begin flicking pages, all jam-packed with graceful handwriting. Spells for ridding gardens of pests and plant diseases. A dual-purpose charm that softens grief and chases away dogged sensations of bad tidings to come. The instructions are most confounding.

Use a bellows to summon a sail of wind. Add mourning bride and asphodel. Crush to a juice. Let drain through cheesecloth into a goblet of rice wine and give to a party of your choosing.

There are notes in the margins, words walled between question marks. A half-finished sketch for a possible fear-banishing draught takes up the last page, calling for *a simmer of snakeskin, ghoul-light, and the bones of a gray rabbit skinned in spring.* I snap the book closed, leaving it on the table, and start poking through an odd sort of mulch piled up on a shelf.

"Now, that's not very polite, is it?" somebody pipes up. "You of all people should know that when you're finished with a book, you put it back in its proper place."

I leap in fright, spilling the mulch into the cauldron, and there, occupying a chair at the table as if he's been there all this time—and perhaps he has been—is a young man.

"Hello, Zelda," he says amiably. "I see you've found Hither again."

THE MAN TAPS the glass of his pocket watch and a mug of tea appears next to his hand. It's hard to tell if he's in his twenties or thirties—he's got a youthful face and thick, rumpled brown hair, but his pale blue eyes wear the weight of the world.

"Hither?" Morgan repeats, as I say, "Again?"

"I created this village quite a long time ago. I call it Hither, and this will be the third time you've visited."

As if in a dream, I look down to see myself dragging over a stool, seating myself opposite—but I don't *feel* any of the physical matter I touch, as I am so out of my body. "I've never been here before."

He magicks up a second cup of tea and slides it across the tabletop. Morgan quickly sits down beside me. "Can I have a coffee?" he asks.

The man makes him another tea.

"You ran away when you were little," the man tells me, stretching out his legs. "Your grandmother was worried about you because you didn't have many friends or an easy way of social things. But I could smell the magic on you—a particularly wild magic, that, by nature, gave you a predisposition for going off on your own. I still can't tell exactly what your gift is, but obviously it's something to do with running around the woods."

"My gift is that I can see paranimals," I manage to reply, the words wobbly. "Enchanted creatures. Are they yours? Are you the Black Bear Witch?" I'm floored. "I thought the Black Bear Witch was a woman."

He smiles. "That isn't your gift from magic itself, that is your gift from *me*. It's been a while since I've been out in your world, in the way I used to be, but I've still got quite a lot of power left in me. When you were a little girl and found my village, you needed a bit of cheering up so I gave you the ability to see the true nature of my animals. But then you found me again, some time later, after one of our four-legged friends was struck down by a car."

"Katrina."

"Yes. I explained to you that my creatures cannot actually die, they merely turn into other creatures or dreams or spells—magic cannot be created or destroyed, only transformed, and all that—which made you feel better. But you wouldn't remember any of that now, naturally. I had to remove your memory of my home, and then I gave you another memory spritz to discourage you from coming back into the woods. Please forgive me. I had to make you afraid of exploring Falling Rock all by yourself. You were always wandering around here, and I worried you'd get hurt."

Morgan leans forward. "So you're the one who gave Zelda her powers?"

The man tilts his head, studying him. "She already had her own powers. What those are, only Zelda can tell us—but the ability to see my enchanted animals as they are and not how ordinary people perceive them; *that* part is a present from me."

"But *why* do you enchant the animals?" Morgan asks.

The man shrugs. "Why not? I like to experiment in my spare time, which I happen to have quite a lot of."

I'm still thinking about *She already had her own powers*, and what that means. What are my natural-born powers, then?

"The ability to hear brays," I say at once. "That's my real power."

"You can hear them?" The witch sets his cup down, blue eyes alight with interest. "That's extraordinary. What do they say?"

"A lot of nonsense."

Morgan is practically halfway across the table, so far is he leaning toward him. "Sir. You have no idea how grateful I would be if you'd give me a power, too."

"It doesn't work that way, I'm afraid."

Morgan's energy is palpable, a froth of fear, distress, hope. "But you gave some of your magic to Zelda. Couldn't you do that again? It doesn't need to be big. I'd be happy with elemental magic, or divination, alchemy, healing. Knotting. Waterbending. Whatever you've got on hand."

The witch cuts off his plea. "I'm sorry."

Morgan's hairline is slick with perspiration. He has to hold himself back from desperate begging, as it might put the witch off more. *"Please."*

I slide an arm around Morgan's shoulders. "Can't you give him *something*?" I ask. "We came all this way, looking for the Black Bear Witch. And that's you, right? You know how the legend goes: you find the lair, the witch gives you magic. Well. Morgan found the lair, so . . ."

The man shakes his head at him sadly. "It isn't your time."

Morgan badly wants to argue. I can see it. But he resists. "What does that mean?"

"It means that your time hasn't come yet."

"But it will? When?"

"If it does, you will find out then."

Morgan sinks a couple inches, not saying a word as he frustratedly combs over this, twiddling with the frayed stitches of the carpetbag.

"And this is not the lair," the man adds carefully, watching us. He folds his hands behind his head, reclining. "When the town was young, my lair was disguised as an ordinary stagecoach inn. The family inhabiting that building now is rather unusual, and I suspect it's because of all the magic I left behind."

I'm confused. "So this village isn't your lair?"

"No. It's an experiment I had to abandon, unfortunately." His mouth twists, wry. "I'd intended for it to be a ghost town in the literal sense. A place where ghosts could come and be corporeal again. Eat and drink and live satisfying lives. But it turns out that the magic in this place can only work for the person who created it, and the poor old ghosts who find their way in are still as invisible as ever."

He rises to his feet, draining the last of his tea. The man is tall and well-built, clothed in older fashions: a loose linen shirt with a dropped shoulder seam, twill trousers held up by leather suspenders. "Now. I'm very sorry to cut this short, but I have some business to attend to." He gives me an evaluating look, a small smile lifting his lips. "It feels nice that you believe in me again."

THIRTY-FOUR

After the third frost, if you see a pile of brightly
colored fallen leaves, step around them and
not over. It could be a goblin trap.

Legends and Superstitions, Expanded,
Tempest Family Grimoire

WHERE ARE WE going?" I ask as the man herds us out of The Drowsing Dragon and down the path into an evening that hasn't changed in spite of all the time we've passed. Surely it should be night by now, but the boxwood bushes along Hither's paths still twinkle golden like lucky coins.

He whistles under his breath, strolling briskly along. "To Whence."

"What's Whence?" Hither and Whence. I like the sound when I roll them up together: *hitherandwhence*.

"It's where you came from." He checks his pocket watch, a soft wave of his hair slipping wayward over his forehead. "I'll head there soon, too, but I've got a nice potion on the boil here, and it'll misbehave if I'm not watching."

"Wait. You're kicking us out?"

"That's right."

Morgan and I put up a fight, babbling over each other. "But we just got here! You're not going to scrub our memories, are you? Since we're technically not at your lair?"

The witch sighs. "Morgan, you're an amiable gentleman, but I know about your podcast. I know you write for the newspaper. You enjoy talking too much, and I can't take any chances; I need to protect this space from prying eyes."

Morgan clutches the man's arm. "You know about my podcast? Do you like it? Which episode's your favorite?" I elbow him before he can ask if the witch subscribes to his Patreon. "We won't tell anybody, we swear. I won't post about this online, I won't write about it. You can trust me."

"I truly am regretful that this is how it must go."

"Oh come on!" I beseech. "What's the harm in us knowing? I'm a witch, too, I'm not gonna betray you. And I still have so many questions. How long have you been the Black Bear Witch? Are you ancient, or does the role pass from generation to generation? And *why* are you called that? Do you turn into a black bear? What other magic can you do?"

"There is no point to answering any of that," he replies. "You'll just forget, anyway."

"I will pay you four hundred dollars to let us remember this," Morgan says. "Maybe more, if I can get a loan."

The witch laughs. It's a gentle, good-humored sound.

Morgan tries again. "I'll give you my car."

"I have no use for a car."

I drag my feet. "How did you get so powerful? Tell us *that*, at least, before you make us go."

And he does.

"As a witch, the older you get, the more of your life you've given to doing what magic wants, and therefore, the more reward magic gives back to you. One day when you are as old as I am, if you hold tight to your magic and don't let it escape you, you'll have riches of your own." He spreads his fingers in the air, as if feeling for a change of winds, and the frame of a door appears beneath his touch. The rest of a dilapidated cabin paints itself into existence around it.

The carved owl is still taking flight. LEAVING SO SOON?

No! There's too much left that I want to find out! "But my grandmother was a witch, she grew old, and she didn't have the power to build anything like this." I gesture to the village. "What did magic give to her?"

"Isn't it obvious?" The man looks at me sidelong, hands clasped behind him. "Magic gave Dottie *you*. Luna. Romina."

Morgan's mouth slumps into a half frown. "How do you know about Zelda's family?"

The man opens the door. "Be watchful where you walk in there," he advises us. "It's dark now, and full of life. I've just let loose a raccoon that transforms into a cloud of yellowjackets whenever it smells pears, and a melanistic red fox that nests on rooftops." He interrupts our monsoon of follow-up questions with a curt shake of the head. "No, no, got to keep on moving. It's time for you to be leaving now."

Morgan and I face each other in a cold panic as the witch presses his hands to the backs of our necks. My body flashes cold. "We're going to lose this," Morgan says in despair. "We won't remember."

"Let him remember," I entreat the witch. "Take it from me, but let him keep this."

The man prods us over the threshold. "You knew how it would end when you started out."

The forest is feral here, overgrown with wide, flabby mushrooms, split trees, and blinking yellow eyes crouched in the undergrowth. "Must be about to storm," I surmise, tipping my head back. "The sky got black awful fast." My feet ache from walking all day, my muscles are sore from carting luggage, and my eyes beg for sleep. Where did the brays go? Can they see us? Are they following?

"You smell something burning?" Morgan asks.

I sniff. "A conflagrinal?"

We check out our surroundings, but it's too dark to make out any smoke.

"Something's wrong with my phone," Morgan murmurs. "Says the time is ten fifteen."

"We should set up camp," I say. "It's too dark, there's no way we're finding the Black Bear Witch tonight."

"Where'd we leave our stuff? I don't remember setting it down."

We shine flashlights through the woods, beams of light revealing a heavy fall of mist. My light crosses with his, landing on our suitcases forty paces away.

"Here, you hold Forte, and I'll grab it all." Morgan lifts the sling from around his neck, handing the gingersnappus over to me.

"Okay, but *hurry.*"

I'm ashamed to admit that the instant he leaves my side, I start to get nervous. And a bit sick? Almost as if he has become a necessity, and I can't function correctly when he isn't within touching distance. Which is ludicrous.

I am all alone.

I love being all alone.

Except maybe not *all* the time anymore. I am failing my own hermit-detached-from-civilization fantasies. I miss my sisters dearly, even though I know that as soon as I get back home, I will hang out with them for all of thirty minutes before I've drained my battery and need to recharge in the attic. I like being able to hear them through the floor, chattering, playing music, being rowdy with each other. I join in now and then, but I don't feel the need to be *right there* all the time. I simply like having my people close.

I pull out my phone, suddenly anxious to talk to Luna and Romina, but I have no signal.

"Thunderation," I mutter, replacing it in my pocket.

There's a small pond close by and I'm running low on water, so I take the opportunity to refill my bottle. The air's chilly, so I expect the temperature of the water to be punishing, but my fingers dip through what feels like bathwater.

"Oooh."

I submerge my arm up to the elbow. It feels so nice that when I draw my arm back out, the air feels too cold. This must be a hot spring. I had no idea there were any hot springs in Falling Rock.

I stare at the clear indigo water, night a thick cloak around my shoulders, thinking about how fresh I must smell after a full day of hiking. I've accounted for every requirement on this trip except for bathing.

Not that my level of freshness matters just because *he's* here. Morgan is safely outside the parameters of my romantic ideal now that I have officially shut down my attraction to him, so it isn't that I'm particularly self-conscious, or care to impress him. This is purely courtesy.

Once Morgan has returned and we've set up camp again, I casually let him know my plans.

"I'm going to take off all my clothes now, so if you wouldn't mind turning around . . ." I should note here that as I say this, I am facing the spring, and it takes me a beat to realize that Morgan has been facing the tent, so it appears as if I've asked him explicitly to turn and watch me strip.

"Uh," he says.

"Actually, I'll get the soap first." I slip past him to rummage through my bags, producing a clean set of clothes. I didn't bring a towel, another failure of forethought. "Is soap harmful to the ecosystem of a hot spring? Stupid question. Yes, it is. Never mind."

Morgan dithers at the mouth of the tent. "Um."

I sail right back out, sans soap. "That's all right. I'll freshen up with dry shampoo once I'm done."

"Er."

When Morgan doesn't turn away, standing there bewildered as if he suspects I might be laying a moral trap, I swirl a finger to indicate that he needs to move. It breaks his trance.

"Zelda, it's the last day of September. That water is going to be, like, twenty degrees."

"It's a hot spring."

He eyes it with new interest. "Really?"

"Yes, and I've been hiking all day. I'm a mess."

"Hm." He steps forward, hands behind his back. "*Hmm.*"

I arch a brow.

Morgan takes another forward step. "It's just. *I've* been hiking all day, too, and if my back's turned the whole time you're in the hot spring, how am I going to protect you?"

"Protect me from what?"

"Bears. Witches. Bear-witch hybrids. Aquatic paranimals."

I hadn't considered aquatic paranimals, which I do not think could survive in geothermally heated water, but then again, until recently I did not know about the existence of birds with wings made of smoke. "I'd hate to be eaten by a hot-spring shark that looks like a minnow just because your back is turned—"

He's already yanking off his shoes. "Exactly. I need to watch you. Watch *over* you, I mean."

"Hold on! Let me go first. And cover your eyes."

Morgan slaps his hands over his face so fast that I can hear it. "Ouch," he mutters.

I have to stifle a laugh. "*Turn around.*"

He obeys.

I shuck my clothing, wad up my bra and underwear inside my jacket, and jump in gracelessly, underestimating the depth of the spring when water shoots up my nose. "Bagh!"

Morgan whirls. "What's wrong?"

"Turn around!" I repeat in a yell, even though from the neck down I'm concealed by water that, I hope, contains lots of beneficial mineral content and no deadly bacteria. But I'm not fully confident he won't be able to see any skin, or the illusion of skin, or even a vaguely human shape.

"Sorry!" he yells back. "I didn't see anything, I swear."

"Okay, I'm fine now. Ready." I keep watching him until he crosses his arms over his chest, waiting, and I remember myself. "Right. Turning. Shutting my eyes."

Splash!

The spring has shrunk. With the two of us occupying limited space, it's very much like a Jacuzzi. An intimate Jacuzzi in the forest, in the dark. I am suddenly overcome with the need to know whether he's fully naked like I am, or if he's got underwear on. I will not dip my gaze below the surface to see if I can tell. And he had better be keeping his eyes on my face. Above my face, even. He should be skygazing.

Morgan is not skygazing. His eyes rest on my face, so he knows when my attention roves over the tattooed constellations that grip his upper arms. His silky hair gleams at the crest of every wave and his skin glows like a pearl. Lips dark and full. The shapes of his eyebrows sharpen when wet. I reflect again on my romantic ideal; it is a very, *very* good thing that this man is not a danger to me.

We're at the edge of October, which means there are three months left in this calendar year for me to—according to prophecy—find my True Love.

When I imagine this person I have yet to meet, I think of

the peace and serenity he'll exude. He will be honest. He will be sincere. He'll clearly communicate his feelings, he will always say what he means (and what he means will always be sensible). Eventually we'll buy a duplex together. I'll have my space, he'll have his, and we can pop in for visits via a connecting doorway. (When I mentioned this vision to my sisters recently, Romina was unsurprisingly aghast. She would crawl under her boyfriend's shirt and live there, if she could.)

My relationship with True Love will be poetry.

"Do you think animals ever get songs stuck in their heads?" Morgan asks.

"What?"

He grins, sliding a step closer. "Just trying to throw you off. You look like you're thinking hard about something, and *I* think it'd be a great idea if we didn't think at all."

"That is such a *you* thing to say."

I couldn't possibly entangle myself with somebody like Morgan. I am a woman of evidence and reason, and all evidence points to him being the worst possible match for me.

He's a boisterous, unpredictable extrovert who makes the wrong recommendations to customers at the shop, recommending the DESPERATE MEASURES candle to anyone and everyone regardless of their needs, disturbing me while I'm trying to work, leaving his half-finished coffee on my stool, rearranging books in the Cavern by color, spinning his chair to hear it squeak, starting a sentence with "Guess what?" and ending it with some outlandish claim. And that isn't even the half of it!

Sawing the violin badly on purpose. Pretending to like me just because he wanted magic powers. Taking notes on coralotes and tabbing them, and the way he looks at me as if I hold all the answers to his questions in my mouth—he looks at my mouth *entirely* too much—and he doesn't mind when I'm not on time because he understands how my brain works. He encourages me to experiment, to live a little, to mix the FOR WEDNESDAYS potion with the FOR SATURDAYS one and find out what sort of disaster it might bring. He rolls my suitcase through the forest and, on Aisling's birthday, helps her to feel like a fairy queen. Wears a monster in a baby sling. Says *I'm only good at this when it doesn't mean anything.*

It is confirmed, then. Morgan does not pose any danger to my heart at all.

He takes a step forward, and I take a step back, swallowing. Tha-*thump*, tha-*thump*, tha-*thump*. My safe-as-houses heart beats in triple time.

"You're staring at me," I manage to say. He doesn't laugh at the quiver in my voice.

He holds my stare until the act feels brutal, until my skin flames and his eyes go dark, dark, dark, and my vision can't make out anything other than him. "I'm always staring at you," he replies.

"It's different now." I can barely hear myself. "Normally, I'm wearing clothes."

"Not in here." He taps his temple, his mouth curving. "I like to imagine you and me making use of that armchair in the Cavern of Paperback Gems. And the only things that cover you are my hands."

I become a dragon, heat lighting me up inside. The response

is involuntary; I think all he'd have to do is touch me in one particularly sensitive spot, and I'd lose myself here and now.

Morgan spreads his arms as he revolves in a half circle, head tipping all the way back until his Adam's apple is a prominent lump in his throat. Air is scarce as I visually trace the sharp line of his jaw, the shape of his arms, his fingers, resting on the surface of the water like katydids.

Still turned in profile, he drops his gaze to my face and that smile becomes serpentine. "You look like you want something."

I try to summon passages from books, but the door to my inner world has shut itself. A sign hangs from it that reads NOT IN USE. COME BACK LATER. I am trapped most wretchedly in the present.

"I want to kiss you," I tell him. My pulse is now painful. "And more. I want everything."

"Take it," he demands roughly, his body knifing through the water as he brings himself to me.

I want to savor this.

All the world shimmers as I raise my hands, slowly, to cradle either side of his face. He closes his eyes at the contact, shuddering out a breath. Then Morgan lowers his head, and we simply stand like this for a small eternity, breathing and feeling, mouths tantalizingly close but not yet touching.

His focus rocks from my eyes to my mouth. As if he can no longer resist, our lips meet at last.

First, soft.

Then, the sweetest burn.

It is such deep pleasure, the rasp of his stubble. The flick of his tongue across the seam of my lips, bidding me to open up. And I do. I had thought, in the moments when I allowed myself to dream of this, that it would be bright colors, frenzy, like the man himself. But his touch is restrained, contemplating each deliberate action before his fingertips skim my shoulders, settle in my hair; as if *he's* dreamed that this moment would be quiet and composed, like me.

So I tilt my head, moving into his body with more pressure, more heat, less inhibition—to make our moment a perfect synthesis of us both.

He guides my touch down his throat, to his chest, to his arms, wanting me everywhere.

"I love these," I confess, tracing the tattoos on his left biceps. "What made you want the stars?"

He watches me explore his body, his eyes feverish. "Stars were the prettiest things I'd seen, at the time that I got them put on me." Morgan leans in again, catches my lower lip delicately between his teeth. Lets go, and drops kisses to the corner of my mouth, the pulsing spot at the hinge of my jaw, the hollow of my clavicle. "That's changed."

I pull him to me, and kiss him harder.

Water rolls from the top of his head off the tip of his nose. It forms jewels at the ends of his hair. They collect on the swells of my breasts, snaking down between them into the black pool. His eyes track the journey, transparent with hunger. I can see the slip and swirl of water reflected in them.

He is magnetic and effortlessly eye-drawing and impossible not to become obsessed with. How did I let this happen? I know better.

"You can take more, if you want it," I murmur into his ear.

"If I want it," he repeats thickly. "You have no idea. You *are* the word *want*. You in this pool, for the rest of my life. That's what I'll think of any time I hear the word *want*."

Morgan's warm body shifts to press against me from behind, and a little moan escapes my lips. I let my head roll back to rest against his chest, and a pair of hands skate down my ribs. I know so much better, and yet I don't care.

A knuckle brushes between my legs. And again. Barely there, just a flutter. I can feel his hard length against my backside and I want so badly to touch him but he pins my hands against my stomach and doesn't let me.

"Please," I say.

Morgan's laugh is soft and wicked, murmuring into my skin. And then his ministrations halt. I stiffen, opening my eyes. Something must have caught his attention.

But then he says, in a rough scrape, "You believe me now, don't you?"

"Believe what?"

His mouth presses a kiss to my spine, between my shoulder blades, and he lets go of a little sigh that I feel in my inner ears, between each rib, the back of my throat.

"Look at what I've gone and done, making myself my own biggest obstacle," he mutters bitterly, then resumes what he was doing previously with a dedication that can only be described as worshipful. I melt against him, boneless . . .

And he stops again.

I'm going to come out of my skin. "*Morgan*."

"Shhh."

His arms encircle my body in a protective way. A way that makes my muscles seize and my heart flip for entirely different reasons. I blink the film of lust from my eyes. "What's wrong?"

Morgan brings his lips to my ear. "I heard something."

I open my mouth to respond but fall still when there's a light crunch in the grasses not far from where we stand, vulnerable and naked in the water.

Something moving, disturbing twigs with their weight. Or a some*one*. Watching us. I try to think which would be worse, a beast or a human.

Heavy green ferns part, the massive head of a tiger emerging. It slinks toward us, five hundred pounds of stealth and teeth and speed, ocher eyes narrowing, trained on mine. I think I can hear it purr as it assesses what a satisfying meal we'll make.

Morgan sucks in a sharp breath, whispers, "Any chance that looks like a unicorn to you?"

THIRTY-FIVE

Sleep under the dog star and dream a wish to life.

Local Legends and Superstitions,
Tempest Family Grimoire

BEAST. BEAST IS worse.

"I see a tiger," I whisper.

Strong hands grip my waist. "So do I."

Whenever I think of the word *panic*, I conjure up lurid colors and high, pounding volume. Bodies running, shouting, pandemonium, confusion. A blur.

This panic is silent. Falling Rock is calm, my vision crystalclear. I have absolutely no idea what to do, the reality unfolding around us so surreal that I cannot think beyond fear. We must be hallucinating. There cannot be a *tiger* in the woods.

Morgan slides his body in front of mine, shielding me. This is a terrible time to be distracted by the ram tattooed on his back, outlined in deep blue dots. He has got a truly magnificent back.

Out of all the ways we could die in this forest, being shredded by a tiger before I've gotten the chance to appreciate all that Morgan's body has to offer has got to be the most unpleasant. "I feel like I'm underdressed for this."

"Shhh," he murmurs.

"I'm so sorry this is happening while we're naked in a pond. It's my fault."

"*Shhh.*"

We've switched bodies. It's the only explanation for why I cannot keep my mouth shut. "God, I love looking at you with your clothes off."

"I appreciate that," he whispers, "and I promise to give you as many opportunities as you want in the future, but please make like a tree and shut up."

"That's not the phrase."

"Trees are very quiet."

The tiger, listening to us hiss at each other, loses interest and prowls around the spring, nosing up to the tent. Morgan tenses, and I know he's thinking of Forte curled up inside, snoozing in his salt circle. But the tiger keeps walking, eventually flopping down on a patch of leaves not far from where we stand.

And it doesn't get back up.

I can't calculate how much time passes before I finally venture: "Is it . . . asleep?"

"I think so." Morgan brings his hands close to his face, and I can guess that he's analyzing how wrinkled his fingers have become. "Staying in hot water for too long is bad for you."

"Being eaten is also bad for you. I'm not getting out."

He laces a hand through mine. "We have to."

I take a deep breath. "Okay. Okay. Oh my god. Okay."

"Here's what we're going to do. I will slowly climb out, get dressed, and then I'm gonna put your clothes over there." He points to a bush on the edge of the spring that's farthest away from the tiger. "Okay? Zelda, we are going to be all right."

"You cannot possibly know that."

He levels me with a fierce look. "If anything happens to me, I want you to run."

A lump rises in my throat. "Don't say that. I'd never leave you behind."

"Remember me as a hero. Tell everyone of my sacrifice. For the statue, I'm thinking bronze, erected in the town square where the trolley is. Tell the statue artist that I want to be portrayed with my hands kind of prying the tiger's jaws open, like this—" He begins to demonstrate his stance with an invisible foe, and while he's busy doing that, I go ahead and roll out of the spring, onto dry land.

Without the buoyancy of the water holding me up, my muscles feel weak from being exposed to warm temperatures for too long. My first few strides are trembly.

The only positive to having my body feel so odd is that it distracts me from the tiger, who is difficult to monitor from this angle. I hurriedly cram myself into jeans and a sweater, tossing Morgan's clothes to him.

"I didn't look," he assures me once he's dressed, moving quickly to my side. He coaxes Forte into his sling and drapes it around his chest.

I'm jostling my backpack on. "Huh?"

"When you were getting out. I didn't look. Okay, I looked a *little*. But I couldn't see much."

I check the tiger, who's lifted its head. It isn't facing us right now, but it's definitely listening, ears pricked, tail thumping.

"Okay, I saw your ass," Morgan confesses. "I saw your ass, and it was spectacular."

"Is this the best time to have a conversation about my ass?"

"You're right. I'll need to set aside half an hour for that conversation, at minimum."

I move to climb into the tent and grab my rolling suitcases, but my brain presses *stop*, shuts my eyes, and inwardly turns me around into another time and place.

I am here in this forest with Morgan, but I am also in Treasure Cove, Virginia, in my old camper van. I am facing my laptop, open to a nearly finished draft of *The Bone Flute*. I am about to paste in a pretty line I've had waiting in the wings since the beginning, saving it for the perfect moment. But when I do, the words don't fit exactly right. The course of the story has changed, and that line doesn't make sense anymore.

The scene dissolves, snapping me back into my body. Morgan is grasping my shoulder, repeating my name.

I tug us backward. Farther and farther, until my magic relaxes. I can feel it shuddering. A *yes, that's better*.

"What are you doing?" Morgan asks. "What about the rest of our stuff?"

I scramble for a sensible explanation. How do I verbalize what I just experienced? "We need to move away," I tell him. "I . . . I honestly don't know why."

Morgan shrugs. "Okay." A smile of camaraderie touches the corners of his mouth. Just as our tent is trampled by a—

No, impossible.

Definitely not.

Except, yes.

An *elephant*.

The tiger bolts and the elephant (!!!!) screams and so do we, tearing out of there with nothing but our backpacks, Forte, and a lantern, leaving the rolling suitcases and tent behind.

"Elephant?" Morgan yells, checking behind him to see if we're being pursued.

"Elephant!" I confirm.

"What is happening?" His arms shoot up in the air. "What is *happening*? I love it! We're probably going to die. But wow, having so much fun, though! Loving this! Brilliant!"

We run, breathing hard with the excess weight on our backs, still wobbly from the hot spring. It would be wisest to hide in the darker parts of the forest, probably, but it's night and we can't see a damned thing, so Morgan and I have no choice but to run along moonlit trails. There is no way we can outrun that tiger if it decides to give chase. If it does, our bodies will never be found, and when we return home Aisling will be the only one who can see us.

"Our stuff," I lament. "What are we going to do without a tent?"

"Remember what I said about my willingness to cover you with my hands? *I'll* be your tent, my queen."

Laughing hurts. "Stop. My poor ribs." I clutch at my side.

"But I also want to be your sleeping bag, so that I'm lying under you as well. The only solution is to clone myself."

I laugh again, and my ribs protest some more. "You're going to make me cry."

Then I remember all the books I've packed, surely destroyed—some of them belonging to the library—and shed physical tears. *The Mystery of the Exploding Teeth and Other Curiosities from the History of Medicine. The Royal Art of*

Poison: Filthy Palaces, Fatal Cosmetics, Deadly Medicine, and Murder Most Foul. Those poor pages! The staff at Moonville Library have already had it up to here with me—I'm going to get a ban.

On and on we run, in the direction of who knows what, propelled by adrenaline. "Are we going to discuss the fact that there's a tiger and an elephant loose in Moonville?" I mention when we finally stop for breath, panting.

His eyes shine. "I *knew* it. All those stories! There had to be some truth to them."

I'd honestly forgotten the stories. They say that a hundred years ago, a circus train crashed in these woods and a few exotic animals escaped. Now and then, hikers claim to have spotted a cheetah or a monkey, but nobody ever believes them because the photographic evidence is . . . shall we say, unconvincing. I certainly thought it was hogwash. You're telling me that you carry a phone in your pocket programmed with the capabilities of an expensive camera, and all you managed to capture of a cheetah is a grainy colorless streak in the distance? Pah. If it was real, it could be proven!

"Nobody's ever gonna believe us," I say, incredulous and exhilarated.

"Not in a million years."

We grin at each other, and I wonder why this feels like such a good thing—Morgan and I believing in something that others don't. Is this how my sisters have felt all along, believing in magic while others scoff from the sidelines? It's like buried treasure. The only ones who are able to appreciate it are those who've discovered it for themselves.

Our legs are tired of walking, but we have to find shelter. We have no cell reception, no tent, and not much food. "All right," I declare, relaxing my muscles. "Show us where to go, magic."

Morgan holds my hand as I'm guided by feelings, a supernatural version of the "you're getting warmer, you're getting colder" children's game.

This way.

Magic shows me the effect of font—how the same sentence can settle differently when set in Garamond versus Times New Roman.

And now that way.

It stirs the smell of old books, organic compounds in the paper breaking down to release faint fragrances of vanilla, almond, and coffee.

Yes, you're going in the right direction now.

Old English words that have fallen out of fashion, antiquated idioms that tickle my brain most pleasingly. Discovering a mysterious book at a flea market that I can't find any information about on the Internet, as if it appeared from nowhere.

Favored words and phrases. *Decanter, night fever, shiny laugh, patina, put the kettle on, quicksilver, tooth in the brain.* I levitate my mental keyboard, typing a few of them out. Each letter floats into the air. I follow the ink so closely that my senses strengthen with each one, until I know intrinsically where to turn in order to continue collecting them.

Emulsion. Emollient. Austere. Alacrity.

Misreading a sentence while editing, and finding I like it better the way it wasn't.

"Slow down," Morgan says with a laugh. (A *shiny* laugh! Ah, there it is!) "What are you going so fast for?"

"I want to catch up." I know that what I've said doesn't make sense to anybody but me. I pull him along, our steps never faltering, never tripping over a root or a plant. Emotions fly swifter and swifter, whirling about me in a warm, wonderful wind, and I let it rush all over.

What do you love about writing? magic asks. Then it shows me the answers.

Popping down research rabbit holes. The aha moment when I find exactly the right term I've been hunting for. How joy can swell a paragraph bigger and bigger until your heart bursts, and tension cinches it tight like an emotional corset. I love rewriting, comparing material to older drafts to see how far it's evolved. Grafting stronger prose over frail areas, stitching it all together with transitions. I love the immortality of storytelling, how my daydreams will outlast me, how in a way I'll exist forever as long as my stories sit on somebody's shelf or in a digital file.

I love how certain songs are irreversibly connected to scenes I've written. Figuring out, with my agent and editor, how to make a scene stronger. Rewriting, deleting, sacrificing to the pacing gods, then taking back my offering because no, I want that in there, I will be indulgent. What a miracle language is. Letter by letter, word by word, sentence by sentence, paragraph by paragraph, page by page, chapter by chapter, all of it culminating in this stressful, exhausting, satisfying, rewarding outlet for all of the noise that collects in my head. It's how I process my own philosophies, grief, desires. A hybrid of pure imagination and diary.

When I break down what writing truly is, it sounds almost magic. Minuscule, tedious squiggles of printer toner, lined up in soldier rows. You stare at the squiggles and forget where you are. They make you fall in love with people who don't exist, they make you livid, they bring you to tears. They disappoint you, make your pulse sprint, make you swear you'll never try that genre again. Change your life. Synchronize your emotions with those of hundreds of other readers spread across space and time, absorbing the very same words, but who will view them through the lenses of their own unique experiences—so that, in a way, nobody reads exactly the same book, and each variation is different still from the original, the one the author created.

Some stories you forget about as soon as you finish the last page, and some you carry in your soul forever, like an imaginary friend you understand so well, it doesn't matter that others can't see them. It doesn't matter that they live only in you.

I think of every time a reader has reached out in a letter to say *It feels like you wrote this specifically for me.*

Something snaps beneath my footfalls, and I kneel to examine a chain of words. *Once upon a time, nobody went into the forest and came out of it alive.*

I feel like I'm awakening slowly, sunbathing in the fringes of a dream. Magic releases my nerve endings one by one, letting me drift fully back into my body. The vivid reminiscences fade to ghosts but don't leave me. They linger.

"Where *are* we?" Morgan is marveling. There's astonishment in his voice. More words break apart under my feet. They're everywhere, fragments scattered among the trees like fallen leaves:

> *The Clock of*
> *   Old and New*
> *was always talking*

There's a soft smile on my face. Tears in my eyes. I've been running with them closed, and now we've stopped.

"At the source," I say, not fully understanding why until I open my eyes again.

THIRTY-SIX

Ghostgill: A creature that looks half ghost, half
mushroom. Shaped almost like a tiny figure pretending
to be a ghost, with a sheet over its head. Eleven inches
tall. Body is white, with lots of folds, like the gills
on the underside of a fly agaric mushroom. They live in
creeks and would pass for plants were it not for
the way they walk, slowly, like starfish.

Paranimals, *A through M*,
Tempest Family Grimoire

W E HAVE FOUND ourselves in an ancient city of
trees so towering that Morgan and I, from the
bottom, can't see how high it goes. Birds trill,
their music filtering down in ethereal echoes. The air is cool
and clammy, mist soaking our ankles.

There is a tall lamp growing out of the soil, with a post of
braided iron. Its gentle light spills onto the mossy floor below,
the night and dense foliage diffusing it to an emerald green.

"Hey, they've got electricity out here!" Morgan raps the
lamppost. "Or . . . hmm. It must be solar-powered."

"That's strange. I didn't put a lamp here."

Morgan peers at me. "Why would you have?"

Black shapes rising to chest level are slow to appear, given the lack of illumination. They're shelves. Square plastic milk crates, rectangular wooden crates, and cardboard boxes have been stacked together in a vertical triangle, like a Christmas tree. They've been carefully decorated with books, and a memory falls into my thoughts like a shooting star into the sea.

The Traveler's Library.

That's what I'd called it.

When I was small, slipping into the woods to build my hideaway. I didn't have quite enough space to be myself at home, and I'd felt like The Magick Happens was Luna's haven more than mine, a special place for her and Grandma Dottie to be an inseparable pair. There wasn't anywhere that I belonged. So I made my own haven out here, one book at a time. I'd stacked my unfinished stories between those by authors I admired: Zilpha Keatley Snyder and Vivian Vande Velde.

Morgan slides a composition notebook off a shelf—the type with black splotches all over a white cover. It's titled *Phantasmagoria* in handwriting that was honestly much neater when I was ten years old than it is now, and beneath that: *by Zelda Margaret Tempest.*

I drape my braid over one shoulder, twisting the ends. "I can't believe I forgot about all this."

Morgan flips through the book. It's barely three chapters long, because in those days I got bored quickly and was too impatient, continually starting over, starting over. Any time I scraped enough quarters together, I was down at the dollar store buying notebooks.

The Clock of Old and New was always talking about how she used to be human, and had butter-yellow hair. That was before the sorceress stuffed her inside a clock.

There was a secret princess inside this clock. She had wooden hair and her arms and legs were wooden, too. One leaf grew from her left knee. If Fortuna could only find the key, she could free the princess.

"This is what I've been hearing," I whisper. "It's . . ." Morgan's eyes are terribly bright as they rest on me. "You." Not brays. Stories. I've been hearing stories—some I wrote long, long ago, and others, I suspect, must be glimpses of stories I still have waiting inside me: books and books and books yet to come.

"Does magic want you to finish what you started?" Morgan speculates, sifting through dozens of notebooks. "Look at this."

Once upon a time, nobody went into the forest and came out of it alive. A little boy named Theodore lived by himself in a cottage at the edge of it, and he could hear dangerous monsters lurking. His father had been dragged away by wolves made of water, who charged out of the sea every full moon.

"Reminds me of waravers," he notes. "Creatures made of water, living by moonlight."

"Waravers, werewolves. Similar sound. That has to be where I took the idea."

Many of my stories borrowed characters from each other, recycling favorite titles. I've got a "Tale of Elixir" about an actual drinkable elixir and a "Tale of Elixir" about a prince *named* Elixir. What an adventure, to tumble through words however I wanted, rolling down hills of them, the story growing bigger and wilder around me like a snowball that picks up more of the world as it goes. "Baby Zelda was quite a prolific writer," he says.

"Easy to write fast when you don't have to care about spelling. Or plot. Or an ending." I grin at him, which he mirrors. "I don't think I actually completed a manuscript until I was a teenager, and it couldn't have been longer than twenty thousand words. I burned it a week later because I'd named one of the characters after a guy I had a crush on and couldn't risk anyone finding out."

"I didn't start writing until I was maybe twenty-two or twenty-three," Morgan tells me. "I started with online reviews, just for fun. These long, stupid think pieces about pizza cutters or whatever I'd ordered. It turned into fiction exercises—like, I'd say that a shower cap I bought made me have dreams about *The Sopranos* every night, or I'd complain that my bicycle arrived without a built-in toaster, as if that was the standard. Some of my posts got taken down for not being verified purchases."

"Of *course* that would be your journalism origin story," I say, doubling over. Morgan blushes with pleasure to have made me laugh. "You troll."

"Those reviews weren't a total waste of time, turns out. I printed a few to show the *Moonville Tribune* when I applied, and they liked them." He tilts his head. "To be fair, they had no choice but to hire me because they were understaffed and desperate, but still!"

"And now you're the entire newspaper," I say simply.

There's no disguising the admiration in my voice, and Morgan stands two inches taller. He straightens an invisible bow tie. "And now I'm the entire newspaper. Speaking of which, if you're ever looking for a side gig, you should write serialized short stories for the *Moonville Tribune*. We don't have the budget to pay you much, but it could be fun."

"I'll keep that in mind." I spy a familiar spine on the shelf, this one of a published book. "*The Magnificent Mummy Maker!* I *loved* this one. I forced Luna to read it, too. Then Luna forced me to read that." I point out *The Forestwife* by Theresa Tomlinson. "We still trade book recommendations."

"Add me to that group chat, please." He thumbs through *The Time-Travelling Cat*. "I think I read this when I was in elementary school."

"Ooooh, yes, me, too." I scan the cover and am instantly transported to second grade, curled up on a beanbag in Mrs. Kipley's classroom. Reading for Pizza Hut's BOOK IT! program. I can still taste the personal pan pizza.

We study copyright pages to discern how old some of these are, impressed by the condition we've found them in.

"How aren't they moldy?" I exclaim. "The pages aren't warped, the paper doesn't feel funky." I bring a book to my nose. "Doesn't smell funky, either."

"While we're on the topic, *how* did you carry all this out here and not get lost? I can't hear any cars, so there's no way we're close to town."

"I'd fill up my backpack. I really couldn't tell you how I didn't get lost. The way I remember it, the trail here used to be straightforward, easy to access." I didn't only bring books. I nicked trinkets from home and the shop to decorate my library with: flattened souvenir pennies, a locket necklace, one of Grandma's hats, buttons, beads, keys, and lenticular stickers with images that change when tilted. A blanket, too, that's stiff as plastic and partially disintegrated now. All of it is dirty and decomposing.

But the books . . .

The books are impeccably preserved.

"I'm sorry, but this is precious." Morgan braces himself for my wrath. "Papaya, you're adorable. I know you don't want to be. I know you think you're a sentient knife. But this is the cutest thing I have seen, ever."

I grumble, secretly pleased. "Young Zelda would have been happy to know I'm visiting as an adult who has real published books on real shelves." My chest tightens as I open another notebook, titled *The Zany Adventures of Zoey Werewolf.* "She dreamed of seeing our name in this library someday."

Morgan brightens. "Young Zelda is about to watch her dreams become realized."

"Oh?" I pitch forward, curious, as he unzips his bag. Removes a paperback copy of *The Heartbreak Vampire.*

I stare at it. My name on the spine.

Zelda Tempest next to *R. L. Stine.* The child in me jumps up and down. She runs and twirls, arms outspread. She can't believe we've done it, we've *made* it, and even if I never publish another book again, I'll always have achieved this.

"Now these are what I consider the classics," Morgan tells Forte as he exhumes Goosebumps books. *"The Ghost Next Door. Ghost Beach. Say Cheese and Die!* I inhaled these sorts of books. No wonder I turned out like this."

Morgan and I rest against the Traveler's Library. He audibly wonders who put the lamp here if I didn't, and how the books are still in such good condition. Then he reads *Ghost Beach* aloud to me until he can't keep his eyes open anymore, nodding off.

When I return *Ghost Beach* to the shelf, I slide off *The Heartbreak Vampire*. It is the most unnerving déjà vu, to be back here again, standing right at the brink of a story. Preparing to tumble in.

I make myself comfortable at the foot of the lamppost, taking in the cover of my book anew, flushed green in a magical glow. How many other humans all over the world have held this in their hands, looking at this same cover?

I turn the pages. Title, dedication.

This one's for Dottie, who taught me about magic.

And I begin to read.

The wood is sweet with rot tonight, and as Henriette draws her breath from it, every living thing falls still.

I can't stop reading. Chapter one bleeds into chapter two, into chapter three. I thought I would hate it, have avoided revisiting it for fear I'd find imperfections. And there *are* imperfections. If I could have another crack at edits, surely I'd find plenty to change. But I can't really care about any of that, because all I notice is how much fun I was having here in these pages. My love for storytelling radiates from them.

Henriette has a dimple in her cheek just below her left eye, like I do. She wears green boater shoes to work, and a silver mask when she's fighting monsters. She is softhearted like Romina, but direct like Luna, and bold like Aisling. She has my grandmother's way of speaking with such sincerity as to nearly embarrass those she's conversing with. Henriette Albrittey is a mosaic of myself and the people I love most in the world, and I am proud of her.

I've forgotten the joy of creating. What a wonder it is, to find it hiding inside this book in the middle of the forest—a book I've had at home, in nine different languages, all this time. I could never bring myself to open it, so afraid I'd be disappointed by what I found, or worse—to feel like I'll never be able to write anything as good as it. But I have more stories in me.

So many more.

Nobody else will ever read this book the way that I do. Flipping open to chapter eleven, I see Christmas in Iceland between the lines. In chapter twenty, a desert sunset on Route 66, snapping pictures to send to my grandmother. Chapter thirty-two: eating a huge blueberry cobbler at a diner in Michigan. Spilling coffee on myself while working at a café. Falling in love more than a few times.

I see my life as it was while writing this story, and the story itself, twisting into one.

I think it's the most wondrous thing, to have captured a time capsule of my past in here without realizing it. It will always be this way. Once I'm finished with my next book, whatever that may be, someday I'll reopen it, and highlights from right now—at that point, my past—will rise from between the lines to say hello. What unrelated memories will I find attached? What will ultimately prove significant in my life today when viewing it in hindsight? I think I'll definitely remember this moment. I think I'll see Morgan everywhere in that book.

I keep reading, long after I should have joined Morgan in sleep, unable to stop now that I've started, so many years after I penned *The End.*

It's just me and the words and the moon and the magic; it feels like wrapping hands around my own heart, it feels like *the best it gets.* Tears splash the pages, and I keep turning them, keep turning.

THIRTY-SEVEN

For a simple good-health charm, sweep basil from your
back porch and fenugreek seed from your front porch.
(If porches are not available, windows will suffice.)

Spells, Charms, and Rituals,
Tempest Family Grimoire

ORGAN, WAKE UP." I tap his shoulder.

"It's you," he says in his sleep, smiling a little.

"Wake up. It's raining."

His eyes open, fluttering as they take me in. "Oh." The
smile widens. "It really is you."

"Come on." I lead him to a cave nearby, which I remember
now that I've revisited the library—and there's a waterfall
around here, too! And a few pieces of railroad track, and a tree
I decorated with necklaces and stuffed animals—at every
turn, a new connection is illuminated. If I stand here long
enough and think, I'll end up with a complete map of the forest
in my head.

"How'd you find this place?" he asks, stripping off his
jacket and spreading it on the dry ground for us to sit on. I
place my lantern alongside. "Look at all that!" He points at
white mineral formations gushing down the walls, frozen in
place.

"Flowstones. I used to call them crystal candles, because they look like dripping candle wax."

We sit side by side, knees up, peering at the beautiful crystals thrown into relief by the lantern's light. The cave feels rather smaller now that I'm fully grown.

"And you were out here by yourself? As a kid?"

I laugh. "Yeah."

"Imagine what you'd do if Ash went sneaking off into mysterious caves."

I bump his shoulder with mine. "That's the difference, though. Her family would notice." Not only Luna, but Romina and me, and to some extent, Morgan and Trevor, too. We're Aisling's village.

"Ah," he says, with a nod of understanding. "And yours didn't?"

"My parents weren't worried about what I might get up to because as far as they knew, all I did was read and climb trees. What kind of trouble could I possibly find? Now *Luna*, on the other hand . . ."

"Golden child?" he guesses.

"Nope."

He mock-gasps. "*Luna* misbehaved?"

"Definitely not."

At his confusion, I smile ruefully. "She was the best-behaved of all of us, but our parents were still the hardest on her. I don't know why. Romina acted up so much that whenever she was good, she got praised for it, and I had my grumpy moments. Luna was expected to be perfect for some reason— they lectured her for any tiny misstep. If she'd tried to run off into the woods like I did, I can't even imagine how they would've reacted. Would've been a blowup."

He winces. "That's why she doesn't talk to them anymore?"

"That's part of it." I still have a relationship with my parents, but we aren't close. I see my mom maybe a couple times a year, and I call my dad on holidays. "What are your parents like?"

"They're awesome, I get along with them great. Which sounds funny to say, honestly, because I used to kind of hate my dad. When I was little, he was tons of fun. I worshipped—and I mean *worshipped*—him. I had friends hanging out at the house all the time because they idolized my dad. When I was thirteen, my parents found out they were having twins, which wasn't expected at all, and things were pretty tight moneywise so Mom had to go back to work. Dad started working longer hours, too—actually, this is why I don't want kids; I fell into the role of third parent because they were gone a lot, so it feels like I've already raised my kids, you know what I mean?—and anyway, I found out that my dad's way of coping with stress was by chasing women. More than once."

"Oh no."

"He framed it as *loving women too much*, like he couldn't help himself. Mom left him a couple times, but always went back. Every time she forgave him, she'd rationalize it as Dad being overly friendly, not realizing he was behaving inappropriately, *that's just his personality*, blah blah blah. He'd say he was sorry and would never do it again. They treated it like a congenital weakness, and not a choice he continuously made."

"Wow. I'm . . . very sorry you went through that. I can only imagine how frustrating it would've been, and how you must've hurt for your mom."

"Yeah." He picks at his sleeve. "It's so weird, because it's like . . . I love him. He's great to me, always has been. Super charismatic, life of the party. He's the guy you call at two a.m. when you've blown your tire in a snowstorm—that's happened before, and he was there in six minutes, wearing pajamas. But I still resent how he hurt my mom. Part of me wishes she'd walked away from him for good, because he deserved to lose her. But the other part of me is happy for how happy she is *now*, because she loves him so much and they seem to be in a good place, so it's conflicting."

"I can understand that. I'm still mad at my mom for selling The Magick Happens to Trevor when she knew Luna was looking forward to inheriting it someday, and sometimes I want to punish her by ignoring her calls. But then I remember that my grandma—and I love her, don't get me wrong—but Grandma wasn't always that nice to my mom. She wasn't *mean*, but she wasn't . . . warm, I guess you'd say?" I trace patterns in the rock, reminiscing. "Totally different when it came to her grandkids. We were flawless angels who could do no wrong. But when I got older, I did notice some coldness between Mom and Grandma, and I know Mom was unhappy because she'd wanted a better relationship with her. After Dottie died, Mom admitted to me that she regretted selling the store."

Luna will never forgive her. I'm not sure if I forgive my mom or not, but I don't want to make her feel bad about it anymore, because I've made mistakes, too.

"Family is complicated," Morgan says.

I hug my knees. "So very true. Speaking of family, how's Forte?"

He takes a peek in the sling. "Awake, but strangely docile? I think he must really love being swaddled."

"Don't let him out. He'll maul my other leg."

We're quiet for a while. Morgan lies down, patting his outstretched arm to indicate that I can use it as a pillow. I'm not one for cuddling, as it makes me hot and I don't like feeling restrained, but it's about forty degrees in this cave so I'll take heat however I can get it.

"I know what you're thinking," Morgan tells me once I've made myself comfortable.

"And what's that?"

"You're thinking about trying to seduce me again."

I roll onto my side, exhaling into his chest. "Curses."

"You couldn't wait to yank off all your clothes and get wet with me. And you kissed my hand when we were high on psychedelic potion."

"You kissed my hand, too, if you'll recall."

"If I recall? Do you think I'd forget getting my mouth on you? Anyway, back to your trial here. You, Miss Boots, dragged me into this sexy cave"—he pauses while I burst into laughter—"and are plotting your next move. I bet you knew the cave was here all this time. I bet you've got a picnic basket with grapes and cheese stashed nearby."

"Grapes and cheese in a cold cave with no mattress to lie on," I reply dryly. "What a fantasy."

"My fantasy is you, Zelda. In it, you're thirty feet tall and you pick me up like I'm nothing. You throw me onto a giant cupcake." He spreads his hands above him, finger-painting the scenario in the air. "I swim in French buttercream frosting. Then you swallow me whole and I live inside you like a symbiotic parasite."

"We shouldn't talk to each other anymore."

Morgan wraps his arms around me and hauls me close. "I feel the same way," he murmurs in my ear, as if I've just confessed that he makes my insides warm and fuzzy. Which he certainly does not. It would be a waste of time to have my insides kindled into warm fuzzies in regards to Morgan Angelopoulos, who is an interference in my path to finding True Love. My True Love would *never* say he wants to live inside me like a symbiotic parasite. I bet he's a psychologist or an archivist. Somebody who takes his job seriously and would never, ever post gleefully incorrect movie synopses in a newspaper under the moniker Moe Angelfish.

I think about my True Love as we drift in and out of consciousness, sleepy and comfortable, lulled by the pattering of rain. Our bodies move closer, closer. I say to Morgan, "I bet my True Love wears a newsboy hat and he's got a proper library in his house," but the syllables get all jumbled up on their way out of my mouth, so instead it sounds like I've said, "I like being alone with you."

Most befuddling.

"I know you do," he whispers. "You're constantly engineering it."

"Am not," I whisper back.

"That's all right." His lips graze my temple, brushing over

hair and skin. My eyes slide closed. "Once you admit to yourself what you want, *that's* when the real fun can begin." He sighs against my cheek.

What I want.

What do I want? I know exactly.

"Is it me that you like?" I ask, swallowing, twisting my fingers in the fabric of his shirt. "Or is it my magic?"

He tilts up my face, commanding me to meet his eyes. "The only thing I want from your magic," Morgan tells me, each word grave and deliberate, "is for it to keep making you happy."

And he kisses me.

My first lucid thought is *Morgan has known exactly how he would touch me, if he got the chance.* He's thought about this. Dreamed of it with methodical thoroughness. I can feel the release of a tight and heavy yearning in the sweep of his tongue, in the way he rolls so that he's positioned halfway on top of me. He's known just how he'd angle his head, anticipating where my hands might wander along his body, how I'd arch mine to seek his.

The kiss deepens, the pressure lovely. It isn't enough. I need more hands so that I can touch all of him at once, I need to be the ground and the air and his shirt, I need . . . I need . . . I moan under my breath when he rubs against me just right, the hard ridge in his jeans notching between my legs, and he stiffens for a second.

His breaths are shallow. "Make that sound again. No, don't, actually. I don't have spare pants to change into."

I hold him tight against me and rock; this time, Morgan's the one who groans.

"Fuck. Fuck, fuck, *fuck*."

"Yes, I'd like that." I'm a flame. All I want is friction and his mouth, I want to see that easy smile fall open into pleasured gasps. I want, I want, I want. "You," I say softly. "I want you."

Morgan stops breathing; my chest is pressed against his, so I can feel it. He stares at me, the emotion in his eyes startling the shadows away; the lantern brightens as though responding to freewheeling particles of electricity, and we devour each other.

He unbuttons the fastening of my jeans. I peel his shirt over his head. Pants and underwear, all our layers, until Morgan is (oh my *god*, magnificent) dropping kisses onto my naked skin. He murmurs curses and praise, firm hands loving my thick thighs, my wide hips, my soft stomach. My fingernails gently graze down his nipples, his abdomen, to the hard cock jutting between his legs, and he shivers.

"I'm finally going to have my way with you," I say wonderingly, half-delirious, and he buries a fist in my hair.

"You're so damned beautiful. Poor thing."

"Poor thing?"

"Don't you realize? You're never getting rid of me."

And with what he does next, I can't imagine ever wanting to be rid of him.

Morgan tastes me, reverent, filling his hands with my breasts, dragging his tongue over my nipples. I stroke up and down his back, letting my knees fall apart as he sinks between them. Words that don't make any sense spill from his lips to caress my mouth as he positions himself at my entrance. "Yes?" he asks.

"Yes."

Morgan pushes into me, slowly, my hips rising up to greet him.

"It wasn't your desk, it was you. It was your energy, it was . . . the magic telling me: *Wait right here. She'll be back soon.* Didn't even know what I was waiting for, really. Just knew I had to stay put in that spot."

A light laugh flutters from my throat. "What are you talking about? Ohhh, my. You feel so good."

"I'm talking about . . ." He falters, his features relaxing into bliss. "Oh, it's only everything. *You.* Sweet lord, Zelda. Do you even know? I'm still not sure you have any idea."

I love that he can't think straight.

"I know that I am feeling incredible right now," I reply. "Don't be offended if I don't come, though, all right? Sometimes I don't, and when I do, it usually takes a while."

"I'm a patient man. We'll see what we can do."

Morgan slows, testing different rhythms and positions. He wants me on top because he's worried my back will get sore (and he's not wrong), but I need the pressure of his weight, I need to feel like I'm sinking. Through trial and error, we find out what my body wants from his, and after pausing a few times so that Morgan can last longer, I eventually sense a wave cresting.

I dig my nails into his hips, bringing him closer to me. Harder but not faster, we writhe together, and ultimately, I suspect my climax is equally credited to the euphoria caused by his words, and not just the way he moves inside me: *You're never getting rid of me.*

He's laid a pillow under my fear, giving it a safe place to land. If he likes me for me, then perhaps it's safe to like him back.

We kiss anew as joy bursts in my heart. I kiss him and touch him, stroke and savor, until we can't ignore that we need to clean ourselves up. So we do; then we redress when the heat we've generated dims to an ember, and he asks again, hopefully, if I've stashed a picnic basket around here.

I rip open a packet of peanut butter crackers. "Sorry, this is all I've got left. Somewhere out there, an elephant is enjoying our granola bars."

"We hallucinated that, right? There's no way there was an elephant in the woods. We're in *Ohio*."

"There were definitely fumes in that hot spring," I agree. "I bet we saw a funny-shaped tree and somehow convinced ourselves it was . . ." I trail off as the vivid image of an elephant trampling our tent stampedes across my memory.

"Nah," we say in tandem. "That was an elephant."

We split my water, polishing off every cracker crumb. "I still can't believe that the first time you kissed me, the kiss was on my hand," he laments. "I'm going to have a stern talking-to with that psychedelic potion."

"If it helps, I definitely would've preferred to kiss your mouth. But I was trying to be respectful toward your father."

He tucks me up against him again. "What a weird and wonderful creature you are, Zelda Tempest."

Through the mist that suffuses the mouth of the cave, I notice small, silvery insects weaving. One of them blows into the cave, landing on the rocks close to me. Its wings twitch as it rights itself, and it flies back out to join its friends.

"Those are supposed to be green," I remark, as Morgan's arm tightens around my waist. "I think they might be paranimals. Or not animals, since they're insects. Parasects?"

"Interesting," he replies distractedly, the rumble of his voice inviting me to snuggle in deeper.

"Want to go have a look?"

"No." Morgan kisses my neck. "I want to be right here."

I smile.

And the rain shivers through the trees and the magic burns in my veins and I want to be right here, too. *I could live right here*, I think.

"Not a bookmark," he says softly, as I'm falling asleep.

"Mm?"

He smooths back my hair, baring my cheek. I feel the weight of his gaze, and his voice is like melting gold. "If you were a gingersnappus, you wouldn't transform into a bookmark," Morgan tells me. "You'd be a galaxy. So bright and beautiful that I could see you from any edge of the universe."

When I dream, I am in Morgan's arms, drifting across space, through implosions of stars and the births of planets, through all the constellations inked into his skin.

THIRTY-EIGHT

Run directly through one door and out another
in the home, thrice before sunrise, and your
True Love will have a lucky day.

Love Magic Misc.,
Tempest Family Grimoire

"YOU ARE *GLORIOUS*," Morgan murmurs to me in the early-morning light, staring into my eyes. "I could look at you forever."

I slide a palm across his cheek. "Good morning. I'd like to get railed again."

"So romantic."

"*Bmm-bmm-bmm-bmm-bmm*," adds a humongous bird, emitting a noise like a faraway beating drum, standing directly above us in the cave.

We scream. The bird seems to realize, *Oh, right, I'd like to chase them.* At least it waited until we woke up to attack us. What a well-mannered monster bird.

"It's a pterodactyl!" Morgan yells, swinging both our backpacks over his shoulders and flying out of the cave, pushing me ahead of him. This leaves me with Forte, hollering in his baby sling.

I wrap my hair into a ponytail as I run. "How the hell is there a pterodactyl still in existence?"

"How the hell are there *any* of the things that we've found lately?"

"Fair point."

It is too early for this news. I haven't even stretched yet. One second I'm drooling on Morgan's arm, and the next, I'm hurtling through the woods. The ground is soggy from last night's rain, my boots slapping mud and slippery amber leaves.

"Is it still chasing us?" I look over my shoulder as the pterodactyl produces a sound that I can only describe as *baritone purring*. "Wait, that's just an emu."

"An emu?" Morgan picks up speed, his face blanched with wild panic. "I'm *terrified* of emus!"

"How are you more scared of an emu than a dinosaur?" I knife left. "This way!"

"I've been thinking." His words are garbled. "I want a property."

"Property?" I tuck a loose strand of hair behind my ear. "I can't hear you."

"I'VE BEEN THINKING. I WANT TO TAKE YOU ON A PROPER DATE."

"Morgan, we're being chased by an emu." I dart right. "This way. Down that hill."

"This is the optimal time to plan a date. Endorphins, running for our lives. Careful of that ditch there."

"I don't think this qualifies as running for our lives. It's a bird."

"Clearly you do not have an uncle with a pet emu named

Gregory Peck, who tried to eat you when you were only an innocent, appetizing toddler."

Four figures tear out of the trees, hollering in surprise when they collide with us. "Run!" they yell.

Morgan and I stop, face-to-face with Luna, Romina, Alex, and Trevor. They're sweaty, red-faced, wide-eyed. Trevor's got a camo bandannna tied around his forehead. "We're already running!" I say. "What are you doing here?"

Luna yanks my arm. "Run in the other direction!"

"But." I point. "Emu."

She points, too. "Bear." We all tangle together in a chaotic herd as we lunge toward a now-terrified emu, who jumps out of our way.

"Right. Bear." Morgan nods, speeding ahead. "Bear is worse."

We're hit with an epiphany at the same moment, stumbling. We grab each other. *"Bear?"*

I tear off in the direction of the bear. Romina shouts at the top of her voice at me that I'm going the wrong way. Morgan races at my side.

"The Black Bear Witch!" I exclaim. "We're going to find her, Morgan."

"Yes! We *are*."

The bear could be anywhere. I keep an ear out for signs of wildlife, but my internal radio only picks up a story I've never heard before. Never written before.

> . . . *a graveyard so ancient that all of its tombstones had long crumbled away like rotten teeth. A house stood upon*

*the hill now, and nobody who lived in it had any notion
of how many bodies were buried beneath them.*

*Downhill the earth rumbled, a hand reaching through
dirt to grasp at air. Rain poured down pale fingers; the
ground shook again and a man's dark head of hair
pushed through. His sole consuming thought was that it
did not matter how deep they buried him, or where—he
would find her. Nothing mattered except for spearing
himself on the sharp gaze of his beloved once again.*

"Later," I promise the forest. "I'll write it all down later, I'll
write everything you want so long as you keep feeding me stories. But right now, I'm looking for a witch."

Where do we go now? I close my eyes. *Which way?* I echo
this question down the chain of my magic. The words rever-
berate as if spreading through deep space, and I feel an intrin-
sic pull to my left.

I turn us.

The magic tugs left again.

"This way."

And then we see it—a large, lumbering shape, unmistak-
ably a bear, but—

But the magic doesn't stop. It keeps tugging leftward, insis-
tent. *I already found the bear! You can leave me alone now.*

The magic shimmers. *This way, this way.*

Morgan and I revolve in circles, but no matter which way
we're pointing, magic keeps demanding me to go . . .

I look left, into Morgan's face. Realization hits.

"Are you all right?" he asks, brow furrowed in concern.

Love magic, Grandma once said, *hangs in Moonville's trees, swims in our rivers. A romantic love grown in Moonville is stronger than anywhere else, and if you're here in near proximity to your One True Love, magic will physically redirect your paths so that they continue to cross. It will make your love burn forever, as bright and true in your fiftieth year together as it did your first.*

"It's you," I whisper.

Morgan cups my face in his hands. "Zelda, you're scaring me. Why are you looking at me like that?"

Him, magic thrums, urging me closer. I follow the sunlit path, and Morgan opens his arms to let me in.

Magic takes me to Morgan. He is my *Where do we go now?* He is my *Which way?*

"I think . . ." My heart thunders, head spinning. "I think I love you."

His arms slowly drop to his sides, stunned as if I've struck him. "Well, Zelda, I love you right back."

I want to say *Are you serious? Do you mean it?*

But I don't. I wouldn't dare question his sincerity, because of course he means it. Whereas I have resting murder face, Morgan has resting I'm-in-love-with-you face. This man is impossible. Frustrating. Overwhelming, at times. But my heart still points to his and sings, *"That one."*

I move to kiss him, but his gaze shoots over my shoulder and widens. "Look."

Hidden behind a drapery of ivy is the mouth of a cave. Leading up to it are soft imprints in the mud. Bear tracks.

"This must be her lair!" I loud-whisper. "We did it!"

He jumps up and down, joyful but endeavoring to keep it quiet. "It's happening. It's actually *happening*. I thought the cave and the lair were two separate places on the map? Guess we were wrong!"

I take a step toward the cave, but Morgan grips my shoulder. His fingers briefly tighten, then release. "Wait."

I look to him in question.

"We've found the lair," he tells me, stating the obvious. "You know what happens next."

I jerk my chin toward the entrance. "Yeah. We go in."

Morgan bites his lip. "She'll make us forget everything to do with finding this place. How much memory will she scoop out? Does the erasure start the moment we *see* the lair, or the moment we're *at* the lair?"

We fall quiet, calculating this.

"Because we've been *at* the lair for several minutes now without realizing it," he continues. "She might make us forget that you said you love me."

"I'll tell you I love you again, after this," I promise. "It's inevitable, because that's how I really feel. You will hear it again."

I watch as an emotion rises within him and he steels himself against it, swallowing hard. "You can go in there if you want to, but I'm not. I won't trade the first time my Zelda says she loves me for anything, not for all the magic in the universe. I want to remember this forever."

My lashes clump together with hot tears. "You have to risk it, though. This is your chance. It's everything you ever wanted."

He shakes his head solemnly. "Not anymore. I've just gotten what I wanted most, and I'm keeping it."

My heart dips and rises and dives. Hurricanes in circles. *This man.*

$$T \quad I$$
$$A \quad S \quad H$$
$$N \quad M$$

This mythical, marvelous, made-for-me man.

I suck in a deep breath. "You saying you love me right back is the best discovery I'm ever going to find out here," I tell him. "I'm not giving that up, either."

Morgan's mouth presses together in a crooked half smile, and then that smile falls gently against mine. I open to him at once, melting.

He's got a kiss that grabs you right by the lungs, but he doesn't use that kiss here. This one is soft and lush. It feels like *Isn't this wonderful? Let's never do anything else.* All points of light in my periphery slide into holy crosses, and my whole body pounds, and I can't stop thinking, *How are you real?*

"Did I tell you," he murmurs, "that I got you a present? It's back at my apartment."

Now is hardly the time. I don't care about presents.

Although . . .

"What is it?"

"A book about huldufólk, the hidden elves of Iceland."

My grip on him tightens. "Really?"

"First edition, printed in 1908. It's got illustrations and smells like a wood-burning stove."

I sag in his arms. "Goodness. Hold me up, I've gone light-headed."

He lays a kiss to my temple, a wicked grin in his voice. "Somebody who owned it in the 1930s used its title page to keep records of their family tree. It's got tons of names and dates."

Kill shot.

"You've finally done it," I mutter woozily. "I'm seduced. You can have anything you want. I'll find a dozen witches and steal all their magic for you."

He laughs.

"After we get out of here, my stunning star," Morgan tells me once I've regained my bearings, "I'm going to put on my finest breathable nylon tracksuit and let you sweep me off my feet, just as you've been dying to do."

So we double back to find our friends and family, holding hands.

WE HAVEN'T BEEN walking for six minutes when we collide with the others. "Why'd you run off?" Luna screeches, pink face sweaty.

"Because of the bear." I point behind us, just like before when we were escaping an emu.

"Lion," Trevor says casually, pointing in another direction.

"Lion!" we all scream, and run for our lives.

Morgan does not allow running for our lives to deter him

from discussing our new romance. "So I was thinking, for our next date, we'll go to Wheatberry Books in Chillicothe," he says. "It's about an hour's drive, and if memory serves, there's a candy shop, an ice cream shop, and a cake shop right around the corner. We'll hit up all three, because I'm a classy guy who treats my lady right, and then get matching tattoos at the tattoo parlor on West Second Street."

I process this while leaping over tree roots, dodging crevices. "Matching tattoos?"

"They don't *have* to match. You can go first, and then whatever happens . . . happens."

"Hang on." Romina grasps my wrists, giving me a full-body shake. "You two are dating?"

"Yes," Morgan replies quickly, before I can answer. "Our first date was at Dark Side of the Spoon. We shared a burger and apple pie. It was devastatingly romantic."

"Awww," Romina and Trevor cry.

I laugh. "That was my date with *Dylan*."

Morgan raises his nose in the air. "I don't remember anybody named Dylan. He sounds unnecessary in the greater scheme of things." He lifts our joined hands, nuzzling a kiss over my skin.

Luna's jaw is dragging behind us. "You and Morgan? Why didn't you tell us? This is so against the code! Your sisters are supposed to be the first to know when you like a guy, so that we can tease you every time you're in the same room. Winking, nudging, innuendos. It's our right."

"Yeah, you deserve it!" Romina piles on. "You teased me so bad about Alex."

Oof. "Can we do this later? Talking while running is hard. Running at all is hard, especially without a sports bra. Two sports bras doubled up, in fact. Have you *seen* my chest?"

"Yes," says Morgan, reverently.

My sisters cackle their heads off.

"Lion's behind us again," Trevor announces.

"I could pen sonnets," Morgan tells me in an undertone so that the others won't overhear. "I'm going to. I'll make you listen to them, even if they're bad. I won't rest until I've got you naked in a hayride."

I am not getting naked in a hayride, but now is not the time for that discussion.

"Is the lion injured?" Luna turns. "If he wanted to catch us, he certainly could."

"Maybe he enjoys the thrill of the chase," Alex suggests. "Going slow so that his prey thinks they have a hope of surviving."

Trevor begins to estimate how many lions we could sustain. "There's six of us," he says. "That's a feast."

"Possibly seven," Romina tacks on thoughtfully. "Is now a good time to tell everybody that my period's a week late?"

THIRTY-NINE

Amorgic moths: Silver, hummingbird-sized parasect
moths attracted to the cables of energy between soul
mates. Appear only during storms, and become
frenetic when feeding on lightning/electricity. Their
mundane disguise is the luna moth.

Paranimals, *A* through *M*,
Tempest Family Grimoire

I N SHORT ORDER, we find ourselves up a tree, with Alex
securing Romina to a branch with his belt.

"This is an overreaction," Romina insists. "I haven't
taken a test yet. And a week isn't much—it could be nothing."
She nibbles on her nails, betraying that she hopes it isn't *nothing*. Romina wants to be a mother, and while I bet she didn't
plan on that happening right now, I know my sister: the only
reason she hasn't taken a pregnancy test yet is that she's already grown attached to the idea that she might be having a
baby, and she's worried she'll see a negative result.

"You might be pregnant," Alex says, uncharacteristically
dazed. "And there is a lion in the . . . there is a bear in the . . ."

"Don't forget the emu," Morgan adds helpfully.

"Whoa, buddy." Luna helps steady Alex when he starts to
sway. He threads his hands through his short hair, eyes widening as he likely begins to compute whether he'll build a crib

with pinewood or oak, and the shortest distance to the maternity ward in Athens.

"Stay where you are, Romina, and think tranquil thoughts, okay?" He begins to climb down the branches. Pauses. "Focus on the sound of the river! Let all of your stress wash away. I love you!"

"What are you doing? Where are you going?" Romina calls, then freaks out. "Oh *no*. You're going to punch the lion in the face, aren't you?"

Trevor gives Alex a thumbs-down as he descends past him. "Booooo. How dare you knock her up at a time like this? We were finally gonna go to Coachella!"

Romina points sternly at Trevor. "We are still doing that. You hear me? Don't you dare sell my ticket."

"Oh yeah, like you're gonna wanna walk around the desert with a big ole watermelon in your stomach." Luna snickers.

"It'll be fine," Trevor assures her. "Lana Del Rey can deliver the baby."

Romina turns to him, excited. "Oh my gosh, can you *imagine?*"

They begin to discuss the likelihood of Lana Del Rey agreeing to be the baby's godmother, and whether she might write songs about a Coachella baby (*Indio Child* and *I Heard the Baby Crying on a Friday Night While Singing About Dying* are top candidates for eventual album titles).

Alex settles himself on the lowest branch so that he can punch any lions in his girlfriend's honor if the need arises.

"If the lion eats you," Trevor tells him, "I'll raise your baby as my own. Don't worry. I'll find a private school just like the one in *School of Rock*, and Little Ro will have the most sublime baby sneaker collection. All the other babies will be jealous."

Alex drags a hand down his face.

"That is comforting, Trevor," Romina tells him, sounding genuinely touched. "Thank you."

I adjust the baby sling, Forte's weight digging the strap into my neck. "You still haven't told us what you're all doing out here in the first place."

"We were worried you might be in trouble," Luna replies, as Trevor cuts her off:

"*Luna* was worried *Morgan* might be in trouble."

Luna throws Morgan an apologetic glance. "It's just that most of your footwear is vintage. And, you know." She gestures to me. "Zel might have left you for dead if you inconvenienced her in any way."

"Hey!" I cry.

"I brought three pairs of sneakers for you to choose from," Trevor tells Morgan. "Since your shirt is pink, I'd go with green. Opposite on the color wheel, for maximum pop."

"Aw. Thanks, man, you're the best. Any chance you brought food, too?"

"Yeah, I brought burritos."

We cheer.

"But I got hungry, so I had to eat them."

I groan. Morgan groans. The lion groans (hungrily).

He's found us and is working up an appetite prowling the base of our tree, shaggy golden mane abuzz with flies. He isn't exactly skinny, which makes me wonder what his diet usually consists of. And how lions (and tigers and elephants) have managed to form a habitat in Moonville's backyard. But, to make the scenario all the more bizarre, this lion has the tail of a betta fish.

It is glorious.

His elegant fins stream and flow as if that part of his body is underwater always. Morning sun pours through his fins' webbing to light them like stained glass, beautiful and fiery. A lionfish. *Black Bear Witch, whoever you are,* I think to myself, *you've certainly got a sense of humor.*

"Aghh!" Romina shouts. "It's back! Alex, punch it! Wait, don't punch it. It might eat your arm. You have the *best* arms."

A chunk of rock *kerflunks* down the side of a cliff next to our tree. More chunks come raining after it. I turn away to avoid dust clouding my eyes. "Falling rocks," I warn everyone.

"In Falling Rock Forest?" Alex pipes up. "Inconceivable!"

Morgan calls him an ass, Romina threatens to fight Morgan, Luna reminds her that she can't fight anybody because she might be pregnant, and somebody yells, "Did you say *pregnant?*"

We all look up. Aisling and Cannon are clinging to the cliff face.

The sound that Luna unleashes is the closest that any of us, on this side of mortality, will get to hearing the gates of hell wrench open. "Aisling Gwenelieve Tempest! You were supposed to stay home!"

"I'm going to be an aunt!" Ash sings.

"Cousin," I correct.

Cannon is in tears. "I'm so sorry! I told her it was a bad

idea. She made me do this. I wanted to stay home and practice tempering chocolate!"

Luna swears. Apologizes for swearing in front of Cannon. "I knew I should've left you two with Alex's mom and Miles. You know better!"

"I'm not sure that I do know better," Ash replies honestly. "I can't believe you were gonna deprive me of seeing a lion." Her right foot slides in its hold, more rocks crumbling away. The shards of cliff bounce and skitter to their deaths far below. The lionfish sneezes as dust billows into his nose.

"Hold on," Luna tells them. "Mommy's coming." She begins to crawl across tree branches, working her way in their direction. The bough I'm perched on wobbles when her weight sinks onto it.

I scrabble to stay in place. "Careful!"

"I'm saving my babies," she hisses.

Crrrraaaaack!

My branch snaps. Luna grabs the one above us and I fall to the one below, swinging upside down with the backs of my knees gripping rough bark. My long hair spills like a ladder for the lionfish to climb, its tips hanging *just* above his swatting paws. "Sit up!" Luna yells, as if she isn't responsible for how I got into this position.

An upside-down Forte falls out of his sling.

"*Pliggguck shhurr!*" he yowls, legs kicking, parachuting into a grand piano in midair. He falls with a melodic *thunk* onto the lion. The piano rattles, yowls, and shrinks back into a gingersnappus, scrabbling back up the tree.

"What happened?" Trevor screams. "Why aren't I wearing a body camera at all times?"

"I think a tree branch fell on the lion," Alex says.

It certainly wasn't a tree branch, but in all the commotion, nobody saw what happened clearly. Or perhaps their brains rejected the sight of a cat turning into a piano. They've endured too much for one day.

My sisters haul me upright just as the blood pooling in my head begins to pound, and catch me when I get the spins.

Aisling risks her grip to get a better view. "Is the lion all right?"

The lionfish is grumbling, fins switching furiously. "I think so," I say. He decides he's had enough of this and lopes off in search of an easier meal. We watch him disappear into the trees.

I inspect Forte, who pins his ears back and scratches my arm. Seems to be in normal spirits.

"Gas leak," Alex is muttering as we climb down. "Forest gas. A mirage. We're all dehydrated. Only way to explain lions in the woods."

Once we're on the ground again, Luna hugs her daughter tight. "I'm so happy you're safe. You are in the biggest trouble."

"The smartest thing to do now is stick together," Alex tells us, as Trevor shouts, "Split up! It can't eat us all if we go in different directions!" Then he bolts.

Madness ensues.

Romina panics and runs after Trevor; Alex panics and runs after Romina. Aisling pounces on the opportunity to escape her inevitable grounding and tries to peel off with a reluctant, regretful Cannon in tow. Luna tracks them down, and soon I hear whining.

Morgan yanks a hand through his hair. "You need to stay with Zelda!" he bellows. "You idiots! She's the only one who can sense where to go!"

We return Forte to his sling, then take off after them.

"This way!" I call, doubtful that anybody but Morgan hears me. "Well, they got themselves here. They can get themselves out, I guess."

"They're going to run into that bear."

"Or the emu." I lean my head on his shoulder. "I'm sorry about the witch. I really hoped you'd get some magic. Now we've lost the opportunity, as well as our tent, and there's nothing else to do but go home."

He kisses my forehead. "As long as I'm with you, I don't care what we do."

He is the most impossible creature in this whole forest, but a different sort of impossible than the definition I've pinned to him so far. He is impossible like a waraver or a unicorn—something you think you'll never, ever find even if you search your whole life, and then one day, you do. I wrap my arms around him, basking in how right he feels. "You are a gorgeous man, Morgan Angelopoulos."

"That's my line." Morgan smiles, eyes crinkling. "Are you going to kiss me now?"

"That is exactly what I'm—" I stagger when my elbow knocks into something solid, and we turn abruptly. There is a cabin. Right beside us.

"Where'd that come from?" he exclaims. "Did you notice there was a house there?"

"Guess we weren't paying attention."

We appraise a steeply pitched roof, black split-log walls, a door with an oak leaf and the words THIS IS A TREE, NOTHING MORE carved into the wood. "What on earth does that mean?" I utter, tracing the grooves of NOTHING MORE with my thumb.

"I dunno. Looks abandoned, though." Morgan checks behind us. "Might be a good place to hide from lions, tigers, and bears." He brushes his arm against my shoulder, winking mischievously. "And from your sisters, so that we can kiss some more in peace."

"Ooooh, yes, that sounds like an excellent plan."

We eagerly tumble through the door, which smells like maple and whiskey, and end up . . .

In a spring meadow.

"How?"

"What!"

"Why?!"

We've teleported to a pastoral tableau of gentle rolling hills, wildflowers, trees pushed all the way back to the edge of the horizon. A topiary spreads before us, glossy shrubs pruned into the shapes of rabbits, cats, bats, and a boxwood creature that might be a mole mixed with a dragon. There are no roads, but there are ponds, and a lone shop that closely resembles The Magick Happens—except without our banner of purple, gold, and green, and the window boxes are overflowing with marigolds rather than Romina's coral bells. Standing out front of it, clutching a threadbare carpetbag, is a tall man with wavy brown hair and suspenders.

"Hey, there!" Morgan waves at him in greeting.

"Where *are* we?" I call out. "It's like we've landed in another town."

"And another season," Morgan remarks. "The temperature must've risen at least eight degrees."

The man sighs, setting down the carpetbag as he ambles toward us. "Oh, for heaven's sakes."

FORTY

Fablefinding: The supernatural practice of
gathering stories lost in nature.

Family Witchcraft,
Tempest Family Grimoire

M Y FAVORITE TIME of year is that dark pocket between autumn and winter, when it isn't freezing yet but the landscape has ceased to be conventionally pretty, after the trees have caught their deaths and it's foggy and gloomy and rainy. The sky doesn't know if it wants to storm or snow. Everyone hates the weather, how the colors of autumn have run together into a blobby gray-brown-black wash. With the leaves stripped, you can see the lovely twists of tree limbs, their unique shapes. I call it perfect tea-steeping, book-reading weather.

"I *hate* this time of year," Romina declares miserably as we collect our drinks from DeShawn and James. Their seasonal beverage truck, The Sleepy Shrew, is only in operation from Halloween through New Year's, and whenever they appear on Vallis Boulevard on October 31, the lines for spiced cider are preposterous.

"There, there." I toast my milky oolong against her hot chocolate. "Spring will be here soon."

"In one hundred and forty-one days," she grumbles, sparing a dark glance for Luna. "I don't know how you can wear that right now."

Luna's dressed in denim shorts and a crochet tank. "I don't get cold."

I poke her. Our older sister is eternally bragging that she never gets cold, flaunting Birkenstocks and halter tops in the dead of winter. Romina and I can't tell if she's committed to the bit and is secretly freezing, or if she should be studied by science.

The chilly air is rich with fryer oil and salt, the Midnight at Moonville festival in full swing now that sunset has begun to paint itself between the trees.

"Ferris wheel?" Morgan suggests. His face is still wet from bobbing for apples. He dunked his whole head repeatedly until I made him stop, and is still sneezing water. Quite proud of his three apples, though.

"Looks like it got stuck again," Luna remarks. We all crane to watch people in the bottom carriages glare at Ivan, who's experimenting with the buttons and apologizing drunkenly. Trevor and Teyonna, seated in the carriage at the very top, couldn't be happier.

We pass a stage where a local garage band is making my teeth vibrate with bass, then a hayride wagon that I drag Morgan away from, coming to a stop in front of Gilda Halifax's booth. She's beaming in the midst of hundreds of individually wrapped traveler's talismans, wearing a spangled silver muumuu and blue eye shadow that rolls all the way up to thin eyebrows painted on with a liner that's closer to green than brown.

"Come get your talismans!" she's crooning. "They're my own special recipe, and I'm the only one alive who knows it. I've been baking these beauties since 1982!"

"She's shameless," Romina mutters darkly.

Luna crosses her arms. "Grandma's going to haunt her for a month straight, after this."

I shake my head. "Vile woman."

We all step in line.

"Six, please," I say sweetly.

"Ahh, it's my *girls*, how very *divine* to *see* you." Gilda smooshes Luna's face between her bejeweled hands. "Come by Bowerbird's Nest later, I've met a man online who'd be amazing for you. Name's Denver. Quite young, in dog years. He carves puppets. They all bear a resemblance to his mother, but with a net worth of six million, we'll let it pass."

"I'll talk to whoever you please if you'll give me the traveler's talisman recipe," Luna replies.

Gilda scrunches her nose. "I couldn't possibly. Family secret."

"It's supposed to be *my* family's secret—" Luna begins, tersely, but Gilda's already moved on to Romina.

"Darling, you've got to touch up your roots. They're crying out for help. How do you like the hat I sent you? You're such a doll, I can't help it, every time I see a good hat I have to buy it for you."

I brace myself when it's my turn. "Zelda, you're looking more and more like Baba Yaga every day." Her eyes fill with sorrow. "But it isn't too late for you. Let's go shopping some time. Let me do something different with your hair."

Gilda tells Alex that he needs to repaint his mailbox, and fawns over Morgan's black opal rings before finally doling out our cakes. "I shouldn't let you have this," she tells Morgan. "We all know how much you like to harass us in E-flat."

Morgan breaks his open, then immediately starts puffing on a whistle.

"I can't believe you still put charms in them," Alex disparages. "Isn't that a health and safety violation?"

"Are you the fuzz, boy?" Gilda rejoins. "Mind your business."

I unwrap my triangular cake, breathing in the sweetness of cinnamon, pumpkin, chocolate chips, and brown sugar. As I've done since I was a child, I take a nibble of each corner before splitting the talisman open to reveal my charm.

"You got the bell, too!" Romina shakes hers at me. "Twinsies."

With traveler's talismans, you get either a whistle or the bell of a jester's hat. If you ring the jester's bell in someone's ear while they're sleeping on Halloween night, the ringer and the sleeper are brought a week of laughter. If you get the whistle, you're supposed to blow it before bed on Halloween night and your All Saint's Day will be a lucky one. It's tradition to give half your cake to a friend, to share the good fortune.

I devour mine in two bites, because I don't share.

Luna studies Morgan as he whistles happily. "What does it feel like," she says at my ear, "to be the sister who's no longer running from love?"

My quizzical expression prompts her to add: "In the prophecy. Remember? When the silver luna moth makes its appearance, one of us will be running from love, one of us waiting for it, and the third will already be in over her head. Romina was the 'in over her head' sister, and I'm the one who's been waiting for love."

My lips press together, gaze sweeping over her face. Doesn't she know?

Luna awaits my response, totally guileless. *Hmm*, poor woman's in for a rude surprise.

My older sister thinks I'm the Tempest who's been running from love, when I have, in fact, been waiting for it. Which means she's the one running. And she has successfully convinced herself otherwise.

"Feels fantastic," I finally reply, clearing my throat. "Can't wait to watch when it's your turn."

Aisling runs up. "Mom! Can I take eight grams of cat's claw bark from the herb drawer at home?"

Luna sighs. "Who are you trying to hex this time?"

"Not a hex. I need it for Samuel."

I blow an involuntary raspberry. "What use does a ghost have for herbs? He can't even touch them."

She tips up her chin, defiant. "You're the reason he needs more, thank you very much. You dropped all of Samuel's cat's claw bark into a cauldron."

I muss her hair. "You and your imagination. Please never change, my darling."

Luna and Aisling follow a path of glow-in-the-dark painted footprints toward home. Our shop is festooned in orange and purple fairy lights. Pumpkins, spider orchids, and scabiosa line the walkway.

I stoop to admire one of the pumpkins.

"These are the pumpkins that grew on top of my house," Romina informs me. "Note how much bigger and orange-er they are than regular pumpkins."

"You did *not* grow these."

"Did too."

"This one has a sticker from Moonville Market still on it."

She picks the barcode sticker off. Pastes it to my forehead. "You think magic can't grow pumpkins with stickers on them?"

I tap her flower crown playfully. "You're right. There isn't any evidence to prove it can't."

She preens.

There certainly is a surge of enchantment in the air tonight. I breathe deeply, my senses compressing it all into a memory I'm going to treasure every time magic resurrects it for me in the future: crisp air, sleeves again, leaves falling, the blush of golden hour, shop windows decorated with black cat decals, love potion number nine.

"My purse!" Romina cries, plucking at her boyfriend's sleeve. "I must've dropped it. Quick, Alex, use your gift before somebody steals all my trail mix."

"I don't have a gift," he insists. "I am not a witch." He pauses, then points at The Sleepy Shrew. "You left it on the concession shelf."

Romina shakes him. "*See?* I told you."

"Deductive reasoning! Not witchcraft."

The two of them bicker, and I wind an arm around Morgan's waist, leading us away to peace.

We switch on our EMF readers, as the veil is thin tonight,

aiming them this way and that. Unfortunately, electromagnetic field detectors are easily triggered by cell phones. At the rate that ours are lighting up, it'll be difficult to catch anything genuine. We stay close so that we don't lose each other to environmental hazards (potholes hidden beneath rolling dry ice, children running amok on toy broomsticks, the beguiling come-hither of vendors who promise Morgan that he won't regret trying deep-fried butter on a stick). We end up in a corn maze, where at last our readings normalize before blinking again.

"Red level five," I report bracingly. "There's got to be paranormal activity present."

Morgan pats down his pockets. "Where's my EVP recorder? I need this for the podcast!"

I've been a guest on Morgan's podcast three times already. We don't discuss paranimals publicly, as we don't want them disturbed or experimented on by anyone, but I'm glad to recap late-night ghost hunting jaunts through town, hoping to cross an apparition.

"Over here, Hot Drama." I follow the red flickers of my EMF reader, Morgan begins to narrate our current situation into his recorder, and we turn a corner only to find that Joan and Wanda, the ladies from the murder mystery dinner theater, have inadvertently set off our devices with their smartwatches.

"Damn it," Morgan mutters.

"We'll come back later, once everybody's gone home," I assure him. Just Morgan and me, skulking through the foggy shadows, inviting dead people to haunt us . . . Truly, if a more romantic date exists, I haven't heard of it.

"Want to go forest for a while?" he suggests.

I grin at his usage of *forest* as a verb, and because he's always itching to get back into the trees, just like me.

Hand in hand, we traverse the bridge over Foxglove Creek, fireflies shining on the water. Black trees beckon, bending toward us.

Zelda, Zelda. We have more for you.

"What will you bring me today?" I ask aloud. Sometimes I'm told my own stories, ones I've forgotten, and sometimes the ideas are new.

"The Magician of More-Again," Falling Rock Forest whispers.

Morgan presses a kiss to my cheek. "Which has it begun?"

"'The Magician of More-Again,'" I relay. He smiles broadly. Morgan is particularly fond of how that tale is progressing.

The Magician of More-Again, the fearsome Woodwitch, and their not-a-cat companion arrived at the Singing Mountains with less than seven minutes to spare.

"They finally made it to the mountains."

Words push up against me like gusts of wind, impatient to get in as we enter the forest proper and become undergrowth.

Hills rolled up in waves, each one bigger than the last until they exploded into gigantic peaks that rang with otherworldly sound.

"When did you first know you were magic?" Sylvia asked him.

Morgan stops at a tree and spreads his jacket over the leaves. He seats himself, then extends a hand toward me. I grasp his fingers, my gaze holding his as he lowers me down beside him. Swallowed up in darkness, he trails a finger down my cheek, naked admiration on his face. I immediately pin the beauty through space, superimposing him onto this fictional magician the woods call Aries. How could I not? Morgan is the perfect muse.

Morgan reaches into our bag for his violin, to pass the time, and for my notebook, which he passes along. I fish a pen from my braid.

Begin to transcribe. My hand dashes across the page, hurrying to keep up. It feels exactly the way it did when I was a little girl, hunched over my notebooks: a bloom of elation, invention, infinite possibilities.

The Zelda of my childhood waves at me from the past, the two of us writing together. I've discussed a few story ideas with my literary agent and editor, and we're all excited to create something new. I plan to have a first draft completed by the end of the year.

My eyes fall closed when Morgan begins to play "In the Hall of the Mountain King." It's the perfect song for this moment.

He pauses after the first few bars. "Can you see it?" he asks, his voice hushed.

"See what?" I whisper back, and—

Norway. Scrubby green fields with mountains in the distance, and all around us, a castle materializes. A vast grand hall wavers like it's reflected in moving water, bright and merry with goblins, gnomes, and trolls so tall I can't see their faces. A troll king is resting in his gilded chair, his right hand clutching a scepter topped with a crocodile's head, an ostrich egg of a ruby in its open mouth.

As Morgan continues to play, more details appear in the scene: the *clink* of dishes upon two long tables, a ladle falling sloppily from its tureen of gravy; the crackle of enormous twin fireplaces on opposite sides of the room, chimney stones jutting in a zigzag pattern; the smell of roast swan, potatoes dripping buttery herb sauce, a fruit tart that wouldn't fit in a human-made oven. Cheese and nuts; breads of such pillowy breadth and depth that I could sleep on them.

My vision hazes, tempo accelerating.

"Yes," I breathe, emotions sharp in my chest. "I can see it."

I can see the song.

I don't know how he's doing it, and from the wonder on his face, neither does he, but Morgan is playing magic.

He keeps playing, one song and then another and then the next, every single piece he knows until he's run out and is making them up; all the while, the forest's stories provide accompaniment and leaves blow down like rain, and I am so relieved to know that I am not even close to discovering all the best impossibilities rainbowing across the universe.

I think back to the Zelda of early summer, berating herself because the words wouldn't come. Of course they wouldn't come. They weren't ready. Everything that I have now, all that I most treasure, arrived in the world on its own time.

He swathes us in luminous music that grows from his soul like the expanding branches of a tree, as I let go and write.

And drift into his lap to kiss him, here and there.

Once I reach the end of the third page, I turn back to the start; freckling in all the fundamental alliteration, lines with rhymes, and crooked door

s.

Did you know that there's magic in Moonville? It bubbles within my coven like a heady brew, fortifying the threads that connect me to my sisters, my niece, my grandmother, my Morgan. It shimmers like his musical heartstrings, running as fast as it can through the forest in my bones. Into my finger tips. Pen. Ink as it gleams wetly onto paper that will someday disperse far and wide across a thousand different minds to recycle into new ideas, different energies, evoking a smile or a grimace, an altered mood—

And in that way, magic belongs to anyone who turns its pages.

ACKNOWLEDGMENTS

I DON'T KNOW WHAT sort of spell I've cast over the lovely people at G. P. Putnam's Sons—Kate Dresser, Tarini Sipahimalani, Nicole Biton, Bianca Mestiza, Ashley McClay, Amy Schneider, LeeAnn Pemberton, Lara Robbins, Christopher Lin, Claire Winecoff, Almudena Rincon, Maggie Leone, Katy Riegel, Vikki Chu, Regina Andreoni, Maija Baldauf, and Alexis Welby—but I hope it never fades, as I so enjoy working with you. You are the tendons and muscles and bones of my stories and without you I can't stand up. Thank you to my agent, Taylor Haggerty, for your guidance, brainstorming, and general excellence; and thank you also to the wonderful Jasmine Brown.

I want to thank my husband and children for all of your bright, sparkling magic; thank you to my writer friends (Martha Waters, I would be lost without you) for making the world dazzle. Thank you, booksellers, and librarians, and Tim Burton, and Diana Wynne Jones, and Hayao Miyazaki, and innumerable '80s musicians (Chappell Roan counts. Morgan would LOVE you, Chappell Roan), and readers throughout the whole of human history—past, present, future.

You beautiful, brilliant readers.

Do you know how special you are? You're why Shakespeare and Jane Austen are household names centuries after their deaths. You carry whole worlds in your hands and hearts; you're the guardians who keep them alive. To the readers who will find these words in 2025 and to the readers who will find them far in the future—thank you for being Moonville's guardians.

It means everything to me.